TRIBUTE

ROBERT LEE JOHNSTON

Also by Robert Lee Johnston

LUCIFER ON LEAVE

(Available 2 July 2018)

About the author

Robert Lee Johnston is an author based in Tropical Far North
Queensland. Tribute is his debut novel.

ROBERT LEE JOHNSTON
TRIBUTE

there is only consequence

ROBERT
SCHOLTEN

This book contains adult content. If you are under age 18, or you arrived here by accident, please do not read further.

Tribute

By Robert Lee Johnston

Copyright 2018 Robert Lee Johnston

ISBN: 978-0-6481855-3-6

A catalogue record for this book is available from the National Library of Australia (ISBN: 978-0-6481855-0-5)

Cover by Robert Scholten

www.robertscholten.com

This book is also available as an ebook from Smashwords, Amazon and iTunes.

For my Wendy.

You are the greatest part of me.

*Amicitiae nostrae memoriam spero
sempiternam fore.*

I hope the memory of our friendship is
everlasting.

Cicero.

CHAPTER ONE: SYD

Rev deftly pocketed the money.

'A donation for you, old mate.'

Syd winked a sleazy wink as the two of them exchanged yellow, scatter-tooth, crooked smiles. Not a penny of Syd's donation would ever see the church coffers. The money feathered Rev's own nest as it had done for years. Too many to count.

Syd thought out loud. 'Cozy's little arse is looking fuggin tighter than your wallet.'

A few of the kids were in his line of sight doing jobs about their cottage-style home. Bugs and John Henry mowing, Cozy and Kenny raking, the girls helping out, picking up and piling the itchy lawn clippings around fruit trees. Stirrup rolled around, messing up and spreading the piles of grass with a smile. The aroma of crisp jungle air and earthy, freshly shorn grass made for a delicious, lung-pleasing alchemy.

Syd's eyes focused cold on Cozy. 'Cozy, looks fuggin good and ready to my eye, old son.'

'Well, he's all yours. I'm glad to be rid of him at last. Just keep him the hell away from here once you take him.' Syd had been watching the kids carefully from a safe distance over the years as they grew.

Jenny fell over and moaned as her knee twisted. She lay in a foetal position, aching as other kids helped her up. Syd preferred boys all day long and usually didn't care for the young lassies, but hearing that moan convinced him to try again.

'I reckon I might take that there blond lass as well.' Syd pointed, as if he was selecting fresh T-bones.

Rev smiled widely, his one good eye focused on Syd after looking where he'd pointed. He knew Syd would come around to pretty Jenny.

'Young Jen has been turning a few heads, Syd. You know I can't let her go for nothing.'

Syd's hand was already in his sweaty overall's pocket, giving his hammer a presumptuous squeeze. He fumbled about and pulled out five hundred more in cash, handed it to Rev.

'Wonderful, Sydney my son. When do expect you'll be done with them?'

'Give us a few weeks, I reckon. The fuggin wet's got me behind.' He adjusted his hardening erection. Syd was done small talking and wanted to get his toys straight home.

'Syd, best you keep Cozy busy. He has a nervous energy that one. It makes him wily and impulsive. He's trouble that boy when he won't sit still.'

'I'll sort his fuggin troubles out, one way or another.' He winked again. 'It's nothing a good fuggin up the arse won't straighten out of him.' He mumbled a low chuckle and then looked the other choice child cuts over again in case he had missed something or someone interesting.

'Nah, they'll do.'

Rev invited Syd into his separate quarters for a nip or two while Cozy and Jen finished up around the yard,

Tribute © Robert Lee Johnston 2016
Email: tributerobertleejohnston@gmail.com

oblivious they'd just been sold. Only Syd was permitted inside Rev's quaint cottage. Rev rarely welcomed well-wishers and visitors (leeches) or ingratiated himself to guests. A purposely crude, mouldy, outdoor round table, accompanied by filthy, faded, bum-pinching plastic chairs, the most uncomfortable set Rev could find, awaited company. Refreshments and tea was never offered. Inside, however, it was impossible not to imagine snifters of port, hot drinks and cucumber sandwiches.

Syd smelled bad to Cozy. His old Land Rover was slow and reeked of sweat and old-man stink. Syd was hard to understand. He spoke slowly and gruffly with a long, deep drawl. His pattern of speech, grunts and groans was an affront to any and every language. Syd swore oddly and nearly every other word. His teeth and breath were rancid. His brown, deep eyes squinted with his face. He'd told Jen to sit on his lap to have a go at steering while he drove and never spoke another word.

Cozy had never been down this road before. The green hills were loaded with fat dairy cows. Thick, rich-green pastures ran down fenced, hilly country into dams or small streams once away from the jungle. Rickety wooden bridges, wide enough for one car to cross at a time, traversed the many creeks and rivers. Dense jungle flourished on the river banks. This is looking all right, Cozy thought. He abhorred the church grounds. But there was a tense undertone in the silence. Cozy couldn't shake the feeling from his troubled gut. It chewed at a compartment in the forefront of his brain. He ignored it and the vile grin on Syd's sharp lips that he couldn't place or yet understand. Instead, Cozy enjoyed the fluorescent green view from his open window.

Jen smiled at Cozy. She also seemed happy to be away from the church. Cozy turned to study Syd's face for a moment. His thick bottom lip was pulling the rest of his face down. Syd's baggy face needed throwing into an industrial clothes dryer for shrinking, and then a hot ironing to remove

Tribute © Robert Lee Johnston 2016
Email: tributerobertleejohnston@gmail.com

his many angry creases. His permanent scowl included solid, harsh eyebrows, tangled with a mess of unkempt, dark-brown hair. All of him, body, face and hands, was filthy. A fat neck above his fat gut. A big, smelly, hairy grizzly. His button-up overalls, always open to above his waist, exposed a sweaty, tortoise-shell-shaped gut moist with sweat; heaving and sucking in lung-whistling, heavy breaths. Red, oxygen-starved blotches blossomed all over his wet, scabrous, sebaceous skin. A man's hat is said to represent how he lives or works. Syd's rotting, sweat-stained, floppy brown hat explained it all. The battered Akubra had from much exposure lost its firm-brimmed stiffness and hung like forgotten clothes on a Hills Hoist around his head.

'Don't you ever be fuggin staring at me, boy.'

Syd focused deep, cold eyes on the boy. His strange words were said with no endings. 'You' came out as 'yer' or 'ya'. The letter K never got a look in.

'I'll slap the stupid-looking fuggin look off your stupid-looking fuggin face.'

Cozy heard: Owwl slap the stup'd-loogin fuggin loog offa ya stup'd-loogin fuggin face.

What's an 'Owl' got to do with my face?

It took a moment for Cozy to connect the dots as he contracted a sudden case of locked-in syndrome and accidentally kept staring. Cozy barely saw Syd move and completely missed his left hand firing off the wheel as it backhanded Cozy's nearside cheek. Syd had rock-solid dry ice streaming through his veins.

'Are you DEAF? I won't fuggin tell you again, Boyo.'

When Cozy opened his eyes Jen's were also wide open, her teeth clenched, her left hand holding Cozy's right, tight with fear and anxiety. The boy tried not to let Jenny see it stung and exhaled slowly and calmly. She had to wipe the beginnings of a fat tear from her face. Cozy turned his stinging face to the open window and could see no more green, no more beauty.

Tribute © Robert Lee Johnston 2016
Email: tributerobertleejohnston@gmail.com

'You ever fuggin back-chat me I'll flog you black and fuggin blue, Boyo. You two'll do what I says when I fuggin says it. If I bloody says it youse two fuggin do it! You hear?'

Jenny's hand clamped more tightly around Cozy's hand, fluttering and shaking. She hardly breathed. Cozy didn't want this crappy, shit-coloured old Landy to ever stop. He didn't want to see where they were going or how Syd lived. Just wanted to keep on driving.

Syd, shoved Jenny off his lap and freed his dick.

'Now, Girly, you'll kiss this till I says stop or I'll fuggin backhand you too.'

Syd's pungent cock smelt sour and the tip was pasty and rotten. He forced Jen's head down violently until she gagged, cried and dry-retched. He grunted and mumbled, joking proudly to Cozy or talking to himself, sort of laughing. 'You just suck the fuggin pus out of this, young blondie. And no fuggin whinging, eh.'

Cozy couldn't look but it was too loud to ignore. He didn't want to hear anyone talking to his Girly like that. Time passed painfully slowly. They arrived as Syd blew his load all over the joint, moaning like a shot bull.

Syd's dirty, small, dank wooden house stank far worse than him. Syd's partner, Deidre, a decaying whale, squat and triumphantly ugly. Her clothes resembled weather-bleached, cum-stained safari tents. She scared the shit out of them. There was a struck match between them, her ropy, unkempt, oily hair the same penny-coloured, dog-shit brown as Syd's. A whale and a pig. The species barrier had been savagely breached the day Deidre was ingloriously conceived.

The walls and windows of her sty were green with mould and stained with dangerously coloured lichen. Filthy dishes and shit stacked the sink, a herd of flies and maggots sniffing around littered cups and cutlery. Rat shit and stinking rat piss covered the joint. Inside were two of the most bullshit, useless farm dogs Cozy ever seen. Poodles.

Tribute © *Robert Lee Johnston 2016*
Email: tributerobertleejohnston@gmail.com

Two large males who loved nothing more than rooting one another, and sitting around the house doing bugger all. She spoke to them like a lover whispering true lies. The mutts' noses always in the kids' or any rare visitors' arses and genitals, drooling and shivering like stroke victims. Trying always to knock the kids over and root them like lonely rabbits.

Two poofter poodles. Overrated, long-haired, ribbon-toting, undisciplined mongrels. They were always demanding food and attention whilst moulting a daily carpet of fleas. Deidre spoke to her beloved mutts as if they were deaf and dumb infants. Only a dog could love this dirty great beast. She swore like a drunken jillaroo ex sailor, who'd lost her wallet. The big cow—yes there were many animals crammed into her rude vessel—barely moved from her couch for weeks at a time.

From a cluttered, rodent-infested lounge, coffee-stained pannikin in hand, she'd yell and scream Syd's name like a python-strangled, pirate-trained cockatoo.

'SYD, GET ME THIS.'

'SYD, WHERE'S ME FUCKING SMOKES?'

'SYD, WHERE'S THAT?'

'YOU'RE A DICKHEAD, SYD. YOU'RE THE WORST FUCKING MAN IN THE WHOLE WORLD.'

'SYD, YA FUCK. YOU DIDN'T GET MY FOOD.'

'SYD, WHERE THE FUCK HAVE YOU BEEN? YOU FUCKING SO-AND-SO.'

Deidre didn't stand to meet the children. Instead she insisted Cozy sit next to her on the lounge; her sweat and other bodily fluids soaked through his thin shorts.

'You'll do just fine.' Her plump paw touched his cheek. 'You got a look about you, don't you?'

She told Jen. 'Come on, come here, hon. My God, you're prettier than an angel.'

Deidre wiped a creamy dollop of Syd's jism from Jen's neck and shirt collar and greedily licked her fat, dripping, pork-pie fingers.

'You two can call me Deidre.'

She screamed, 'YOU DONE REALLY GOOD, SYD!'

Syd, scratching his balls through his overalls in a way that wasn't easy for the kids to watch, appeared in a doorway, and they smiled at each other. Smiles that would turn even a cast-iron gut to rusted dust.

'Have you two bathed together before?'

They shook their lowered heads.

'Well, from now on in this house we'll bathe together. C'mon, let's go.'

The kids would rarely see the garbage bins, or Deidre's lounge, empty. She heaved her massive self out of the lounge chair; its flannelette material stubbornly clung to and peeled from her flesh for a second or two. The couch's stretched fabric clung like Glad Wrap to the exposed skin her clothes refused to cover.

A copper pipe, pig rooted, kicked the house and rattled loudly when the water, rusty at first, was forced into life. As the bath filled, Deidre made the kids undress her, and then each other, and forced them to stand around the discoloured tub, washing her body as she spilled out of the bath. Naked, she was, to the children's eyes, frighteningly ugly. They'd never seen so much woman or known that much woman was even possible. Deidre had folds and layers upon folds and was almost shapeless. She barely fit into the poor, rust-stained tub. Deidre smelt foul, of a thousand wet arseholes or a year-long homeless armpit. She clearly hadn't washed or used soap for a while. Jen and Cozy had to wash her sweat-pimpled back. Then her even dirtier front. Syd furiously jerked off that great big prick of his; the bloody thing was bigger and fatter than Cozy's forearm. Deidre, a wet, beached turtle on its back, pathetically waving limbs to Syd for help. When she struggled out, Syd got in. He was

muddied and red with filth. They had to clean him too. When he was done he made the kids get into their foul bilge water. The kids had to clean each other just the way Syd wanted. 'Eyes wide open.' Jenny looked how Cozy felt: mortified.

Fuck, Cozy thought. We've only been here half a bloody hour.

It was about to get worse. Syd oohed and aahed his hillbilly drawl. Deidre asked to look at Jens' hands. Then she violently pulled Jen to the foot of the tub, dragging and sliding her halfway out so her bum was pointing to Cozy's end. She locked her fat talons under Jen's armpit, shoving Jenny's face into her swollen guts. Syd manhandled Cozy's right arm, positioning him behind his twisting, kicking friend. Syd grabbed Cosy's wrist firmly with one hand and with the other stretched out the boy's two largest fingers. Cozy held his breath and thought Syd was going to bite them off, but Syd lustfully sucked on them. Cozy was repulsed and confused when Syd spat on his fingertips. Syd drove Cozy's fingers repeatedly and without remorse into Jen's anus.

Cozy tried to resist.

Syd was too rough, too strong.

Cozy screamed apologies to Jen when she jumped and screamed.

'Don't you fuggin apologise, Boyo. Little bitch is going to have to get used to getting that fuggin arse reamed. Little tiny fingers first ...' He grasped his hard-on. 'Then this fulla.'

Cozy wanted to kill them right there. Big Deidre sat, fat on the edge of the tub. Her legs spread wide as she could. Her guts hung, repositioned manually, over one thigh. She fingered herself like some ancient, rattly steam engine as Syd ejaculated onto the children and into the bath water.

They left Cozy and Jen in tepid, tainted water, too freaked out to say or do a damn thing. Jen's face slowly, painfully scrunched up. She burst into tears and hugged Cozy tightly.

'I'm so sorry!' She was a wreck.

'No, Jen. I'm sorry!'

'Cozy we're in trouble, aren't we?'

'I know, mate, I know. We got to get away from this house.'

As the shock and weight of their predicament bore down, Jen vomited a little in the bath.

'What did we do wrong, Cozy? Why are they so mad at us? How come we're in strife?'

'I don't know, Girly. But whatever we did it must've been bad. Are you okay?'

'It stings a bit down there, but I'm okay. Please, Cozy, you can't call me that no more. The way Syd said "Girly", it sounded horrible. Please don't call me "Girly" no more.' She wiped the snot hanging from her nose. 'He's going to hurt us more, isn't he, Cozy? What are we going to do? They're bad. We need help.'

Cozy felt hollowed out, cold. No one would help them. Not here.

'Cozy?' she whispered, looking confused.

'Yeah?'

'Your eyes have turned bright green.'

He faked a smile to ease her. 'Well, you're whiter than a ghost.'

They sat at opposite ends, rubbing feet and toes nervously in shock.

'Fucking pig swill.' Cozy pulled the plug and emptied the swampy water and all its floaties, refilling the tub with clean water to try to wash away the filth surrounding them, invading them, staining them. After a few minutes' peace, Syd opened the door. 'Fuggin hurry up. Time you two were to bed.'

Jen looked for a dry towel each as Cozy pulled the plug. She found two wet, used, cold towels on the floor. Both were stained and stank from the previous users. Cozy was looking forward to his bed and getting away from this heavy

Syd reckoned, 'I fucked the guts out of it ages ago. Killed it.'

He wasn't lying. The only thing uglier than her vag was her expansive, sulphuric arsehole, long since shagged out. Her sphincter had ages ago packed up shop, packed it in and legged it forever and a day, after seeing that donkey-dick of a cock, a-knocking, a-barging, a-huffing, and a-puffing at its door. All that was left in its absence was a fist-sized, rusty old bullet hole surrounding pinkish, reddish flesh, that was her prolapsed innards. They easily herniated their way out of her arse whilst her poo poo valve was on the lam. On long service leave, sipping cocktails beside a pool out in the sun on a secluded, exotic tropical island with all the other morose, close-fisted, terrified bum holes relocating to start afresh.

Her overripeness gagged the kids' throats and lungs. The greasy, cottage-cheesy bits decomposing, hidden in her many crevices, were to blame. Their eyes nearly fried, chemically burnt at the sinful amount. If Syd had ice in his hardened veins then Deidre had sour, fetid, maggot-ridden cream flowing through hers.

Fly blown, wriggling ice cream.

Deidre had a true love in her life, other than her mutts. One surprising feature. Despite her deep, long-burning, ingrained racism, she adored 'Little Michael Jackson'. She cared none for the other members of the Jackson Five, often saying, 'Those fellas have no talent, shit voices, and can't dance a step. Those useless black bastards just hitched their stinking wagons to little Michael's gravy train. That lazy bloody mob are just using the boy.'

She delighted in Michael's white teeth when he smiled, adored his voice and the way he danced. It was a sick infatuation. She constantly ordered the kids to walk, dance and talk like 'Little Michael'.

Syd, however, hated constantly hearing about the 'cocky liddle shit'.

Tribute © Robert Lee Johnston 2016
Email: tributerobertleejohnston@gmail.com

Cozy told Jen, 'I bet that ... I reckon, if Deidre was ever to get a hold of the poor bastard, Little Michael Jackson's black arse would turn bright white with fright, and turn him off girls forever. She'd fuck his shit up.'

Within days, Jen and Cozy were five shades filthier, inside and out. After a week they stopped asking why and adopted a fatalistic attitude. Many tortured tears were shed in those first weeks. They attempted unplanned, spontaneous escapes. Syd always found them walking the lonely, muddy road back to Tribute.

Syd and Deidre's demands became more and more depraved and destructively powerful. Before long Cozy and Jenny were tied naked to chairs, table legs, the bed, to each other, spending all day and night kissing, pulling, licking, fingering, sucking and fucking whatever was presented to them. Unable to shift from their binds. Syd often turned them onto each other, demanding they do all he asked. Jen and Cozy slowly became mindless, soulless, almost boneless products of their carers' tempers and boundless imaginings.

***

After a few weeks Jenny asked, 'Cozy, if we died here now, you reckon, would we go up to heaven? You know God can see all this. When's he going to help us, Cozy?'

Cozy shrugged defeated shoulders, too beaten to respond.

'It's just ...' She paused. 'I just feel like I've done something dirty, and real bad, you know? And I know it's wrong, Cozy, wrong in my heart. What if that's why God isn't helping? And we get punished for this forever? What if God says I'm no good and there's no place up there for kids like you and me? So even when we're dead we still won't have a home, never have a place that's our own forever, Cozy.'

Cozy looked into her light-blue eyes welling with grief. Her shock was brutal, ebbing and flowing. He got mad seeing her so, and pleaded, 'Fuck me dead, Jen. We's just

nine.' Cozy choked on the words. 'This ain't our fault, Jen. What can we do? We's just kids.'

The lost tear spilt from her eye. Cozy changed tack and whispered powerfully, 'I've been thinking how to get us two out of here.'

She held her breath and looked around. 'Where will we go, Cozy?' Her mood shifted.

'Don't know, Gir— Jen, but really, really fucking far from here. Fuck this dump.'

Jen smiled and repeated, 'Yeah, fuck this dump!'

Just as the plan was coming together they were bundled into the Land Rover and, without a word, driven towards Tribute. Crossing one of the many rickety crossings, Syd hit the skids, pulled the Landy up and killed the motor right in the middle of the empty bridge. He spoke gruffly. 'Me and Deidre went fuggin easy on you two. If I ever hears one fuggin word, if I hears even a whisper of what you both did … I will drive this fuggin truck into town and get the pair of you little shits and never fuggin bring you back.' He stared down at them. 'We'll keep you both. I will cook you and fuggin eat you, and feed your guts and bones to the fuggin dogs.' He whispered menacingly, 'You two fuggin savvy?'

They nodded, shitting themselves, believing Syd's threat completely.

'Not a fuggin word.'

They were dropped off to a sigh of disappointment from Rev and a 'Get away inside you two!' Syd grinned and they exchanged common pleasantries.

'To your liking, Syd?'

'Yeah, I trained them up good, mate.'

Stooping, he wheezed as he laughed, murdering the English language. He added. 'You could slide your fuggin arm up to your elbow in the lassie's arse now. She won't blink or flinch. All loosey goosey. Well, Rev, I'm in a hurry. My civic duty is done here for a bit, me old China. I'll see you in a few months. I got to fuggin go.'

Tribute © Robert Lee Johnston 2016
Email: tributerobertleejohnston@gmail.com

'God bless you, Sydney.'

Rev's all-time favourite proverb was composed by Thomas Fuller, MD:

A woman, a spaniel and a walnut tree.

The more they're beaten, the better they be.

Over the years Rev had fiddled with the proverb and created his own abomination:

Loose women, stray dogs and orphans, you'll see.

The harder they're beaten, the better they be.

***

Bugs, John Henry, Kenny and Evie were at the table playing monopoly.

Jen and Cozy could hear the laughter and hysterical cheating as they approached the cottage door. Jenny stopped in panic under the verandah. She looked at Cozy and held his hand tightly. They suddenly looked ruinous, unkempt, and felt sickly. Their blond hair was as filthy as the clothes on their backs. Two sorry bodies still burnt and hurt down there, making walking hard. Apart from being sex toys for five weeks, they were worked within inches of their endurance while being cruelly starved; fighting greedy roaches, flies and the ribboned poofter poodles for any leftovers.

Jenny's breathing was short, sharp and shallow, her pulse racing from adrenaline. Shaking, hugging Cozy, fearful she would pass out at saying the words out loud. Jen spoke softly, 'He said he'd kill us, Cozy. Eat us. I'm sorry, Cozy, for doing all those things to you.'

Cozy squeezed her. 'I'm sorry too. For everything. I promise those poofter fucking dogs and them two pigs won't eat us. I hate them! I fucking hate them.'

'Cozy?'

'Yep.'

They released each other and looked into each other's face.

'We can't tell anyone.' Jen looked towards the door. 'Cozy, I don't want them to know.'

She smiled and it looked so completely out of place. It hurt Cozy to see her still so achingly beautiful. An innocent, blinding beauty. Even covered in dirt, worry and grime it was a hell of a smile. Cozy grinned. She closed her eyes and gently kissed him.

'I love you, Cozy.'

Cozy was in shock, his lips unresponsive, his eyes wide open.

Jen opened hers. 'I didn't want Syd to be on my lips, Cozy. I much prefer you.'

Sometime later, Cozy would think she knew the others would sense what had happened to them both. She replaced all that crap with something sweet, so they could end on a high. On her terms. A defiant act. They straightened up the best they could and went inside.

'FUCKING JESUS! WHAT HAPPENED?' Kenny yelled in fright when he laid eyes on his litter friends.

John Henry was up and over. 'Holy shit.' He was worried instantly, and asked if they were okay. He didn't wait for an answer but gave them each a once over, grabbing Jen's skinny arm gently. 'Let's go to the sink, Girly.'

Jen flinched at her ancient nickname. 'Henry, all of you! Don't call me that name no more. I never, ever want to hear that name again.'

Henry was confused. The pack always called Jen, the youngest of them, Girly. It was cute and sweetly used. He apologised sincerely and tended to Jen. Very soon they would all feel that 'Girly' and 'Boyo' were indisputably derogatory.

Stirrup skipped in to say g'day, his tail wagging when he heard Cozy's and Jen's voices. But as they came into his sight his tail stopped wagging and he rushed to them, worried. He knew. With one look he knew. They were hurt and hurting. He was softer than a daisy investigating their recent past

Tribute © Robert Lee Johnston 2016
Email: tributerobertleejohnston@gmail.com

with his nose. His face dissolved, offended at what he smelt. Stirrup was confused. Not by Jen or Cozy, but by the evidence procured in his canine brain. A moving picture, an up-to-date biography of scents. He could smell bruises, semen, cuts, shit, piss, and blood. Totally out of character, Stirrup sniffed their genitals. He recoiled in shock at the damage done there. Stirrup never let Cozy or Jen out of his sight. He felt he failed his pack. It wouldn't happen again.

'What the fuck happened to you both?'

Bugs was distressed at their state. Shirts and shorts were torn; blood, fluid and shit stained them beyond recognition. Evie, after her initial shock, was all over them.

John Henry, doctoring Jen, asked Evie to bring fresh clothes and hot water. And after seeing Jen's boney ribs standing proud, he added, 'And please, Evie, get them some bloody food.'

'Why have your pants got blood all over them?' Evie asked innocently. She was on her way to the freezer, where countless stacked Eta 5-Star margarine containers were filled with leftover soups and stews from the local Meals On Wheels service.

Bugs, in deep thought, asked sympathetically, 'What the fuck's going on, man? You both look like shit.'

Jen and Cozy hadn't realised just how shitty they actually looked until they saw the others. They hadn't noticed their own decline. Compared to what was happening it didn't seem to matter.

Food appeared in the form of bread and soup. Leftovers had never looked so good. After they had eaten, John Henry stripped their bloody rags and forced them to have showers so he could clean all their cuts. They answered no questions. After John Henry was satisfied they were patched up, Jen and Cozy went to their long-missed, separate beds and slept deeply, without dreams.

Cozy woke to movement and the boys sitting on the edge of his bed. Cozy whispered tiredly and huskily, sleep lining his throat. 'Oi, Oi bunjees.'

'Hey, how you going?'

Cozy yawned and shrugged.

Bugs wanted answers. 'What the fuck happened, Cozy?'

'Whatdyamean?' He tiredly rubbed his eyes.

'Fucking hell, Cozy. Jen's been crying and screaming out all morning.'

Kenny added in disbelief, 'Saying how some old bastards were fucking youse.'

Cozy looked to Jen's empty cot, panicked and shot bolt upright. 'Where is she? Does Rev know?'

'Nah. Henry and Evie took her to the river to settle her down.' Bugs paused. 'Is it true, man?'

Any strength Cozy had left suddenly and completely left him in front of his blood brothers. He broke, crying, choking on words of fire and hot coals that escaped his belly.

'They're worse than fucking pigs, them pair.' The boys all had a hand on his shoulder or back, patting him, comforting him as tears and snot dripped onto his shirt.

Bugs was crying. They all were. 'You're fucking joking me, right?' Bugs spat.

Cozy told them how he'd 'kill us, eat us and feed our bones to his poofter fucking dogs'.

Kenny felt he should say, 'Jenny, already said.'

'Hey, boys?' Cozy had their attention. 'If you ever see that fucking Landy coming up the road youse run flat fucking out and just head into the jungle. Drop whatever you're doing and fucking leg it. Run and don't stop. I promise I'll find you.' Cozy looked deeply into their wounded eyes. 'Promise me.'

They promised.

When Jenny had woken earlier that morning Kenny lost his shit. Jen was a walking corpse. Her broken, starved body

Tribute © Robert Lee Johnston 2016
Email: tributerobertleejohnston@gmail.com

and shattered face was too much for his mind to digest. All the young ones had to play with Rev, and he forced all of them to suck on his tiny dick. Syd and the big heifer sounded like seven extra flavours of shitty fucked up to Kenny, and this was beyond any of the suffering they'd already put up with. They all wondered who'd be next. Kenny went Tourette's, swearing out loud as they made a way through the jungle towards Jen, John Henry and Evie.

'MOTHER FUCKING DIRTY FAT FAGGOTS. MAGGOTTY ARSE FUCK, FUCKS. FUCK. PUTRID FUCKING POOFTER TOE RAGS.'

His voice echoed and ricocheted through the scrub. Henry and Evie were at the river, near a scrub turkey mound the size of a small car, supporting Jen, and had heard the whole shitty yarn. Jen had settled down some. But then she saw Cozy. She held him as the pack rubbed backs, hugged and cried closely.

'It's okay, Jen. We'll be okay.'

'I'm sorry. I told them all, Cozy.'

'Don't be sorry, Jen, ever. Syd'll never find out.'

'You promise?'

'I promise you.'

Jen's breathing eased and her tears settled. They broke the scrum's embrace. Bugs and John Henry built a fire to warm their wits. The kids sat around it on the forest floor. Jen and Cozy answered all their questions. Eventually they ran out of them. They sat in a fire-induced coma for some time, staring into the red heart of fire.

Kenny asked, 'Who the fuck does that shit, man? I didn't even know blokes could fuck blokes. And ... why the fucking hell?'

'Cos we're young, weak, and available,' Jen wisely supposed.

Henry added grimly, 'And it's cos no one gives a fuck whether we live or die. No one to tell and no one to care.'

Tribute © Robert Lee Johnston 2016
Email: tributerobertleejohnston@gmail.com

Jenny shrieked in terror, 'NO. DON'T TELL ANYONE, HENRY. NO ONE CAN EVER KNOW. EVER.' She settled down. 'No one but us.' Jen hated the thought of others hearing or knowing.

Cozy wasn't really listening. *If that fucking hillbilly ever touches any of us again I will kill that buck-tooth fuck, then spit roast those poofter fucking dogs for smoko.*

'What's up, Cozy?' Bugs could see he was in thought.

'I was just thinking. I'll kill those animals one day for what they've done.'

'How you going to pull that off, mate? We're just kids, man!'

'I'll think of something.'

Evie had a thought and shared it with the rest. They all wished she hadn't. 'What if Syd and Deidre aren't the only ones? What do we do then?'

Jenny turned pale at the thought and looked crook. Cozy panicked, eyes turning a bright green. *Ah fuck. I hadn't thought of that.*

'Fucking nothing's what. Fucking squat,' Bugs reckoned.

They got scared. None of them were immune. It seemed that eight or nine years of age were Syd's induction years. There were many more Syds and Deidres to school them. Soon they reluctantly became acquainted with each of them. One by one. No one was immune.

No one.

Over the next four years Rev was very well paid. By Cozy's eleventh birthday he had became a regular at the houses of Syd and a few others that were on Rev's books. Each of those six kids had done time at Syd's and paid dues at all the others. Syd still had a preference for Jen and Cozy, though he went through all of them. They were on his constant rotation. His once rundown, overgrown farm serviced by cheap, child labour, now was one of the best on his road; weed free, manicured and well fenced. Syd and Deidre became more rodent-like as they aged. Their house

Tribute © Robert Lee Johnston 2016
Email: tributerobertleejohnston@gmail.com

was still a pig sty. At thirteen, Cozy and Jen were getting too old for Syd's liking. Both their arseholes were numb to him now and he wished both were young again so he could feel their arses twitch and panic. Gradually, Cozy's beatings took on a bloodier tone. Syd would pick up whatever was handy: power cords, belts, brooms, paint tins, lawyer cane, timber. Anything! Swing it, throw it and hoick it in his direction.

One day he reached out and searched for something, anything, and found a handle. A wooden handle to an old bullock-team whip, belonging to the previous land owner, who introduced the first bullock team to Tribute. It soon became Syd's first choice and personal favourite. The damage it laid on satisfied his need for carnage and blood. Soon he preferred whipping Cozy more than fucking him. Jen wore all the fucking; he wore the whip.

They consoled each other whenever they had moments alone. Without Jen, Cozy would have thrown himself under a fast-moving hungry slasher or into the path of a bone-thrashing rotary hoe.

Before Syd, Jen and Cozy's first punishment by a stranger was when they were five years old. Young Jen and Cozy had never been on a farm before and everything was larger than life and brand new. Rev had fallen ill with a lung infection and fostered all the kids out to regular 'trusted' churchgoers. Jen and Cozy watched on, hidden, as the woman of the household cut the heads off a few chooks. The dying chickens' bodies danced a merry, headless dance, running around. Jen thought it all looked pretty cool and had an idea. The sturdy, capable woman took the collected, gutted birds towards the house. Cozy and Jen raced out to the vacated, bloody chopping block to have a go. Cozy pulled the sharpened axe from its tight lodgings.

Jen eagerly got down and lay with the back of her neck across the well-used block.

'I want to go first! Then I'll cut your head off!'

'Righto, Girly.'

Tribute © Robert Lee Johnston 2016
Email: tributerobertleejohnston@gmail.com

She patiently lay there, neck exposed, smiling up at Cozy. A mischievous, cheeky, excited smile at the fast-moving, cloudy sky. Cozy raised and arced the blood-spattered axe head high above and behind his head.

'Hey Girly, you stay still now.' He lined up her throat.

The stocky woman turned around to see what they were doing. 'God knows why,' she'd later say. She shit her breaches, dropped the chooks.

'COZY! YOU DROP THAT FRIGGIN AXE, THIS SECOND!'

Cozy, swinging, and Jen, lying there, got a hell of a fright. Jenny, panicked, rolled and put her hand on the chopping block to get up. Cozy, startled, let go of the axe. It fell through the air cleanly, thumping deep into the thick wooden stump.

Cutting straight through Jen's index finger. Slicing the poor thing off at the second knuckle. Her trigger finger, her pointer. Her nose and bum picker. She squealed and held the stump of her digit, wide-eyed, running on the spot. Screaming loudly. Their eyes watched, as if at a three-player ball game, from Jen's finger, to each other's face, and then to the fast-approaching mad woman.

She was upon the kids, all steamed up. 'I'LL FLOG THE BLOODY FEATHERS OFF BOTH OF YOU.'

A rooster, her number one cock, scavenging around the yard, saw something bleeding, wiggling deliciously in the grass. Like a condor or albatross trying to get airborne, he flapped, running on the wing. With a stabbing motion he picked it up with his beak and gobbled it down.

Jen screamed bloody murder. 'OH SHIT. ME FINGER.'

Cozy yelled towards the puffing, angry train of a woman, pointing. 'The rooster! Look.'

The bird necked the finger as if sculling a shot. It ran off. Jen, seeing this, fainted fast away. Cozy and the old girl chased the bird, which took off in fright and panic, yelping and nervously clucking as chooks do when two people chase and frighten the crap out of them. The proud rooster

Tribute © Robert Lee Johnston 2016
Email: tributerobertleejohnston@gmail.com

coughed, wheezed and croaked on the run. Stopped suddenly. Fell over. Dead. Choked to death on Jen's bony, witchetty-grub-look-a-like fingertip.

Then the sturdy, angry woman chased Cozy. 'Get here now! You little shit!' She flogged the white off both Jen and Cozy with an open hand for that. Triplets of WHACK WHACK WHACK. The old girl was more cross at losing a prize rooster than at any injury caused to Jenny. Nevertheless, Jen never, ever lay across a chicken's chopping block again.

The new levels to which the suffering of the children rose made her farm look like a sunny day at kindergarten. On Syd's farm, Jen became proficient at stitching Cozy up during his early whippings. Cozy had an unexpected vasectomy. The whip tail or thong snaked around his thigh on impact, up under his shorts. The whip's tip sliced through his scrotum. Tiny kiddy's nuts and some stringy looking bits fell out of the boy, out of their sack, as the pain and blood loss stunned him. Completely winded him. Syd didn't hang around and left Cozy there in the yard crawling to a shed while bleeding out into unconsciousness. Jen found Cozy and stitched his nuts back into their ball-bag as best she could with needle and spool—bright yellow thread—and hoped like hell he'd wake up. Bristly, yellow, cotton pubes on a bald nut sack left a scar jagged and thick. Jen saved his life. Cozy was put back to work the next morning. Whatever was cut or destroyed took away his ability to father children. Perhaps for the best, he later thought.

Bugs's skin had now and then tasted the whip too. Somehow it was not as satisfying for Syd. It broke Bugs quickly. Cozy was much more fun to break. Challenging. Better sport. No first fleet cat o'nine tails or triangles. Just a simple, single-strand, plaited raw-hide, bullock-team whip. Saved especially for the rebellious boy. A long wooden handle the height of a full grown man helped to gain mechanical leverage. Absolutely lethal in the right or, in Syd's case, wrong hands. It ran through flesh like a straight-

edged butcher's knife cuts paper. New strikes soon overlapped old ones and gave shape, pattern and depth to a disturbing metamorphosis.

Cozy kept his promise to Jen and they ran away often. Deidre's poofter poodles would track the runaways down and, after flogging Cozy and fucking Jenny, Syd threatened them, 'I will fuggin shoot youse next time you do a runner.'

The time Syd shot Cozy, Jenny and he were legging it down the long gravel driveway. Cozy felt the projectile from Syd's straight-barrelled old bolt-action .22 rifle slam into his body near his lower back, a few centimetres from his spine, instantly dropping the boy. His right leg would not obey any orders.

Jen was screaming at Cozy, crying, 'SYD'S COMING.'

He was loud. 'You don't fuggin listen, BOYO. You keep running away, don't you? Just like your slut of a mother. She ran as fast as she could. Like them falls you were born beside, where they found you at. It never stops running. Well, I'm a fuggin dam wall, Boyo, and I'll pull you up. All but fuggin too quick.'

Jenny lay over Cozy, hanging on, protecting him angrily. 'LEAVE US ALONE, YOU.'

He grabbed a fistful of her hair and dragged her kicking and screaming to the house, leaving Cozy there in the mud and gravel to hear it all. 'Your fuggin arse might pucker up a bit and tighten like it used to after that, eh Girly?' He laughed to himself, thinking he was funny.

When Syd was finished with her, he fell asleep. Jen searched for Cozy. He'd crawled with his elbows to hide in the back of the tractor shed. She had raced around and found some tweezers, some bi-carb soda and Dettol. She fished the lead out, and a piece of his shorts it took along for the ride. Jenny stitched him up. She stole two sleeping pills from Deidre's bedside table, gave them to Cozy and he drank them down. Both slept the night, broken and scared, in that old tractor shed.

Tribute © Robert Lee Johnston 2016
Email: tributerobertleejohnston@gmail.com

Syd stood over the kids, kicking Cozy's knee. He opened his eyes. The agony he woke to was worse than the initial shot. His body vibrated in pain as it stiffened and locked.

'That was a fuggin pea shooter, Boyo. Next time you pull that fuggin shit I'll shoot you with a real fuggin rifle. Next time, Boyo, it will run right through your dopey fuggin head. Now get away, the both of you, and milk them fuggin cows.'

The kids milked all morning in silence. Cozy fell to his knees in that dairy and cried, bawled out of control. Not in pain. It was more like self-pity mixed with bleak insufficiency.

Jen came to Cozy and pulled his head gently onto her lean belly, stroking his hair. 'It's okay, Cozy, it's okay. Okay?'

Cozy disagreed. 'No, Jenny. It's not.'

They stayed right there till he settled. He looked up at Jen and smiled a halfway, inward grin. 'Remember what I said to you all the first time we came to this fuck hole?'

'Yes, yeah I do. You promised we'd run away, and you kept your promise to me, Cozy.'

'No. Remember I told you all I'd kill that fat fuck one day if he ever hurt us again?'

She inhaled. She was nearly thirteen. Almost four years had passed since they admitted to their mob what had happened that sad day, around a fire in the jungle. She looked into Cozy's eyes and recited Syd's words: 'I will feed ya gutz and bones to the fuggin dogs!' Jen was still scared by the words.

'I know how I'm going do it as well. I'm going to kill Syd.'

Instinctively she looked around and then whispered, 'Syd's going to die?'

'No, Jen, I'm going to kill him. I will let the tractor do it.'

'How?'

Tribute © Robert Lee Johnston 2016
Email: tributerobertleejohnston@gmail.com

'It's taken me forever to think of it, but I'm going to kick the tractor out of gear on that steep hill at the jungle-and-swamp paddock.'

'But won't you be on the tractor too?'

'Yeah, but nah. I'll jump off as soon as I kick that gear stick. He won't be able to find any gears once it takes off.' The old tractor had little to no brakes. 'Three hundred metres of steep hill will surely kill him when he busts into the scrub.'

'What if he grabs you?'

'He won't, Jen, I promise you. His hands'll be full. He'll be too busy getting control and steering the old girl. I'll do it when it next rains.' He secretly hoped Syd wouldn't find a gear. 'And if that fuck does manage to jump, a tyre will run his fat, slow arse over for sure.'

'But that tyre could hit you!'

'Nah, I'll be right, sitting on the mud guard so I'm half ways there, see? And I'll get well away jumping from there. I'll be quick. He'll have to jump from the driver's seat somehow. It'll look just like an accident.'

'What about Deidre, Cozy?'

'Fuck her. That fat slut can rot and suffer in her safari-tent knickers. She's good as dead once Syd's gone. I'll tell Syd there's a heifer bogged in the swamp and only the tractor can get her out.'

'Will Syd believe you?'

'Yeah. Why wouldn't he?'

He thought for a moment. 'Jen.'

'Yeah?'

'I'm going to kill Syd. Until he's good and fucking dead.'

Thomas Fuller, Gnomologia. The author, RLJ, has changed the text.

Tribute © Robert Lee Johnston 2016
Email: tributerobertleejohnston@gmail.com

CHAPTER TWO: THE FOUR BOYS

Seems contradictory, don't they?
Your mates.
They are! My Australian oath they are!
Take it from me, there was never such dogmatic, obstinate,
prejudiced, pig-headed sons of a twisted mallee root since mates
were discovered.
Yet I stick to them;
I can't get rid of them; they are inside my skin;
They're me ... bother them!

Thomas Dodd, quoted in The Australian
Worker

They were cheeky brats, up for anything, filled to the brim with beans and benevolence, completely, fearlessly adventurous.

Some were ten, the others nine, surrounded by loud rainforest and a fast-flowing, deep river bend. A wide, safe eddy broke off from the quick-moving tongue offering both

slow- and fast-moving water to play in. It was day four of the latest plan. They'd successfully wagged school all week thus far, swimming, fishing, smoking, laughing, running free and having fun.

Tribute's inhabitants and their children have for generations been rote-taught the inherent dangers of the forest, and its many mine shafts. Urban myths and haunted stories of unfortunate lost children wandering into the jungle, forever disappearing, kept other children at bay. They diligently obeyed and stayed away. Once the inseparable pack of kids heard those imaginative tales, the inclination to investigate became irresistible to their impoverished minds. They stayed and played. And they diligently disobeyed.

They knew each other before time or memory. They were family, though not a drop of blood shared. They happily did everything together, school, and the obvious wagging of it, playing and joking around. And, of course, footy. They lived under the same roof, and so ate together every day and every night, except when some were fostered out.

Bugs was the heaviest; he was their team's prop. He wasn't the tallest, but what he lacked in height he made up for with bulky, solid width. A bull child. Even his hair resembled that of a wildebeest or scruffy buffalo. John Henry was the tallest; he packed in at second row, so was very athletically built, even muscular. His face was sharp boned and classically handsome, with huge, brown eyes and dark, shoulder-length hair. Kenny and Cozy were the smallest and slowest to physically mature. Their baby faces gave the pretence of softness and innocence. Handy, because they were anything but. Kenny was cute, but Cozy was awkward and adroitly offensive. But just as your favourite bad smell requires two sniffs, Cozy's indelicate looks exacted a second scrutiny.

Tribute © Robert Lee Johnston 2016
Email: tributerobertleejohnston@gmail.com

Girls weren't on their radar yet, so taking off on their pushbikes, barefoot and helmet-less, filled empty time. Dodging, without crashing, the precise, sniper-like attacks from a tribe of renowned, no-nonsense, local bullies. They possessed a loathsome predisposition for violence when breeding. The bullies were feathered, beaked, territorial, and terribly bloodthirsty. Tribute's many swooping magpies were a brutal, anger-addicted gang of louts.

Running wild was a daily event. The ten-year-olds hated school—the books, the teachers—but mostly Rev and his orphanage.

'Rev'll kill you if he finds out you stole his durries.' Kenny's grin widened as Cozy handed him a ciggie out of the stolen Craven A pack.

Cozy offered Bugs one. He reached out and cackled to Kenny, 'They taste better when they're stolen. Ha ha. Especially from Rev.'

'Chuck us one, man.' John Henry was stoking the fire. 'Just don't get fucking caught. You know what he gets like.'

Cozy knew. He wished they were all sixteen, so they could legally leave this shit and just live here. The dream of emancipation was already burning within them. The fire, like the boys' dream, was far too big and blazing away. John Henry lit his smoke with a burning stick, blowing smoke rings into the still air with a homely grin. 'This'd be a great place to live. Lots of thick jungle. Plenty of rivers, and fish to eat. And, best of all, no adults telling us what to fucking do all the time.'

'I could live here,' Cozy agreed.

'Piss easy. Just need a big fuck-off tarp and a bag of rice and spuds.' After a moment's thought Bugs rubbed his belly and licked his lips. 'And some Tim Tams or chocolate.'

Cozy was nursing sore ribs and some welts here and there. He had just come back from Syd's. Syd had recently taken Cozy and Evie for a spell. The boys had decided to wag school and catch up with Cozy to make sure he was okay.

Tribute © Robert Lee Johnston 2016
Email: tributerobertleejohnston@gmail.com

Cozy shivered, chilled at the thought of Rev finding out he had stolen from him again. Rev wasn't as physical as Syd, but he wasn't that far off it. The boys' smoking pissed Rev off. John Henry noticed Cozy, locked away in thought, and smiled reassuringly. 'Deny everything, Cozy. Lie always.'

Henry's dog, Stirrup, a young, chunky, big-boned blue cattle dog dropped a well-chewed stick at Cozy's dirty, bare feet for him to throw into the fast-moving water. Stirrup looked eagerly into Cozy's soft eyes and then energetically shook water all over everyone and everything. He picked up the fat stick and told Stirrup, 'That's a branch, not a stick,' and pegged it as hard as he could. The insane Stirrup charged through them and the rude camp and then leapt at full pelt off the bank. Airborne, his tail spinning furiously like a propeller, he belly flopped with a massive splash. They laughed. Stirrup went everywhere with them. He was a calm, thoughtful, polite dog until John Henry was threatened or afraid. Then that blue dog would become courageous and savagely dangerous. He loved and protected them, and was happiest hanging around his pack when they ran through the jungle or swam. He walked to school every day with Henry and waited at the front gate until the bell rang, freeing him. Whenever Henry came into sight, Stirrup would run, smile, canter, skip, trip, roll and greet him as a wild piglet greets his mum's tit—one-eyed tunnel vision, with yelps of joy, grunting uncontrollably with excitement and happiness. He wasn't a licker or a sniffer, and never once tried fornicating with anything other than female dogs. He was a perfect gentleman.

John Henry reminded the boys, Kenny in particular, of the time they first saw porn a few years ago. John Henry and Cozy had found a hidden stash of Playboy magazines in the shed of a foster couple they'd been staying with. The boys ran without fear over old trucks and machinery and a couple of conveyer belts used to move bulk grain. Up on a mezzanine floor they discovered, along with a tonne of

Tribute © *Robert Lee Johnston 2016*
Email: tributerobertleejohnston@gmail.com

other shit, forty or fifty stick magazines. The seven- or eight-year-olds nearly fell off the second floor when Cozy opened the pages. They had no idea. Afterwards they felt educated, perhaps more mature than their less grown-up, tender kin.

At the very spot where they now sat, Henry had announced straight out to the others, 'Me and Cozy found a big stack of Playboys the other day!'

Bugs's head had spun around so quickly it nearly came off. 'Fucking when? Where is it then?'

Henry reached for a few favourites stashed in his school bag.

Kenny's young eyes and jaw were wide open. He barely blinked after a few of the tatty-eared Playboys were broken out. Kenny read aloud slowly, squinting, 'Blah blah blah. Her clit was swollen ... Hey, Bugs, is there only one hole? And what's all that hair, and this clit thing about?'

The boys giggled and shifted awkwardly.

'There's two holes, man. I'm sure. They piss out that clit thingy,' Bugs knowingly informed them.

Kenny asked, 'Two? Plus this clit thing! How do you know, you know, what to do with them?'

'I don't know, mate,' said Cozy. 'You sure there's only two, Bugs? It makes no sense, man. They got a hole to piss and a hole to shit, right?'

'Right.'

'Shouldn't there be another one somewhere?'

'No, man, there's only two.' Bugs was positive.

'You sure?'

'Yep.'

'I don't know. Shit, boys, we're going to need a tool box and a bloody mud-map to deal with all that crap.'

'I bet there's only two, Cozy.'

'Righto, cos I seen this filthy slag once. She couldn't wait, so pissed in front of me out back near the church. And I'm sure, man, I saw a third.'

Tribute © Robert Lee Johnston 2016
Email: tributerobertleejohnston@gmail.com

'Bullshit! I'll win, cos you only ever hear them old fellas say pussy and arse. They don't ever say some third hole's name.'

'Yeah, but those same old fellas tell you to piss all over your bruises and cuts to fix them up. You're going to believe them? You're the same bloke who told us catfish eat cats, and dogfish eat dogs. What was it again, Bugs? What is it that lionfish and … sperm whales eat?'

Bugs belly laughed. Kenny asked Cozy, very confused, 'So when is the right time to, you know …? When do you know it's the right time to piss in their pussies?'

Cozy flicked a twig at him. 'Who told you that? Was it, Bugs?'

'Nah, I don't think anyone told me. I just sort of thunk it. Isn't that what you do if you love them?'

The other boys fell about. Henry choked on his words. 'Don't … Don't ever piss in a girl's pussy, man. Shit. You sort of thunk it!'

'Fuck!' Embarrassed, but not understanding why, Kenny joined in the merriment. He was still confused. 'But … So girls don't piss on our dicks when they love us, and when we root them?'

Bugs cried, he was laughing so hard. 'No pissing, man, you or her. When you finally get a root, no piss. FULL STOP.'

They were weak from lack of oxygen. Cozy's eyes watered and his guts were sore. Kenny's face contorted in horror as he yelled, 'FUCK ME DEAD! They're so bloody confusing and horrible.'

***

Cozy kept throwing the wet stick for Stirrup, who showed no sign of slowing down.

They talked about the future. The boys were always in various stages of trouble, but Bugs the 'ring leader' always

had to be the first to do any- and everything. First to smoke, first to steal or do something risky or daring. Because he was physically more mature and powerful than most kids, he got his way with them. Bugs's plan was to do as little in life as humanly possible that wasn't fun. On this point he was firm. Others were here to do the heavy lifting. He would pick the low hanging fruit. Bugs, for now, was the toughest of them and had a mean streak. He loved stirring people till they lost their shit and fought. He liked firing the other boys up saying stuff like: 'Did you hear what that crusty cum-stain over there said about you? He reckons you're fuck all. You better do something about him. I fucking would.'

He was an excellent stand-over bloke, and he was only a boy. He had plenty of time and opportunity to practice and improve his technique. In their late teens, if Cozy was training for a tough fight and Bugs was holding the heavy bag for Cozy's coach Bernie, when Bugs saw Cozy tire he'd say stuff like: 'You remember when all your shit was stolen that time? Your house trashed? Well guess what? It was me! You remember when some gutchy slag crashed into your car, wrote it off, then took off and didn't even leave a fucking note? Well, fucked if that wasn't me too!' No robbery or crash had happened, but Bugs was at his best at these moments.

All the boys started footy a couple of years earlier and were loving it. Now playing under tens, they were all pretty deadly. Cozy had taken up boxing the same year he started footy. His coach was a battle-scarred, old-school, ex Aussie champ. The scars he wore were testament to the many battles he waged. His older brothers, all bloody seven of them, boxed. And though not being the most naturally gifted, Bernie worked hard and trained diligently. He won many titles with no more than horse-hair gloves. He fought pro at middleweight and, from all accounts, had power to burn in both hands. Stories were passed around boxing

Tribute © Robert Lee Johnston 2016
Email: tributerobertleejohnston@gmail.com

circles about his knocking out unwilling beasts of burden with a single punch.

Bernie had the wobbly boot on, on his way home from The Middle Pub, and saw Cozy having a blue, fighting bare fisted after school hours 'behind the dunnies' with some bully who had, a day or two before, punched Kenny in the head. Bernie raced through a gate on his walk home past the school and broke it up. 'You whooped him good,' he announced after the bleeding meat-axe staggered off hurt. 'He's a lot bigger than you. You rattled his chain didn't you, little mate? You got great feet, but your punches are shithouse. How old are you?'

'I'm nearly eight. I won but.' Sticking up for his victory.

'Seven, eh? Do you want to learn how to fight properly?'

He had a kind, no-nonsense smile. His face had been smacked a lot and his nose was a pumpkin-looking thing, all big, busted and broken. Cozy's young body was tingling from the after effects of adrenaline.

'I don't want to fight if I'm going to wind up looking beat up and ugly like you. Did you come a gutser? Didn't you never duck?'

'Ha, that's a corker. You're funny too, are you? See, I can teach you how not to get hit.'

'Well, why didn't you learn it then?'

'Cos, kid, I liked getting hit.'

'You liked it?'

'I loved it.'

'My name's Cozy.'

'Cozy, is it? What's your last name, Cozy?

'Withazed.'

'Withershead?'

'Nah. With-a-zed.'

'With-a-zed? Jeez, can't say I have ever heard that one before. Me, I'm Bernie.' Shaking hands, Cozy noticed twisted, knurled fingers and ripped-up, scarred knuckles.

Tribute © Robert Lee Johnston 2016
Email: tributerobertleejohnston@gmail.com

'Do you have a boxing club, Bernie?'

'No, Cozy. I don't usually train anyone, little mate.'

'Well how come you want to train me, then?'

'Cos, little one, you see, you're a fighter. You may not know it yet, but I can see it as plain as this big old nose stuck on my face.' Cozy smiled. 'And not every bloke can be a fighter. People think they are, all the time. Think they can. But, Cozy Withazed, only a few understand the cunning behind it.'

He seemed really smart and softly spoken to the boy.

'I got a bag hanging up outside, some gloves, and a skipping rope. If you want to rock up, that's all we need to start.'

'I got no money, Bernie, to pay you, and I would have to ask Rev. But he will say yes. He's happy to see me not bothering him.'

'Well you go ahead and ask this Rev. Is he your minister?'

'Nah, yeah ... sort of. He looks after all the orphans from around here and there.'

'Are you an orphan, Cozy?'

'Yeah, but I can still fight, right?'

'If your Rev says yes, then sure. I got a lawn that needs mowing every now and then. So if I teach you to box, you mow my lawn. Deal?' He offered his hand and Cozy sealed the deal, extending his.

For months, Cozy ran and ran and ran. He mowed when the grass grew, then ran and ran, and, for fun, ran some more. The boy skipped rope and was taught one single punch to practice for now, a left jab. He wasn't allowed to move his right hand from his chin while cradling a squash ball between his chin and his lifted left shoulder, hiding and protecting his jaw from any opponent. In time, Cozy had what Bernie called 'a safe left jab to die for'. He stung the heavy bag with machine-gun-fast, barrel-straight jabs, but still wasn't allowed to throw a right. His footwork was

Tribute © *Robert Lee Johnston 2016*
Email: tributerobertleejohnston@gmail.com

sweetened by adopting a safe technique but a dangerous style. Bernie's lawn, which doubled as a simple boxing ring with four star pickets and a rope, was looking all right too, with a little of Cozy's elbow grease.

Bernie and Cozy watched every fight they could together on the telly, and Bernie would explain what went right and wrong in each bout. He always asked Cozy if he'd seen anything he liked. The answer was usually anything both 'Sugar Rays' had done. Cozy also admitted a secret love of Roberto Duran and his awkward, confronting, no-nonsense style. Bernie noticed a switch flick in Cozy while watching Duran's 'Hands of Stone' bash and brawl. Poor Cozy cried like a spanked baby as Sugar lost when these two, his heroes, first met, fisty gloved.

Soon Cozy was drawing power from his feet, from his toes, through his calves and legs. Emulating his beloved heroes, able to connect the rotation of his sinewy torso and new tummy muscles with the power of his bony fists.

Bernie would smile. 'That's it. It's looking sweet as a rosy-pink peach that punch. Can you feel it snap? The energy? The power?' Cozy nodded. He could feel it. Every week he was getting better, tougher, faster and fitter. Bernie reckoned it was time to beef up his left arm's bag of tricks and learn left hooks and left uppercuts. Bernie was pretty excited with the kid's jab. 'Nearly, bloody, perfect!'

***

Stirrup growled fiercely and became tense, looking deeply into the dense jungle behind the camp. The boys looked in that direction. The ten-year-olds could hear something bearing down on them.

Bugs was startled. 'What the fuck's that? It's bigger than a tree kangaroo or a pig!'

They were all up. After a moment looking they saw Sarge's blue uniform in the greenery and all six foot four of him.

'ARGHH BE FUCKED.' Kenny squealed. 'IT IS A PIG.'

Stirrup took off, a flaming, heat-seeking missile, and grabbed Sarge's trouser leg, barking, until he got a mouthful, and then growling once attached. Sarge yelled, kicking his leg out, his broad face sweaty and grimacing. 'GITOUTOFITYAMONGRELBASTARD.'

Stirrup had a good hold and wasn't letting go, giving the kids enough time to escape, as they shot off into deep scrub, scattering like sheep shit. Once out of sight Henry whistled and called, 'Stirrup! Come here, boy.'

Stirrup let go of Sarge and took off after his master, proud of his toothy self. Sarge wasn't so happy. Hat in hand, his thinning black hair didn't look at all dignified or 'policey', tangled with jungle trash and wet with sweat. The school had rung him, saying the boys had been skipping school again the last three days. 'Find them for us, please?'

Sarge knew the young fellas would be in the jungle somewhere. He wandered the trails until he heard them near the river. He got a glimpse of them as John Henry's blue dog suddenly appeared, meaner than a wild grizzly protecting her cubs. He smiled to himself as the little buggers predictably ran off.

'You little shits think I got nothing better to do? Youse have ruined my bloody uniform.'

The boys could hear him, plain as day, complaining and grunting as he crashed and blah- blah-blahed his way through the scrub. It was as if a clumsy, uncoordinated, slightly retarded, big-foot was loose.

'You cheeky bastards. Where are you?'

The runaways listened, barefoot, silently hidden in various spots. Sarge walked, hands on hips, right in front of the tree behind which Cozy was hiding. Sarge turned his back on the kid. He was so close Cozy could reach his holster

and gun. His legs went weak. It was terrifying but also exhilarating. Then Henry flew past Cozy! Sarge turned heel and took chase. In hot pursuit of Sarge, Stirrup nailed him again.

'FUCKNHELLDOG! GITOUTAIT!'

Stirrup was pissed, nipping at Sarge's heel and getting a grip now and then while Sarge captured the villain, John Henry. Henry surrendered, worried Stirrup might cop a kick in the guts and get hurt. The trio had circled around and were now right next to Cozy. Stirrup came over to Cozy to see what he was doing, just as Sarge booted Henry hard, right up the arse. Henry yelped. Sarge smiled. Stirrup growled, left Cozy, and had another crack at Sarge's strides.

'Fucking piss off, Stirrup!' Sarge complained. 'Where're those other three bloody clowns, Henry?'

'I don't know.'

Sarge looked into the jungle, straight past Bugs. 'RIGHTO! IF YOUSE COME OUT NOW I'LL KICK YOUSE ONCE, JUST LIKE I DID HENRY! IF NOT! I'LL GET YOU THREE MONGRELS TOMORROW. AND IT'LL BE DOUBLE, YOU WATCH! LOOK! I GOT YOUR SCHOOL BAGS.'

'SEE YOU TOMORROW THEN, COPPER!' Bugs yelled into the trees behind him, scattering his voice as Stirrup, Sarge, and John Henry left.

Sarge was true to his word. He was at school waiting for them to arrive, or not. He kicked them all, Henry included, up their absconding, tender, ten-year-old arses, three times on parade in front of the whole school. When Bugs complained he'd said he'd only kick them twice, Sarge reckoned, 'That was before you all were smart arses about it.' Then the four boys were publicly dressed down by a displeased headmaster. They were sent to his office, where they held out hands to receive six cuts each from a fat man and a cured, thick length of lawyer cane. Crack, crack, crack on each of their calamitous hands. To top it off they got a

colossal hiding from a loud, socially embarrassed, unimpressed Rev when they got home later that afternoon.

Still, they reckoned it was well worth it. And the boys grew to 'like' those expertly stashed, dog-eared Playboys more and more often.

CHAPTER THREE: START FIGHTING

"Run like hell."

Pink Floyd – Song Title.

'Your eyes, man, they turned stone cold! Fuck me dead, man, you just ...! You fucking ...! You're a fucking thrashing machine, man. You demoralised the fucker. Did you even get hit? You just ate him up!'

'Yeah, I got hit.'

'You did?'

Bugs sounded surprised over the applause as he leant on the ropes in Cozy's corner. It was the young fighter's very first fight, a hometown fight.

'It was like watching a Great Dane eat a fucking kitten! He didn't stand a fucking chance!'

The young fighter's head throbbed. A messy, unorthodox, massive right hand had landed flush on Cozy's

chin, rattling him, sending a curtain of bright purples and dull greens across his vision.

Bugs had missed or simply forgotten that bit. Bernie was kneeling next to Cozy, taking gloves off and wrapping a towel over his shoulders. He told the boy he done good then asked how his head was.

He nodded. 'It's okay.'

He reminded Cozy, 'Go over and thank and congratulate your opponent, now he's awake. Remember to be a gent, Cozy.'

Cozy's age-for-age, weight-for-weight, eight-year-old, taller opponent was awake. He was heavily concussed. He didn't know where he was or who Cozy was. Cozy smiled and thanked him for the fight.

His coach said, 'That was a great fight. I'll have to remember your name. I'm Brunker, Jack Brunker. This your first fight?'

'Yep.' They shook hands, Cozy's still bandage-wrapped. 'I'm, Cozy.'

'I'll say! You owned the ring tonight. Old Geoff here's had over twenty bouts and you won that fight pretty easily. He simply doesn't have your feet.' He looked into the boy's eyes. 'Or your eyes.'

It struck Cozy as strange that Bugs and now Jack had brought up the same thing.

'Funny, cos now they're warm and innocent. How do you do that?'

'I don't know.'

'You want to fight again, Cozy?'

'Yeah, Jack, I want to.'

'Does Bernie still play heaps of Tom Waits and Bob Dylan when you're training with him?'

'Yeah he does, all the time. I really like the stories they sing about.'

'That's good, mate. I used to hate it, until I got a bit older. Bernie's a fine coach and a good man. Stick with him,

Tribute © Robert Lee Johnston 2016
Email: tributerobertleejohnston@gmail.com

Cozy. I'm sure you'll win a few more yet and, most probably, fight of the night.'

'Did Bernie train you, Jack ...? Wait up, is that a thing?'

'Yeah. He was my coach years ago. He only trains a few here and there, so he must like you. And yep. I reckon fight of the night is yours tonight. We give the best fight of the night an extra special trophy.'

Cozy's heart beat faster. 'I didn't know that. I've got to go, Jack. Pleasure to meet you both. I hope Geoff's okay.'

'Righto, Cozy. He'll be right. It was good to meet you.'

Cozy's smile, his little hands still bandaged, his fighter's cool composure and the way he walked in his boxing ring made Jack laugh. Shaking his head he asked loudly, 'You're trouble, ain't you, Cozy?'

'That's what I keep hearing. See you next time, Jack.'

Jack winked respectfully and nodded. He shrugged in amazement after Bernie and he traded a certain look boxing coaches give one another. Bernie made his way over to thank Jack and his young son, Geoff. The wink means a million things in boxing talk.

Fucking hell, Bernie.

We got a live one, boys.

Lucky bastard!

Who the fuck?

Where the fuck?

How the fuck did you stumble onto him?

Bernie didn't have to say much. He whispered to his dear friend, 'Jack, believe me, son. Don't I bloody know it? Christ!'

They watched pure energy pour off as Cozy left, bouncing over the top rope.

'You're going to have your hands full, Bernie.'

Bernie came down to the change room once Cozy had finished showering.

'You did great, little man. Just relax now and take in the fight at your own speed. It'll all come to you in little

Tribute © Robert Lee Johnston 2016
Email: tributerobertleejohnston@gmail.com

moments and flashes. And it'll slow down for you in your head, I promise. You just got to let it in and see it properly for what it is.'

Cozy hugged him and smiled. 'Thanks, Bernie. I will. I felt all right out there.'

'You looked pretty much at home, little mate.'

The boys came in, whooping and cheering.

'That fucker was gammon. That was fucking awesome! You were a fucking animal out there! Did you see that shit, boys?' Bugs looked at the other two. 'Did youse see it?'

Both asked almost at once. 'Are you okay?'

Bugs answered for Cozy. 'Course he's okay! Weren't you fucking watching? He's better than okay!'

Kenny was calm. 'I barely saw your feet touch the ground. You fucked up gravity.' Henry agreed. 'You were just too fast, way too fucking quick. You made him look slow and gangly.'

'He's a fucking machine!' Bugs was happy. 'Did you see his eyes when the bell went? Holy shit! I never seen you like that!'

'Scary, man,' agreed Kenny.

'You looked pissed off, bloke. That gammon, southern fuckery didn't stand a chance!'

Cozy looked up into Bugs's face. 'That gammon fuck nearly knocked me the fuck out.'

'What? He hardly laid a finger on you.'

'Man. He got me good, with a bomb. You must've missed it. Fucking hurts like hell.'

***

Cozy loved going to away fights. Visiting strange new towns and fighting strange new heads. Bernie would let all the kids pile into his old Ford. Tom Waits and Dylan religiously played. Bernie let Cozy listen to his own AC/DC in

Tribute © Robert Lee Johnston 2016
Email: tributerobertleejohnston@gmail.com

the car before stepping into the ring, helping the fighter in him to divine strength and expel fear. Once the boys forgot to bring their music so Cozy turned up Tom Waits, loud. Tom's fury stoked Cozy's ambition. Tom humbled the boy into accepting his own weird, savage ways.

Bernie would shout the youngsters food all day long, whatever they wanted, making sure Cozy ate plenty of pasta while stuffing chunks of chocolate in his gob as the fight drew nearer. Cozy loved the post-bout, late-night drives home. Won or lost. Listening to, and memorising, Tom Waits. Artfully dodging Bernie's elbow as he expertly wrestled the three-on-the-tree, column shift gearbox into action.

CHAPTER FOUR: "BEEN DOWN SO LONG".

The Doors - Song Title

God's sledgehammer, Rev, was mad.

The kids had been playing up like second hand whipper snippers.

His animated peroration could easily scold the devil up and out of a haunted mine shaft. The tall sack of bespectacled, chain-smoking, yellow-fingered, one-eyed shit was ramming all his toothy, godly crap down the kids' necks. The two girls and four boys, each of them barefoot, wasp-waisted, and tighter than black paint on white undercoat.

No children were allowed unsupervised in Rev's church, until the age of sixteen. He could not tolerate youthful interruptions, such as crying, whispering, burping, or farting, during his Sunday sermons. The road to the church ended at the church. The roof's steep, red, sharply apexed roof was always a challenge for local painters to coat. Five steps wound up either side of a covered, spacious

Tribute © Robert Lee Johnston 2016
Email: tributerobertleejohnston@gmail.com

landing and two open doors greeted Tribute's believers. Wall-mounted fans ticked and rotated soothingly, keeping the tropical heat and flies at bay. Premium, local, top-shelf timber had been selected for Rev's pulpit, the pews, and the adorned walls, and covered the floor. As the day grew hotter the floorboards would groan and complain. With Rev's preaching, the floor could never get a word in edgeways. The orphans were only allowed under his apexed, hallowed roof to clean and tidy. His churching them involved a monthly gathering under the verandah of the children's cottage. Never to praise his Almighty God, thank Christ. It was his heavy, flowing, menstrual venting of an infected spleen and shitty liver. He declared this day during his lectureship that all of them were innominate, then ranted angrily.

'You will have no atonement or respite for your impish petulance. You can't hide from Almighty God. If our Heavenly Father wasn't so, the world would be overrun with vagabonds, wastrels, and indentured reprobates such as your sad, pitiful selves. You are all far too foolish and brazen of late. You children are unprincipled and unutterably ... unparalleled. Heed unto my warning. I will have you fictile! I will decoct the bloody lot of you!'

The children barely understood a word he was regurgitating. When regular churchgoers on Sundays heard his long, self-serving sermons, half the educated people seated on their pews never knew what the hell he was on about. For the six kids most of Rev's one-eyed crap went in one ear and out the other. But, now and then, some of his words stuck. His sentences continually had the kids scuppered by the fourth or fifth big word. They tried not to worry.

However, Rev, along with his Almighty, fierce God, were leviathans in those half-dozen tiny, insignificant lives.

Cozy was thinking to himself, What the fuck is decoct? What the fuck is a wastrel? Atone for what, fuck knuckle?

Being born? Sounds like he just looked up U in a dictionary and listed shitty words to call kids.

Cozy asked the boys closest, in a hushed whisper, 'You reckon Rev's just making words up?'

They earnestly shushed Cozy, telling him not to make them laugh.

None knew the definition of Rev's razor-sharp words. Cozy got out his old dictionary later and looked up those words. They all knew what a whore was. Rev always called their sluts of mothers loose, lustful fornicators and beastly sinners, so they were familiar with that salty delight. Cozy particularly wasn't keen on the word indentured. Decoct frightened the collective shit out of them.

Jen asked the rest, giggling, 'Who says "unto"? Unto me, unto you. Go, Rev, unto the jungle, and lose yourself unto a short jump unto a deep mine shaft.'

They all shuffled with tight-lipped smiles. Prisoners of war mustered on parade would have been proud of those kids. They dropped their rebellious heads, pretending to be solemn and remorseful, hiding their shit-eating grins. Upon hearing Jenny, Kenny burst out laughing at Rev's lecture and all the dispositional judgement given, then just as quickly bottled his reaction. It was too late. Cozy was already laughing along with him.

'What's so funny, you two imbeciles?' A heatwave shortened his mood.

Rev focused a nicotine-stained, yellow-brown index finger and a hawk-eye on Cozy and then Kenny. His weeping, shithouse eye eventually following and catching up. A little bit of fresh pus oozed from it. Three bright, blue-arse flies, miniature Spitfires, swooped in greedily, attacking Rev's blind spot, and gorged on eye pus, until they irritated him enough to swipe them away. His eye had contracted some type of malady when he was a child.

'Nothing,' Cozy, disgusted at the flies, lied. Rev was pissed now. He swatted and fumed, trying to find the words.

Tribute © Robert Lee Johnston 2016
Email: tributerobertleejohnston@gmail.com

Bugs covered the two lads. 'Cozy just asked what "unto" means.'

'It means "to"!' Rev's face darkened red. Heat rose from his temper, fogging his glasses. Annoyed, he took them off and polished them furiously with a hanky. Kenny was confused. Shaking his head, he looked pathetically at the rest, shrugging.

John Henry asked, 'Why didn't you just say "to" instead of "unto", then?'

'Because, stupid little boy, one of us happens to be enlightened and educated!' He gathered himself. 'Also, one must be able to express oneself using the unique gifts Almighty God, in his wisdom, so bountifully bestowed. Something you untenable children wouldn't understand, being found so lacking in fight, spirit and bereft of talents.' His hollow pigeon-chest exhaled. Veins throbbed swollen upon his sharp, thin-skinned temples.

John Henry whispered, 'Rev, the chosen one … but he can't find any fly repellent.'

The few that heard snickered.

'Dear me! Years of thankless devotion, just to raise you, you, you lot.'

Perhaps he'd run out of insults … But, no!

'You apish heathens need an electrifying culture shock. All can plainly see you have no hope, no heaven, no saviour, no faith, no education, no virginity or chastity, no morals, no family, no one and no thing!' He took a deep breath. 'You're not smart. You're not at all clever or good at or for anything. None of you are needed, loved, or clean. You're all filthy and stained. You're blank, soiled sheets! You're nothing. All you have is what I give to you. Do any of you ever ask yourself why you're not adopted? It's simple! Because everyone in this wide world can see—can sense—how tawdry and vile you truly are. So do not, children, provoke or stupidly bite the one hand that feeds you. This hand has sharp, powerful teeth.'

Tribute © Robert Lee Johnston 2016
Email: tributerobertleejohnston@gmail.com

Finally, he arrived at his point.

'If ever anyone, and I mean anyone, asks you what the orphanage is like, what it's like to live here, you will politely smile and say, "It's fine." Understood? Bugs, Cozy, you two are forbidden from now on to ever be without a shirt, at school, here or around town. None of us need to see the punishment the Good Lord saw fit to dispense you. It is your burden alone to carry, not mine nor anyone else's. Your ugly, profound unsightliness makes the rest of us sick to the stomach. If you children refuse to obey me, one may be forced to destroy all your meagre, petty possessions and toss them and yourselves to hellfire, you apish horde of miscreants.'

'Unto hellfire,' John Henry whispered, still stung from Rev's insult. He corrected the exulted, Cyclopean one.

Rev had heard whispers that one of the children had complained to a teacher about his lecturing and sermoning of the pack of misfits. That was what the kids called it when the sick, seedy-eyed fucker, drunk and bold, smelling of hard liquor, would wake one of them and drag them, tired and reluctant, to his own private quarters late at night. Without his pants on, he'd "sermon" over them.

Rev hated the jungle and the jungle, him. He proved a Latin proverb true: Natura abhorret vacuum. 'Nature abhors a vacuum.' When the kids hid in the forest, or their foot-falcons became too fleet-footed for Rev to catch, he'd bring in deputised trouble shooters. Callous, hard, pious men like Syd who gladly found them, caught them, and then screwed them over. Flogged them black and blue for Rev, Queen, Country, God and Co. God was indeed everywhere. Rev was told everything by those who knew him. Mostly, Rev's Almighty God, had an almighty, size-twelve boot, kicking one or all their arses. His God was a strong, lead-footed, vengeful bastard.

It was time for the kids to repay Rev and his one dribbling eye some dues. When they were too young to

work, they cost him money to 'raise'. Selling their labours once they were old enough was Rev's just compensation. They thought this happened to every kid.

Rev routinely avoided adopting out a half dozen kids into their teens to prop up his meagre income, telling prospective parents they were old, diseased, sickly, damaged goods, from contaminated, fouled stock, far beyond the Good Lord and His salvation. 'Resentful, untrustworthy monsters! Incarceration is surely their pre-ordained future.'

The orphanage's constant stream of unwanted babies was always homed quickly to keep his trade secret and locals in the dark. To them he appeared pious and civically minded.

The oldest kids in the orphanage, now fifteen and sixteen, were being disposed of into juvenile boys' and girls' prisons, or they simply, quietly and, quite understandably, ran away. No longer wards of the state. Free and now off the books, so to speak, no one cared about their fate.

Cozy and his mob, now eleven years old, were Rev's next stable of groomed whores, greedily dispatched. He would repeat the pattern once they were too old.

Evie asked herself often, 'How long has this been happening?' The system felt old, cyclic and rehearsed to her.

Rev's rabbiting-on ended with a final threat. 'You children, worthless, forgettable whelps! One can easily let you slip one's mind. Satan will have a hot seat in the deep bowels of hell for each of you while this monkey business is ongoing. If it's the devil and eternal damnation you seek, we can start today. Why don't we start with removing all your linen and bedding, all your toys and books: everything to which you have an attachment. See how you like those apples? Maybe I'll forget to accept food for you wretches, and turn the water off. You will, every one of you, bathe in the green river, like the filthy, un-evolved animals and pigs you are. I will insist the power be shut down to your cottage.

Tribute © Robert Lee Johnston 2016
Email: tributerobertleejohnston@gmail.com

Everything you have, you love, is Almighty God's, and, therefore, mine. I will not tolerate unbelievers here! Nor blasphemy nor any criticism towards the church, Almighty God, our humble orphanage or myself. I will send for Syd, and you will never ever be heard of again. Now be gone, the lot of you, and best you little shits heed my warning!'

The children went back inside, shaken, scared, and impotent. They may not have remembered or understood all the flash words, but they knew they were well and truly rooted.

Later that night they learnt some new words from Cozy's old dictionary. Cozy discovered Rev was full of shit, and had used both the words 'innominate' and 'fictile' incorrectly. All of them had names, and they weren't made of clay, by a potter.

Cozy reckoned, 'What a wanker.'

He found and liked the word 'self-righteous', particularly with 'fuck' after it: self-righteous fuck. It rolled off his tongue easily. He felt he should thank Rev, in a way, because without Wan-Bung-I's (their Chinese name for him) keen, corrosive vocabulary, Cozy may never have discovered his first and greatest love: his stolen dictionary and its many wonderful words.

They each felt a coarse noose tightening roughly as they waited for the gallows floor to drop them swiftly into a pre-heated, pre-arranged seating plan. They weren't unbelievers at all. Rev got that wrong. The kids didn't doubt for one moment a word he preached. Each hoped like hell there was a merciful, loving father. None were able to see it in their heads or feel it in their hearts and soul. Once they saw a picture, a glossy fashion magazine's cover of a blond lady dressed in white, lying on a bed of white sheets. White curtains, white walls, white everything. The woman looked weepingly beautiful. Her minx-like face, hidden from the camera's view, made them all think she was an angel.

Jen was certain. 'That's what angels look like.'

Tribute © Robert Lee Johnston 2016
Email: tributerobertleejohnston@gmail.com

They desperately wanted to be close to the lady in the photo.

What chance had a bunch of eleven-year-olds of trying to figure out God and angels? They had weird, almost philosophical discussions. No matter what, Cozy still wanted to stab Rev in his one good eye with a roasting fork.

'I can't love no God that hurts me, calls me names. Fuck Rev! I like Pops' idea better.'

Pops was a clever, wise aboriginal elder the kids knew.

'Pops' god never once called me a filthy bastard. Never once called my father a dead-shit drop-kick, or my mother a diseased whore.' To Cozy it just made sense. All Rev's big words and threats didn't impress him. 'And I don't want to go to heaven if that bung-eyed, hawk-eyed fuck's going to be there, or Jesus and his fucking almighty, poxy father. How can we miss those other two fuckers when we ain't never had them? How can you miss what you've never had?'

Even Bugs couldn't answer that. The thought of hell wasn't any better. It occupied a great deal of conversation and thought. Not only had they been turned against any merciful God: they slowly turned against the whole human race. Particularly grown, sexually active men.

Bugs sighed. 'We're fucked either which way.'

They hopelessly hung their heads.

Kenny spoke sadly. 'I'm sick of getting ragged on, and being every bastard's mongrel fucking dog.'

They were truly rooted. They had to swear secrecy, more or less blackmailed with fear of religion into cruel silence. What would the consequences be if any of them reneged against Rev and his Almighty God? Little brains stewed. Rev didn't have to boil kids in a pot to 'decoct' and extract their essence.

The kids made a song up that night. Now and then the girls skipped, or double dutched, with ropes tied to a tree. They jumped to the beat of the slow, disturbing, catchy

Tribute © Robert Lee Johnston 2016
Email: tributerobertleejohnston@gmail.com

jingle, with an ever-increasing tempo after each cycle. Until it was impossible.

Don't sweat the petty stuff.
Don't pet the sweaty stuff.
Don't say yes.
Don't say no.
Syd will get ya then ya won't know
Which way's lost,
Which way's found.
If ya miss a beat
He will tie you down.
(Faster)
Don't sweat the petty stuff ...
(Etc.)

A verbal spear impaled the boy's heart. A truthful Doors song "Been Down so Long" being thrashed on the local radio, sprang to Cozy's young mind. That song, the bluesy hook, that chunky feel, the groove, the strength of lyrics Jim Morrison sang as if he had smoked barbed wire, and the music The Doors played, suddenly struck home.

Cozy loved those men and their language.

Tribute © Robert Lee Johnston 2016
Email: tributerobertleejohnston@gmail.com

CHAPTER FIVE: POPS, THE DINGOES AND COZY

"If you look proper like
You will see
I promise."

Pops

You will need one very important ingredient if you want rainforest, namely rain and shitloads of it.

Tall, peaky mountains won't hurt if it's thick, impenetrable jungle you want. It was always raining in Tribute. Worse still were the 'in-between' months of merciless, humid, damp, smoky fog and general mistiness, pouring off the mountains as if spot fires were lit or huge geysers constantly billowed out. It was enough to drive each and every child mad. Solid rain for nine months, and then the trees would drip for another three. Some years were like that. Christmas time, however, was always bright, blue and swelteringly hot. The sun was so close to land up in that

mountain range this time of year it fried any bright whities to a smokestack-terracotta red.

On those sweet, rare, sunny days, the gang left the hot, airless, mouldy confines of their communal quarters as soon as the sun rose and escaped into the jungle to one of their favourite swimming holes, leaving in their wake the soul-crushing humidity and the tall, apexed roofline of the church.

The rivers ran clear and deep all year long. The swings, shallows, rapids and huge water falls kept locals cool and entertained. All of the mob could swim like swamp rats. No one ever taught them. Around here people just sort of learnt to swim when they first crawled through the puddles. The creatures of the forest always attracted the children's keen attention. So too the river life. They'd fish, chase turtles, get chased by big, old, evil-looking eels and angry, wet, swimming snakes, exploring every part of the river system and its many tributaries.

The jungle was also home to a segment of the local aboriginal population who weren't interested in living in any town or settlement. They longed to live as their ancestors, on, in and from their country. They were always gentle, generous, thoughtful and friendly to the kids. They would get a little pissed every now and then and tell old dreaming stories which captivated their childish imaginings. They pointed out animals the children had missed or couldn't see: birds and their nests, lizards, snake hides. No doubt the odd tall tale was thrown in to make the youngsters laugh and wonder. Cozy loved them. The kids absorbed all the information they offered. They loved that the aboriginal men swore a lot, and didn't care if they did too. Being a mob of starving shits they greedily ate up all and any tucker they were offered: scrub turkey, black brim, perch, turtle, catfish, and their favourite: scrub turkey eggs, depending where they were and what they were hunting. Never once did the murder of crows' empty tummies ever call it bush tucker. It

was just tucker. When those kids caught a whole heap of fish they'd always drop a few off to that older mob. They taught the young ones how to share completely.

On certain days, the kids were shown which roots made the tall spears they carried, how to track dinner and back track so as not to disappear in there forever. The older mob, the parliament of owls, would tell the boys they'd make 'goot hunters and would be bloody goot liddle blackfullas'.

The boys, in particular, loved going with the wise men to their secret fishing spots, often places the wandering, nosey kids had never come across. There was a good feed at every spot and the old men knew precisely when the next good feed was due. Through time and close association, the kids learned what berries and jungle fruit could or couldn't be eaten, which ones to wash out if patient and/or desperate. They learned how to make and find cover, to find termite larvae and extract water from wait-a-while. The children became confident bush boys and girls.

Dingoes and cassowaries quickly became Cozy's favourite wildlife to watch or see. The cassowary was old Pops' totem animal, along with the black brim. He taught the boys some old traditions. How it was an aboriginal person's duty to protect their totem animals from harm and over hunting. Everyone received a totem and every animal, in theory, was husbanded and protected. If you follow that train of thought further, in theory no Australian animal should ever go extinct. Pops reckoned that those born here and naturalised should have a totem animal each to nurture, to speak for, to protect and connect them to this country.

The dingoes, the pure-breeds, were becoming scarcer. They were slaughtered by farmers and more and more cross breeding with domesticated runaway dogs was diluting ancient blood lines. Cozy and Pops loved tracking this one particular pack of dingoes. Usually fairly solitary animals, this pack was different. The pack sensed they were coming a

Tribute © Robert Lee Johnston 2016
Email: tributerobertleejohnston@gmail.com

couple of hours before they arrived. This mob of dingoes had known Pops and his ancestors for countless generations and didn't seem to mind a tiny, eleven-year-old migaloo coming with him, so the quadruped, canine family carried on as normal.

Pops reckoned this pack was different from the others, and didn't tolerate any stray dingoes, or especially domesticated dogs, trespassing in their territory. They would never let them join the pack. They lured strays by sending out the bitch while on heat to bring them to ambush. It was as if they knew domesticated dogs didn't belong in their scrub, a balance had to be maintained, the threats annihilated. The males of the pack, four great, prickly-eared, stout, healthy boys waited in hiding for the imposters following lustfully the bleeding bitch. The ripe bitch would gallop to a prearranged position, a relatively clear, steep gully, hard for even a nimble dog to climb. The four bonded boys waited downwind atop the ravine, perfectly hidden and dangerously silent.

Pops was doing a post-mortem on the grisly scene. His broken English required a keen ear. 'See dat girl dingo? She ran to dat stray mob der, den turned tail like lightnin and run like the debil, eh! Den she bolted into dis gulch. Look ere, see?' He pointed to found dog tracks left by the dingo boys downwind above their hot-pit trap. 'Dem dricky, dem bugga.'

They made their way to the opposite side of the gully and found where the boys had lain in wait. 'See, one be ere, eh.' They could plainly see the disturbed forest-floor trash where one lay or sat. His tail had swept the jungle's litter aside, wagging in thought and expectation of the murder to come. 'Eh look, another one ere, look.'

Together they soon found all four of their hides. So bloody clever, Cozy was thinking. The boys and this particular female were a beautifully rehearsed unit. She was

Tribute © Robert Lee Johnston 2016
Email: tributerobertleejohnston@gmail.com

a staunch matriarch. 'She ebil dat one, eh. Real bitch of a ting.'

Pops told Cozy that the female had made those dogs run until near exhaustion, in their excitement to be first at her. Smart, clever girl. The stray pack of three malnourished shepherd-kelpie crosses would have been no slouches.

'Dey was tinkin with der dicks.' Pops laughed. 'Not dis one!' He pointed to his brains. 'Ha ha! Dem horny fullas not tinkin straight. Dem tree yelpin and cryin, chasin dat bitch. Dey didn't eben know four killers jus waitin for em, ere on da high ground. Den dat bitch, she call out to her boys when dey was right ere. Right where dey agree before da hunt. Dat's when dem four come a rollin real heaby down da hill.'

The dingoes let none escape. It was a vicious, dog-eat-dog, no-holds-barred, shit-fighting bloodbath.

The bitch was the first to attack them, Pops pointed out. 'Must've scared da fuckin bejesus out of em!' He chuckled.

The strays were ripped to pieces. Fleshy, large, lumpy pieces. There were even a few bits missing. The pack had found and eaten the strays' hearts and lungs. Left a hell of a mess. A message of pain and blood to others.

'Must've bin loud,' Pops reckoned. 'Ip dogs git torn up in da jungle, and ip no bugger hear him? Did dat eber happen? Ha ha ha.'

Cozy imagined the pain the poor mongrel bastards suffered. Other than Syd and Deidre's poofter poodles, Cozy loved dogs and found it hard to look at. It was difficult to tell whose blood-stained, dripping body parts were whose. Cozy found a brand new respect and admiration right there and then. It dawned on the boy that those mates of his were, in fact, pack members. His own human mob of dingoes. They had to defend themselves, like this pack threatened intruders. To diabolical death if need be.

'Dem cunning dat mob, eh Cozy?'

'Do they want to be just left alone, Pops?'

Tribute © *Robert Lee Johnston 2016*
Email: tributerobertleejohnston@gmail.com

'Dat's all eberting wants, mate.'

Hard as those dingoes were, Cozy respected their solidarity, mateship and loyalty towards each other. 'Are they family that mob, Pops?'

'Yeah, dey better den family but. Dem a tribe. Dem hunters and survivors.'

Cozy liked his analogy.

Pops nodded his head in thought. Something bright and out of place caught his eye. 'Look ere. One of dem big boys hurt. Look see?'

There was a thick blood trail on the ground. One of the males had had his velvety right ear torn off. Pops soon found the soft, smooth, ripped-off ear. Cozy worried and Pops could see it.

'Hey, yer eyes jus turn green again. Owd you do dat?'

'I don't know. Will he be all right?'

'Em be right, mate,' Pops promised.

If he was sure, then so was the boy. The old man buried the ear shallow in the jungle's soil, returning it to the ground the dingo came from. Then he and his young mate climbed out of Dead Dog Gully.

'Em be easy ta spot now, dat one-ear fulla, eh?'

'If I was a blackfella, Pops, I'd want dingoes to be my totem.'

He cackled loudly. 'You'd make goot liddle blackfulla; a proper goot one, Cozy.'

Now and then Cozy would see that one-eared dingo during his jungle wanderings, and soon came to see a lot of himself in the brave, shy dingo.

He's scarred, just like me. He was born in the jungle, just like me. He was forced to fight, just like me. His family are his pack, just like me.

Cozy fell deeply in love with that native hound and soon named him 'Louis', as in 'King Louis'. George, Henry and William stood fast beside him, sharing the throne. The female or queen he named 'Cunning Cleopatra' or 'Cleo'.

Tribute © Robert Lee Johnston 2016
Email: tributerobertleejohnston@gmail.com

Cozy tried his best to emulate Louis' stoicism and fearless pride. Louis would receive many more jagged scars before his canine reign was up. Both boy and dog were young in their respective lives. Princes of the jungle: youthful, resilient and strong. Even thinking about Louis gave Cozy a burst of strength. The child connected forever to that orange dingo and his pack.

'Do you ever sort of feel the cassowaries? You know, like ... I don't know ... Don't worry.' Cozy gave up, not able to find the words.

Pops guessed the missing words. 'Course I do, Cozy. If him hurtin then I be worry n hurtin too. When him strong, I peel strong! Why you ask dat for?'

'Sometimes, no, nearly every time I think of Louis, I feel better. I feel like I'm somebody.'

'You somebody. Dis your forest, Cozy! Louis born in dis jungle, just like you n me. That makes us deadly fullas, somebody diffent. Not every bugger's born in da jungle, you know. Pity you a whitefella. You would've made a goot protector of dem dingoes, I reckon. But you always member dis ting: if dis forest's Louis's and your mutha, den dat'll always n foreber make you brudders. That's somethin! That makes someone real special.'

'Brothers like you and me?'

'Yep, jus da same ting!'

Cozy smiled. 'I like that.' Cozy stopped walking mid step.

'What, Cozy?'

'I think I hate God, Pops. I prefer totems and returning to country. That'll do me, I reckon.'

'Dey believe God, I believe spirit and dreamin.' He spoke quietly. 'My spirit always free in ere an will be foreber once I gone. Don't eber let em steal or break yer spirit, Cozy. Dem take all yer got. Dem fullas took eberting from my mob. Dey took our land, our cer'mony places, my people, our youngins an pickaninnies. But dey neber git dees.' He held

one hand against his heart. The other pointed to his head. 'Dees always mine.'

Cozy nodded.

'You'd make a bloody goot blackfulla, Cozy. Yer always askin proper goot questions n listen proper.' He chuckled. His voice sounded keen. 'I ear yer hab a win and fought pitty goot, eh?'

'Yeah.'

'Goot on yer. Hey hey! My jungle champ's deadly, eh?'

'Nah, I just got lucky's all.'

'I hear em pitty bloody goot, dat odder bloke?'

Cozy gave Pops the gossip about his recent fight and how he nearly got cleaned up early in the piece.

'Randell him name, eh? A blackfella? Him be me nepu.'

'Your nephew? Really? I didn't know. He was real deadly, yeah. He was quick and had a good, fast jab. He just had heavy, lazy feet and I cut him off easy.'

'Randell, him always bin lazy, dat black bastard! I heard yer got a nick name: Typoid Cozy. I like dat one. Funny, eh? Dat scary, dat name, ha ha! Goot name but! Scare dem nex fighta goot n proper a name like dat one!'

'My name don't do any of the fighting, Pops.'

Pops smiled at the wisdom and shook his head. 'Cozy, you'd make a bloody goot proper blackfulla!'

Tribute © Robert Lee Johnston 2016
Email: tributerobertleejohnston@gmail.com

CHAPTER SIX: COZY SHOWS UP

"Welcome to the Jungle"

Guns and Roses - Song Title

Spawned, unnamed, alone in the thick, leafy trash of a dark, misty rainforest, an endless canopy of green.

Completely surrounded by dense jungle, amongst the under growth and wait-a-while, given life near a noxious patch of stinging trees, seen only by curious native creatures. Unwanted, unnoticed and left for dead. Unceremoniously. The noise of a large, rushing rapid feeding a great waterfall close by, and the mysterious jungle's wildlife served as the infant's introduction to the universe of sound.

The nurse that found the infant boy could see dirt and mulch still clenched in a tiny fist, up his nose, in his ears and mouth. She opened the doctor's tiny practice at 8 am. She appreciated the cliché of a baby wrapped in newspaper on the doorstep, abandoned and left helpless. With no one around, she tut-tutted and picked the baby up.

'Who have we got here, then?'

Tribute © Robert Lee Johnston 2016
Email: tributerobertleejohnston@gmail.com

She soothed and cradled the child as she prepared the practice. When the doc arrived she helped cut the newborn's long umbilical cleanly and washed and dried him. She gave him a gift to keep, a nappy. Then she wrapped him up, safe, found and sound. She warmed baby formula and proceeded to bottle-feed him his first meal. She called the police, a local copper known to all as Sarge. He called all the surrounding hospitals for any trace of a mother. She was never found. Shirl placed the infant in a crib on her desk as phone calls were made and arrangements sorted.

Patients soon arrived, and a local older woman asked Shirl, when the infant giggled, 'Who's baby's that, darl?'

'I don't know. We don't know. No one knows yet. I found him here on the top step. Just showed up out of the bloody blue this morning.' Her sweet voice still held traces of disbelief. The two noticed how quiet and alert the baby was and how interested and comfortable he appeared, smiling at them.

'Lucky it's not raining, eh Shirl?'

'Yeah, you're not wrong, Dotty.'

The darkened heavens opened up just then, and thick, heavy raindrops fell like gravel.

'Speak of the devil! It's a boy?'

'He is. You know, I haven't ever heard a newborn baby laugh before, in all my years nursing. I never even heard of it. Did any of your three, Dotty?'

'Nah, can't say they did. Took them a few months, from memory. But each of them could cry the bloody banshees out of house and home.' They both smiled. 'Shirl, what you going to call him? After all, love, you found him. He needs a name, don't he? We can't very well call him "I-don't-know" can we, girl? He won't get terribly far with a name like that, the poor dear.'

Shirl laughed with her dear old friend. 'I wouldn't have a clue what to name him, but he looks warm and cosy in there, doesn't he? Out of the rain in his safe, cosy crib.'

Tribute © Robert Lee Johnston 2016
Email: tributerobertleejohnston@gmail.com

Grinning, Dotty, Shirl's lifelong mate, agreed and pondered. Then she looked around and whispered. 'Well shit, Shirl, "Cosy", it is. "Cozy", with a zed.' The old ladies smiled proudly.

'G'day, Cozy, I'm Shirl. This is my best friend, Dotty. Welcome to the world, little man.'

Cozy smiled at Shirl, reaching for her fingers.

'Look, Shirl, Cozy's smiling. He knows his name. It's a good name, darl. He and I both like it.'

Word travels fast within Tribute's sparsely populated communities. A few rumours here and there, and generous spoonfuls of bullshit, marinated and seasoned the yarn each time it was told.

A local, a young bloke, had gone for an early morning run around a lovely, rough-cut track. It circumnavigated a postcard-beautiful creek and an ill-tempered waterfall. He needed to water and tend his half a dozen plants, growing secretly in the abundant sunshine provided by the fall of an ancient tree or two recently. The felled trees cleared the sun-choking canopy, revealing sky not far off the track. The fresh morning air, crisp, cool and clean in his lungs, he could hear the comforting roar of the falls as the trail he ran brought him closer to it. A lively time in the forest is early morning. Lizards ran and birds sang. Parrots screeched and shrieked. The always constant insects roared. It was a heavenly time of day in the jungle. He tentatively hopped across the mossy, moist, slippery boulders to the deep pool of clear, clean mountain water oxygenated by the loud waterfall. He knelt, cupped his hands and gulped down the cold, sweet, untainted water.

He thought he heard a noise against the resounding falls, but couldn't place it at first. He stopped drinking to focus. Nothing. It was probably some strange bird call. Then a second time! A high-pitched, squealing giggle.

'Is someone there?'

Tribute © Robert Lee Johnston 2016
Email: tributerobertleejohnston@gmail.com

Other than the waterfall, silence again. He made his way to where the noise seemed to originate. This time he definitely recognised a human giggle. It sounded like an infant. He easily followed the trail of joy, until he stumbled upon a newborn baby, giggling at a pair of lapis-lazuli Ulysses butterflies, flapping and gently kissing his face as they sweetly landed upon him.

'HOLY SHIT! JESUS CHRIST!'

He looked around, calling desperately for a mother. He even cooeed. The newborn still had blood and shit all over his little, wrinkly body. Seemingly, the whole forest floor was stuck to him. His long umbilical cord had obviously been bitten off.

'Fuck a duck! How the hell did you get here, kid?'

Without thinking, he scooped up the child and jogged back along the track and into town, where his car waited. As he puffed and ran he said, 'Bugger my plants! I'll run you to the doctor's office straight away, little mate.'

It was still early and no shops were yet open. No morning traffic buzzed about. He wanted to wrap the kid in something warm, but his only option, other than his wet, sweaty shirt, was a dry newspaper atop a street bin. It contained yesterday's stale chips. He shook them out and wrapped up the baby.

'Sorry, little mate. Your first nappy ain't real flash, is it?'

He smiled as the boy cackled at his voice.

'You don't seem too worried, do you? How bloody long you been in the jungle?'

He placed the little bloke on the steps, not knowing what to say, think or do next.

'I'm so sorry, little fella. This is all I can do for you. Shit, I just learnt to drive, little man. I'm a kid too, you know? I can't keep you. I would if I was able, but me, I'm just a kid me bloody self, you understand, little one? Shit, me balls were about as smooth and hairless as yours a year ago. When you're grown up I'll shout you a beer or three and tell

Tribute © Robert Lee Johnston 2016
Email: tributerobertleejohnston@gmail.com

you all about today, okay? I'm Kev. People around here call me Lacey. It's good to have met you! Good luck, little wild man. I'll see you later. I promise you, righto champ?'

He shook a tiny hand. It hung on tightly to his first friend's index finger. Lacey got up off his haunches and slowly, reluctantly left.

'Good luck, little mate. I'll see you around, eh? I promise you.'

No one knows how long the little fella was in the jungle before Lacey found him. Surely no more than a day or two. Sarge was forced at the end of the day to ring the local church orphanage, when no mother could be tracked down. The state took possession of little Cozy, after a short stint in hospital.

Shirl went home that afternoon and told her kind husband how she had found and named a baby boy. Cozy, with a zed, had a constant, calm, cheeky smile. After, in his gentle arms, she asked him solemnly, 'What's this crazy, big old nasty world got in store for little Cozy, love?'

***

Bugs, John Henry, Kenny, Jen and Evie would soon follow, due to unfortunate circumstances, all of them babies, some abandoned with names and birth certificates, others not.

In a small farming town, the kids would grow up in a world of warm cattle piss and hot, sloppy bullshit. The church was surrounded by thick, wonderful rainforest. Its call was never far from the children's minds. Every spare moment they were in there: the tracks and shacks, the haunted, deep, dark mine shafts. They were everywhere. If you knew where to go the scrub provided endless entertainment, food, and tonnes of water. It was the mob's playground: cuttings, fallen trees, natural oddities,

Tribute © Robert Lee Johnston 2016
Email: tributerobertleejohnston@gmail.com

waterfalls, vines hanging over creeks and ancient, dry river beds that cut deep, ravenous ravines into the landscape. They could climb and swing like lemurs, and swim and dive like native cormorants. They'd hide from one another, chase one another, swim, run, explore and discover.

Some older Aboriginal men dwelled happily in the forest, hunting, fishing and sometimes drinking. From time to time the kids would bump into them. The kids liked them and they liked the kids. The children knew all their young grandkids and learnt what they learnt. Sometimes those old men would tell Cozy, when they were drunk, that he was a bit like them.

'We's bon in dis jungle, too. Yer native of dis bloody jungle. Dis jungle is our mudda and yours too.'

The thought never ever left young Cozy's head. Those old men taught them all to hunt tree kangaroo and fish. It was here that the kind, wise elder, Pops, took a shine to Cozy and let him in on dreaming stories, on how the mountains, forest and rivers were formed, and how his tribe came to be. Cozy asked many difficult questions, so old Pops probably didn't have a choice. Still, Cozy loved all his yarns and listened intently. Especially the Quincan stories. Pops taught him how to be seen, found and, even better, become invisible in his forest; how their mother could provide, nourish, and even hide the child, or anything Cozy asked of her. Pops told the boy what really happened when his mob first met white fellas. It differed greatly from what teachers later tried to put over on him in school. The most important things he taught the child was how to be humble and patient. Cozy loved every second with him. He saw firsthand how destructive plonk and sour alcohol could be to sweet, fine old men of any race. Grog had the power to either render Pops mute, or turn him into a desperate swimmer in a cesspool of bitterness and hatred.

Tribute © Robert Lee Johnston 2016
Email: tributerobertleejohnston@gmail.com

'Dem white CUNTS,' he'd yell into the scrub, his angry echoes bouncing back. 'Dis our HUNTIN ground! Dis our CEREMONY land!'

Bile and whisky paralysed Pops, and often he would pass out on his forest floor. Cozy's heart felt heavy and his mind guilty, ashamed for being white when Pops spoke that way.

He'd see Cozy when he sobered up and tell him, 'Hey, I don mean you, Cozy, when I yell at dem bastard Quincans. You're my shiny brudder. We jungle brudders. My tiny, shiny white hunter. Dis ere is the only peaceful place I got in my whole country, right ere.'

The boy understood.

'Cozy, yer mudda.' He paused. 'She always alive, always talkin n listenin at the tame time, alway lovin. She can hear yer heart, den frightin yer fears n enmies way. You ask her any question. Any bloody question you want, eben dem real tough one, she'll answer.' He spoke with reverence. 'She bin ere foreber, Cozy, know eberting. Peel eberting you peel. No good up ere?' He pointed to his head. 'She'll help you. She goot n wise, Cozy, genrous n loyal to her pamily. Me n you we connect to her; we her boys, me n you. You could go all da way to da moon, dem stars der or dat bloody Mars. She'll pine you. Cos we connected, you undstand? You see?'

Cozy nodded.

'HEY HEY, he sees!'

Cozy Withazed learned a lot about loyalty, love, love of country, soul and life from that kind, sweet, bony old man.

Pops aged fast and all that drinking did him no favours. Cozy saw a lean, fit, proud warrior and hunting man turn into a high school, science-room skeleton. Drained of life, withdrawn, syphoned and destroyed. Cozy stole all the food he could from the church and foster homes, plenty of eggs, cheese and milk. All he could carry. He avoided school. Instead, he hunted and fished for Pops' favourite tucker. The old man's appetite waned until a budgie ate more.

Tribute © Robert Lee Johnston 2016
Email: tributerobertleejohnston@gmail.com

Cozy begged him, 'Pops you got to eat. Have some brim I caught for you, cheese, and some bread. I've seen guppies eat more than you. Please eat.'

Pops reached for the young fella's hand and held it very gently. 'You're alway smilin n by rights you shouldn't.'

Cozy shook his unkempt, shoulder-length hair and pleaded again. 'Please eat something. Please, old man?'

Exhausted and uninterested, Pops whispered, 'Not hungry, eh Cozy. I'm goin to see our mudda. She callin out fer me to come ome.'

'No, Pops, no! Don't listen to her! This here is your home, here with me. Don't orphan me, Pops!'

The eleven-year-old was stricken and panicked.

The old man gently squeezed Cozy's hand. 'Don't you worry bout me, liddle hunter.' His voice was friendly and calm, tired and quiet. 'I got to tell you secrets, Cozy. Jus tween you n me, okay?'

Helpless, hopeless tears burst from Cozy and snot ran as from a busted water pipe.

'I name dat rapid wit ole time ceremony for you. You know which one, eh?'

Cozy smiled sadly through tears. 'I know which one.'

Pops flashed white teeth. 'Your birth place. It's yer waterpall now. Don let no blackfella or whitefellas tell you diffent. I dun dance a special old-time ceremony for you. Now yer my real brudder. I gib you skin name.'

Pops told Cozy his skin name, and what it meant.

'You got to choose a totem animal now, Cozy, but I's already reckon I knows what yer goin to have. We pamily now. Dem Dingo, yer pamily now. We a tribe now, you n me."

Cozy couldn't hold back his overwhelmed emotions.

'Cozy, listen goot now. Listen to me. You member all I taught you, brudder. Cos I be gone soon.'

'No, Pops, don't say that.'

Tribute © Robert Lee Johnston 2016
Email: tributerobertleejohnston@gmail.com

'It okay, mate. I neber orpan yer, eber Cozy, I pomise, okay? You will see me in da jungle here n der, hidin dem shadows like I showed you. You member?'

Cozy glanced down and nodded, pale and in too much pain to speak.

'If you loog, you'll pind me. Hey, you loog proper now!'

Pops knew he was dying and didn't want Cozy to see any further. 'Hey, Cozy, you go git some elp now.'

Cozy took off in a flash.

'Hey, wait up! Wait, mate. Cozy, come ere a sec, come ere.' Cozy knelt beside him. 'You're a bloody goot kid, bloody goot hunter and tracker. You're goot brudder to me. I want thank you, Cozy. My tiny, shiny brudder. I love you, Cozy.'

'I love you, Pops.' Cozy tried to be brave. 'I don't want to go, Pops. I don't want to leave you here, or want you to go.'

'I know. It okay, Cozy. Hey, if eber you feel sad or lost, my frien, you come in ere to fine yer way out, okay? I'll fine you. I pomise. Don't you eber be scared of nuthin. Eber. Pomise me now.'

'I promise.'

Cozy hugged him for the last time, for at least a minute, and whispered, 'Thanks for teaching me. Can you say hello to our mum for me, and tell her ... I love her. I love my name, my totem, my falls. I love you, Pops. I'll miss you, old man.'

He patted the boy's back. The child let him go and legged it, hoofing it through all the jungle shortcuts to the doctor's practice. They informed Sarge and he had Cozy show him where Pops was.

By the time they found Pops he was long dead. Cozy knew he was dead before he saw the body.

A large, bright, brave male cassowary, stood in their path in front of Pops, with two downy chicks at dad's feet. The chicks had their heads down, bums up, as if praying, or in submission to Pops.

Tribute © Robert Lee Johnston 2016
Email: tributerobertleejohnston@gmail.com

Cozy yelped. Shit. He stopped in fright. He looked around for a suitable tree to climb. The male cassowary, Pops' own totem, moved away with his babies in tow. Like silk sliding, he majestically revealed Pops' body behind his own large, feathered frame. The huge bird and his chicks turned unfazed and angelically made their way into the undergrowth, elegantly disappearing a few steps in.

Their mother had made sure Pops' body was kept safe by dispatching a stoic, loyal sentry, a sweet beast by his side to protect his body, keeping guard over her beloved warrior son.

Cozy's feet wouldn't move an inch closer, and as Sarge and the ambo bloke sorted it out, he turned tail like the huge bird and vanished from Sarge's view, bolting to the river. Once there and settled he realised Pops would be fine. Everything he ever wanted or needed was here. Whenever Cozy was upset or lost, and life got out of control, a walk in the jungle cleared everything up for him. The distraught child spilt many tears into the evolving, perpetual beauty of their mighty green river for his old friend.

***

The next men to influence Cozy's life, in a fatherly fashion, were just as wise, as patient and insightful.

All good blokes, Cozy believed. Tom Waits, Bon Scott, Jim Morrison. Cozy never met them, never would. The three men fed his soul and shook his beliefs. The characters in their songs were Cozy's father, mother, siblings and archangels; apostles, friends, uncles, aunties, lovers and coveted enemies. Like blood family they were always there for him, dependable, able to sooth the fire in his guts and nurse his addiction to anger. Protecting his heart with truth and bravery.

Cozy listened proper.

Tribute © Robert Lee Johnston 2016
Email: tributerobertleejohnston@gmail.com

CHAPTER SEVEN: THE WHIP

A whiplash screamed out.

Cozy wanted to be in his forest.

Tribute the town was simply named. Around the town gathered a dozen or so spring-fed 'tributaries', mountain streams, lakes and reliable creeks, that eventually feed all year long into a large, moody, mighty green river.

Tribute's nature and inherent beauty was forged long ago, from horrific, violent energies. Aeons of sleepless turmoil and relentless turbulence. Sonic booms of heat exploded, and sun-orange lava boiled. Pestilential destruction steamed from within, igniting maniacal explosions of toxic, chemical chaos. Sky-choking smoke reached high into the atmosphere and rained confetti-black ash upon the scorched earth. All the while, simmering away, dangerously coloured lakes of poison and fractured sulphur-stinking craters grumbled and bubbled in evil cahoots with a thick, foggy, never-ending venomous haze, fashioning a shimmering, mosaic horizon.

Granite cannon balls, the size of small towns, too aggressive and impatient to wait in line, burst forth like carbuncles or angry pimple heads, creating and destroying, tearing land and ranges asunder, rearranging the stricken landscape. Huge, volcanic boulders, thrown for kilometres,

Tribute © Robert Lee Johnston 2016
Email: tributerobertleejohnston@gmail.com

trailed vapour across a ruptured, dense sky. Blazing meteors skipped across the eerily hidden moonlight. While ravenous fires, palely mimicked by those of today, raged for centuries.

All destructive energy must go somewhere, and over the ages and millennia the lifelessness and death slowly receded. Ash settled and hardened into deep, ox-blood-red, fertile top soil. Lava trails, pock-marked craters, and blow-holes became fresh water rivers, deep, clear crater lakes and all-consuming swamps. Inspiring waterfalls now gracefully fell where once angry molten lava percolated. Disorder gave way stubbornly to progress, and living things finally gained a foothold. Dark, haunted skies of ashen grey and pied shadow finally yielded to divine, golden fingers of sunshine. Light, and the lost, glittered moon, found their way through.

The raw power mother nature released all those years ago was still evident today in Tribute's energetic rivers and fast-flowing rapids, quenching the thirst of a timeless forest. Tranquil lakes and rugged, misshapen landscapes still bore the scars of her terror-forming, terraforming anamorphosis.

From the horror came a birth. From the deep, heavy ashes rose spectacular forest and a fertile jungle abundant with wildlife, rare with inherent, exotic diversity. A heavenly place of water. A land that bore much punishment now shone like a precious jewel. Tribute had been forged into a deeply complicated, visibly scarred, historically rare gem.

The imagery caused Cozy to wonder. Can any worthy jewel come from the pressure, power and savage energy expended on me? Can the immortal, stubborn life that persevered and rebuilt ancient, evil Tribute rebuild me?

The whiplash screamed out. Jungle couldn't protect Cozy now.

It stung at first with its brutal percussion. It was a thick, ten-foot-long beauty. Its gradually thinning end tapered to the width of a pencil. It was Syd's 'Sweet Thing'. No scorpion's scourge or deadly spiked tips required for this monster. Wet and heavy with Cozy's blood, it tore deeply

into flesh, muscle and nerve receptors, cutting a deep swathe through everything in its path. Light and heavy at the same time. Brutality and delicacy. Cozy assumed he was building resistance to the punishment; maybe getting tougher.

Often people who are involved in serious, traumatic accidents feel no pain. The condition is called 'battleground analgesia'. War is always a common breeding ground for this affliction. It's a life-preserving, human mechanism, probably bought on by endogenous opiates. So potent when compared to the more ineffective, laboratory-grade, hospital morphine.

Pulpy, raw connective tissue and nerves were repeatedly ripped and sliced off Cozy's spine and rib cage. As the nerve tissues disintegrated and decayed so did the capacity of his pain receptors. Pins and needles started to make their prickly hot presence known all over his body, as if fine, red-hot coals had been stowed under his clothes.

Blind Freddy could see this crap was going to catch up with Cozy. Cozy kept asking himself, How would this all un-fuck itself? How do I un-fuck this situation, man?

He was tired of asking. Weary of long-term rumination.

Only his ears could register the whip's voice now. He could feel skin split apart, but little or no pain. It was happening to someone else. Nothing made sense. Metronomic repetition, an annoyingly predictable cycle, was bringing him unstuck. His shorts filled with warm, fresh, slick fluid. Thick, sharp-edged furrows directed blood and serum, as gutters direct water into flooded storm drains. He was at an emotional snapping point. Cozy's sympathetic, short-term arousal was overwhelmed, and his near unconscious mind teetered between gallant insanity and, sadly, irresistible death. An internal combustion of reprisal burst; the lump in Cozy's throat burned exhaust red.

The whip took another draft and breath of fresh, clean air, whistling away from Cozy's body, its repugnance clearly

Tribute © Robert Lee Johnston 2016
Email: tributerobertleejohnston@gmail.com

audible. The thong struck along an older scar, and a bee's dick from the last, tearing a thumb width of skin that now hung from his lower back, dangling onto his hamstring. It drove in deep and heavy, as if someone had just passed him a bowling ball from a flag pole. The tail cut around his torso and across his stomach. Exposing ribs. Crimson gore ran thick off Cozy, warm, bright ink pooling at the boy's feet and misting the air with fine red, spray-painting his torn body with bloody, sun-shower droplets. Falling to his knees, Cozy begged Syd, God, anyone, to knock him out.

Inbred, toothless fuck. He's winning. Cozy knew it. One day, fuck knows, I will gut this cunting fuckery. And revel and dance amongst his rip-torn innards. I'll proudly carry his bluntly severed, decaying head around in a fucking burlap sack, till damnation, like a medieval madman.

Cozy wanted to threaten him, scare him, roar and bellow at Syd. All he could unfortunately muster was, 'You retarded, hillbilly fuckery. For fuck's sake.'

Cozy thought surely he had no more blood to give. On his knees, he hadn't the strength to rise. A spitting-hot flashpoint of noise and insidious venom winded him again. Piercing flesh, as the whip rang out, reaching inside his lungs, sucking the very last of the oxygen from his emptying sails. Cozy was wrong. There was more blood to excise. He simply would not, could not pass out. He wanted it, searched for it, found it, just couldn't grasp it.

He wondered, Did I just trip out? Flashback? Or did I flash forward?

The whip, a sinister talisman, tossed Cozy into another atmospheric dimension. A mute, visual world, too fantastic for words or dialogue. The boy staggered in through the outdoor for a brief moment.

Syd savoured seeing Cozy still, emasculated, downed, unable to run from him and his long, plaited length of greenhide. He was wounded, grounded, broken, and Syd could strike the young fella at will. Cozy would not drop

lower. For no one. A pyrrhic act. He was slurring, talking to himself. Just ... Fuck. Knock me out. Please. Just fucking knock me out. He found a deep, defiant breath. Fucking knock me out, you scabby, toothless, drooling, inbred fuck for the dogs.

Syd smiled a king's evil, repulsed at the boy's plight. His teeth, or lack thereof, were a burnt-out picket fence: a black one here, half a one there, a yellow bit, and a brown, rotten, derelict, dying stump or two way back. He drooled, leaked spit like a burped baby. Syd wiped the saliva dribbling from his twisted lips with his forearm, standing triumphant over the child, powerful, satiated. And with satiation came disgust.

The long, strong, blue-gum handle helped support his hefty weight, like a spear held by a tired indigenous hunter of old.

Cozy, dazed, laughed. HEH HEH! Syd the big man. The great, white warrior. HA HA HA!

With that, Cozy's breath was truly knocked out. He'd been well tenderised. Puffing like a landed fish he tried to be strong, tried not to cry. On his knees, his arse flat between his feet, tired elbows on his thighs. The sun-congealed blood slowly dried on his pale, forsaken skin. Instead of asking for sweet unconsciousness, Cozy wished to die, wanted to stop breathing. He needed a break from the world, from this and that, and everything in it for a minute or two, a whole day, maybe longer. Cozy wished to stop thinking, to stop feeling. He valiantly tried to remain still, but his body's toxic chemical cocktail wanted him to get up and run away. RIGHT NOW! His body wanted to run fast and far. Tired legs wouldn't, couldn't, get the boy up. Two hours Cozy knelt there, blood fusing to him in the sun, unable to control his muscles. They rebelled strenuously, panicked, and fired against his will. Cozy bellowed like a bull calf in a branding cage.

Tribute © *Robert Lee Johnston 2016*
Email: tributerobertleejohnston@gmail.com

For no reason at all, maybe blood loss, or perhaps the beginnings of losing his outcast mind, particular sights and thoughts entered Cozy's head. A farm, a special farm. Special to Cozy. The boy realised from his time on this other dairy farm that every animal on Syd's farm, even his herd, was scared of him. Syd's girls were skittish and came across as uncooperative and stupid. They were neither. No radio played soothingly in their dairy. Every morning and afternoon Cozy had to walk miles, rain or shine, to round them up. The girls would split up, with those poofter poodles annoying them for sport. Each day twice a day they'd baulk at the bails as if they were the entrance to a slaughter yard. Syd and his arm-length piece of poly-pipe ensured the herd resisted strenuously the dairy and being milked. Anxiety spread through the girls like a ritual dose of Epsom salts and castor oil. Their many guts would turn to water, and they'd shit and piss on cue everywhere. They hated being touched and would lash and strike out when Cozy tried to milk them, or just happened to wander into their firing zone. Heavy, cloven feet landed like chucked stones. Some of the clever ones could lift their leg and turn their hip in such a fashion that human heads came dangerously into hoof range. No kind words were heard here. Syd always called them bitches, and yelled 'dirty sluts' at the ladies. The pumps' rhythms sounded beastly and maniacal. Syd's old dears had agreed to rebel on mass and made his life as miserable as theirs.

The herd Cozy milked on this other farm were happily waiting for him at the dairy, when he woke and trudged off in the early-morning dark and cold to find them. He stood there with one of the farmer's red dogs as the sun rose, too stunned to say a word. He rubbed tired eyes, thinking he must still be asleep.

Cozy informed the farmer as he turned up, 'I didn't have to round them up. They were all just waiting here!'

Tribute © Robert Lee Johnston 2016
Email: tributerobertleejohnston@gmail.com

'They wait every morning and every arvo to get their pats. You know, there's pork, home grown bacon, tomatoes and fresh eggs for brekkie at the house for you. I thought you were still in bed. When I saw your room empty I figured you might be introducing yourself. You go eat, mate. I'll milk them. I got you here to relax not work, Cozy.'

Cozy could not believe what he was hearing. His mouth and his bottomless stomach imagined food. Food, food, glorious food! The farmer patted Cozy's back like a kind uncle. His smile was true. He wasn't at all twisted, this one. He was a genuine, kind man that never made any child feel small or uncomfortable.

'Nah, I'll give you a hand to finish with the girls first, mate, then I'll hook into all that pig you got waiting for me.'

'Well, it won't take long to milk them with us two fine, young, fit-looking bulls working together. Then you can eat all the bacon you want.'

Cozy was grinning, spinning in confusion. Their pats? Bacon? Fine bulls? Relax?

Cozy's belly was unusually full, full as a goog. Everything felt wrong and well out of order. Every girl in his bails had a name or was affectionately called 'sweety', 'darl', 'old dear' or 'ole girl'. There was no poly-pipe. No tormenting, angry dogs here. Each of the sweet, big heifers waited calmly, eager to be met, patted and asked about their day. They were serene, doe-eyed and passive with each other, kind to the farmer and young Cozy. Fluttering dark, long, luxurious, Bridget Bardot lashes as the radio informed them of the world's recent goings on and tasty gossip. While smiling and chewing their cud, it looked for all money as if they were silently discussing the juicy news of the day, nodding or shaking their heads wisely. Ruminating peacefully. Jolly and placidly composed, they barely shit or pissed once in the dairy. When the farmer saw Cozy being careful around their feet he assured him they had never struck out. Not one of his heifers ever tried to kick Cozy. The

same machines hissed, sucked and pumped away, but because of the light and energy it sounded like a swinging big band or a funky, folk-music festival. The farmer never raised his voice around his cattle. He never hit them or cursed them.

No amount of cruelty could achieve the results he reaped. Cozy reckoned the milk tasted better from his happy herd. The love and patience the dairy farmer had for his land and the life around him repaid his efforts a hundred times over. He adored his milkers. His horses would come to a single call, his dogs to a single whistle. His huge bull was docile. Nothing feared him. Cozy had never seen friendly pigs so fat and happy, never seen dogs so loyal, eager to please and work. Every animal respected their owner and rewarded him with compliance, great milk and fresh, flavoursome meat.

He was killed in a tragic farm accident, that kind man. Cozy missed him and his farm.

Syd gasped, spent. Too tired to yell, he grumbled lowdown, castigating the boy between heavy breaths. 'Fuggin stay there, you bastard. And stay out of my fuggin sight, or I'll give you another fuggin flogging. Look at the state of you. Fer chrissake, Cozy, clean yourself up, Boyo. You're making me sick to me fuggin guts!'

All Cozy heard was: Fuggin blah, blah. Fuggin blah.

He felt as if he'd just run a marathon. Breathing was his only thought as endless hours passed. Pain spread like spilt paint. Thick and all consuming, slowly reaching out. Then throbbing to a uniform, predictable low rumble. The intensity increased with every heartbeat, burning deeply and sharply into raw flesh.

Fucking flies.

Hundreds of the greedy bastards were buzzing around and getting into the mangled mess. Each one landing was a short, blunt knife, stabbing. Cozy reached behind, dispersing a shadow of flies, Mexican waving as they hurdled his hand

with a dark ripple, momentarily distracted from their free, hearty feast. He felt the rat's tail of skin dangling and spilling low levels of his depleting oil. If he'd had a full-length mirror Cozy would have seen firsthand the carnage.

Cozy, defeated, shook his head and grunted. Abused by Syd, Rev, the fair State and society. The injustice and futility debased and insulated him simultaneously. He was turning crystalline, tortured into wrack and ruin and transformed, with much heat and friction, into glass. Tainted, toughened, blood-stained glass. Cozy was feeling pretty ordinary kneeling there in Tribute's red dirt. If he'd had a lighter and enough petrol, he would have burned the whole world down.

Tom Waits once asked Cozy in song, 'Why are the wicked so strong?'*

All Cozy knew was you should never give motivation for a vendetta to a hurt, defeated, lost, crazy kid. Nothing matters to a colonial-child, who's hurting, got nothing and no one to lose. Nothing.

It's rumoured that people with a sense of humour have a better sense of life. Cozy was struggling to see the funny side of these savages.

One day. One bloody, fine day, he thought, I will test their sense of life and humour.

Each time Cozy walked by the tractor shed, whether Syd's 'Sweet Thing' was in his sight or not, his mind's eye saw the whip hanging, waiting for him, hungry on its rack. He could feel the whip's starved gaze on him, like the Mona Lisa's eyes.

Cozy couldn't for love nor money get the scars off his body. He would never get accustomed to the whip's noise. He couldn't erase that sound from his mind.

Ever.

Tom Waits lyric – Mr Siegel

CHAPTER EIGHT: I HOLD A WOLF BY THE EARS

Auribus teneo lupum.

Necessity is said to be born from calamity, and when the gap between sane and completely screwed up is as wide as a fingernail.

How do you stay normal? When people push you over the edge, and then keep on pushing? How do you not snap? And keep balance? Do you drink? Or play sport? Do you count to ten and breathe?

Cozy was thinking and wanted to know, Who the fuck will stop me, when one day I lose my shit? Where do they think this is going? Do they know what they have hatched? One of them knows now.

The kids had all been struck with fear, confusion and relief. Cozy confessed to the boys and Evie that he'd killed Syd that morning.

Tribute © Robert Lee Johnston 2016
Email: tributerobertleejohnston@gmail.com

That particular morning was wild, wet and woolly. The grey, heavily laden clouds promised downpours. Jen and Cozy milked the miserable, dripping, drenched herd and, by 9 am, had decided today was the day Syd had to go. Their gum boots were full of rainwater by the time they had walked from the dairy back to the house. Cozy, still dripping, mentioned to Syd that he'd seen a heifer headed for the swamp block yesterday arvo, and then heard a cow bellowing late in the piece, last night.

'Fuggin hell, Boyo, bloody well do something about it then. Fugg you, Cozy! Get off your arse and have a fuggin look. Use your fuggin shit for brains. Do I have to tell you every fuggin thing, Boyo?'

'Righto, Syd.'

The rain was falling heavily. Syd couldn't see that Cozy walked to the tractor shed and smoked a couple of Deidre's rancid Craven As, while those two inhaled and devoured a hot breakfast that could feed the orphanage for a week. All the kids save Evie had taken to smoking, like wet shit takes to white sheets. Jenny hated the long, rainy days stuck inside with those two. Far too small a house for a girl to have any privacy. Always in plain sight. She asked Syd, 'Where's Cozy?'

'He's gone, Girly, looking for some fuggin cow he reckoned he could hear last night.'

She avoided freaking out and getting overly excited. 'Oh, okay.' She hoped this day was possibly the day.

Swinging open the door about an hour later, Cozy caught a whiff.

It stinks like a rotting fucking horses' stable in here, he thought, then smiled small at Jen.

'Syd, there's a heifer bogged. I saw her in the swamp. Not far in, but enough to make it bloody hard.'

Jenny held her breath as she listened to the lie.

'Of all the fuggin days. Fuggin hell. Fuggin pissing with rain. Fuggin cold. Fuggin swamp. Fuggin stupid bloody cow.

FUGGIN HELL! Go on, warm the tractor up, Boyo, and get my good thick rope.'

Cozy could smell cooked eggs, onion, toast and bacon over the house's noxious stench. He was starving, but tight, nervous knots and butterflies ran amuck. His stressing guts wouldn't let him swallow a bite even if he tried. Not that the greedy porkers ever offered.

Jenny smiled as Syd left. He's completely oblivious to Cozy's lie. Syd is always too busy looking at Cozy's arse to notice his eyes.

Off they went on a rusty-roofed old Fordson into the mist and rain. On a tractor it takes a bit of mucking about and a few shut gates to get to the hill-encased swamp paddock. As the old diesel bellowed and hummed, Cozy had a mile of time to decide and, if necessary, change his restless mind. In first gear, high range, they went pretty fast for the trip to the top of the last long, steep hill. Syd pulled the old girl up and slotted her into a slower, low range, then again selected first gear. They ambled off and moved no faster than walking speed down the steep incline. The idling diesel engine gave ample resistance, safe against the earthly pressures applied. Until, that is, Cozy bravely kicked the gear stick as hard as he bloody could to get it out of gear and into neutral.

Nothing! It didn't budge.

Shit.

Syd saw him do it and was about to react by clubbing or grabbing Cozy when the second lash did the job. It was if the tractor was fired out of a huge cannon. Cozy was a bit shocked how fast it was getting away. Scared as a bear-hunted salmon, he leapt confidently from the slippery, muddy guard. His chest palpitated as the finality drove home. Hitting the ground like a sack of wet chook shit, he winded himself while simultaneously driving a knee into his face. He could hear Syd yelling. 'FUGGIN HELL!'

Tribute © Robert Lee Johnston 2016
Email: tributerobertleejohnston@gmail.com

A fast-moving gearbox refused the low range gears, complaining angrily with a sickening, metal-eating grinding. The non-existent brakes were all but useless. All the same Syd had the pedals pressed all the way to the floor. The bumps, gentle at walking speed, became motocross jumps at the speed Syd was travelling. A tight left turn lined with ancient scrub awaited him at the bottom. No way he could get the tractor around the bend at that speed.

Could he?

The diff screamed in agony. Two or three old-man-emu red tulip oaks would be in the path of Syd's new turning circle. Cozy inhaled anxiously. Adrenaline slowed the whole process down for him. Every sense tuned up, paying attention to every variation, calculating all possible outcomes. Syd gave up on the brake, gears and clutch and tried to steer the weighty cruise missile to safety. The tall, fat rear tyres were throwing up rooster-tails of thick mud as high as the tractor's roof.

'AAARRRGGGGHHHH! FUUUGGG!'

An almighty crunch scared the bejesus out of Cozy. In his last-ditch, desperate efforts Syd realised he wasn't going to make the turn. He tried to get his fat old barge arse out of the seat and bail. Getting out of the seat was hard enough for a skinny kid like Cozy, with levers, roof attachments and the steering wheel in the way. If you were fat arsed like Syd, you had Buckley's chance of getting out at speed. Syd was thrown violently into the steering wheel as the tractor snapped in half at the bell housing on impact, ramping the buttress before tackling the tree head on. The gear sticks and steel under the steering controls busted Syd's legs as they met the tree trunk at violent speed. Smoke and steam rushed skywards as an unhappy, garrotted motor sung its last tortured, sickly note. The hand throttle, shaped like a drum stick next to the steering wheel, punched a huge hole in Syd's neck, ripping his Adam's apple wide apart. Cozy ran and slipped arse up down the hill, half expecting the old fella

Tribute © Robert Lee Johnston 2016
Email: tributerobertleejohnston@gmail.com

to leap out and hunt him down. Maybe strangle him to death. When Cozy arrived, Syd lay motionless on the floor of the cab, bleeding and broken. The kid stood there like a stunned mullet just watching him, waiting. Syd was conscious. His paws grabbed at his bloody throat, trying to hold it all in and together. Cozy initially gasped at the amount of damage done, the amount of blood spurting out, and worried the tractor would explode, as in the movies. It never did. Syd just slumped there winded and stunned, helpless, moaning, gurgling and bleeding.

Syd knew he was fucked. Cozy knew Syd was fucked.

Syd's gurgling grew louder, thicker and wetter. He groaned when his eyes found the boy.

'Fuck you, Syd. Fuck you, man.' Cozy surprised himself at the timbre and finality in his tone. Syd could only blink.

'I should cut that cock of yours off and force feed it down your fucking neck hole. You're a fucking animal, Syd. I dreamt a million dreams, plotting and planning what I'd say to you in this situation right here, right now. It all doesn't matter a fuck now we're here. All that matters is you die. I ain't going nowhere, till you're dead. I ain't getting help for you, till you're dead. I ain't doing shit for you, but standing here watching you, making sure you die, till you're dead. Cunt of a day to die, Syd. Cunt of a way to die, Syd.'

Cozy lit a cigarette, Syd's eyes angry when he saw the pack was Deidre's. Cozy tormented and teased him. 'Whatchafuggingunna do 'bout it, you rapist fuck?'

He wasn't listening. The boy was talking to a carcass.

'Fuck you. Fuck you forever, Syd.'

The cold winds blew green with murderous envy as Cozy took it all in and smoked a few stolen durries while surveying the wreckage. He tried to keep the cigarette dry under his hat. The warm smoke felt good in his lungs. He raised a hate-filled face to the downpour, opened his mouth to let some in, opened his eyes and looked up into the bleak, dark, dead sky. Cozy spoke loudly and very carefully.

Tribute © Robert Lee Johnston 2016
Email: tributerobertleejohnston@gmail.com

'Have I got to be the mongrel bastard to do all your dirty work, you old fuck? You fucking made Syd. Where the fuck does he fit in your grand design? I bet you pass the buck again with him now he's been freshly dispatched back to you. I got to do what you and the devil never would? You want to stay out of the swill? Be clean and dry, old man? I get it. I'm slowly, slowly seeing your form and getting it. You, you, you're a cruel, fickle old man, ain't you? Feeding us young ones, kids, to swarming-hungry, starving fucking vultures. One day, you selfish hypercritical fuck for the dogs, and I bet you soon rather than late, you're going have to answer me. Hear me ask questions other kids won't, don't, ask you. Can't ask you. If I don't like them answers, Jack ...' He lowered his voice. 'I'll take you for one last ride too, you gutless, cowardly, old man? You'll be next. One day, it will be just me and you, old boy.'

The righteous sinner waited to be struck dead by hot bolts of godly lightning, or to be fatally maimed for his irreverent blasphemy. Cozy shook his head, sickened, smiling at the blackened heavens.

'Nothing? Ha! You'd just send some other fucker to do it for your demented arse anyway. You cowardly fucking amateur.'

Cozy broke down, crying hot; not for killing Syd, not for hating God or widowing Deidre. But because he'd been pushed to this very point. Cozy couldn't let Syd hurt him or any of the others ever again, not in good conscience. It was killing Cozy, watching Jen, all of them, harden and stiffen in every facet of life. Cozy convinced himself, as the eldest, it had to be done. He would have killed one of the kids. Surely, it was just a matter of time. If Cozy were a dingo, he would have eaten Syd's granite heart. Cozy felt better and a tonne lighter. He walked up the hill and took a good, last look at the shit fight born at the bottom.

'Fuck, that was scary,' he said out loud.

Tribute © Robert Lee Johnston 2016
Email: tributerobertleejohnston@gmail.com

Being in no particular hurry he made his way to Deidre, smoking in the rain the whole way back. He just walked straight into the house, smoking, dripping water all over the joint, gum boots still on, dragging mud and fresh, green cow shit in. Syd would've had him whipped for that. He just laid it straight out cold onto Deidre. 'Syd's dead. He crashed the tractor. He's fucked. You're going to need an ambulance.'

She started blubbering and yelling and screaming to herself. 'WHERE? AND WHERE ARE ME FUCKING SMOKES?'

Cozy grinned, pulled her fresh, fat pack out of his pocket and lit one. 'If you can catch me, mudguts, you can have them. You sick, fat, diseased whore.'

Cozy pissed himself laughing, tormenting her.

She yelled out. A reflex. 'SYD, COZY'S FUCKING ROUND, AGAIN.'

Cozy thundered and growled. 'No Syd here, you simple, fat fuck.'

Jen was in disbelief and tears. She didn't say boo. She just stared at Cozy, silently crying, and nodding her head over and over. He ran and got that mongrel bullwhip off the shed wall, some diesel, and, determined, he burned Syd's 'Sweet Thing' to ashes in the dry, empty tractor shed. Sarge arrived soon after and asked the boy what they were doing down there after talking to Deidre.

'We thought a heifer was swamp bogged and went to have a squiz.'

'Deidre said you were acting strange when you got back to the house.'

Cozy let a moment hang in the air … and gently lied. 'Yeah, I was shook up after watching Syd crash the tractor, and bleeding and that.'

Sarge was already disgusted at the state of the house. Syd's body would tip him over.

'You know, Cozy, this is the second time you've led me to a body. Do you remember that time?'

Tribute © *Robert Lee Johnston 2016*
Email: tributerobertleejohnston@gmail.com

Cozy recalled easily the day the cassowary dad and his two chicks protected Pops' body.

Sarge drove the police four-wheel drive to the top of the steep hill. 'You right, son?'

Cozy, for the second time in as many minutes, lied. 'Yeah, I'm okay. I just haven't thought of that day for a bit.'

They got out into the shitty weather. It was, if anything, worse.

'Shit!' Sarge reckoned as soon as he eyed the wreck at the bottom. 'We'll leave the truck up here for now and check how slippery and boggy it is down there first. We don't want to end up in the scrub, do we mate? You're bloody lucky you got off it, Cozy. That could be you down there.'

They slipped tits up, sliding like beginner rollerbladers down to the site. Sarge got muddy. Cozy panicked and tried his best not to let it show. He was sure Sarge would find some clue. He even imagined Syd leaving a vivid, blood-stained written message. IT WAS COZY. Or, BLOODY COZY DID IT.

'You can wait here if you want, Cozy. Best I continue down on my own, eh?'

The youngster had seen enough of that scene. 'Righto.'

The ambulance pulled up next to the cop truck and Sarge politely yelled out to them that Syd was no good, well and truly cactus, and not to worry about needing to revive him. After realising the ambulance would get bogged it was decided to stretcher him up. They all had a hell of a time getting his wide load out of the twisted machine. Then up the sodden hill. They dropped him a couple of times, hauling that huge, dead-weight hide. All were red faced and puffing once his body was finally slipped into the back of the ambulance. Cozy stepped up into Sarge's Toyota when the ambos took off.

'What a bloody mess. Poor bastard didn't stand a chance.'

Tribute © *Robert Lee Johnston 2016*
Email: tributerobertleejohnston@gmail.com

Cozy, hat in hand, agreed, shaking his wet head. 'Poor bastard.'

'Bloody farms kill a lot of people, Cozy. Never painlessly either, mind you. Bloody dangerous places these.'

Cozy nodded and agreed. 'Bloody dangerous.'

'I'll take you kids back to the church. It'll be no place for kids around here for a bit. His missus will need some time and space.'

Deidre was good as dead without Syd around. No Jackie-Jackie doing it all for her hateful guts. Maybe those poofter poodles would eat her. Cozy could only hope.

'Did youse end up getting the cow out of the bog?'

'Nah, we didn't get there in the end.'

'Hmmm. I reckon the truck will get us down there and back up. It'll be a bit bumpy but, Cozy. You'll be okay?'

'Yeah, I'll be right.'

'Okay, let's go find her and see what we can do, eh?'

'Righto.'

The spanking new Toyota sure footedly traversed the steep hill. They passed the silent wreck. Rain had washed hydraulic oil and Syd's blood onto the ground around it, staining the earth. It looked as though the beaten tractor was bleeding. Cozy felt bad having to involve the hard-working, reliable machine.

'Poor old tractor,' Cozy whispered.

'What did you say, mate?'

'I was just feeling sorry for the old tractor's all. I loved driving that old girl.'

'She's buggered now, mate. I don't reckon nobody'll drive her again.'

The police truck got to an empty swamp. 'Where did you see her, Cozy?'

'I didn't see her.'

'Deidre was sure you'd seen a heifer bogged in the swamp.'

Tribute © Robert Lee Johnston 2016
Email: tributerobertleejohnston@gmail.com

'No, I never saw it.' Cozy, reminded himself to keep cool. 'I told Syd I could hear something. I thought it was a lost girl in the scrub, or one bogged down here,' Cozy lied again. 'Syd heard something not right through the night as well.'

Shit. Shit. Shit. Far too many lies, he thought. He was trying his hardest to shut up, screaming at himself in his head. Fucking shut your big, fucking, dopey mouth, Cozy.

It rebelled against his will and went on. 'Maybe, she was just lost? Bellowing and, you know, missing her mates.'

Sarge was looking for tracks.

'How many ways into the scrub, Cozy, other than the way we came in?'

Nervous, he thought Sarge was onto him. Cozy suddenly felt like a sickly murderer, filthy, closeted and shadowed, like Syd's house. The boy's guts didn't feel sick, though. They felt clean, justified and defiant. He ran with the latter feelings.

'Heaps, eh. Scrub paddock's bloody fence ain't done being fixed yet.' That much was true. 'So the bitches keep going bush, and start legging it even deeper into the swamp when we, and those mongrel, poofter dogs, go after them, then they hoof it even further in.' Cozy tried to sound matter-of-fact as possible.

'Shit, they can get in and out of here lots of ways, then?'

'Yeah.'

'Well, I hope the poor thing is okay and back with the herd. Let's go, eh Cozy?'

'Righto.'

Cozy was relieved. Sarge was just worried for the heifer, not catching him.

The hill climb back would be a challenge, and Sarge gassed it at the bottom. They slithered and spun all the way up. It was excellent fun and really rough. He drove amongst

Tribute © Robert Lee Johnston 2016
Email: tributerobertleejohnston@gmail.com

the herd on the way back to the house. 'Anything look out of place, Cozy?'

The kid feigned a serious look amongst the milkers. 'Nah, it all looks right to me.'

Once back, Deidre wanted to know what Sarge had seen. That gave Cozy a moment to get Jen on the same page.

'Jen, if Sarge asks you if I saw a cow in the swamp you got to say you were listening when I said, I heard a cow in the scrub block. Okay? You got to say, Cozy heard it.'

She was happy Syd was dead, and showed no emotion in front of Deidre. 'Okay, Cozy.'

Her smile made it all worth it. It made Cozy smile. In fact, Sarge did ask Jen a few questions as he drove them back to the orphanage. She lied, saying what had been arranged, and then added she wasn't really taking that much notice.

They opened the door to a surprised mob. Jen went to greet Evie and the young ones, and Cozy the boys. Evie, John Henry, Kenny and Bugs … Everyone were speechless. They knew Syd had to go.

Defiantly, Bugs broke the silence, smiling and slow clapping. 'Fuck Syd.'

'Syd's dead?' John Henry whispered in disbelief.

'Uh huh.'

'You killed him?'

'Uh huh.'

It was an alien thought to them all. They inhaled the granting of the wish, pleaded and begged for so many times before.

Kenny asked, 'You sure he's dead?'

'I'm positive.'

'And no one saw you?'

'Just his God, me and Syd.'

Evie asked if Cozy was scared.

'Fuck, yeah. I was cacking me daks.'

'Was it fast?' Kenny needed to know. 'Was there blood? Shit! What was it like?'

'I don't know, man. Scary, I guess. He was yelling once the tractor took off. I was sure he was going to get up mad and dust himself off, and get into me. There was so much blood, man. He just sort of gurgled away; you know, kind of moaning. All busted up and twisted, leaking lots of oil. Then he just stopped breathing after a bit.'

Jen, still couldn't believe it. 'Holy shit, Cozy. Syd's really gone, isn't he?'

'Yeah. I just stood there freaking out a bit, half winded, just watching him. Then I sort of snapped back into focus to tell him what for. And he was already dead. The sound of him drowning was gone. Man, that fat fucker had lots of blood. So much blood.'

'You okay, Cozy?' John Henry asked.

'I feel bad now, man, real rotten in my guts.'

Henry reckoned, he'd be okay tomorrow.

Bugs was rapt. 'Fucking awesome, Cozy.'

'You don't think I'm a fucked up unit, or some animal? I feel real sick in my guts, man.'

'Fuck no. That beast needed destroying, bro. He was so stupid he wouldn't know if a tram was up him till the bell rang. Look what that fool's done to us, then take a gander at all the people he's fucked up that we ain't never met, never heard of. There's probably more than we could poke a burnt stick at. Nah, man, he got his, perfect, I reckon. And it ended with us. No others will never be fucked with by Syd. Ever. That's just guilt and shock, mate. It's normal, I reckon. It'll go away, mate. He was never going to stop, Cozy. He was an animal. I got to go strangle a brownie.' Bugs left for the dunny, happy as a bastard on Father's Day.

Evie had to ask, 'So, Sarge doesn't suspect you?'

'I don't think so. He even admitted to me that lots of people die on farms.'

***

Tribute © Robert Lee Johnston 2016
Email: tributerobertleejohnston@gmail.com

That night Cozy couldn't sleep. Cruel thoughts gathered in his head. He felt his blanket pulled back, and opened his eyes to Jenny's silhouette climbing into his bed. She looked so much older than their youth suggested, so bright eyed and pretty to watch. Her eyes welled up and matted her lashes.

'I never got to say thanks properly for today, my Cozy.'

She had his hand in hers, face to face. Cozy smiled and reassured her. 'You've saved me so many times, doctoring me and stitching me up, taking that bullet out of me.' He smiled. 'Let's call it even.'

She placed her head on his skinny shoulder and wiped her face. She looked at Cozy, sniffling, and sweetly whispered. 'Deal.'

She touched his body. And it was unlike anything Jen or Cozy had known. Unlike when Syd or others made them do things to each other. Different, somehow, but the same, sort of. It was very revealing, confusing and a bit scary. Jen knew all his scars. She found them all easily—she herself had sewn most of them up—and lightly traced them with her nine nails and finger tips. It felt to Cozy as if she was trying to gently erase them and magically rub them away forever, as he had Syd. For the first time in their short lives they made love. It was clean, fresh, forgiving, kind and absolutely non-destructive. They were momentarily liberated from the fear and desperation to which they'd been condemned. They felt dissociated from the world around them. Heat dissolved, caramelised and moulded them into one. All that had been taken, robbed and stolen was filled with guiltless, bottomless pleasure. The young lovers lay there all night, stroking each other's hair and skin, kissing, and breathing each other in warmly. Together and tenderly they became sexually mature, aware. Aware now that sex could involve love and joy. It was a concept they both took and needed time to absorb.

They had never seen adults love gently or decently. Syd and Deidre never once displayed the niceties of affection.

'I needed you, Cozy, and wanted to come to you. I was thinking so much I couldn't get to sleep.'

'Me either. God, that was so different. You know, to the rest.'

She purred. 'Yes it was, Cozy.' Her teeth shone. She arched her back. Smiling, she repeated, 'Yeah, yeah it was. I wasn't expecting that. Cozy, you felt great, all of you.'

They just lay there. As the sun came up she stole his T-shirt, put it on, and left for her bed.

They kissed softly. 'Mmmmwwwaaa. Thank's, Cozy. I'll see you.'

'See you soon, Jen.'

Cozy slept soundly with Jen's light scent on his pillow.

Tribute © Robert Lee Johnston 2016
Email: tributerobertleejohnston@gmail.com

CHAPTER NINE: EVIE, JEN AND THEIR WILD

COLONIAL BOYS

Tobacco-haired, brown-skinned Evie. 'Tenebra.'

Blond, porcelain-pale Jen. 'Candidus.'

Concealment, obscurity, and dark. Radiant, beautiful, and white.

Evie was three months Jen's senior, Jen being the youngest of the gang. The two were best mates, and loved one another's company. They arrived at the orphanage within a few weeks of each other, named, unweaned, crawling babies. Besides the four boys, the girls pretty much kept to themselves amongst the younger girls and babies, without being distant. All the while remaining helpful, supportive and generous. Remarkable really, considering their Darwinian environment. Both loved the Stones, and 'Ruby Tuesday' was their favourite song, although they sounded like decrepit tom cats fighting at full lung when they sang. They had fallouts and fights. Freakishly loud ones and painfully ignorant, silent ones. At times completely hating each other's guts, as is a young girl's wont. Their

sisterly devotion to each other was safely above any thoughtlessness or petty antagonism. Like most sisters and best friends, the girls were chalk and cheese. Jen's skin was paper white. Evie's altogether browner. Jen's hair platinum, dishwater-bubble blond, long and slightly curly. Evie's the colour of rosewood, earthy shades of roasted coffee and tropical timbers, rifle straight. Jen possessed a fast-burning classical beauty. Evie was a thinking man's pretty, her face thoughtful and considerate. There was something about Evie. Even though the kids were in their awkward, gangly, early years, everyone could tell those big eyes of hers would be there forever.

Jen's brittle exterior had the power to render every boy she met needing to help her, if she wanted it or not. This alone made her untrusting of compliments and off-the-cuff stranger's remarks. Her generosity was heavily outweighed by her non-sociability. Sadly, Jen appeared lost to some. Her pack knew otherwise. She was a deep thinker. Her mind was a naive, innocent place and easily stunned by garish behaviour and sights; a dead cat run over on the side of the road would affect her heart, dreams and mind for days and sometimes weeks.

Evie was patient and pragmatic. She rarely swore and never complained. Her temperament always seemed to be relatively unaffected. The kids again knew otherwise. Evie could see that dead cat and be happy it had lived until the point of its demise. She accepted naturally the animal's death, and figured it was happier where it now was. Evie could deal with any tough emotions, while the other kids turned acidic and porous. She had not been spared from the likes of Syd and his grubby peers. The explosive children always sought appeasement. They were reactive. All except Evie. She sometimes came across as aloof, maybe slightly removed, far above anything thrown at her. Perhaps, like all of her herd, she thought she didn't count. Don't believe that. Evie had no trace of the children's ingrained lack of

self-worth. Evie had pride and possessed something the kids couldn't put a finger on at such a tender age. Dignity. Not snobby or stuck up, like some of the spoilt, prissy students at school.

Evie could put terrible things in a place inside her mind that was hard to visit. It was impossible to stay there. She had a magic ability to never look back. She could move on without hot, residual emotion. Evie was smart, rarely did her block, or blew a head gasket. She was wonderfully innocent and seemed, to strangers, disguised or slightly obscure. A thoughtful girl who made for a fantastic, level-headed, devoted friend.

The boys' hormone-addled heads thought Jen was sexy and hot, but Evie was beautiful. Stunning! Her honey-tanned back was broken up with a triangle of freckles, and a couple of stray ones here and there. If you dot-to-dotted the triangle, it would be bigger than a man's fist. Cozy loved the way they looked with her burnt, glazed skin in the background. When she wore a bikini or singlet you could see the freckles plain as day on her right shoulder. Her teeth looked whiter and brighter because of her skin.

All Tribute's young blackfellas, they loved her and reckoned, 'Eh! Dat tan one der, she loogs all right!'

All the boys loved her.

Jen's true, sometimes hard-to-access smile could melt a slab of solid ice from a kilometre away. Evie smiled honestly and easily. Her smile made people feel comfortable and important, whereas Jen's panicked boys' hearts, intimidating many with its mind-erasing beauty. Evie's eyes expressed all her inner feelings. She was easy on the eye and easy to like. Her deep-thinking common sense saved all their arses, more than once.

The boys imagined how pretty Evie's mum must have been, on the outside at least. How anyone could give Evie up amazed them. She, like all the kids, couldn't remember her mother's face. Some kids reckon they can remember being

Tribute © Robert Lee Johnston 2016
Email: tributerobertleejohnston@gmail.com

born, their early days. None of these pups could remember shit. Each child still searched the face in the mirror for features resembling their father's and mother's. Cozy didn't search faces for his own family or doppelganger, but did it all the time for Evie and Jen. He often wondered if they were local women they knew or saw about, perhaps a dark secret in plain sight. None of the kids could find answers. Rev, his hawk-eye and the dripping one, black with heavy bags underlining his sockets, must've known something, but he always rattled off the same old spiel. 'You all just showed up in the system one day. Only God knows how,' he'd lie.

Evie always thought, Bullshit! Our mothers know.

'Be grateful and thank the good Lord for the church and people like me, or you'd have nothing. No use dwelling on the what ifs. Many children have it far worse than you blood-sucking parasites.'

Unlike Cozy, most babies showed up wrapped and nappied, without leeches, dirt and a rainforest of murderous intentions. The rest would argue that at least he knew where he was born. Bugs asked Cozy and everyone all the time, 'Where do you reckon I was born?'

Cozy couldn't say.

'Jesus, man, what happens when I meet and fuck some chick, then she turns out to be me sister or cousin?'

That always cracked Cozy up. He'd tease Bugs. 'You wouldn't never root your sister, Bugs. She'd be too fucking rough. Even your third cousin would be pig-dog bloody ugly, and not far enough removed from you.'

He'd get lost in thought and tell Cozy, 'You know what I mean, eh?'

'I know, bro. I get it.'

Evie didn't care or waste time thinking about those things. She hated her mother and that was that, no matter how beautiful or pretty she may be. Looking back wasn't Evie's thing. Her mind had much more important goings on. She firmly believed she would never again suffer like this

Tribute © Robert Lee Johnston 2016
Email: tributerobertleejohnston@gmail.com

once old enough to gain control of her life. She promised herself this and tried not to become bitter or sullen. And hoped, if she was ever a mother one day, never to re-enact or mimic her past. Her children when they came would be loved and protected.

Evie and Jenny studied while the boys ginned around smoking pot, drinking, and generally mucking about, rooting their lives away. Evie was the polar opposite of every human they'd ever known, and that was exactly why she was loved so deeply by all who knew her.

Evie was Cozy's touchstone, his link to sanity through many complicated, testing years. She had the strength to calm, pacify and love Cozy when nobody else dared or could. She knew he could never hurt her or, in fact, any woman and so threw herself with much personal risk into many fist fights, bloodier than your butcher's boots. She pulled him from the brink of being snapped, or snapping some poor bastard in half. Not once did she worry about her own safety. She never worried about Cozy getting hurt, but she knew he was like a strung-out, desperate junky around blood. Evie, never backwards about being forward, bought it up to Cozy himself, asking if he was aware of his surroundings.

'Babe, do you know what's going on, Cozy?'

Cozy loved blood. Not like in some cheesy flick. Its metallic iron taste left a once-civilised Cozy vampiric, fierce, and hellishly thirsty. Rendering him a blood-lusting, juvenile delinquent.

Evie worried so, whenever Cozy got his taste.

It was a primal, years-old chemical reaction that few could stop. Even the boys couldn't contain Cozy's heathen. Jen was too scared to react, and froze in panic when Cozy was in that state. Truth be told, any woman could stop him easily. Cozy loved and respected women. He hated seeing kids, girls or women hurting. All except Deidre. But he wasn't Cozy anymore when he tasted blood.

Tribute © Robert Lee Johnston 2016
Email: tributerobertleejohnston@gmail.com

He was transformed, in direct contrast to his sweet, soft name. It became like the name of Lucifer, which inspires thoughts of brimstone, darkness and evil. Its true meaning forever tainted. The word's true meaning, Cozy pointed out to Evie, was 'shining one', 'son of the morning', 'morning star', 'son of the dawn', and, most bizarrely, 'bearer of light'. The opposite of most people's thoughts on the exiled archangel. Cozy's light, comfortable name became similarly two toned, defaced of light, and possessed by shadows.

No longer soft and cosy, but ugly and terrifying.

Cozy had a God-given gift, a technical ability to ground his enemy, expending as little energy as possible with maximum effect. The barbarity of the energy he released was devastatingly explosive, and always bloody. He made sure the thought of challenging him never entered his opponent's head again. If you don't believe in evil spirits, or soul possession, you haven't seen 'Typhoid Cozy' fight. The nickname was coined by a stunned ring announcer when he saw Cozy in his corner. He was a boy of nine, with maybe as many fights under his tiny belt. Pacing eagerly, he cut a restless character, impatiently wild and long haired, with a pitiless, inward smile. The host called him a cosy looking devil.

The master of ceremonies was actually thinking out loud and told the crowd, 'He's a cosy looking devil, isn't he?' Not even realising he was using the fighter's name. Then the realisation dawned. He spoke more confidently. 'He's a bloody virus. Everyone say g'day to … Typhoid Cozy.'

Evie hated that smile. A patricidal, homicidal, suicidal smile.

It was impossible to think of Cozy without thinking of Tom Waits. Tom's stories were always playing when Cozy was home. It was a nice change from the rock and roll they all adored, providing a dark sweetness to balance their tastes. Depending on the day certain songs or phrases had the power to lead them happily away, or to overwhelm

Tribute © Robert Lee Johnston 2016
Email: tributerobertleejohnston@gmail.com

them. Some were at first reluctant to let Tom inside. Nevertheless, Tom helped them escape, and to draw out emotions too deep to purge instinctively.

If death and loveliness, to use Tom's words, were coming for Cozy, it would be on his terms in a fighter's squared ring. This was the only language he knew, the only power, currency and control he'd ever known. His eyes changed from glinting blue to bright green. And that blood-thirsty Spartan smirk, an I-know-something-you-don't smile. A smirk his opponents quickly came to fear, revealing an unquenched, evil side, with a concentrated stare that promised, 'When I go, fuck it, I'm taking you with me.'

A look he well knew tempted honest, seasoned fighters and true warriors alike.

Cozy would say to Evie, 'You're the strongest of us all. The weight always looks light and graceful on you.'

Cozy was wrong and in his heart he knew it. He had seen Evie lowdown, weak, tired, sick; sick of life and all its shit. If Evie carried that weight or load gracefully, Cozy carried punishment and violence with the same aplomb. The kids had seen grown men punch him so hard curious onlookers yelped in pain. Evie had witnessed the collisions, the recoils, as his head snap back on impact. Evie had heard his muscles tear, and bones break from bloody fists. He never stayed down. So many times she had cried out loud, or silently wished, and whispered in fear, begging him to stop, just give up and lose. He didn't, and wouldn't. Even Syd struggled to turn that bright luminescence off. Cozy was a rubber ball, and energetically bounced back up to his lively, murderous feet if he touched the blood-art canvas. This, after all, had been where people condemned him: on the ground, malleable. In the streets with the rotten garbage, amongst the lowest, filthiest denominator and malingerer.

Evie liked to think when he got a reminder, a taste of his gutter dirt, every ounce of him knew it was wrong, and they were wrong. Cozy visited canvas rarely. Never stayed.

Tribute © Robert Lee Johnston 2016
Email: tributerobertleejohnston@gmail.com

It cut the pack deeply hearing Cozy painfully piss blood, seeing the bruises, the cruel concussions, the deep lacerations. Cozy's blood.

Evie never saw him get knocked out cold. Cozy would tell her that bruises and cuts helped him see the punishment. The blood and damage done gave him access to the mess he felt inside.

'I can't understand pain unless I'm physically hurting.'

Cozy would try to reassure young Evie, saying that boxing gloves were like the big, soft pillows they'd smack each other round with as kids. 'Just a grown-up pillow fight, really. It's fuck all. Nothing to stress out or worry about, Evie. If it ain't a whip, a rod or lump of timber, it ain't fuck all.'

The whippings ripped and ate up much of the meat on his back, his nerves so badly damaged he could barely feel a soft or medium touch. And Evie thought ... No, she knew it was getting worse. He knew it too. The girls could touch his back and he didn't register they were there. Evie played, tickled, experimented with him and his increasing pain resistance all the time. He only responded to heavy pressure on his skin's surface. He was losing a sense. His sense of feel, his sense of soft touch, was declining. Evie didn't want to believe it, but it was rapidly progressing. Syd's scourge was ever and always developing.

Evie had heard of a dog that reminded her of Cozy: the Dogo Argentino, banned in most civilised countries including Australia. A seriously serious dog with its sense of pain purposely bred out. Fighting, bleeding, dutiful, hateful devils. Cozy was becoming that dog breed. He humanised it, personified it. Dogo Cozy. Though Evie was sure he'd prefer a dingo for this analogy. The thing about Cozy, Evie concluded, was that he was a better person than he thought he was, much smarter than he knew or let on.

His battered-eared, out-of-date dictionary, with the original owner's name crossed out, had been with him for as

Tribute © Robert Lee Johnston 2016

Email: tributerobertleejohnston@gmail.com

long as Evie could remember. Words were, to Cozy, what shiny was to Bugs. When Cozy thought out loud he was articulate and well spoken. He had learned from much tribulation to dumb himself down, so as not to stand out or make waves. He believed it was not wise to be wiser than necessary.* Other than when boxing, he hated being the centre of attention.

He once broke into Rev's quarters to seek books after noticing shelves full of thick, important-looking hard copies. Sadly, most were bible related, so he stole a Latin dictionary, filled with ancient phrases and quotes, and Rev's false teeth. The book inspired his mind with age-old, timeless thoughts, which he memorised and repeated fluently. His favourite was a quote from Virgil's Aenied: Flectere si nequeo superos, acheronta movebo. 'If I can't move heaven, I will raise hell.'

The second time he broke into Rev's, he found a book called The Devil's Dictionary and stole, to throw away into the forest, Rev's new, replacement dentures.

The book gave the child a different perspective upon the meaning of words. Making confusing words understandable. Cozy would often quote a Latin saying to Evie, or The Devil's Dictionary's spin on a word, and point out its eloquence and perfection at summing up certain situations. Rev's vicious tongue had sparked in Cozy an early curiosity about language. An obsession with words. Some of the most intelligent, earthy conversations Evie ever had were with Cozy, when no others were around, when his guard was down or he was too tired to care. His imaginative, cryptic, left-of-centre thinking was entertaining and enlightening. Adults loved his enthusiastic conversations. Cozy could find a common thread with any man, any woman. His spirit was contagious and easily harvested. Cozy had an old soul, indentured to a young, beaten body. His body, was thirty years too young to look like it did. Things seemed to sting him more because, unfortunately, he had a

language to describe and understand his predicament. A fool wouldn't fathom or contemplate the murky depths into which he dived. His strength of mind, his ability to plan meticulously, and to see things through—sometimes beautiful things; sometimes things that were truly disturbing—were his ultimate strengths. He was much deeper than he portrayed. But he was unstable.

Evie and Jen loved him to bits, but he hated too hard.

Kenny. Ha! Kenny was so lovable. Wonderfully gentlemanly and old-fashioned shy around girls. If Jen or Evie injured an upper thigh or their lower bellies he had to look away, blushing. If he accidentally walked into the shower and one of the girls was in the nuddy or semi dressed he swore loudly, became anxious and flustered, apologised, and then was fast away, leaving a whirlwind of talcum powder with which the girls had fogged the whole bathroom. Then it would take a day or two for his eyes to meet those of his victims again. Kenny was too polite to look at skin or any revealed part of a girl's bodies when they were swimming and a top came off, or a bit of something accidentally poked out. Anything that caused Jen or Evie grief would profoundly affect Kenny. He was strangely asexual, or unavailable to the girls. Both adored him and his cute, tanned, infant face. When Kenny fell for a girl she would find a soft, sensitive soul, incapable of hurting woman or child; loyal, but seriously rebellious.

He defied an old logic: the deepest rivers flow without sound. His softness was equally matched by his bursts of volume, wildness and his confidence in front of the boys. They gave him extra strength to be himself. He was a living, breathing contradiction. Kenny loved order, worshipped perfect and proper process. But he was a habitual procrastinator. Therefore, he got nothing achieved ... perfectly! His brain was a tough act to follow, though was nothing if not busy. Evie had a crush on him and had trapped him at school, locking the door in a dark, empty sports room

as seven-year-olds and savagely kissing him. Jen also loved him from time to time and once or twice did a similar thing. He liked it and the girls did too, but, to them, he was their sweet, shy little Kenny. He was their soft, toy-brother doll. Both loved him far too much to be his girlfriend. He looked suspiciously like a roadie for Bob Marley, Bugs reckoned.

Bugs's face animated every emotion he felt. He pulled faces and exaggerated certain feelings. He could make the others squeal with laughter. His wickedness was criminal and multi-faceted. He could make people feel regal and recognised, as if he grew up in their home town, or pumped gas at their local servo. Conversationally swift, with a familiarity that was sometimes comforting to folks when, in conversation, he struck a familiar name or street where they grew up. Other times this was equally worrying.

When Bugs grew bored his eyes became weighty, and he resembled a cheap man's Marlon Brando, as in The Godfather, with his unimpressed, slow blink, and a slight snarl on his large lips and heavy face. On a dime, he could turn his snarl into a wide-eyed smile, eyebrows high, and he would cackle like a crazy woman. He always found a place to insert the latest word or phrase, 'gutchy' being his latest favourite. Bugs and Cozy noticed everyone using the word 'bro' all the time, and not only with friends. People called strangers 'bro' regularly. So Bugs, taking the piss, wanting to be original and slightly cryptic, called Cozy 'Bro-Frazier', 'Bro-Hammad Ali', etcetera. Cozy would respond with, 'G'day, Bro-Nads', and the like. Each time they saw one another, the mental race was on to outdo the other. Some of Evie's personal favourites were 'Bro-Lapse', 'Bro-Migo', and 'Bro-Thel'. Some that failed made her laugh too, as when Bugs called Cozy 'Em-Bro', trying hard to make it sound like 'embryo'.

Bugs's guitar skills were impressive and always improving. A man who once fostered him noticed he was drawn towards his guitar and kindly taught Bugs a few basic

Tribute © Robert Lee Johnston 2016
Email: tributerobertleejohnston@gmail.com

chords. He gave him an older acoustic guitar he had little use for. Bugs loved playing. The axe was always within easy reach. If something important happened, Bugs could hastily put words and music to the event. He would pick out a juicy riff, usually bluesy, Leadbelly-ish, if he was teasing. Once Evie smacked her head into a corner of an open cupboard door and swore loudly. Bugs sang, and played a riff:

Evie hit her head.
Da da da dum dum.
She yelled, bloody cupboard! Fuck me dead!
Da da da dum dum.

Any and all were fair game to his humour. The girls loved it when they were relaxing, maybe reading, and Bugs was summarising the day, picking and strumming away happily. It was if he was sweetly serenading the household.

Bugs never wore jocks! They were barefoot as children, their ratty clothes donated and then duly handed down. Fresh underwear for the girls, in particular, was a constant struggle; nevertheless, they all had undies. Bugs just never liked them. His legs were always spread, and he was not at all gun shy. Bugs's spuds, the eggs, nested amongst a hairy patch between his thighs. Every time a kid turned around, the bloody things were there to frighten the bejesus out of them. Jen and Evie had many a cold-sweat bad dream in which his commando, free-wheeling, saggy testicles played a leading role. Both girls had woken screaming, then pissing themselves laughing at the tattooed, dream-memory image of his monster-sized, rusty-pubed plums bouncing after them down a dark, endless alley. Oddly, they weren't even attached to Bugs. Just a big blob of wrinkly balls resembling a headless, badly plucked chicken carcass.

Jen once woke up screaming, 'RACK OFF, HAIRY LEGS!'

No matter how much the girls or the boys teased him or complained he was never embarrassed. Bugs was completely at home in his own skin. They all tried to emulate his self-belief, not his exhibitionism, but only Bugs

Tribute © Robert Lee Johnston 2016
Email: tributerobertleejohnston@gmail.com

could pull it off naturally. Eventually and unbelievably, the kids just accepted those balls malingering around. Still, it induced belly laughs when he fell asleep in a chair and all his tackle innocently poked out to say g'day to all and sundry and let them all know how it was hanging. With Bugs snoring a timber mill, the kids would, without getting sprung, throw towels, pillows and clothes over his crotch to hide his meat and two veg, like basket ballers shooting three pointers. Now and then, Cozy retrieved a broom stick or a long curtain rod and, from a safe distance, tried tentatively to tuck it all back into Bugs's shorts, as if Bugs had leprosy; or as if he was coaxing a cobra back into its basket. But from afar, ready to run when the offended brute came to life. They giggled hard, trying not to wake Bugs while steering Cozy remotely.

Bugs would protect the girls if it came to that, although only if the odds were heavily in his favour. There was a touch of yellow in Bugs, a whiff of the coward, and self-preservation was always foremost in his mind. He often felt one way and acted another. His ability to stand over people diminished as all the kids outgrew his short arse. More often than not Bugs relied on Cozy for the rougher stuff or, at least, had Cozy back him up in a fight. Cozy was his wall. Cozy wouldn't see him hurt or beaten. There was a greedy, self-imposed, almost granted entitlement owed by the world to Bugs. Often he would tell his friends, 'If everyone in Australia gave me a single dollar I'd be right.'

Cozy and Kenny would ask, 'Why the fuck would anyone want to give you a buck?'

'Cos I fucking suffered more than them, and it's only a dollar. Most fuckers wouldn't miss that. It's the least they could do for me.'

Crooked was Bugs's straight, and others' straight was there for him to twist and corrupt.

Stirrup loved them all, but only liked Bugs, and the feeling was mutual. There was a subtle distance between

Tribute © Robert Lee Johnston 2016
Email: tributerobertleejohnston@gmail.com

them. Bugs just wasn't a hands-on-with-dogs bloke. Stirrup was left with Bugs when once everyone but him was randomly fostered out. John Henry reminded Bugs to feed him and change his water each day. Bugs grinned lazily and looked at Stirrup.'I got two words for you, dog. Dry. Food.'

Henry instantly reacted, as any kind dog owner would. 'Fucking feed him properly, Bugs!'

Stirrup understood Bugs, and, though it was a joke, it exposed to Stirrup a careless, uncaring, empathetically stunted, arrogant, greedy pup. Stirrup would never let Bugs suffer in front of him, and, of course, there was a begrudging love between them. Neither would Bugs let any harm come to Stirrup. Unfortunately, it would take suffering to snap either of them into action. The weird thing was if anything bad ever happened to Stirrup, Bugs would cry all day like a kid with his dick stuck in a zipper.

Cozy was his closest friend. Cozy, running a distant second to any available action or fresh entertainment. Whereas Cozy and the other boys shared everything they had—money, ciggies, lollies, toys, books and food—Bugs could easily not share a thing and pig out. Not directly in front of them. He would cunningly disappear momentarily and then return sneakily with chocolate-stained teeth or smelling of smoke. Cozy's heart broke every time he noticed Bugs's selfishness, but he never brought it up. He wouldn't know where to start. And Bugs wouldn't give a fuck, or change. His greed for what he didn't have and his need for bragging rights and leading the way were vain and self-inflating. He loved to rub salt in and remind the boys if he had performed some act they hadn't. He despised any of them taking his glory by experiencing something cool and remarkable before trying it himself. Once he'd had a crack at it, whatever it may be, his attempt would be so much better than his lowly predecessor; the day sunnier, the conditions better, tougher and altogether more life threatening; and any people involved far cooler than his lowly litter mates.

Tribute © Robert Lee Johnston 2016
Email: tributerobertleejohnston@gmail.com

The end result easily surpassed anyone else's achievements to date and for the perceivable future.

Bugs was also a comfortable, conscienceless kleptomaniac; a human bower bird that had to have anything shiny, and preferably not his own. He was consumed by the shiny and tactile. Quite handy, really. If one of the girls misplaced something, you could be sure Bugs had picked it up and placed it with his gleaming, ill-gotten treasures under his bed. He wasn't always aware that he stole and often emptied his carrot-filled pockets of forgotten booty.

Cozy asked him once, 'If you don't know you stole it, is it actually stealing?'

Bugs sometimes stole sweet, pretty, girly stuff for Jen and Evie. He never admitted to nicking these pressies but they knew. His unprovoked, random generosity at times could be disarming and revealed a kind side to him the girls adored. No doubt if the stolen goods were in any way useful to him they would never have seen them, but the effort and the thoughtfulness endeared him to them. His timing was a thing of beauty. Often the warm gift would turn up at Evie's or Jen's lowest moments. He may not show it but he loved them all with a kind of love that, like him, was a little twisted and obscure. All the same it was out there, and as real and comfortable as his jocklessness.

Evie loved them all dearly, but was in love with John Henry. She adored hanging with her wild colonial boys, but time with her Henry alone consumed her mind and body. He was growing taller and more handsome, and with new, well-developed muscles appearing almost daily. She became lost in his big, brown eyes and huge, warm smile. She shivered as butterflies danced a jig in her tummy. He turned every girl's head. Lately she had noticed, when his shirt was off, his stomach muscles firing and tensing every time he moved, laughed or spoke. Cute, curly sprouts of body hair had made an appearance, making her excited, curious and goose

Tribute © Robert Lee Johnston 2016
Email: tributerobertleejohnston@gmail.com

pimpled. They knew each other's bodies from spending extended time with Syd and his kind. John Henry's eyes would apologise to Evie for every trespass inflicted. His beautiful eyes always remained sympathetic, soft and other worldly, reassuringly focused into Evie's, protecting her and taking her magically far away from their cruel predicament. Cozy's eyes at times like these would turn bright green in a flash of friction and heat, reminding her of those of a wild, hateful, untameable panther. Henry's would remain brave, a sunset of melting chocolate and soft down feathers. What you saw was what you got; stable, reliable, deep, loving and his big, never-ending sweet heart. He smelt like the boy angel who fell from heaven, and Evie smiled at something Cozy would often say about people falling from heaven. 'So did Satan.'

Evie disagreed, laughing with him. She and Jen once saw a picture of a statue, a kneeling Lucifer, wrapped delicately in his wings, recently captured and chained. She and Jen both reckoned, 'He's so bloody hot. Tropically hot!' The flustered, slack-jawed girls decided Lucifer was cast from heaven because he was damned for his wicked good looks, and sexy, hot bod. Henry smelt that good to Evie. She considered what it would be like to kiss him without an audience. Her belly tingled with nerves. All at once she felt nervous, wanted, beautiful, desired and emboldened, imagining his big brown eyes staring into hers.

Evie thought, Bugger it! I'm going to kiss him right now. Jen kisses Cozy all the time and a lot more I bet. Henry will be mine.

Quintas Curtius Rufas.

Tribute © Robert Lee Johnston 2016
Email: tributerobertleejohnston@gmail.com

CHAPTER TEN: JOHN HENRY COMES GOOD.

Stirrup went to footy training twice a week with John Henry.

While John Henry toiled sweat, Stirrup eagerly watched from the side line, occasionally coming on to the field to stare down and growl at some poor bloke who had, in Stirrup's mind, tackled John Henry a bit hard. Everyone had seen this happen a million times, and team members joked that Stirrup was staring at some of them, daring them to have another crack at Henry. Soon it became a habit at training; if anybody tackled or bumped John Henry, they had to look over their shoulder. Stirrup would not be far away. As Stirrup got larger, a rope had to be employed to stop people's arses, socks and boots, calves and Achilles being ambushed and torn apart.

John Henry, compared to the rest of the kids, was really smart in school. He could easily absorb and understand information. Some teachers liked him. His quick wit and confidence was too much for some. He smoked a little weed now and then. When footy season started, he barely

Tribute © Robert Lee Johnston 2016
Email: tributerobertleejohnston@gmail.com

smoked at all. When the yearly footy break-up party started, so did John Henry. Although this year he would continue playing on, as he had been selected to represent a combined team from his competition to play teams from afar. He fit perfectly into his new outfit. He was a solid player, a bloody good bloke, funny, and an absolute live-wire on the field. Every bus trip would see him pack a stereo and four or five AC/DC albums, playing them loudly all the way to the games, getting all the boys on board fired up. In no time every kid on the bus knew the lyrics to 'Big balls', 'Ride on', 'She's got balls', 'High voltage', 'If you want blood'. The boys couldn't hear those tracks and not think of junior rugby-league road trips, whether playing alongside Henry or watching him play.

John Henry's game was becoming refined. He cut people in half when he tackled them, softening them up nicely. Coaches and players alike shit their footy shorts when they saw him pole-axing blokes. His name was soon thrown around among the people in the know, higher up in the circle.

They told him, 'You're so young, and the whole world's in front of you. Keep your head down and your bum up. Keep training. We'll keep an eye on you, and when you're seventeen, we'll be wanting a bloke like you around.'

John Henry knew he could get even better and decided to turn things up a notch or two. He'd just won his first on-field punch up. Bravely he slipped, weaved and bobbed and couldn't be hit. Henry smashed a fist into the bloke's guts and he went down, fight over. Life was looking pretty good. The others followed him to the rep games on a commissioned school bus, with family and friends of the selected players. The brothers couldn't have been prouder. Henry played out of his skin and won best forward that year and player of the final, even though his team ultimately lost the decider. Rain had bucketed down before the last game and the field was a mud pit within five minutes. You couldn't pick out the jersey colours or make out numbers. Long, steel

Tribute © Robert Lee Johnston 2016
Email: tributerobertleejohnston@gmail.com

tags were screwed in, and most tackles were slippery and soft. Not John Henry's. His ability to fell ball runners with crunching power was evident when his victims grunted, moaned and sometimes squealed like girls as he lined them up and slammed the involuntary shit out of them. His running game was gutsy and brutal. His attack hurt defenders. And, because he grew up with all the boys always throwing a footy around, his ball skills were silky smooth and faultless. Note books came out, his number and name recorded. They were still kids when John Henry was approached by three different NRL scouts that recognised his talent. They loved him; his character, his sense of loyalty and humour. They all wanted a big hand in his ongoing development. His future was looking bright, and he tried not to get overly excited or big headed. In fact, the boys showed much more excitement than he ever allowed himself.

Cozy was stoked. 'Holy shit, man, you're going to the top, brother.'

'I can't believe it, man. Did that just happen?'

Bugs hugged him aggressively. 'Fucking oath it happened!'

Kenny joined in the celebrations. 'You beaudy. You're a fucking legend, man.'

'God, boys. I can't believe it.' He had to sit. 'It feels like a dream.'

The boys nodded and couldn't wipe off their proud smiles. They knew how hard he worked and admired his perseverance and dedication. John Henry was absolute in their eyes, deserving and rightly rewarded. He sat there and absorbed all the possibilities. All he had suffered and endured would be soon be left far behind. His sunglass-bright future illuminated deeply buried thoughts and hopes previously dismissed as daydreams or wishful thinking.

'I'm on my way, boys. Just got to keep doing what I'm doing. Them scouts are keen and asked me what I want to do outside of footy. I told them I always wanted to be a vet,

Tribute © Robert Lee Johnston 2016
Email: tributerobertleejohnston@gmail.com

and get this, man. They promised they'd help me go to university and get the education I need.' It was overwhelming him and the makings of tears formed in his eyes.

'Be buggered,' said Kenny. 'One of us going to university! Who woulda thunk that?'

'I can't believe this is happening to me, boys!'

Bugs told him, 'Fucking believe it, brother. You earned it.'

John Henry let his head fall back and breathed deeply. Because it was his last game for the season he asked, 'Which one of you tight bastards is going to mull up and blow me out?'

'That's more like it,' Kenny agreed. 'Let's burn one end to end, my friends.'

That night they slept well. When they woke, John Henry, Cozy and Bugs were ordered to get their shit together by Rev. A farmer wanted help and Stirrup was to stay behind because the farmer had large, aggressive pig-dogs. He wasn't like Syd at all, this one. This particular farmer just liked to work them to the bone. The rainy weather meant their clothes were always wet, and Bugs and Cozy caught slight colds. The rains kept coming, and the whole farm was a series of giant, muddy lakes and puddles, every inch soaked. The boys walked barefoot everywhere, through muddy puddles and standing lakes of water. After their labours they had many cuts and scrapes. Not that they gave a toss. It was far too uncomfortable walking around with gummies or boots full of water. Barefooted worked better.

In high rainfall areas lurks a silent killer called leptospirosis. It's a mongrel of a thing. Under a microscope it looks frighteningly like syphilis: an evil-looking, microscopic spiral worm. Rats and rodents are common hosts of the killer. When they drink from puddled water they sometimes piss in it. If you happen to walk into that particular puddle

Tribute © Robert Lee Johnston 2016
Email: tributerobertleejohnston@gmail.com

with an open wound, with that rat's piss in it, it will get into your bloodstream. At the start its symptoms are identical to the flu. Many people make the fatal mistake of assuming it's a common cold or flu. The sweats and chills dehydrate you, and you lose your appetite, can't keep anything down. The wormy critter attacks your internal organs. You find out when you start coughing up and pissing blood, by which point your almost beyond saving. You must recognise lepto quickly and seek treatment. Treatment is a cheap, plentiful antibiotic. Total organ failure is what kills you; usually your kidneys fail first, and then your liver. The rest soon follow suit. Leptospirosis shuts down everything … Fast! Death comes as a welcome relief. Even if you see a doctor early enough he'll still say, 'You'll think you're going to die, you'll want to die—but you won't.'

Lepto is a mean mother. It kills dogs, men, beasts. You could be the fittest bloke, fitter than a mallee bull; you could be young, old, in-between. This murderer doesn't care. It destroys life as quickly as a chainsaw fells trees.

Bugs and Cozy got rid of all the snot and phlegm their colds had generated and, predictably, John Henry caught a cold. For a day or two he was snotty and drowsy. Day three he was coughing like rats in a chaff bag. On day four he couldn't get out of bed. The farmer was annoyed and whinged, 'It's just a fucking cold! Get the fuck out of bed and get to work, boy!'

Henry looked pretty crook, so Bugs and Cozy let him sleep, hidden in the hay shed, while covering his chores. When the boys came back at lunch to check on him he was terribly hot and sweating his arse off. His clothes were soaked. Cozy swore he saw steam come off of him. They had never heard of lepto before and suspected nothing. People often used to call it 'Weil's disease', but over time that was adopted as the phrase to fall back on when a pet cat or dog was run over. 'Wheels' disease.' The boys didn't put the two together. Bugs and Cozy tried to get Henry to drink some

water. Bugs raced to the bathroom medicine cabinet for some aspirin. It was all he recognised. Cozy wished like hell that Jen was there or Evie. They'd know what to do, how to make him come good.

The farmer yelled after them, 'Get back to work. Lunch is over.'

They left John Henry there all day to sleep it off. He hardly knew they were gone. When they returned he had gotten so much hotter and paler. He was moaning and saying sentences that made little or no sense. He was surrounded by vomit. All the water and aspirin had come up. They couldn't get him to walk so they carried him to his bed and stripped off his sweaty clothes. Bugs tried to get him to drink but soon needed a bucket when Henry chucked it up. Cozy and Bugs showered him and they slept in the same room. They threw mattresses on the floor around Henry's. The night was tough. His body rested but it wasn't sleep. He was in stacks of pain. When the sun came up John Henry had turned a sickly pale and wouldn't wake. Cozy gently forced Henry's eyes open and the whites were discoloured and glazed yellow. He and Bugs shook their heads. What the fuck is going on here?

Cozy informed the farmer. 'John Henry's real crook. Sick as a bloody dog.'

He took a quick look for a second from the bedroom doorway. 'He'll be right. He's just got the flu. Let the lazy bastard sleep it off.'

By that afternoon, when they'd finished all their jobs, he'd gotten much, much worse. Cozy and Bugs pulled the sodden sheet off him and the bed was soaking with sweat. And around his dick was red-orange piss. It was obviously watered down blood. They raced to the farmer.

'Henry's pissing blood!'

His eyes widened. 'Arrgghh SHIT!'

Tribute © *Robert Lee Johnston 2016*
Email: tributerobertleejohnston@gmail.com

He got to John Henry's bed and saw the sweat and bloody piss, and then lifted him up. 'We got to get him to hospital.'

The nearest hospital was fifty kilometres away, and when they arrived the nurses instantly recognised lepto. They gave him medicine to stop him vomiting and hooked a drip up to a vein. Then the boys were kicked out of the room.

The doctor confirmed to them on the way out, as nurses whizzed and whipped around him, 'Your brother, Henry, he's a very sick little man, and it's going to be a rough night.'

John Henry died two hours later. Killed by rat piss, a puddle, and some dopey farmer who didn't know what it was. Until it was too late. Bugs and Cozy were told by the doctor that if they had brought him in a day or so before, they could have saved him. With cheap, abundant antibiotics.

The farmer had left as soon as he dropped the three boys off, leaving them alone in a strange place. He said he would be back to pick them up later. The doctor, assuming the young fellas were brothers, let them see Henry one last time to say goodbye. He left them alone with their friend. Their world was on fire. They cried, wailed, yelled and broke down. Then the boys walked. They 'borrowed' a 'For Sale' sign from out front of a house beside the highway. They gathered closely under its protection, tripping each other up. They hitched, yelped and moaned the fifty kilometres back to Tribute in the pouring, killer rain to tell the others.

'Bugs, mate, Evie and Stirrup ain't going to like this news one little bit.'

Tribute © Robert Lee Johnston 2016
Email: tributerobertleejohnston@gmail.com

CHAPTER ELEVEN: STIRRUP! COME HERE, BOY

Stirrup could hear the boys crying long before they came into sight.

He was already missing his master terribly, and his sharply honed canine senses knew something wasn't right. Stirrup ran, anxiously hopeful, into the dark and rain to welcome them. He searched and sniffed for his master as Cozy explain to him Henry's death. All three of them stood motionless, bar the shivering, soaked to the bone in the black rain. Bugs and Cozy patted and hugged Stirrup, crying, explaining to him what had happened and hopelessly apologising. Stirrup's tail stopped wagging. His gut instinct was hijacked by the horrific news. All three made their way to the verandah. They towelled down after removing sodden shirts, and gave Stirrup a once-over to dry him off as well, before entering.

They explained to the others what happened. One look at Stirrup explained it all; his head heavy and listless, his tail down with grief. Evie wouldn't accept it. NO! she yelled over and over, long and loud. Each of them was paralysed with

the discovery of a fresh phantom limb. They had no language to describe the loss they endured that day. It was too sad. Too encompassing. They all felt as bad as Stirrup looked.

Bugs and Cozy got cleaned up and warm. Cozy's shower did little to wash away the day. Jen and Evie collapsed, sobbing, exhausted, after screaming and wailing. No one could stop crying. They huddled together on the floor, unable to rise. Brave Stirrup licked children's tears and nuzzled them as his heart was torn in all directions. He understood perfectly what had happened. He worried now about his babies fretting and he started to grieve, fret and worry himself. Like all of them, he blamed himself. Stirrup's kind soul and stoic spirit were tortured and whittled out of him in that tear-filled room. Everyone he loved, his family members, was hurting, and his beloved owner was up ahead. Stirrup dearly wanted to see him, to be with him, to share the next adventure together and protect him.

Stirrup, orphaned one Christmas, was given to Rev as a puppy by a kindly older lady, to keep him company on long, rainy Tribute days. Rev accepted reluctantly and quickly disliked the animal, and the pup him. Stirrup always had a wonderful nose for bad eggs. When the pup and a five-year-old Henry, a pup himself, laid eyes on each other, the shared attraction was instant. They became best mates forever right then. Rev soon realised the burden of a pet was lifted from his shoulders, so let Henry keep him. Stirrup loved all the kids, but John Henry was his great love and he John Henry's.

Stirrup had a wicked sense of humour, a strange thing to say about a dog and even tougher to explain. The kids were always laughing when playing with Stirrup, even more so when they watched Stirrup and John Henry playing together. They had similar senses of humour, and Stirrup's smile was a thing of pure beauty. Each day he'd walk them to school and wait at the front gate all day for the bell to

Tribute © Robert Lee Johnston 2016
Email: tributerobertleejohnston@gmail.com

ring, to hang out with Henry and the pack. He even knew what day of the week it was, and when school holidays started and finished. Stirrup worried his feathers like a clucky mother goose when Henry was fostered out to Syd, or to other farms where Stirrup wasn't welcome. He understood what damage was being done. Stirrup could smell and read the trauma inflicted on his boy, his Henry. Stirrup hated not being able to protect his brother child. What he enjoyed best of all were the one or two foster families that would let Henry take his clever, well-mannered dog. The farms were theirs to explore and roam. No harm would come Henry's way with a protective Stirrup at the end of his bed. Not that these families ever tried. Stirrup just wanted to be close, and alone as often as possible with John Henry. No matter how busy Henry was he always made time to hang out, play and enjoy Stirrup's company.

After Henry's death, Stirrup refused to eat. Every day he pined and fretted more. Stirrup worried so much his eyes looked tired and beaten. Any energy he'd had was long gone. Life slowly and heart wrenchingly drained from his disposition and condition. He loyally called out to Henry with a heart-breaking, long howl. Stirrup had many voices: happiness, sadness, and joy. That hurtful noise was Stirrup crying. No patting or stick could comfort him, nor food tempt him. Pleading words were not heard by Stirrup as he lay beside Henry's empty bed. The kids begged; they begged him over and over, and bawled for him to eat, to drink, to please not give up. Cozy promised Stirrup he would do his best to make him happy. He gently nosed Cozy's face and smiled for the briefest moment. Then Cozy saw his smile fade as Stirrup's orphaned mind wandered to his John Henry. The gloom returned to his eyes as he exhaled and forgot forever his smile. Cozy hated seeing his spirit break. They all did. The girls spoiled him and tried tempting him lovingly from the brink. They weren't of much help to him. They were all so damaged, in the same boat and tarred

Tribute © Robert Lee Johnston 2016
Email: tributerobertleejohnston@gmail.com

heavily with the same brutal brush. They all died a little, so loved was John Henry.

After the funeral, three days after Henry died, Stirrup was far from himself. The burial he attended on the church hill cemented in his mind that his Henry wasn't coming home. Stirrup came to each of the orphans, finding them hidden in various spots after the funeral, and comforted each of them individually. The young ones hugged him and confessed all the things kids confess to wise, sweet, brave, beloved dogs. Knowing full well they wouldn't tell anyone. He big heartedly nuzzled each of their necks and inhaled their youthful, wonderful, sweet scent as the children breathed him in.

Each of the youngsters were unsaddled, un-stirruped, when Stirrup died during the night. They liked to think he had been saying goodbye to the pack and gone to join Henry. John Henry must have needed Stirrup and called him. They woke to Stirrup not waking, and any reserves of group bravery left swiftly. It was too much to handle with grace. Stirrup's broken heart killed him. No way in hell could they could bury him in the grounds of the beastly orphanage cottage. Stirrup and John Henry should be together forever.

Bugs and Cozy carried Henry's Stirrup to the grave site, to the church's very own hill cemetery, hallowed for all Tributarians, no more than a hundred metres from the orphans' cottage door. The mounded soil of Henry's grave hadn't settled, and the sight of piled, fresh, red earth, covering their blood brother, brought with it flooding tears. It was too hard, so cruel, for them to lose them both so soon. If they were breaking any godly laws or commandments by burying a boy's dog with him on consecrated, hallowed ground, Cozy told them, 'Well, shit. God, that pussy, is just going to have to look the other way tonight. And fucking deal with it.'

Cozy and Bugs dug, but not too deeply. They didn't want to disturb Henry. All the same, they dug deeply enough

so no one would ever know Stirrup loyally lay there. Each took their turns saying goodbye. Jen and Evie had brought some flowers they'd picked, along with a nice big stick for them both to play with. They all cried, and kissed and hugged Stirrup. Each told that heart-broken dog, wrapped in John Henry's sheet, how much they loved him. Let him know he was the best, funniest, bravest, kindest dog in the whole world. He and his love would never be forgotten. They confessed their love for him and hoped they'd see him soon. They knew, as they laid him carefully at his best mate's feet, that the two of them would have had it no other way. It was the single, sweetest thing those kids did.

Henry and Stirrup together forever. That always made Cozy smile. Cozy didn't know who had said 'every boy needs a dog', but he agreed.

And every dog needs a thirteen-year-old 'Wild Colonial Boy'.

Tribute © Robert Lee Johnston 2016
Email: tributerobertleejohnston@gmail.com

CHAPTER TWELVE: JENNY BABY

Jen was in an ever-constricting world of hurting. She had just recently gotten her periods, and then they just as suddenly stopped.

She knew she was pregnant. Jen also knew it could only be Syd's or Cozy's. The damage done to Cozy, to his balls from the whip, made her lean heavily towards Syd. A secret sickness grew inside Jen's pale, bright-white belly, faster and larger than any baby ever could. Poisoned and violated on every level, she was determined to kill any filthy spawn of Syd's living inside her.

At any cost.

Each day she tried to consciously convince herself to reject any foreign body inside her. She tormented her mind with horrible memories. They became a weapon she set upon herself, destroying her from within. Jenny was angry and tired. Tired of: 'No good.' No good news, nothing good. Tired of the slaver's shackles, the pain, the imposition. Tired of the cycle of hopelessness. Exhausted from a lifetime of uneasy instability. Worn down from seeing her and her

Tribute © Robert Lee Johnston 2016
Email: tributerobertleejohnston@gmail.com

closest friends' lives having absolutely no cause, effect, or consequence. She felt no purpose and wondered if any good man in this world would accept, understand and truly love her. Could he look at her and see just Jen? See her innocence? None of her childhood? None of her abuse, the shit, fluids and blood? Could a great man understand the hateful sound of a murderous whip, the horrors, and hear the language repeated when she was weak, feeling ugly or down? 'Suck the fuggin puss outta this, Girly.' And so on? The word 'Girly' still made Jen cringe. Would she have to censor herself and keep her shadow in darkness? Keep secrets? Lie? Could she love a good, real man? Even recognise him? She doubted it. Jenny had never been taught how to love ... or to be loved.

The boys didn't count in that way, not like that. Jen wanted, of course, a life of her own. She had dreams that right then seemed a hundred lifetimes away. Her hatred for men like Rev, Syd—for men in general—was overpowering, becoming firmly entrenched and deep-set destructive, making the loss of John Henry, one of the rare men she truly loved and trusted, even more potent. Food tasted stale; her sense of smell grew tainted and sulphuric. She craved a new start, a family of her own that wouldn't hurt her. If it was Cozy's baby she would have that family. But in her deepest guts she knew it was Syd's, could feel it, slowly convinced herself she could taste it, sense it. Like vigorous cancer it grew, consumed and corrupted. The others noticed her shifting moods and hardening heart. She appeared withered and defeated. They did their honest best to cheer her up. Evie spent lots of careful time with her. They all did. They held her when she broke down, and tried to shoulder the heaviest of her burdens when she was without strength. After weeks of gently prying and prodding, Jen gave in to Cozy.

'Syd's still alive, Cozy. Living in my tummy!'

Tribute © Robert Lee Johnston 2016
Email: tributerobertleejohnston@gmail.com

The news stabbed the very heart of Cozy. A hating fire incinerated his mind.

Christ! I killed that piece of shit. He's six foot under. Yet here he is, large as life, fucking with us again. Reaching out capriciously from death and wherever fuckers like him go. Syd, the infamous, simpleton-fuck won't cease. Fuck it!

Cozy understood at once why she had been peculiar lately. He felt ineffective and worthless for not picking it up, sensing it earlier. He tried to convince her that it was his and, between all of them, they could have a family, better than they had ever dreamed as kids. Everyone would help. Mainly, Cozy told her it wasn't her fault and she had done nothing wrong and he, all of them, would do anything she wanted to make her happy. He told her he loved her no matter what. They could and would find a way.

'We always find a way, Jen.'

She smiled for the first time in ages. Cozy didn't buy it, not for a second. Jen, bless her cotton socks, tried but couldn't. It was a dry, halfway smile. For three and a half months she tried to see a way out, a way ahead. Then she finally shut down.

She prayed for a miscarriage, punched herself in the stomach, self-harmed, long before it was 'a thing' or popular, by cutting her stomach and self deeply. She fell downstairs purposely and swallowed a bunch of pills she found. Jen was robbed of her excellence. Not only that, thieves stole things that have no words. Truculent pilots who carelessly directed Jen's life created malignancy where there was once bright comeliness. Dread and foreboding stripped her of life. It was like watching a monogamous bird that had lost her loyal, lifelong mate pine, fret and worry itself into an early grave. The mob was watching Stirrup all over again, and any kind words were just as powerless to their Jen, their sweet baby girl, as they had been to John Henry's kind old hound dog.

Tribute © Robert Lee Johnston 2016
Email: tributerobertleejohnston@gmail.com

While all this shit was going down Jen was sent to a newish foster family, a loving couple who kindly took some of the kids every now and then. It was Jen's first time. As soon as she arrived she needed to use the toilet and noted a bunch of rifles proudly displayed on a felt-lined wall mount right next to the bathroom.

Sleep eluded Jen all night, from a mixture of nerves and fear. She stared at her bedroom door apprehensively, fully expecting it to open, and the cowardly male of the house to sneak silently into her bed. It never opened. It was a nerve-wracking, nightmarish night. All her hope faded within the dark, all her love was spent, all of her heart was black and breaking. She couldn't live with this mess another second. Jen couldn't visualise her future. She hated everything about herself. Then she cried painfully for hating so powerfully. She wasn't like that. She liked to feel happy. Hate was wearing her out, anger exhausting her.

The rest of the house slept. Jen slipped out of bed and silently made her way over the timber floor to her bedroom door. Her hand froze on the door knob. She was thinking … God knows what. The lady of the house awoke, hearing the squeaky bedroom door open, and smiled to herself, hoping young blue-eyed Jenny was comfortable. She and her husband had never seen a girl child attack food quite the way Jen did. Her belly must have thought her throat was cut. She quietly attacked her roast and gravy dinner like Vikings of old attacked village virgins. She assumed shy Jenny was getting a drink or going to the bathroom. She heard Jen's light feet alarm a creaky floorboard on the way to the toilet. Sure enough, moments later she heard the same telltale floorboard whinge when the sad-eyed, pretty girl made her way back to her warm, safe, soft, cosy bed. She thought it strange no toilet flushed. Perhaps Jen was politely keeping the noise down or simply needed a drink.

The couple had tried but couldn't have kids. They felt warm and effervescent knowing there was a child in the

Tribute © Robert Lee Johnston 2016
Email: tributerobertleejohnston@gmail.com

house. Jen, a good girl. The lady recognised with a single glance Jenny's ingrained distrust. The girl's lack of assurance needed lots of honesty, patience and uncorrupt love. The straightforward woman was excited about the days ahead, and a chance to gain Jen's confidence. She so dearly wanted to see her smile and hoped some cute, new, plump baby geese, a few soft, yellow ducklings and chirpy, day-old chickens would soften her up nicely and reveal Jen's pretty teeth.

She was a good old stick, a kindly, sweet woman. Her husband a virtuous, humble, faithful protector, a large, fun-loving, tender, massive-hearted, jovial gentleman. A real man, perhaps the only gentleman Jen had ever met. He would never hurt any woman or child, or see them hurting and suffering under his roof. Jen's bedroom door would never open with treachery in that warm house.

Jenny tippy-toed as tall as she could and reached for the largest rifle on the rack. She hadn't realised how heavy the rifle would be. It took a moment to take the strain and lift it out of place. She closed a squeaky bedroom door behind her. Jen sat teary eyed on the edge of her bed, momentarily lost with the loaded thirty-ought-six. She held the barrel under her chin with both hands. Her big toe searched for the trigger. A secured safety switch prevented the trigger from moving. After a moment's inspection and fumbling in the dark she disengaged the safety. Jen's big toe repositioned itself and found the trigger. All the life inside her was loudly extinguished.

The couple hit the ceiling as the sound blast filled their home.

The youngsters never saw Jen again. Grief exulted them. They loved her; they knew she loved them back. But sometimes, love alone isn't enough.

Jenny had patched Cozy up so many times the boy felt he had betrayed her by not solving her problems earlier. His first thoughts were, I'm weaker than nun's piss. If I had killed

Syd six months earlier, if I could have stopped Syd sooner and not waited, cowardly, she'd still be here. I failed her. Completely failed her. I'm a fucking coward.

Her bubble-blond hair, sweet smile, and kind, tortured heart were memories. The world took another great chunk of their small lives, diced their hearts and tossed them carelessly away.

They didn't know what Jen felt that day. All they knew for sure was that she never felt again.

Jen was buried in the same hillside cemetery, near John Henry and Stirrup. The earth above John Henry and Stirrup, hadn't settled yet. Syd's grave was, sadly, also nearby. They were thirteen, closer to twelve than fourteen, and two of them were gone from view.

The coffin that held for eternity their girl-friend was too small.

Then, sadly, the pack consisted of only four.

CHAPTER THIRTEEN: ROSIE HIGH SCHOOL

Syd had been dead for a while now, and all relaxed a little knowing Deidre and he were out of the picture.

The vacuum created with Syd gone and two deaths in as many months visiting Rev's stable stung him financially. He would engage others from his secret flock-of-freaks to earn a bob.

Most of the kids had started high school this year, the others the year before. Compared to the rest of the students they were unruly. Being physically punished by teachers had no grand effect. They wagged school all the time. Cozy had been boxing for five years now. He wasn't the flashiest but knew the basics well. The orphans were bottom of the rung in social circles at school and were tested by older boys. Soon they found other kids to pull that shit on. The shame of being publicly flogged by thirteen-years-olds was unbearable. Bigger boys with backyard, mozzie-coil-green, Indian ink tattoos, pushing their weight around soon stopped, and in no time the boys were forgotten about and left alone. The principal's office, however, became a second home for them. They played a little rougher than most but never hurt anyone but themselves, unless provoked.

Tribute © Robert Lee Johnston 2016
Email: tributerobertleejohnston@gmail.com

Each day for lunch they would meet up at a tree now referred to forever as 'the-smoke'n-tree'. Bugs had recently traded carrots for joints, and admitted the joints were much tastier. By now the boys were smoking a fair bit of weed. They had taken to it well. It dulled their pains, making them feel upright. They'd toke on a nice, badly rolled joint, smoke a ciggie or two, chat to girls. In no time flat they were selling weed to everyone. Other than a couple of kids who could steal a bud or two off their parents, the boys had the monopoly sewn up. The profit made out of 'the smoke'n' tree' was bloody handy when you were starving orphans.

Bugs, ballsy, calamitous and nowhere near his usual orange, carrot-influenced-skin-colour self, could sell any size bag of dope in a fully attended classroom, right under the teachers' noses, like some secret MI5 operative.

Bugs, Kenny and Cozy completely corrupted that whole school, and soon saw a hundred kids chuck whities, some funny, some hilarious and some not so very much. The flavours, the smells, the feel, and the availability of quality weed soon made them amateur connoisseurs. The next year, bucket bongs became their preferred smoking utensil. The boys fell in love with sticky-sweet, chunky hash that year, though dank, seedless buds were their favourite mainstay. Alcohol became a daily presence in their young lives. Too young to buy it, Cozy and Bugs would steal it easily enough. They would disassemble the louvres of a bottle-shop window once a month and grab enough to last. The Middy pub was fair game too. Their thieving ways stopped as cannabis money rolled in. There was no shortage of blokes old enough to buy it for them, of course, for a bud or two.

Cozy's boxing skills were slipping as he partied and fart-arsed about. He did okay, but just scraped by as the boys blackened lungs, souls and livers. Three teenage boys smoking every day, all day, soon consumed an ounce a day. With no sign of slowing down. They woke to bucket bongs

Tribute © Robert Lee Johnston 2016
Email: tributerobertleejohnston@gmail.com

stashed close inside the jungle and took a stack of joints to school. Rev was blind to it for now. He suspected something was going on when things the kids couldn't afford started appearing. He was sure they were stealing from him again. Tribute was slowly growing, but not fast enough for his liking. Rev needed a few more Syds around. The town itself was just big enough for people to mind their own business, and sufficiently small, poor and guilty for people not to look too far from their own homes or troubles. Teenage boys in his midst was a headache he didn't need. Rev shook his head and mumbled to himself, 'I despise teenagers.'

Needless to say, they didn't last long at high school, getting suspended at first until finally expelled and pissed off once and for all.

The boys had been selling a butt load of pot to all sorts of ex school mates. A local senior girl was dating a bloke from the city a year older than her, with a car and licence. She approached Cozy up town one day to score some dope for him while he was up visiting. Cozy agreed and met the fella. His name was Howie, a cool, solid, shorter lad with tatts and a slick city style. He looked a bit weird but was piss funny, and Cozy got to know him well. Later Cozy had a heap of mull for sale when Howie showed up out of the blue, looking for an ounce. Cozy mentioned he had a shitload of pounds if he wanted some. Howie thought about it and agreed. If they took it to the city his mum would buy a few.

'Your mum smokes weed, man? How cool's that?'

'Yeah, I guess. She's a strange tractor me mum. Crazy as.'

'What do you mean?'

'You'll see, Cozy.'

Cozy picked up four of Lacey's sweeter pounds. Lacey had become a close friend of the boys over the years. Howie drove Cozy to a nondescript, leafy two-storey Queenslander that resembled every other house on the street. They parked underneath and made their way upstairs, through

Tribute © Robert Lee Johnston 2016
Email: tributerobertleejohnston@gmail.com

the back entrance. Cozy smiled when he noticed a phrase on a wall inside when Howie opened the back door.

Home sweet

Ramming the point

Home.

Cozy shat his pants. There were four women, aged between nineteen and twenty-five, almost naked, wearing skimpy lingerie. They all sweetly said g'day to Howie, and then asked who Cozy was.

'He's my mate, Cozy. Cozy, say g'day to the girls.' He introduced them by name.

Cozy extended a hand, eyes firmly fixed on the floor. He was suddenly very shy and nervous.

A dark, pretty Chinese girl, in purple undies and bra, spoke in broken English as she shook his hand. 'What cute name you have. How old you, Cozy?' She put her hand under his chin and lifted the child's face to hers.

'I'm fourteen, in a month or so.'

'You thirteen?'

'Nearly fourteen.'

Another lady in white underwear with short-cut, blond hair, long skinny legs, and giant tits came to meet the youngster. 'What are you doing here?'

'Howie needs some smoke, so I brought a few pounds with me to unload.'

'Shit, you mean to say you're thirteen, here to deal drugs, and you have pounds to sell?'

'I'm nearly fourteen,' Cozy quickly fired.

Howie interrupted, asking where his mum was. One of the girls yelled out, 'Rosie!' And soon his mum appeared, introducing herself to Cozy with pleasant small talk.

He asked her and Howie, very confused, 'What's going on here?'

Rosie responded with a question. 'How old are you, Cozy?'

Tribute © Robert Lee Johnston 2016
Email: tributerobertleejohnston@gmail.com

One of the girls answered for him. 'He's nearly fourteen! Such a little cutie!'

Rosie wanted to know, 'Do you go to school? Where are your parents, Cozy? Aren't they worried where you are?'

Cozy lied. 'I go to school now and then, and my parents, they don't worry what I get up to … for pretty much as long as I can remember.'

'That's no good. I'm sorry to hear that.' Rosie looked for the words. 'Cozy, this is my house of business. I run a brothel here from my home. All the girls you see, and a couple you can't that are busy, live here and work for me. Do you know what a brothel is, Cozy?' The girls giggled a little.

'I think so. Is it to do with prostitution?'

'That's right, Cozy.'

'I see, so you're a madam?' Howie seemed unfazed by the line of questions.

'Yes I am. You're very clever, Cozy. You must read a lot?'

'I got a couple of books.'

'Well, Cozy, just like dealing pot is dangerous and secretive, so is prostitution and being a madam. No one can talk or blab to strangers what goes on here, do you understand? The police like to catch us girls.'

Her tone was of an adult talking to a toddler. Cozy wanted to let Rosie know he wasn't a kid.

'They're piss weak, aren't they? That works great for me, Rosie. I can't stand police, or big mouths. Can I ask, Rosie, what Howie's dad thinks of all this? Is he cool with me being here?'

'Yes you can, Cozy, and no, he isn't upset you're here. I got knocked up when I was sixteen in my home town near Sydney. Howie's dad took off once he found out. And I was kicked out of my parents' home. I was homeless, barefoot and three months pregnant. I had to find a way to start over again. I hated the man that abandoned me, and all men for a

Tribute © Robert Lee Johnston 2016
Email: tributerobertleejohnston@gmail.com

while, because of him. So I used them, Cozy, to make my money and buy all I need, for myself. I raised Howie on me own, all these years, no help from no one.'

'Shit. I'm sorry about bringing all that up, Rosie.'

'That's sweet of you Cozy, and never mind. All is good, handsome. All is good. So, Howie tells me you have a few elbows to sell me.'

Rosie was older, smart, but pretty in a tired kind of way. She was sandy haired and seemed sweet to her girls, kind and soft eyed towards Cozy as she offered him a drink. All the girls were now fawning over him, giggling. Telling each other how cute his long hair and baby face were, flirting playfully and taking great joy in watching the boy blush and wriggle.

'Yeah, Rosie. I bought four pounds for you.'

'What's a kid your age doing with that much smoke?'

'I don't know. Like you, I have to make a living one way or a-bloody-nother.'

Rosie looked hard into his eyes. She chuckled and then considered Cozy's face. She noticed the scars. 'Do you box, Cozy?'

'Yeah, how do you know that?'

'I know a lot of men, some of them fighters. I can tell. Are you any good?'

'I scrape by.'

The thick scar behind Cozy's ear, running down to his shirt neck, caught her attention. Cozy could feel her eyes focus on it. She inspected more closely. Shocked, Rosie asked, 'What happened to your neck, Cozy?'

Howie moaned. 'Mum, stop asking so many bloody questions and leave him alone! For Christ sake, back up a bit, old girl.'

Rosie, a good old duck, sensed a clipped, broken wing. The other girls all investigated his neck. One or two lightly stroked the half-hidden scar.

Tribute © Robert Lee Johnston 2016
Email: tributerobertleejohnston@gmail.com

Rosie asked sternly, 'That's a whip scar isn't it, Cozy? Who did that to you? Your father?' She was searching his eyes for a reaction.

'Nah, it's just an old scar from when I stacked me pushie as a kid.'

Cozy looked away, so as not to let her see his telltale eyes change colour.

'Will you let me see your shoulder please, Cozy?'

Howie saved Cozy's uncomfortable, panicked arse. 'Mum! Leave Cozy alone. You're embarrassing me. Do youse want his pot or bloody not? Sorry, Cozy, I told you she was a bit different.'

'I'm sorry, Cozy. Once a mother always a mother. Let's have a look at those pounds of yours.'

Cozy sold lots of dope to Rosie and the girls. Howie knew how much money was coming in from the brothel and saw with his own eyes the different drugs such a job required. He stole speed from Rosie and swapped it with Cozy for a sack or two of sweet, fat buds. He had seen the girls use needles often enough, so he stole some of those too. He showed Cozy what they did. It was wonderful, Cozy told him. When Cozy got back to the boys and the orphanage, he introduced them to what he had discovered. Bugs was impatiently racing to try it out, especially as Cozy had beaten him to it and knew something he didn't. Bugs needed to catch up.

'What is it?'

'It's speed. Old mate calls it go-e.'

'Whatdya do with it?'

'You inject it.'

'With a needle?'

'Yep.'

Kenny yelled, 'Fuck me dead!' when Cozy, produced a fist full of needles.

Bugs asked, 'Where'd you get all that from?'

'From a whorehouse, in the city.'

Tribute © Robert Lee Johnston 2016
Email: tributerobertleejohnston@gmail.com

'A what?'

'A brothel.'

'Bullshit!'

'No bullshit!'

'Fuck me. How? How'd you get into a whorehouse?'

Cozy explained his weird meeting with Howie and his mum.

Bugs asked, 'How do we do this, man?'

Cozy showed the boys what Howie had taught him. Bending up a spoon he performed the ritual. He dug the pick into his own large, hose-like vein. They asked him to do it for them, and he easily found their thirsty, virgin veins to milk blood from, before gently squeezing the plunger, releasing the solution into them. The three boys enjoyed the instantaneous, lifting effects. 'Holy crap', 'Cool', and 'Jesus Christ' were breathed out. Rushing from the liquid's ecstasy they felt shiny and clean. Happily, their worries were far below. Injecting didn't feel at all dirty, which surprised the three novices. Answers and possibilities seemed much closer, and they overlooked their pasts as a new element of reality crept through their chemically enhanced bloodstreams. They asked lots of questions about how speed was created, its worth and ... where the hell had it been all their lives! Cozy would get some more off Howie for the upcoming fourteenth birthdays, but for now they had plenty to tide them over. Of course, they talked about the girls in the brothel. They discussed in detail what they looked like and what they wore. Cozy mentioned Madam Rosie and her careful paranoia.

Cozy gushed. 'That blond, tall one, with the big tits. I reckon I could've roasted a pumpkin in her bloody bra.'

Bugs asked Cozy enviously, 'Bro-Hammad Ali, who the fuck do I got to root, shoot or electrocute to ever meet a "madam" of a whore house?'

CHAPTER FOURTEEN: FUCKING BLOODY KIDS.

Maybe childhood ends when reminiscing begins.

Perhaps it's over the day children lose their soul. Sadness and loneliness lodged itself so deeply that the pack of teenagers, fifteen years strong, hadn't completely, truly, really laughed out loud since John Henry, Jenny and Stirrup died. They often discussed why they made all that effort. All they fought, struggled and suffered for, only to pay dearly, the ultimate, eternal price. For what? They also remembered great, good times together, success, life, laughs and love.

A huge downside of Tribute's small population was that if the tiniest thing went wrong, Sarge didn't have to be Dick Tracy or Sherlock Holmes to find the culprit. Sarge was usually bang on. He knew well before he got to any crime scene who the culprit was. There were only a few mad fish to choose from in this small, backward pond.

The boys were on a stealing streak. Five years ago, while they were all of ten years old and Jenny, John Henry and Stirrup were still kicking around, shit was cheap, but it

was still way out of the reach of the children's meagre means. If an object cast a shadow or wasn't bolted down, it was fair game for them. The boys combined, criminal form was clean and silky. Their plans were always well considered and never spur of the moment if they and their starved bellies could help it. Sarge figured it was the kids when they shoplifted and stole, but really didn't know for sure, and could never completely prove it. Loyalty, secrecy and silence were the friendship's backbone. And they denied everything, always.

Young, greedy, glutinous lungs loved puffing and sucking on cigarettes. The boys begged, borrowed and stole their daily 'Chinese drawback' and 'bum puff' hits.

Above the front door of one local shop was suspended a bell. It clanged to alert the owner, whose house was attached to the shop, that a customer had arrived.

Bugs was sure. 'If we can shut that bloody bell up, that whole shop is ours to rob while old mate's watching Days of Our fuckin' Lives on the telly.'

Henry squatted down, Cozy climbed on, then Henry stood upright. Cozy was sitting tall on John Henry's strong shoulders, while Bugs ever-so-gently opened the door. With it slightly ajar, Cozy could now fit a hot little hand around the bell. He was dampening the clapper with his thumb. It fit like a bum in a bucket. Once secured, Bugs opened the door wide. Cozy gently and silently let go of the bell once the door was jammed open with a milk crate. John Henry ran out the front after he let Cozy back down to keep cockatoo and an eye out with Stirrup. Bugs, Cozy and Kenny were in like Flynn. Kenny and Cozy stretched their shirts out, forming bowls, as Bugs digitally raped the smoke stand of over thirty packets, then another fifteen or so various packets of rolling tobacco. The gut-worm-ridden-kids attacked with SAS-like silence and determined fervour. Bugs filled the now-sagging shirts with anything and everything within his reach: chewing gum, lollie bags, lighters, pens, Tally-Ho rolling

Tribute © Robert Lee Johnston 2016
Email: tributerobertleejohnston@gmail.com

papers, chips. Everything. Bugs and Cozy grinned toothy grins knowing their guts and lungs would be satisfied in the immediate future. At the same time their devious eyes looked to the mechanical, old-fashioned till. They could hear the TV's chatter, and the shop keeper was no more than a metre or two away, grunting now and then while eating lunch on his couch. Bugs and Cozy could see his shoes as he leant back in his comfortable chair. Both of them took a huge, scared breath. Kenny, seeing hungry eyes and daring grins, shook his head, mouthing silently, No, boys, leave it. Fuck you two, Mary-Lou.

Bugs dropped what was in his hands into Cozy's shirt and snuck to the till. This could get bloody tricky, he thought.

Kenny nervously scarpered outside. Bugs held his hand in front of the money drawer, and the two boys exhaled slowly in unison. Bugs pressed the open button. The drawer opened with the sound muffled, as the live audience on whatever show the shop owner was watching burst into laughter. Bugs prevented the cash drawer from fast hitting the register bell. The tiniest ding was barely audible. Once the exposed drawer was savagely ravished, they legged it out the door, leaving the entrance and the till wide open behind them. They were pretty good kids ... once you got to know them. They were just always, endlessly hungry. In fact, stealing never sat well with most of the lads. Bugs, on the other hand, always afflicted, suffered a life-long predisposition to kleptomania.

By fourteen and in no time flat their tastes had expanded beyond the smoky worlds of cannabis into powders, needles, alcohol and, their latest favourite, the local wild mushrooms, laced heavily with a powerful, LSD-type chemical. The boys weren't aware of the inherent dangers of the injectables and powders they consumed. How could anything that made them feel so good be bad for them? They were too young to be suspected. The general

Tribute © Robert Lee Johnston 2016
Email: tributerobertleejohnston@gmail.com

public, schools and state, may have thought their generation was too young and innocent to need educating about such adult things. Students weren't 'sexually educated' until they were fourteen or fifteen. By then, half the girls were already barefoot, smoking, and heavily pregnant. Made for fantastic show and tell.

The boys smoked weed more and more, while studying less and less. They didn't fit in with people their age, or anywhere to be honest, in school or around Tribute. School became a running joke as the boys grew more and more out of control. They were taking a hell of a lot of time off. They weren't dumb, they just weren't interested. They had been told often enough that they were useless. They became aware early in life that they weren't anything special.

One day, when Cozy and Bugs had been expelled from school for a while, Cozy heard his name called. The voice was loud, mean and agitated. He could make out his name amongst the noises and echoes reverberating through the forest. Then he could hear clearly, 'I'M GOING TO WHIP THE FUGGIN WHITE OFF OF YOUSE.'

Cozy and Bugs had been expelled for six months from school while being fostered at Syd's. It was for something stupid. Smoking ciggies, pot, drinking or rooting around, more than likely. Being on a farm meant that no mail was home delivered. The letter to Syd informing him of their expulsion needed to be signed and returned. It had to be picked up in town at his post office box. The boys knew it, and opted not to tell him they had been pissed off from school, again. Instead, they offered kindly to pick up the mail for him each day. They dressed and prepared, and then pretended to go to school every weekday. Once the bus had dropped them off out the front of the school each morning, they went downtown and stole what was needed for the day, including the mail, and headed off into the scrub, ripping the letters up from the school. For weeks letters kept turning up, the boys collecting them and ripping them up.

Lots of them. If Syd had once looked inside their school bags, he would've found no assignments or pens; instead, dunny rolls, smokes, comics, magazines, chocolate, weed. Maybe one book for subterfuge. One day while Syd was in town he bumped into the high school headmaster in the supermarket. He politely asked Syd if he had gotten around to signing Bugs's and Cozy's paperwork. Syd reckoned he hadn't seen any mail from the school and soon the penny dropped.

He thought, Cheeky fuggin bastards. Then, with a sly wink, he told the headmaster, who happened to be a fiercely devout man and a loyal friend of Rev's, 'Leave it with me, mate. I'll follow them tomorrow, and sort this fuggin shit out, once and for bloody all.'

Bugs and Cozy were sharing a stolen chocolate bar and smoking a nice, big, fat, carefully rolled joint after they'd mucked around with a tennis ball Bugs had pinched to stave off boredom. Celebrating day forty-five, a mighty-fine effort, they both agreed. They must have gladly torn up fifteen letters each. The boys had only been in the shady jungle, beside the river, an hour when Cozy heard his name called. Then they heard Bugs's name called. It was Syd. Wide eyed and frozen, they didn't know which way to run. They looked at each other. Both were at sixes and sevens. They were thoughtlessly trapped and hemmed in by a fast-flowing, dangerous rapid.

'I FUGGIN HEARD YOUSE. YOU BASTARDS. YOUSE FUGGIN STAY THERE,' came bellowing from the scrub. Every forest creature could hear Syd crashing through the undergrowth. He knew the scrub.

Cozy, aware of the trap, told Bugs. 'We're fucked.'

Their ears tuned in, trying to locate which way he was coming at them. The lads were very stoned, with heavy, bloodshot eyes. The sweet, dank smoke wouldn't leave them. It clung heavy in the breezeless jungle. Cozy was keenly aware just how strongly it smelt. They could hear Syd

Tribute © Robert Lee Johnston 2016
Email: tributerobertleejohnston@gmail.com

out there somewhere in that thick wall of green. Cozy got a bead on him, and then he broke out right in front of them. They were startled and instinctively moved backwards. Then they got a squiz at the branch Syd wielded, using it like a machete or cane knife of sorts.

'Youse fuggin stay still, youse pair of bastards.'

He was looking at Cozy, knowing he'd run if he saw a gap. Cozy looked around for an escape. When he looked back, Bugs was on the ground. Cozy heard, and felt, a blunt thump. Purples and shades of blackish-greens filled his vision. Cozy was there, but not really. The branch had connected solidly with the base of the back of his neck. Cozy could make out the forest's silhouetted canopy. His head lolled about like that of a broken doll being carelessly carried. His pained, heavy eyes fell into focus on Bugs, being dragged unconscious on his back by his shirt collar over the forest floor. Cozy slowly realised they both were. His sight faded again, this time with a terrible thought that even his mighty jungle couldn't protect or save them now.

Syd's whip tore hunks and chunks off their hides when he got them home. He never ever tied them down to any objects or triangles, like on Moreton Bay, or among the Death Fleet Convicts. Sometimes he forced them to fetch the whip for him without running away, tears, or complaint, and hand it respectfully to him. Mostly he'd just sneak up on them and CRACK! CRACK! Once on the ground, they were his for the taking. Often he didn't even have to hit them because the 'cracker' he had carefully knotted into the fall, for effect, sounded like point blank blasts from a twelve-gauge shotgun when he warmed up or missed. Young boys tend to shit themselves and react instantly by hitting the deck. This time they were already knocked senseless, so neither could run. Syd let them fall to the ground in a heap when he dragged and man-handled them out of the Landy. Then he walked in no hurry to the shed, to the wall where

his 'Sweet Thing' hung. He came back to the ute yelling, and laid into them with the bull whip.

He hit lots of places the kids' reflexes wouldn't normally allow.

A talented bullocky could, with his whip, as an old saying goes, 'flick a fly off the leader's hoof, without him ever noticing'. Syd wasn't that good by a long shot. But his precision and technique were, over time, improving.

Bugs's and Cozy's backs looked, everyday, all day, like everyone else's backs, with a shirt on. Shirtless they were remarkable, from their shoulders to their hamstrings. Cozy reckoned they received, over the years, about an equal number of lashes, but their configuration couldn't be more different. Both were shit fights in their own unique way. Like a finger print, the pattern of whip strikes was unique. Each snaked, cut and graffitied differently from the last or the next. A pitiless, rude, crude art. A plague on men and young, cursed boys.

You could be derived from the toughest stock in the world. You might have boxed, or be a proficient martial artist, or even done a stack of time. Maybe you work a gruelling, physical job. Maybe you're the hardest bastard you know. Getting whipped hurts every single human body every single time, no matter who the hell you are, or think you are.

A callous, murderous whip is just moments away at any time from laying a mortal stroke. It will sting like a bitch at first. A sharp-edged burn works its way from your inside out. Imagine a slithering serpent of fire under your skin, melting its way out of your flesh, industrious and busy. It relentlessly consumes every tiny cell and region in your head. Pain, demanding all your attention. Panic sets in when you realise this is just the first of many. The beginning. When struck again expect two savage-eyed, hating, blazing serpents. Suffer ten or fifteen lashes in its wake, and skin splitting across your once smooth back reveals skeleton. By now you

Tribute © Robert Lee Johnston 2016
Email: tributerobertleejohnston@gmail.com

will have shit your pants and tripped out. Thick, body-temperature, slippery blood, tainting your soul, soaks and gutters into your shorts, puddling in your underwear. Running warmly down your leg as though you have pissed. The worst for Cozy personally was his blood drying, caking, curdling and forming a thick red-custard skin in the sun and open air. Pulling, tugging, always feeling exposed and filthy. Then the evil rhythm. A far-off beat you sense in your body. It's your pulse racing, softly at first. So softly. Each accented note brings an exactly equivalent volume of stabbing, intensifying pain. A kick-drum loud in your ears, until your whole head fills with its destruction. The throbbing pulse gets worse over the next minutes, hours and days. At week's end each upper-body movement, each sharp or deep breath, tears sensitive, traumatised, lashed skin, as easily as ripping a newspaper page. A single sneeze will break you. You can't sleep on your back or your sides once the whip strafes around you, finding ribs. Sleep becomes defiantly hidden and when, from sheer exhaustion, you do crash out and roll into your natural sleeping position expect to wake with your clothes, pillows or sheets welded deeply to your flesh, fused fast, by the blood in your weeping lacerations.

Bumping your back, or a friendly slap on the shoulder, releases a tsunami of pain. Even when the scars have grown over it's remarkably like the pain of a stinging tree. Much later you still get days, every now and then, when it feels as fresh as the day it was laid on.

Too much whipping will kill you. Fact.

You can lose it all on the receiving end of that monumentally dark instrument. And just because your brain's protected by bone, that doesn't mean it won't hurt you there. That noise. The sound gets into your head. Into the bloodstream. A whip gets a taste of you. Then a taste for you.

One of the best ways to maintain a greenhide whip is to simply keep it regularly wet with blood. It keeps the

thong, the rawhide leather plaits, happy. Keeps them tight, supple, keen. Gives the whip weight and SNAP!

A bullock-team whip has a long, hardwood handle, usually red myrtle or spotted gum. As long as the grim reaper's scythe, six to seven feet tall. The thong is about ten feet long. Compared to a normal-handled whip ... That's like comparing bullets to cannon balls.

This particular bullock-team whip, despite Cozy's best efforts, had a taste for him.

CHAPTER FIFTEEN: BUGS GETS WHEELS

John Henry and Jen had been gone for about three or four years.

Evie still hadn't really recovered. None of them had, or probably ever would. All the kids splintered a little, or shut down one way or another.

Bugs got his licence first and his baby-shit-yellow, two-door Datsun.

'The Datto' may as well have been the V8 hardtop from Mad Max. Bugs would press the heater button and accelerate, pretending the supercharger that wasn't there fired up and, with much exaggeration, pinned them to their seats. All of them only just fit in it, fighting, laughing and arguing over who bagsed the front seat. While cruising along, Bugs would give the boys a worried look, turn the music down and blip the throttle a bit, making the old Datto surge.

'Can you boys smell fuel. Smell trouble?'

They would wind the windows up and sniff the air for traces of petrol fumes and trouble. Only to discover the dirty

Tribute © Robert Lee Johnston 2016
Email: tributerobertleejohnston@gmail.com

bastard had dropped his horrid guts, and the young blokes were sniffing it all up, much to their dismay and his pleasure.

'Shit, man! Be fucked! Air! Oh God! Wind the windows down, boys!'

Thousands of happy kilometres ticked over in that little beast. It was reliable, and not too suss looking. All their lives the boys had waited for this moment, this freedom. By now they knew between them nearly every smoker and dealer in town and so shifted, with a spring in their step, huge amounts of local weed, the poundage of which would have easily outweighed the Datsun. Once the speakers were removed from the rear pillars, they could easily stuff two pounds into either side and then, four screws later, the speakers would be back in place. There was always somewhere to be. Kenny, being a mechanical genius, kept the little motor well fettled and loved; any problem was mended before it became a headache. The Datto never broke down and ten bucks juice would last a week around town.

The music they cranked out of those speakers was never ending and golden. Tonnes of Floyd, Zep, Joplin, Stevie Ray Vaughan, Bowie, Miller, Easy Beats, Vanilla Fudge, DeVille, Marley, Stones, Humble Pie, Rodriguez, Tom Waits and, of course, anything Bon and Malcolm laid their hot little hands to. You name it, those kids knew it back to front, inside out.

Since leaving the orphanage, Cozy was picking up a bit of work with a cooler foster family that liked him. On one of their tractors was a blue flashing light, almost exactly like that on a cop car. He thought, Beauwwdy, unscrewed and stole it.

Evie was sitting in the back with Kenny. Cozy was riding shotgun. They had screwed the light onto the top of the Datto. Kenny had wired up a crude switch and they hit town. Whenever they saw someone they knew, Bugs would swing around, follow them and then flick the switch and pull them

Tribute © Robert Lee Johnston 2016
Email: tributerobertleejohnston@gmail.com

over, while flashing his high beams. If the kids didn't know them, they would take off past them laughing, with mongrel heads, and their rusty bum freckles, out the windows. Of course, they'd all pull over, and Bugs and his passengers would piss themselves laughing at how much the driver shat, and their own lack of giving a fuck. Cozy saw a lad their age, Simon, a good bloke, a fella they'd known all their lives. His shitty, four-door Torana was driving about doing bog laps. Bugs got in behind him and lit him up. Simon pulled over and was fishing around for his licence when Bugs and Cozy raced up silently to his door, hitting the roof loudly with flat palms. Bugs yelled, 'GET OUT WITH YOUR FUCKING HANDS HIGH.' Old Simon and his girl nearly shat themselves. When they realised it was the boys, they laughed so hard they nearly pissed themselves as well.

'Ah fuck! You cheeky fuckers.' He chuckled. 'You fucking got me. You fucks are mad!'

Bugs rolled a large joint. Evie and Kenny joined everyone to 'partoke', saying g'day to Simon and his girl, having a giggle at the prank. They stood around the Torana, catching up. Simon warned them, 'Crazy, mad fuckers. Don't let Sarge catch you.'

The blue light was still flashing brightly and the two cars and the tribe were on a quiet back street having a merry old yarn. No one noticed a legitimate blue light join it. Everyone was far too busy talking shit and toking on that big, tasty bunger.

Simon heard clearly, 'I knew it'd be you bloody fucking dickheads.'

Sarge slammed the cop door and caught everybody's attention. Cozy, mid toke, threw the rest of the joint as far as he could downwind, after scrunching it out in his palm.

Sarge grunted. 'Simon! ... Fuck off!'

Evie and Kenny innocently slipped into Simon's back seat, knowing Bugs was going nowhere. Cozy stayed as the Torana fired up and obediently fucked off, into the night.

Bugs was screwed and Sarge was blunt. 'Are you two bastards crazy, or just plain fucking stupid?' He looked disapprovingly at the convincing blue-light imposter. 'Turn that fucking thing off now!'

When Bugs did, Sarge ripped the wires Kenny had hooked to it, over the bonnet from the battery and held under a windscreen wiper as they snaked up onto the roof.

'You two are the biggest, dopiest fucking clowns I ever met. What were youse thinking?'

'Don't know.' Both young men shuffled.

'Who's bloody idea was this? Fuck it. Don't tell me. I don't want to know the answer to that. All fucking night I been getting calls 'bout some dickheads pulling people over and fucking off, having a good old time, thinking it was a great big fucking joke. I knew it'd be you two fucking clowns! Do you two know how I knew?' He reached over the roof of the Datsun and tore the light off. 'Cos you're both fucking dickheads! I asked myself, who do I know that'd be this fucking stupid? Two dickheads' names sprung instantly to mind. Can you two guess who I thought of?'

They shook heads as Sarge dressed them down.

'Well, it was you pair of wankers, of course.'

He walked to his cruiser and threw the fake police light angrily in through the open window. Years later, Evie overheard Sarge telling someone this very story. She heard him admit he couldn't help but piss himself laughing as the boys followed him to the cop shop that night. He had a tear in his eye from laughing so hard. 'They're good value and keep me entertained, them two fools.'

As Bugs's Datto follow Sarge and his cruiser, under orders, to the cop shop, the boys asked each other, 'What's going to happen here, man? Maybe we should leg it and just keep going.'

They were shitting a bit. Once they had arrived, Sarge pushed, threatened, yelled, and, for the umpteenth time in their lives, kicked them both up the arse. He didn't,

however, charge them. Instead they had to wash his cop cars for a month of Sundays while he supervised, moaned, bitched and whinged to the lads about how every time that fucking phone of his rings at three in the morning, when it's pissing down rain, every time he's hungover or sick, he's got to get up, answer that fucking phone, get changed, and track down a pair of fuckwits.

'You're starting to piss me off a bit, boys. Impersonating a copper?'

'We're just trying to have fun, you know? Liven the joint up a bit. We were just having a laugh and not hurting anyone. It's so fucking boring here in this fucking shit hole, Sarge.'

Sarge got more annoyed. 'Cozy, I don't give a fuck if you're bored. Fucking find something to do.'

Bugs put his two cents in. 'There's nothing to do here, Sarge, I shit you not. We're going stir crazy, man. We done it all a million times. It's no excuse; it's the bloody truth.'

'Look, if you blokes want to be dickheads do it out of town where no one can fucking see. If no bastard complains and my phone isn't ringing off its hook, I'll look the other way. Just stop being fuckwits round town. For fuck's sake, boys.'

Both agreed. 'No worries.' And, 'Righto.'

'Nobody is to get hurt. If I don't hear about or see it and no one's hurting, I don't give a fuck what you do. Now, you little shits, fuck off. And let me get back to me bloody bed.'

'Righto.'

'No worries.'

Bugs complained, once in his car. 'He just wants us out of town so he can bludge his arse off. No bastard does anything out of town. We'll be doing fuck-all out in the middle of fucking bum fuck.' Bugs changed up a gear, and wore the devil's grin. 'Fuck Sarge, Cozy. He can get fucked.'

Tribute © Robert Lee Johnston 2016
Email: tributerobertleejohnston@gmail.com

Both lads were gifted equally with an award Sarge gave out each and every month. A write up in the local rag, The Tribute Police Report.

He would make public any wankerish behaviour he'd encountered, along with what he was targeting in the coming month. He also tallied how many crimes had gone down and who he caught for what. All crap really.

'The Dickhead of the Month Award' was compulsory reading, piss funny, and dearly beloved by all. People just had to read it. Everyone adored that part of his report. Toss the rest. For Sarge, it was a chance to use his upper-class, ex-city tongue. He loved words, punctuation, grammar, using animals and collective nouns, for his analogies.

Bugs's and Cozy's read as follows:

Tribute © Robert Lee Johnston 2016
Email: tributerobertleejohnston@gmail.com

DICKHEADS OF THE MONTH

This month the honourable award will be split two ways in a dead heat. I'm sure the whole community has heard about Bugs and Cozy pulling over unsuspecting motorists with a light that imitated perfectly a police blue flashing light.

By all recorded accounts they happily pulled over about twenty locals. Who knows how many lives these two shiny, new, monumental dickheads actually disrupted with their horseplay and foolery.

Twas three in the foggy morn when my phone rang, and thusly kept ringing. Being brain dead, thoughtless teenagers, the boys used Bugs's own shitty little yellow car, which was instantly recognised.

On pulling you all over, locals witnessed four heads, a bum and as many limbs and fingers they could spare out the windows, apparently not being particularly friendly nor saying hello, having a merry old time. Therefore, Kenny and Evie get a special 'dickheads' mention this month as well.

Bugs's dim-witted, dopey best mate Cozy had found and took possession of the aforesaid flashing light and between the two came up with the idea. Cozy's excuse? He admitted how they were, and I quote, 'Bored.'

right up the arse! To further punish the boys and relieve their troublesome burden of boredom I have them washing the squad cars every Sunday until I'm satisfied.

No charges were laid.

They disrupted not only myself but inconvenienced a lot of you also. I invite you all, whether they pulled you over or not, to bring all your vehicles to the station—cars, trucks, milk tankers, tractors, motor bikes. Hell! Bring your children's tricycles and pushbikes, your crappy cockatoo cages and your filthy dogs that hate being washed. That should provide fun for all. The boys will happily wash them and have them looking like new in no time.

'NO FEE CAR/DOG WASH SUNDAYS!'

For the whole township I will gladly provide water, detergent, a sausage sizzle, shade, chairs and soft drinks.

So come on down. Bring the whole family. The kids and the oldies will love it. Let's all take full advantage of Bugs and Cozy's combined stupidity with a feed and a bloody good laugh at their expense.

This month Bugs and Cozy win hands down the embarrassingly auspicious award of: 'Dickheads of the month!'

See you all at Sunday's car wash.

Locals got a good, long laugh when that got around. It wouldn't be the last stupid thing those two did, or the last tale to be broadcast over the dickhead of the month channel.

Sarge's warning to them soon went by the wayside. Soon all the boys had cars fish-tailing up the streets, doing burnouts, drag races, hand-brakies. Their stupidity drove Sarge ballistic. From the cop shop he could hear them all leave the pub, hooning around town, carving out donuts on the cricket and footy ovals. It was even more fun in the high school grounds and under the covered concrete areas. He knew it was that mob. They'd race on the shitty old dirt roads, dodging fully laden milk tankers mid battle. The old beasts were sideways most of the time. Kenny had a full-time job modifying the cars.

'Just pay for the parts you want, and I'll put them in for free.'

Fondness would only take Sarge so far as the pack grew. They were getting a bit too wild, too much trouble. He knew it. Everything was done on a larger scale now; more horsepower, more alcohol, much more dope being sold; better drugs, better cars; the whole time working less. Sarge stepped up his searching efforts on them, their cars and passengers, only to find empty pockets and nothing in the cars. He suspected, but couldn't quantify his suspicions. That pissed him off no end. He decided to hone in on what he perceived to be the weakest link. He was wrong. Kenny was solid and brutally loyal. Sarge gave up. Kenny was a lot tougher to crack than his looks suggested.

Sarge had to be careful how he approached this lot on foot. They were runners. If he was going to catch them, he'd have to be quick and have a plan. If ever the boys saw him coming they'd split and disperse like shrapnel from a grenade. And even though Stirrup had been dead for years the boys would still yell, 'GET HIM STIRRUP.'

Tribute © Robert Lee Johnston 2016
Email: tributerobertleejohnston@gmail.com

Sarge would freeze in old panic for a millisecond. Often just the time needed to get away. Sarge would stop to make sure that bloody dog wasn't up for destroying another pair of his strides or taking any more chunks out of his arse.

'FUCKING BLOODY KIDS!'

Tribute © *Robert Lee Johnston 2016*
Email: tributerobertleejohnston@gmail.com

CHAPTER- SIXTEEN: SEVEN-FUCKING-TEEN

Sarge liked the kids and kept an eye on them his whole life.

A mad fanatical supporter of all the local sports and teams, he knew everyone and their dogs. Sarge had the gift of foresight and he knew: Blind Bloody Freddy could see the power this lot radiated. He ran a hand against the grain up his stubbled face, pondering heavily. He had mixed feelings: pride, sadness, hope and helpless wishing. He hoped Kenny would be okay. He loved the boy dearly, and wanted more for him than Tribute could ever offer. Had even, years ago, tossed around the idea of adopting young Kenny, sending him to a boarding school and separating him from his murder of crows. He couldn't, wouldn't, follow through and tear that cackle of hyenas apart. They'd had each other as brothers since first shitting in the nest. They were thicker than weeds, and tighter than an Arctic man's arsehole in icy water. Kin to each other, each other's mob, one of Tribute's local tribes. They gravitated to each other the moment they met and had stayed in each other's blazing orbit ever since. Most people in town saw the orphanage as a harbour for the wretched and didn't want their own kids hanging around unruly, strange, irrelevant children. They swiftly nipped any

friendships in the buds. As the roosters grew up, Sarge noticed their strengths and weaknesses.

Sarge thought out loud, 'Seven-fucking-teen.'

He'd seen them all shattered at the funerals, unable, like loyal, huddled elephants, to leave. They were far from okay after their rapid-fire losses. But their remaining strengths combined to bring out the best from them. A healthy, bacterial symbiosis, each almost defenceless without the others. These boys and the two girls could swear a bit. Shit, they could swear! He'd overheard the word fuck and cunt used in all their colourful glory; and some not so colourful. As verbs, adjectives, pronouns, adverbs, commas, phrases and full stops, in every sentence, almost every second word. Ending often with 'ing', 'ism', 'ery', 'ed' and 'full'. It was unusually ineffective, powerless, and inoffensive to them.

They spoke shit all the time, as kids do, but when the moment demanded they could converse better than most adults. They could disagree but still understand the other's point. Sarge had always been proud of the fact that each of the kids had his own mind. He loved his pod of pelicans. He was forty-three, he still drove a heap of shit, and didn't know what he wanted from life. They were seventeen and had it figured between the three of them. Sarge was no fortune teller but his guts, bones and common sense dictated that the boys would do some time. He knew it like fire's hot and water's wet. Their only hope was that if one of them went, they all went to protect each other and preserve their rare, bacterial culture.

Sarge glanced once more at the night scene as he slowly drove the patrol car past. They looked rebellious under a street light, leaning cool, standing or sitting on or around Cozy's two-door. The kids no one wanted. The same kids who'd push-start your car with a laugh and a friendly, 'No worries, righto.' The same kids who'd pick up anything you dropped and hand it back to you, or carry the groceries

for one of the old dears who was struggling in the rain. They were shits. Bloody big-hearted shits. No imitation, completely genuine and non-counterfeit. They had something the whole town overlooked while looking down on them; or they just didn't care to see. The youngsters had strong, non-treacherous hearts, each of them in their own way. And when they combined, they made fierce, loyal friends. The ones you had for good, or bad, forever.

Sarge turn his mind to a quote he read or heard somewhere: 'What society does to children, children do to society.'

God help Tribute. Whatever trespass Tribute had suffered or endured in its past wouldn't amount to a speck of budgie shit compared to this impetuous mob's mischief. If Jesus wept over Jerusalem, his heart must be breaking over Tribute.*

When the boys were joeys, fresh out of the pouch, Sarge was there. He was there for Cozy's first fight. For John Henry's first game, and his last. He was always in uniform, making his presence known for the home games and fights. He it was who had taken Cozy to the orphanage when he was found by Kevin Lacey, and delivered to the doc's clinic. He forcibly removed Kenny and Bugs as babies from their families, who starved, shook and beat them.

Kenny, an infant, was admitted by him to hospital. The diagnosis: Shaken Baby Syndrome.

Kenny flat lined on their arrival, his retinas haemorrhaged, and a section of his brain suffered the same fate. Straight to surgery he went.

He retrieved Jenny, crying, a bloodied babe, from a fatal car accident. Her family dead. Jenny's parents themselves orphans. Evie's young, single mum—a lovely lass known to all in Tribute—committed suicide after being abused and mentally tortured by her pathetic boyfriend.

A helpless, youthful Sarge had to hand all the tykes into the orphanage, along with many, many other rug-ratting

Tribute © Robert Lee Johnston 2016
Email: tributerobertleejohnston@gmail.com

ankle biters, abandoned and mistreated. He had proudly coached them all at junior footy when they were kids. Henry, Bugs and Cozy had shown Kenny a thing or two about fighting and being hard along the way.

Jen the Sweet.
Evie the Love.
Bugs the Ego.
Henry the Wise.
Kenny the Heart.
Cozy the ...

Shit, that was a tough one. Cozy always had been unknowingly confident. The cocksureness of that great, Greek, mythical dragon Hydra. A multi-headed, snake-like creature. Fathered by hundred-headed Typhoon. Knowing full well when one head had been cut off, two would grow back in its place. With that said, there was a determined, gathered humility, or inadequacy, in him; a typically Australian attitude, fast disappearing from our great landscape and its colourful characters. Cozy was blindly fearless. Sarge witnessed him take on all comers; saw him as a man-child, meaner than a goldfield Chinaman, all of fourteen, shovelling punches into fully grown men.

His coach, Bernie, was a top old bloke, tough and true. A fantastic Aussie character, and a recognised legend of the fight game. A fine, dear, wonderful friend to Sarge. Old Bernie forgot more about boxing taking this morning's dump than most learned in a lifetime. Sarge often shared yarns and a rum or two with him at The Middle Pub, 'The Middy'. The pub, Tribute's heart, is, of course, situated in the very middle of town. The only pub for miles and miles.

'Cozy's a bloody good'n. He's sharper than a sewer rat, got a killer's cold heart, and eats raw human flesh off the

Tribute © Robert Lee Johnston 2016
Email: tributerobertleejohnston@gmail.com

bone. Those poor kids he fights ... Bloody hell, Sarge, they'd have a better time of it fighting leprosy or polio.'

After Cozy got his fighting name Bernie remembered an old tale. He told Sarge the story, as wise, fine old men do, about 'Typhoid Mary'.

Sarge hadn't heard of her.

'She was a cook, a tiny, evil, pretty Irish petal of a thing from all accounts. Poor, humble Mary worked as a cook in some richer New York households way, way back in the day. Quite unknowingly at first, she was accidentally killing kids with typhoid, harboured inside her without any knowledge, effects or symptoms. House to house Mary'd go, doing her job every day, at first oblivious to the carnage she spawned. She carried on even when she found out about all the kiddies dying slow, painful deaths. She ended her days in a bitter quarantine. An innocent-looking, sweet-faced, invited killer. It's funny, cos when Cozy first gets in the ring, invited an' all, mind you, and takes his first, deeply held breath, sensing death, and smelling spilled blood, and then smiles that great, bold, disarming smile, I think of the world's young Irish rose, Typhoid Mary Mallon from Cookstown. Cozy, that kid's the male version of tender Mary, baby faced and naïve. He don't care to recognise or even accept the damage he's done.'

Shit, thought Sarge, if some bastard with money would just back him one time, give him a chance, maybe even some love, he'd shake the world champ up, I reckon. He asked Cozy once if he'd ever thought of going pro. He would never forget what the bastard told him as long as he lived.

Cozy was shocked. 'Fuck that, Sarge. Man, I don't do this for money. I just do it to hurt fuckers, legally. I don't need a cent to do that shit. I do it for free. I like amateur cos I'm fighting strangers. Mostly I'm fighting complete unknowns. Fighting some poor, gritty bastard who wants to get somewhere, be someone. You don't know if they been raised by rod, ruin or riches. You never seen them ever fight

Tribute © Robert Lee Johnston 2016
Email: tributerobertleejohnston@gmail.com

before, so it's all brand spanking new, a new risk, a new world. An unknown quantity. Stranger versus stranger. It's scary, Sarge. Who knows what they know? Which way it will go, or pan out? Who knows how hard they'll fight to win, or what they'll ultimately sacrifice if they lose? Nobody knows. That's the way I like it.'

Cozy went on with a calmness that seemed ancient and pure, 'A bit of fear and uncertainty reminds me I'm beatable.'

Sarge was speechless. Truly, Cozy was forged. Carved from ironwood, this kid. A chainsaw would blunt and spark on his gidgee bones. He relished the risk of defeat, demanding his equal. Patiently, patiently waiting. Meticulously searching for his better; his unbeatable foe. Or even worse. What if he was trying to quell, quiet and satiate his own hungry, untameable host? He reminded Sarge of a big, solid black mastiff he'd once owned, a perfect gentleman. A placid, even-tempered giant. But when the dog, or Sarge, was threatened. Mate. Lock your door, hide your women, and head for the hills. Then climb the biggest bloody tree you could see. A man-eater was loose.

Anger was Cozy's power, pure anger. Hatred, his fuel. Sarge thought of various moments and scenes, special memories locked away in a Cozy boxing vault. Little, powerful, amazing things banked along with memories of John Henry, pole-axing and breaking players in half on the footy field. Along with great teams and treasured athletes of his and Tribute's past. Sarge had them tucked safely away forever like mental polaroids. Of Cozy's face, grimacing for a millisecond as he landed a heavy hook, eking out another pound of power. A flashpoint memory, that reminded him of a frenzied shark's face as it fatally lunged, teeth exposed. Or a big cat's intense, squinting focus, going for the throat of a gazelle. Cozy's left hook. Shit! Such a brutal beastie of a thing, so sugary sweet. A handy weapon in his full arsenal because of its savage speed and power. Cozy, a very busy

Tribute © Robert Lee Johnston 2016
Email: tributerobertleejohnston@gmail.com

fighter, set the metronomic pace of a blue-arse fly. Most fights didn't go for more than a round. More often than not, spectators would be at the bar getting themselves a drink as the fighters were being announced, and by the time a bloke got back to his seat and sat down, the bastard had knocked his opponent out. The blood. Holy shit. Sarge remembered all the blood. Cozy cut his opponents easily with his snappy speed, ending many split, bloody fighters and bouts. With a glance he could accurately assess his opponent. See a sharp, bony brow to bust, a soft nose to break; see through a glass jaw, or a vulnerable midsection. In the ring an ancient, caveman brutality dwelled inside the man-child. Even when he was a junior boxer, a tiny novice youngster all of eight, Cozy would say, 'I love knocking fuckers out!'

In this child, in a squared ring, lived a heartless, cold, emotionless monster. An ugly, nightmarish monster. Rare in boxers nowadays. That dangerous volatile mixture of killer instinct, killer hunger, and, most important of all, killer hunting.

A youthful, cold-blooded, huge heart, and a Phar Lap-like resolve pumped frosty, icy blood effortlessly through Cozy's veins. Right at this minute, he was a very young man: strong, young and lithe. A sleek, muscular, rope-veined jungle cat, finally into his prime. A virus to life, to flesh and to mankind was 'Typhoid Cozy'.

Sarge remembered the many losses, and a fight that Cozy very proudly, happily lost on points. A gentleman bested, out skilled, and humbled. He congratulated and thanked his opponent with a massive hug and heartfelt smile. Cozy may have lost the decision that night, but he won the fight. His opponent was terribly busted up, hurting and bleeding. He and his coach thought Cozy had won. Not one fighter left his bloody square ring without a new level of respect, admiration or worse … crippling fear. Crowds felt it. The coaches, refs, his opponents, they definitely felt it. He may have lost a few of his hundreds of fights, but he won

Tribute © Robert Lee Johnston 2016
Email: tributerobertleejohnston@gmail.com

every opponent's heart, honour, respect, and, forever, his friendship.

The kid couldn't stay down. Sarge had never seen or heard of anyone knocking him out. He could fight 'off his feet', keep going when he wasn't compos mentis. Unshakable, natural fighting instincts. Even senseless he was a wild scrapper. Cozy was a hard-headed, determined bastard. He boxed extremely cleanly, a trait shared with John Henry as a football player, before his passing. An ingenuous fighter using honest, rehearsed, artful talent to combat any dirty fighters.

Refs loved adjudicating over his fights. Once, and only once, Sarge saw Cozy completely lose his shit and get nasty. It was bloody spectacular! In frustration some bloke threw Cozy out of the ring through the top two ropes. He landed painfully. Cozy's face was not dripping blood, it ran. His head was getting butted and forearmed, and sharp, bony elbows struck his face. Cozy was getting pissed and decided he'd 'hurt the son of a bitch, bad' for his un-sportsmanlike breaches. Sarge couldn't count the punches in the combinations Cozy threw, and to this day people still argue over how many punches that kid could throw in thirty seconds. For his loss of composure, Cozy was disqualified from boxing anywhere in Australia for six months. But it was scintillating boxing. Epic. Once-in-a-lifetime fighting. People who witnessed it were too afraid to blink. Cozy kept going and going like some articulate, savage, blood-spattered poem. The crowd watched, slack jawed, sensing the bout was coming to its end. Three judges put pens down and themselves became fans. Cozy would not let his prey fall. He shouldered him, forced and man-handled him into the ropes, punching his face over the top rope until he fell unconscious out of the ring, awkwardly, to the ground. Ref was trying to stop the fight, the poor bastard. Cozy's opponent's coach and corner man had thrown two towels in. Cozy had driven him with his body weight as his

Tribute © Robert Lee Johnston 2016
Email: tributerobertleejohnston@gmail.com

thunderous right hand shoved as much as punched him over the top ropes. The fall was ugly; no arms helped break the long, awkward drop. His head copped it all.

Until that point the ref was watching poetry in motion. An old pug from way back, to him Cozy was beautiful to watch. Old school discipline, impeccable footwork. Cozy's clever technique contemporary, with a respectful tip of the hat to the old masters. Slippery, elusive, violent, hungry, and dangerous. Both Cozy's hands stung. His body shots were pin-point accurate. When he found his opponent's solar plexus unprotected, Cozy dug heavily into it, and folded old mate like an accordion. That left hook of his, be it to the head or body, was a game changer, game ender, and nearly tore old mate's pig-iron jaw off its hinge. The ref could've watched this kid box all day long. He later commented to Bernie, 'You can't out fight a boxer.'

Smiling at Cozy, he had tried pulling the pin on the bout as Cozy somehow punted his opposite number over the top rope. The blue—now black, and bloody blue—corner wasn't up or even in the ring for the ten count. Though he ultimately won because of Cozy's many obvious fouls, Cozy's opponent wouldn't really wake properly for a day or two. Cozy turned to a silenced, stunned audience, bleeding heavily from many cuts. Barely able to stand, he flashed his default, friendly smile. Shrugging his shoulders at the lack of noise, as if to say, 'Sorry, you lot. I tried me bloody best.' Sarge, with the whole crowd, erupted. They had just needed a minute to take in what they had seen. Many agreed it was the most beautiful, fantastic, athletic display anyone from around here had ever seen. It was sublime, almost perfection. Cozy lost the bout, but won the fight.

That had been two years and at least fifty fights ago. Today the fighter scrubbed up polished and lethal. Sarge thought back to a night in the Middy when the kids were fourteen or so, right before John Henry died. The kids, bored and skint, sat out the front of the pub, just ginning around,

killing time. The pub's upstairs accommodation provided guests with a spacious, covered verandah. The verandah, constructed from the abundant local hardwoods, provided townsfolk and patrons underneath with a few bench-style wooden seats, offering respite from the wearisome tropical elements. It covered the sidewalk for the entire length of the pub. The whole pub was finished with fine timbers such as red cedar, silky oak and the finest, deepest, kauri-pine bar. Some big bloke went outside for a smoke, and the big fella started taking the piss out of the boys, teasing them, calling them 'chicken leg shits-a-kids, bum-fluff balls, the mongrel bastards no one wants'. That sort of stuff, easily standing over them. Cozy told him kindly, 'Settle down, old cock.'

When the big fella wouldn't, Cozy got up, smiling, real friendly and peaceful like, and then quickly looked around for any witnesses, probably Sarge and his cop car. Cozy had no idea Sarge was having a drink, in his civvies, off duty, a couple of open windows down from the front door, at a table minding his own business. When he heard the big bloke joking at the kids' expense, he thought young Cozy would easily talk his way out of this. Sarge choked on his rum when the blond boy taunted him.

'Is it just you tonight, you fat fuck?'

The big fella laughed confidently at the boys. 'I'm all I'll be needing. Sit down, boy, or I'll give you and your mates a smack in the head and sit you down.'

Cozy's smile was now evil. 'Nah, fuck it. I'm up now, barge arse. I'll have a crack. You don't talk to my mates like that. And besides, you got to catch me first, you chico-roll-eating, butter-ball mother fucker.'

The big fella sneered, a little shocked. 'Cheeky little shit. Didn't get enough fucking floggings as a sprog, eh? I'll catch you, kid, then I'll wring your scrawny bloody neck. I'll bend you over my knee and flog you in front of your little

Tribute © Robert Lee Johnston 2016
Email: tributerobertleejohnston@gmail.com

girl-friends and teach you some manners, with one arm, Boyo.'

Kenny, comfortably seated, yelled and laughed out loud. 'BOYO? You're in big trouble now, you silly fat fuck.'

Young Cozy, till now innocent looking, moved fearlessly forward. Sarge knew the kid's face well, but he always looked twice when he saw the hunger take Cozy over. He looked nothing like Cozy Withazed. No single feature resembled his usual self. If a police artist was to sketch that hateful face and a wanted poster was printed, it wouldn't be recognised as the town's sweet Cozy boy.

Cozy told him, scratching his forehead, slipping out of his thongs, 'Righto, no worries. Sounds fair to me. A duke each it is.'

Sarge hastily knocked his drink over, got up and headed out the door to break it up and save young Cozy's arse. He was one or two steps too late. Cozy put his right arm behind his back as agreed. Reneging on his word, the big fella clenched both his fists.

'I thought you said, we're only using one arm?'

Lard-Arse punched furiously, hopelessly missing his fast-approaching, elusive, one-armed opponent.

'How's your footwork, big fella? You been doing any sparring lately, fuckface?'

Barge-Arse tried to react, as did Sarge, far too little, far, far too late. A step or two behind. Easily slipping the sloppy, telegraphed punches, Cozy's left fist had already exploded violently into the big bloke's face with a nasty, twisting left jab that snapped his nose like a dried branch. The fist recoiled like a fired shotgun and cloned the punch perfectly seven or eight more times. All exactly on that busted cartilage that kept crunching and caving under Cozy's force. The big fella unceremoniously fell slowly to the concrete footpath, his head jolting back and forth like a busy speed ball. Nose-broken tears ran from closed eyes, and plenty of claret leaked from his redesigned snout. He squealed a little.

Tribute © Robert Lee Johnston 2016
Email: tributerobertleejohnston@gmail.com

Cozy, his back to Sarge, knelt and wiped his ox-blood-red-covered left knuckles on old mate's shirt. He was snoring, miles and miles away. Cozy rolled him on his side and whispered to him cheekily, 'Just you shut your huge mouth and have a little sleep now, big fella.'

The boys went back to whatever crap they were talking about before the melee, not missing a beat. None had got up to help, knowing Cozy would be all right.

Kenny laughed at Cozy and complained far too loudly. 'Piss weak! He couldn't knock a rump steak and a stubby over, that gutchy fuck! A good root and a fart would kill him. Boys, what was the nickname we gave that big, fat, male blow-up doll in that sex shop window that time? You remember? In the city that time.'

'He's got a face like a dropped pie, hasn't he? "Blow-Job-Bob" was his name, mate,' Bugs reminded him.

'That was it! I thought he looked familiar! Ha ha. We should piss on him. That'd wake Bob up! HEY, BLOW-JOB-BOB, YOUR PIZZA'S HERE! HA HA HA! CHICO-ROLL-EATING, BUTTER-BALL BLOW-JOB-BOB.'

The boys then asked each other quizzically if 'Blow-Job-Bob' meant that he gave the blow jobs, or received them.

Kenny was repulsed, looked at the big fella's ugly mug and yelled, 'Fuck that choice! Shit, he hasn't carked it, has he?'

That teenage cheek of theirs was funny no matter how old you were. They playfully argued and teased one another as the big bloke lay arse over head on the hard, cold footpath. A bunch of kids joking amongst themselves, paying no attention to their surroundings.

Sarge asked them, 'Did you boys see what happened here?'

Cozy lied, bold-faced, a bit shocked to see the local copper standing there, even out of uniform. 'Shit! Fuck! Sarge. Nah, yeah, we just got here, mate. He was already laying there, sleeping. I rolled him on his side, just now.'

Tribute © *Robert Lee Johnston 2016*
Email: tributerobertleejohnston@gmail.com

Sarge saw the big fella breathing and winked at Cozy. 'Fucking dangerous, eh, that footpath? He must've been pissed and tripped over, Cozy.'

'Yeah, fucking dangerous all right. He'll be right but I reckon, Sarge.'

'Righto. No getting into trouble, you mob of galahs. See you later.'

They all obliged Sarge with a 'no worries, catch ya'. He rang the ambo from the pub's phone. The big bloke wouldn't try that ever again. Cozy. 'Typhoid Cozy' was the hottest ticket in town if you liked the fights and the fight game.

He and those boys had far too much heart. As their father figures were few and mostly shithouse rats, Sarge would now and then impart wisdom by simply repeating Cat Stevens and Bob Marley lyrics to them. 'Take your time. Think a lot. Respect women. Be patient, be cool, be smart. Work hard. Laugh a lot. And for fuck's sake, you mad rooters, use condoms.' He'd throw them frangers like they were boiled lollies.

He didn't have to wait long for his premonitions to take shape. Cozy was a magnet for violence. Kenny for girls and motors. Bugs for whatever the hell was going on. All three together were highly charged police magnets. A small town and one copper with nothing to do. And the boys getting ever braver, un-loveably older, tougher, riskier, ever crazier. Each outdoing the other. Plenty of laughs, broken bones, charges, and injuries would go on their permanent records. Dull wasn't a word used to describe what Sarge and this mob's likely future had in store.

'They're going to keep me busy, those bastards. I wish they could've stayed ten and lovable forever.'

* *The Reverend Fred Nile. MLC. The author, RLJ, has changed the text.*

Tribute © Robert Lee Johnston 2016
Email: tributerobertleejohnston@gmail.com

CHAPTER SEVENTEEN: THE HARDTOP SINGS

The new motor was finally completely built.

The old one was overheating, smoky, and slowly dying. Cozy took it off the road for a complete body and engine overhaul. Kenny had been busting his ring, fettling the great six-litre lump for months. The two-door's slick new paint job was shining, and now it would go over the pits for its registration after the weekend was over and it would be on the road. The young fellas were up all night installing the motor and, when it had started, tuning it with greasy fingers.

It sounded tight, fruity, fat and throaty. They smiled, kicked back, rolled the last of their pot into a joint and victoriously smoked it up. They were much too excited to sleep and no weed was not an option.

Bugs informed the rest, 'Lacey's got some fresh buds and he'll still be up. It's only 1 am.'

He was right.

Cozy ran a hand through his hair. 'Sarge'll be in bed. We could stick a few litres in to run her in and make sure the

Tribute © Robert Lee Johnston 2016
Email: tributerobertleejohnston@gmail.com

old girl doesn't have any teething problems. Fuck him, I'm keen.'

'Righto,' everyone agreed.

Lacey was up and glad to see the lads. He cast a complimentary eye over the hardtop, telling Cozy she was a beast and the new power plant sounded fat.

'I'm just babying it, you know; running it in to loosen her up a bit.'

Lacey laughed. 'Fuck that. Just hold her flat.'

They went inside to smoke and drink. Cozy just smoked. After talking shit for a while, Cozy was getting tired and wanted to head home. The young blokes got some weed off Lacey. It was freshly picked that day and needed drying. The uncured weed quickly stunk the coupe out.

Cozy was barely revving the motor. They were in no particular hurry and putted along. At 3.30 am they had the road to themselves and it was only a twenty-minute drive home. All was good with the two-door and everything worked perfectly. Some headlights appeared behind and rapidly closed in. The same headlights as Simon and Glen's, two local lads, who had the very same model as Sarge's cop car. They were best mates. Simon and Glen and would no doubt be brothers if one of them had a sister for the other to marry.

The boys were hoping like hell it was one of the lads and not Sarge. Simon had bought a new car after he wrote his Torana off, spectacularly, going down the range on a steep, sensationally sharp corner. Glen, in the front seat, grabbed the dash and anything solid to hang on to. He reckoned the Torana pig-rooted, and then tank-slapped out of control, going way too fast and heading over the edge, getting them airborne.

'FUCKING HANG ON, SIM'S! WERE GOING BUSH BASHIN', MATE!'

The hairpin turn was now referred to forever as 'Simon's Corner'. If you looked properly, you could still see

Tribute © Robert Lee Johnston 2016
Email: tributerobertleejohnston@gmail.com

his Torana's rusting, shattered carcass nestled in the tree tops. The shaken, un-winged pilot and his dazed co-pilot simply grabbed their bag of weed from the busted-open glove box, got out through the now glassless windscreen and, palpitating like heart attack victims, carefully climbed the fifty feet or so down the tree to roll a well-earned, fat, nerve-soothing, celebratory, life-affirming joint ... or three. It would be nice to think they landed gracefully in the treetops like a sleek bird coming home to roost. But the old Holdens, they were never really good at flying, and the old girl crunched up like a drunk's kicked can. 'Crunched' being the operative word. It was an odd thing, seeing a mate's car parked within a jungle's canopy.

'Please be Simon. Please be Glen,' Cozy wished.

It turned out Simon and Glen were on the charge all day long, blind. Smoking fat, stinky nuggets and heavily tripping on a couple of tasty, wild acid trips they consumed at Glen's joint.

'No fucking way it was me, Cozy. I couldn't drive with those trips in me. I was off my tits,' Simon told Cozy later, and laughed when he heard the makings of the story. 'And ole Glen necked a third one. And shit got a little crazy-freaky for a bit there and hard to remember after that.'

The hardtop passed through a small town and Kenny got a good look at the following car as it went under some street lights and squealed, 'FUUUUCK ME. FANG IT. IT'S THE BULLY-MAN. FUCKING SARGE.'

'Sarge hasn't ever seen the two-door's new colour. It's got no plates on it. Could be any fucker, right?' Cozy snuck it into second, blipping the throttle to catch the cog, and waited to see what happened when his foot flattened the accelerator to the floor

Such a beautiful motor, fresh, tight and powerful. They shot off, pinned to their seats and headrests. The blue light flashed on but the cop car's six cylinders quickly ran out of puff. Cozy watched the mirrors as the flashing light lagged

Tribute © Robert Lee Johnston 2016
Email: tributerobertleejohnston@gmail.com

further behind. They were soon into top gear and going fast. Cozy had never driven this motor before tonight, and he already loved it. The way it clung to the bitumen! The quicker the coupe went the better it sat on the road. Cozy still had to use all the road, though, and the dry, dark, moonless night ensured he knew if something was coming the other way. If it had been daylight the two-door never would have been able to use all those corners and all that tarmac. The odd car they came across, going to shift work or whatever, approached at such a rate that Cozy would see it, and then they were upon it, having to overtake on crests, blind corners and in all sorts of shitty places. Their missile approached so fast they had to overtake.

'Bugs, should I overtake?'

'I don't know! Bro!'

Cozy would have to fly by or crash into their rear end.

When they had left home for Lacey's, Kenny raided the mower's tin of fuel. Barely ten litres. They hadn't been planning on a high-speed police pursuit. Cozy didn't want to take the new donk over fifteen hundred revs. But here he was, redlining every gear. The crests, gullies, trees and hills flashed by, and they were fast approaching a small township, three or so klicks from Tribute. The hastily made plan was to backroad it from there to home. Take the next right to get off the beaten track of the main highway and kill the lights. Two more crests and they'd be there. The heavily leaned on, six-litre-plus motor was gulping fuel at these rpms. It shot over the top of the last crest with all four wheels airborne. They heard the golden, smooth motor uncharacteristically miss a beat. It was barely audible, but being so highly strung they all felt it. Then again. She surged with renewed vigour as any unspent fuel sloshed around, only to starve altogether. Cozy slipped the two-door into neutral and coasted down the last hill, the planned turn off just within grasp. Cozy hit the anchors. The power-assisted brakes were of no use. He clutched, dropped it into top gear

Tribute © Robert Lee Johnston 2016
Email: tributerobertleejohnston@gmail.com

and let the engine brake them. Then third, then second, taking the corner too fast and sideways, washing off speed. A drop of fuel found its way into the motor, the coupe hammered up the hill as the engine gasped and sung its last, slowing to a silent, panicked stop. Bugs bailed out and piss-bolted into the black, foggy night. With all the carrots he had consumed throughout his life, one may assume his night vision was first class. Bugs legged it, flat out, straight into a taut, sharp, four-strand, barbed-wire fence. Catapulting him backwards onto his surprised arse. Ripping him up good and bloody. All Kenny heard through the open door was a grunt, a thump, and a mad 'FUCKING HELL' from the darkness.

Kenny was folding the passenger front seat forward to get out of the back when the blue-flashing police vehicle pulled up beside the two-door, the roof spotlight on brightly.

Sarge had the brace and bits. 'Bugs, you fucking stay there! Who the fuck is driving? Cozy. You little shit! Get the fuck out of that car now!'

Sarge shone his torch into the back seat and saw Kenny. 'You three fuck wits.'

Cozy got out, and Sarge manhandled the oldest teenager into the side of his car, punching him in the breadbasket. He dropped Cozy, winded, and then picked him up, really mad and shaking.

'Twenty-two years I been in the force. No one's ever fucking done that to me! I ain't never been that fast, or seen anything that stupid. You are a fucking moron Cozy.'

He punched Cozy in the guts again.

'If you three bastards had cum for brains, youse wouldn't fill a fucking flea. Whose fucking car? Is this your old two-door?' Cozy was too winded to speak and just raised a hand.

'You're in big fucking trouble, mate!'

Sarge could smell dope and he strip-searched Cozy on the spot. He threw him in his highway cruiser, along with

Tribute © Robert Lee Johnston 2016
Email: tributerobertleejohnston@gmail.com

Bugs. He called them wankers and clowns as he strip-searched Kenny. Bugs cleverly unrolled the bottom of his jeans. The nog was wrapped in its folds. He hid the bud under Sarge's own seat. Sarge opened the door to search Bugs and threw Kenny in, complaining he could still smell pot. He strip-searched Bugs, found nothing and threw him back in the car, where Bugs reached again under the seat, found the big, wet, stinking bud and rolled it back up into the bottom of his jeans leg. Sarge searched the hardtop and made a mess of the new interior. Cozy whispered, 'Bastard.'

Sarge opened the cop car's back door. 'Get out and fuck off.'

Bugs asked if Sarge was giving them a lift home.

'I'm not a fucking taxi service, you smart arses. Find your own way home, you pair of fucking mung beans. Fucking dickheads.'

They grinned and made Cozy a sad face. Kenny, head down, raised a dread-locked Rasta's fist for Cozy as the police vehicle left.

Cozy didn't say much and wished he could say the same about Sarge. He was all bile, piss and warm vinegar. Mad, because he couldn't charge the other two with anything.

'I'll have another bestselling dickhead of the month this month. I might call it cockheads of the month this time. And them two imbeciles. Fuck. You watch, Cozy. They'll get a decent bloody spray and all. The fucking three of you haven't got enough brains between you to get a headache.'

Sarge was shaking his head at the stupidity, the audacity, finding Cozy's eyes in his rear view. 'Kiss your fucking licence goodbye, Cozy. You just fucked yourself, maybe for years. You broke a million fucking rules out there, and drove like a fucking maniac. It'll take me all night to write you up. You little shit!'

Sarge's gaze hardened. He growled, 'No fucking one has ever done that sort of shit to me before! Ever.'

Tribute © Robert Lee Johnston 2016
Email: tributerobertleejohnston@gmail.com

Cozy knew he was in the shit, and wouldn't get to drive his car for a long, long time. He was gutted. Not for being caught. Fuck it, he thought, I'll take that on the chin. But for running out of fuel. Cozy reckoned he'd had the balding old fuck.

'Yeah, you mentioned that. You're fucking lucky I ran out of fuel, old man.' Cozy smiled cheekily in his mirror. 'You had no chance—fucking Buckley's—of catching me in this piece of shit otherwise!'

Cozy should have kept his mouth shut because 'BLAH. Blah, fucking, blah' was all he heard the whole night. Cozy's mouth, and not knowing when to shut it, had made Sarge demonstrably madder.

The lad didn't deny he'd done it, but the speed Sarge booked Cozy at was bullshit. Flat-out bullshit. None of the boys had got a chance to look down at the speedo. They were all shitting so much, no one looked after about one-sixty. But Cozy reckoned he was doing a hundred and ninety on that old, busted-arse road, tops. Not two-forty, like Sarge claimed to the judge. Two-forty. Pigs arse. Cozy thought Sarge was just a little bit excited and tad vengeful there. Later, Cozy and Kenny did it on a pair of Kawasaki Z nines and got to two hundred. It was scary, and both agreed it was much faster than what they did that night. The judge wasn't very happy either. Cozy's licence was now a thing of the past.

Sarge got lucky that night. He had been called out to a minor accident in the early morning. On his way home, the boys happen to pull out right in front of him and handed themselves to him on a freshly painted platter.

Bloody lucky.

For Sarge.

Tribute © Robert Lee Johnston 2016
Email: tributerobertleejohnston@gmail.com

CHAPTER EIGHTEEN: "AT THE BEATING OF A DRUM"

Poem by Henry Lawson

The boys went fishing, up bush, for twelve days.

They were going to get drunk, smoke and live in isolation, with a bit of fishing thrown in.

There was no hurry, and nowhere else to be. They'd just recently pulled in a smallish patch and celebrated with a trip up the coast and a half pound of their most prime buds.

It would all be over soon, and the three of them in cells.

They borrowed a Land Cruiser ute from Lacey and dragged his little tinny on a sturdy trailer. Every day the boys waited for the tides so they could catch lunch. The fishing here was always awesome. Rivers, estuaries, beaches and mangroves meant they could be fussy and target particular species. Coral trout, grunter and barra were high on the to-

eat list, as were the plentiful, fat, fresh oysters. The last days were fast approaching and they trolled around the beaches. Bugs and Cozy were telling Kenny a yarn, joking about what they had seen together a week or two before. Kenny wanted to hear it again from Cozy, start to finish, and for him not to leave out a single detail.

Bugs was working part time at the local bakery on Tribute's main drag, just cleaning and odd jobs, to impress the judge. He was asked to go in after lunch on a Sunday to clean up. He was there as Cozy walked past with a bag of mince and some groceries. The main street, apart from Cozy, was deserted. Not a single car. Bugs rapped on the shopfront window as he passed. Cozy went in to see how he was going. One of the three large, street-facing windows was a one-way mirror, and being a tourist town, none but locals knew that people were usually working on the other side, while uninformed women and men preened hair and adjusted dicks, clothes, bits and tits.

The boys were talking shit when an old, dusty, beat-up Ford station wagon pulled up, and a sexy young woman in a bright, light dress got out. She darted here and there in obvious distress. The girl was looking for a toilet, and everything was shut. She frantically raced back to her car, parked right in front of the mirror behind which the long-haired louts stood. She looked at herself in the mirror's reflection, checked the road for traffic, shrugged and, rather defeated, shook her head. She lifted up her skirt with one hand, pulled her panties across with the other and squatted and pissed next to her car.

Directly in front of the lads.

Bugs and Cozy belly laughed without making any noise because she was just there. She frog-hopped up and down a bit, drip-drying, and then got up and pulled her panties back across as she let her dress fall. All the while she looked at her reflection, smiling back at herself. Relieved and comfortable, she went for a walk about town. Once she was

Tribute © Robert Lee Johnston 2016
Email: tributerobertleejohnston@gmail.com

out of sight the boys, wide-eyed, looked at each other. Bugs yelped, 'Holy shit, man!' They burst out laughing.

'I got an idea,' Cozy said. They raced outside, Cozy still holding the bag of mince and picking up the bakery's tomato sauce bottle on the way out. Cozy dropped an egg-sized, roughly shaped piece of minced meat on the wet piss puddle she had left running hot into the gutter. He added an artful dollop of 'dead horse'—tomato sauce—for effect, while Bugs kept an eagle eye out. When she headed back to her car to be on her way, Bugs and Cozy waited, hidden silently and invisibly behind the mirror window. They giggled like kids binging on sugar.

The woman, who was really pretty, walked gracefully, without a care in the world, to her driver door. She looked down at her puddle of piss to see a fresh, hideous, blood-clotted lump of gristly flesh on the ground. Internal-looking flesh. Her jaw dropped. Without delay her dress was up and her bright-yellow knickers across again, as she bent over to examine herself. She ran her hand across her exposed vagina to make sure her guts hadn't dropped out. She reached further back, spread her butt cheeks, and then proceeded to check her bum hole. She checked her undies for any skid marks or traces of fresh blood and evidence. It took some time to convince herself that the fly-blown, bloody innards hadn't passed from her orifices. She exhaled, very confused. The look she gave herself in the one-way mirror, alternating between the mincemeat and her mirrored self, was priceless, with Cozy's and Bugs's noses an inch away from the other side. She mouthed silently to her reflection, 'Fucking hell!' As she covered up, Bugs and Cozy were shaking and rocking, biting down their merriment and laughter.

They laughed for days.

They were spinning the yarn and talking shit. Cozy was yapping away to Kenny when Bugs got hit by a fat mackerel. He shut the motor down and reeled him in. Kenny and Cozy

Tribute © Robert Lee Johnston 2016
Email: tributerobertleejohnston@gmail.com

kicked back, watching the large fish fight and keeping an eye on the beach and headlands. An unprotected inlet cut sharp into the landscape and the tinny followed its shape. They were embarrassed at how much rubbish and how many plastic bags marred the otherwise pristine, isolated beaches. Exactly why it was called the tip. There were old thongs, all left footed of course, and drums and barrels, both plastic and rusty steel. Bloody messy.

Cozy spotted three closed drums, washed ashore. 'What the fuck's in them do you reckon?' Cozy asked the dreadlocked one.

'Fucked if I know?' Kenny told him as he swept his dark dreads back out of his eyes.

Bugs sat down again, after Cozy help him gaff and stow his prize Spanish mac. He ripped the outboard into life in his far-too-short stubby shorts, wearing no jocks as usual, and a hairy ball-bag hanging out for all the world to see. A joint in his mouth and a beer between his knees, he asked what they'd seen, throttling off the noisy outboard to hear what the boys were saying. Kenny pointed, convincing them they should go closer. Large rust holes were obvious in one of the drums. They were bored, and Bugs, being the captain, said, 'We got fuck all else to do. Let's check it out.'

He beached the tinny, killing the motor on the way. Kenny kicked empty drums, calling them 'poofter bastards'.

They wondered what used to be inside them. The snap-lock lids were locked on. Kenny kicked a football-sized hole in the thin, rusty guts of one drum to reveal a stack of empty, sandy plastic bags.

'Check this shit out.' Kenny was excited.

Bugs concluded that whatever was in those bags didn't stand a chance once old-Ma-ocean got in.

Another drum was buried and almost invisible, the lid slightly exposed. All of them figured it would have its guts rusted out, but had a squiz anyway. They dug with sticks and hands to reveal the bulk of the forty-four-gallon drum. There

were no holes that they could see, and it was still sealed. After a bit of rooting around they managed to open it. Inside were countless bags of powder, dead-dog, dingo-dick dry. They backed up a step and checked over their shoulders, looked about, and then out to sea. No one was on the remote coast and beach but the three boys. They quick-stepped around the barrel. Bugs tore open the top bag and, holding the drum's edge, plunged his whole face in, excitedly snorting. He raised his face covered in fine powder, like a freshly dusted pastry, and grinned through his make-up. 'Fuck me dead, boys. It's coke! So much cleaner than any crap we get.'

'If that's dried bat shit or ajax he's in trouble, bloke,' Cozy said to Kenny. Then Cozy's own head was in there sniffing, snorting, sampling, judging and tasting. Off their chops, the boys energetically moved the barrel out of the high tide's reach.

'Fuck it, let's camp here tonight.'

It was going to be a long, sleepless night. They sat on old jetsam, milk crates and discarded twenty-litre drums. The stars, the fire, the half-moon. The salty big-blue crashing, and a gentle sea breeze keeping them cool, as the coke's fireworks raged in their heads.

Bugs broke out of his rolling-tobacco pouch a sheet of twenty acid trips. He figured a couple of trips each would help the celebrations kick off.

'It's going to be a wild one,' Kenny told them.

Bugs was relaxing opposite the boys, bouncing ideas off the large fire. Plotting something, grinding his teeth to contain his body's peaky rushes. He looked his mates over very seriously. A durry in two fingers, a cup of rotgut in one hand, a fat joint in the other, a trip in his gob, half a bottle of bourbon, large bag of dope and a pack of rollies between his feet. Not forgetting for a moment, the heaped cocaine on one steady knee. And, of course, his spuds out for ships cruising any side of the Pacific to see. He reckoned really

Tribute © Robert Lee Johnston 2016
Email: tributerobertleejohnston@gmail.com

seriously, with a sly, sarcastic grin, 'Lucky us blokes have no addictive traits, eh?'

How they laughed! They locked arms and danced, singing ditties around the drum like kids playing 'ring around the rosie', witches around a brew, or hippies dancing around a fire at a full-moon party.

Cozy voiced their thoughts. 'Holy shit, man. What are the odds?'

They couldn't believe their luck. They waited to wake up from this vivid shared dream or freaky trip. But each time they checked the drum and looked under the lid, it was there. It was real. It remained real and was still with them, acid or not.

They discussed, thoroughly tripping, how the coke arrived there and where it may have come from. The other barrels had the same markings. They must all have had coke in them at one point. They spent the next day beach combing in each direction from the find, hoping for a twin sister or, even better, triplets. Bugs searched on water in the tinny, Cozy walked south, and Kenny north. If there were orphaned drums to be found one of the young blokes would discover them.

No more drums were found and it was getting late. They fished and caught enough to camp with the barrel again. The next day they started to shift it all back to their main camp. The forty-four-gallon drum was too brittle to tow or man handle, so they decanted the contents into smaller vessels. Whatever they could get their hot little hands on. Kenny fashioned a funnel from a discarded twenty-litre metal drum, and they poured the coke into drums, paint tins and any other suitable rubbish which they washed out and dried in the sun. Anything that washed up on the shoreline that could hold coke or the coke bags. They had no clue how much cocaine was in that drum. It kept coming out like clowns out of a mini. It wouldn't run dry. There were countless trips ferrying coke back to the main

Tribute © Robert Lee Johnston 2016
Email: tributerobertleejohnston@gmail.com

camp. They had to think of a way to load up the truck without it spilling out the windows and getting their lucky arses caught. They tried to calculate how much it would be worth, and there was a shit storm of serious long division in the sand and complicated oral maths. The answer was: A big, fucking, chunky wad, divided into three.

They shared heavenly moments of euphoria, joy, disbelief, followed by hellish bouts of fear and paranoia that were crueller than a holocaust winter. They considered a million reasons why the coke was there, some plausible, some absolute rubbish. They could agree, however, that someone, and who the fuck knew how many of his mates, would know it was missing and may well be looking for it.

'Nobody just misplaces four barrels of coke, man,' said Kenny.

'I agree.' Bugs grimaced. 'Man, it would have taken a while for all that rust to set in, and then the tides to eat all that coke, eh? It must've taken months for the sand to cover that drum. Let's have another line, a session, a durry or two, a few drinks, and have a little think about this.'

Whoever owned it was not going to be an interior decorator or some flower arranger.

'Could be bikers,' Cozy suggested, 'fucking heavy importers from some eastern European hard-as-fuck country. Or, even worse, a cartel of Mexican cut-throat "essays" and "homies". Shit, it could be any bastards.'

Kenny disagreed. 'Steady, steady, bloke. It could be some small-time, one-off sort of guy or outfit, you know? We're focusing on the nasty end of the spectrum a little too much, perhaps? He could, after all, be a piss-weak fucking nobody.'

Cozy thought about it and said, 'Well, I'm just going to think the worst, and anything less will be a bonus.' They decided they had to be very careful, very quiet. They would be set for life if they did this smartly. Their damper, the last

bit of mackerel, a freshly caught grunter, and some bourbon went down a treat.

'If we get pulled over with all this,' Cozy cautioned them, 'we'll never ever get the fuck out of jail. We got to be cool. No bullshit, mother fuckers, if we get pulled over.'

Kenny agreed, wide eyed. 'This shit's a live, primed hand grenade. Waiting for us to slip and drop-it-hot. People will lynch us for this shit, man.'

They carefully loaded the tinny with the live, primed hand grenade and secured the tight-fitting boat cover over the top. Then they filled the truck with all they could live and breathe around. They abandoned camping gear to make room. There were jars, buckets, Eskys, tins, bags and their greedy noses stuffed with powder. They were shitting themselves, so they placed the last trips of acid on their tongues.

Bugs reckoned, 'It'll calm us down.'

They passed—tripping off their tits, and charging like rhinos from thumb-width lines of coke—through the sleepy, old, outback, one-cop towns. The boat and muddy, dirty truck let them blend in. They looked like every other bloke and his truck full of mates getting away fishing.

Bugs told the lads, 'Nothing to see here, C'ntstables.'

With enthusiasm they sang "Have A Cigar" with Pink Floyd, pouring from the speakers.

They agreed not to sell any around Tribute, and to tell no fucker. Except, of course, Lacey and Evie.

'Remember that brothel in the city, boys? All that speed? I bet those girls could shift a butt-load, for us,' Cozy suggested

No bikers or gangs, they agreed, or they may wake up dead.

Kenny asked, 'What if someone comes looking and recognises the coke?'

It was a ripper of a question and it just hung there for a bit, like a horrible, wet, unwanted fart.

Tribute © Robert Lee Johnston 2016
Email: tributerobertleejohnston@gmail.com

All three spoke at once. 'We lie.'

They alone would know the truth. Everyone else would believe what crap was fed to them.

Once home the boys split the stash three ways. Rumours and bullshit stories were quickly made up to protect them, and modest quantities sold cheaply to out-of-towners who had no ties in Tribute. They couldn't put a dint in it, no matter how much of it they snorted, traded or sold. It never seemed to come to an end. Later, in prison, the young brothers were offered coke that originally came from their drum. The quality was sublime, if hands down the line hadn't stomped on it. If you tasted good coke around Tribute or in prison during those years, it came from that barrel.

Lacey was using heavily and selling for the lads while they rotted in prison.

'We should fuck off out of town for a bit when we get out.'

'You said it, bro.' Bugs nodded and smiled at Cozy. 'When I get out I want to see some stuff. You blokes are the only reason I stay in Tribute. Go for a road trip, I reckon, sleep in my swag whenever, wherever. Maybe see old Sydney town.'

Kenny and Cozy joked about how different life would be around Tribute without Bugs's ball bag hanging out all over the place.

Kenny teased, 'They're a local landmark.' He pretended to give a stranger directions. 'Yeah, mate, yeah, you just take your first left there and go down the road a bit, and then turn right, at the big, hairy, white plums. You can't miss them!'

'Ha! I bet you miss them and dream of them. You'll want photos and regular updates.'

Kenny grabbed a butter knife off the table and held it up. 'Stick this up your date. That's a bloody nightmare, mate!' They thought the unintended rhyme was clever.

Tribute © Robert Lee Johnston 2016
Email: tributerobertleejohnston@gmail.com

'I might make me way to Tassie.' Bugs was dreaming out loud, and pushed aside what was left of the nightmare that was their riot-causing, stores-exhausted prison lunch. Watermelon and onion salad. The 'salad' being the onion. 'A nice fireplace, see some snow, catch a proper meal, a sweet-looking chick, and a good-looking trout or two.'

'Not a bad idea,' said Cozy, 'as long as you don't confuse your good-looking trout with your sweet-looking chick. The women there might look and smell a bit like fish too.'

Kenny asked, 'Are you boys doing a runner?'

'Nah. Once we get out I might go to Amsterdam, man, just for a month or so. You want to come?'

Kenny's eyes widened and his grin broadened. 'Fuck yeah, Cozy! Let's go to Amsterdam, bloke.'

'Fucking oath. Fuck Tribute. Fuck this continent for a month, man. Viva la Dutch.'

'Ha, that's wrong.' Bugs chuckled.

'Mi casa es su casa?'

'Fuck youse. They speak a heap of English there. It's a port city.'

'Even fucking better, man.'

Bugs changed his mind. 'Amsterdam does sound pretty bloody awesome.'

Tribute © Robert Lee Johnston 2016
Email: tributerobertleejohnston@gmail.com

CHAPTER NINETEEN: LET'S BE JUDGED

There was a darkness stalking the boys' hearts and stomach.

Today was their last day of freedom. After lunch they would feel liberty's sweetness no more. The length of time without it was still to be determined. The seventeen-year-olds had over four hundred charges between them. Not to mention the hordes of other victims and countless charges laid as a result of the drug squad's widespread operation. Some that were ensnared the boys knew, or had seen around the traps; the rest were strangers to all. They had one unfortunate commonality. They had all met the same nark during the last twelve months. Norbert, to steal a character from The Fabulous Furry Freak Brothers. Norbert the Nark.

That old judge had been seeing a fair bit of Cozy recently and two months ago he warned Cozy and his mouthpiece not to front him again anytime soon; not without a toothbrush. Cozy was still on probation. The boys'

small-time solicitor assured them she was a fighter, but this mess was not winnable.

The operation was triggered and warrants presented at 5 am. And the drug squad pigs raided every house involved, uproariously, at precisely the same time, so that no warnings could be sent to others. Detectives tried to turn the boys against each other, telling each of them that the others had given up this or that. They stayed staunch and would have none of that. Then they wanted the three of them to elaborate on the gathered police information. The boys had a firm rule when it came to being interviewed by filth. 'Tell them fucking nothing.'

They got a good laugh when Kenny saw, written on a bit of their paperwork on the interview table, a sentence from Sarge: 'Don't believe a word those three tell you. They'll all fuck with you!'

The boys believed it was the coppers' job to find information not theirs. They admitted nothing and aggressively lied. Make them earn their tucker, they reckoned, like the rest of us. They bet that 'no bastard cop will ever come along and volunteer for any of our horrid, shitty fucking jobs'.

The surveillance included many photos of them exiting Lacey Knickers's residence, with garbage bags full of cannabis. Cleverly staked out on a mountainside near his farm, the cunning bastards used powerful lenses to record and photograph all Lacey's comings and goings. The boys claimed the bags contained dirty clothes. They'd done their washing there. No pictures of clever Lacey handing boo, or anything, to anyone. None of the boys gave him up. Not a single charge could be laid on Knickers. The drug squad boys were filthy. They knew it was all coming from him. This whole shit fight had gone down to catch Lacey. They failed. The boys never let Norbert meet Lacey once in that twelve-month period nor mentioned his real name. They always

called him Dealer McDope or Farmer Fudd if there were ears close by.

Lacey was shit scared by all the recent goings-on. He became paranoid and wilted. His heart was broken, watching the three get put through the Law's grinding mill. He would stop sniffing cocaine every day, stop injecting speed, and lay off the chemicals and acid for a bit, once they were gone. The boys knew they were going down, and Lacey thanked them a million times for keeping old school, for keeping him and his new girlfriend out of it. He felt guilty as hell. The huge hangovers the lads went to court with were testament to their last night of freedom at Lacey's.

Fucking maggot nark! Filthy, fucking, dirty rats! Dirty slags!

And of course that golden, Australian oldie, spoken slowly with its bespoken, guttural slang, drunkenly, in equal measures of hate, disgust, exasperation and disbelief: Fucking pigs.

These were the phrases thrown around the table.

'When you blokes get out I'll shout you all a trip overseas somewhere nice to thank you. And don't worry, I'll sell that giant bag of coke you left me so you got some cash waiting.'

He looked them over, sadly.

'I should be there beside all three of you tomorrow. You three made me a bloody fortune.'

'Man, I'm glad you got away with it. Hey, we did all right out of you too you know.'

Cozy truly was happy he hadn't got caught. They all were. Bugs blew out a thick, potent cloud of Lacey's finest. 'Shit, bloke. I'd have diddly fucking squat without your elbows.' He smiled as the flavour pleased his every taste bud. 'It was cheap, it got everyone bent, and it was endless. Man, don't feel bad. We could've said no and walked away at any time, mate.'

Tribute © Robert Lee Johnston 2016
Email: tributerobertleejohnston@gmail.com

'When we get out,' Kenny suggested, 'we should fuck off up bush and grow some excellent dope. You know, camp on the patch for the whole duration. Yeah, we had lots of dope here, but the quality we were selling, man, it could've been better. If we lived with the crop, we could manicure plants, water more regularly, tend the sick, and piss the males off sooner. Grow huge, fat crops. Four footy fields sort of thing. Cos fuck it! If I'm getting locked up, I'm going to make it worth my while. Fuck these fucking pigs. If we do a row, or a couple of years even, we got to grow when we get out.'

Cozy shook his head. 'Fuck, man. We haven't even gone in yet, and you're talking about getting out. You're mad, bro. When we finally get out, Sarge, man, he's going to have such a fat, he'll be hot, beady-eyed and hard. Sarge will be all over us, like Bugs's jewels on a stool.'

Bugs laughed. 'Oi, don't bring me into it.'

'I don't know what to think, mate. Cozy, I'm a … I'm a bit scared.'

'Me too, Kenny.'

'Me three,' Bugs admitted.

Kenny exhaled. 'Do you reckon he'll send us to a boys' home, Cozy?'

'I don't know, mate. Hope so.'

'You reckon we'll do a dime?'

'What does that mean, Kenny?'

'I don't know. I was hoping you knew. Fuck, man, we're only seventeen. Cozy, if that judge sends us to prison. We'll be the youngest fucking inmates in there!'

Bugs saw the two getting worried. 'Boys, we just got to stick together, just like always, just like forever. If anyone fucks with one of us, they'll have to get through all of us.'

Cozy folded a little. 'I'm shitting myself.'

'FUCKING OATH,' Kenny yelled far too loudly. 'I'm so fucking worried for tomorrow.'

Tribute © Robert Lee Johnston 2016
Email: tributerobertleejohnston@gmail.com

The music stopped right then, and a weighty, bombed-up silence just hung there. All the soon to be convicts tried to look into the future. Heads down, trying to catch a glimpse of the next few years of their condemned lives. The colonial boys had to be in court at 9 am. Only eight hours of freedom left. Cozy snorted another dog-leg-thick line and packed another cone. He turned to see Evie was still asleep on the couch. 'Let's hope that mean old judge gets some sweet, tight, slippery pussy tonight. How do you blokes reckon judges like to fuck?'

Bugs grinned. 'That's easy, mate. Exactly like Rev. With boys.' Then he added, 'With our luck I bet his missus is holding out on him cos he forgot her birthday. Maybe he didn't take the garbage out yesterday for the umpteenth time. And some son of a bitch ran over his dog. So he's nicely pissed off for the morning.'

They all laughed and bloody hoped not.

Lacey reminded them to be small and quiet in jail. 'Eagles may soar, boys, but how many times do you hear of a bloody chicken getting chopped up in a plane's propellers?'

Cozy chuckled while cutting them each an extra-fat line. 'Fucked if we're sleeping tonight.'

A medley of Fuck that! thundered back at him.

They were all six months or so away from their eighteenth. Effectively juveniles. But they knew the beak wouldn't be treating them as such, and nor did he.

Lacey took Cozy aside. He confessed, with a stagger and a slur, about the day he found a baby that was Cozy. Cozy wasn't expecting that, and didn't quite know what to say.

'Lots of people tell me they're the ones that first found me.'

'After I found you, I was so spun out, man. I had to tell someone, so I told my mum. We noticed Tribute's rumour mill kick into gear. I promised you as a baby that day,

Tribute © Robert Lee Johnston 2016
Email: tributerobertleejohnston@gmail.com

wrapped in fish and chips paper, when I left you all dirty and mud stained at the doc's, that I would tell you the truth, and I sort of been waiting for, you know, for the right time to tell you.'

He went into convincing detail and hugged a dazed, speechless young man. It was weird and took Cozy time, maybe years, to comprehend.

Instead of telling the boys Lacey discovered him, Cozy told them he had rescued one of the boys and wouldn't say which. They had spoken about why he never adopted or fostered any of them before. And on hearing the news, they rightly decided he had already done his part early in the piece. It felt too weird for Cozy, admitting it was him that Lacey found.

In court, Norbert appeared and then spilt his stinking nark guts.

Bloody un-Australian, Cozy thought.

The boys kicked themselves hard and often for not recognising a rat-bastard in their midst. Arriving at the courthouse Bugs told his mates, 'We should have known, man. Did youse notice Norbert never shouted us a drink? At home ... or in the Middy. Not once.'

'That bastard wouldn't shout in a croc attack,' Cozy reckoned.

Kenny added, 'Yeah, but he squeals like the fucking pig he is.'

Unable to look at them, Norbert, the piece of shit, even had the hide to say they had forced speed and acid upon him, and he'd 'mimicked' smoking all that herb he'd toked up with them. Kenny wanted to projectile vomit bile and bilge water onto him. The smile he gave the boys when he claimed that lie revealed to them that he had loved every second of being bent and twisted with them. So out of it he'd have to crash all night on the couch, only to wake and dig in all over again. The judge who presided over the half a dozen little towns surrounding and including Tribute told the

court that he had never witnessed such bravery and intestinal fortitude, such dedication, as Norbert exhibited. Especially being under the heavy crossfire and influence of these three vile, wicked recidivists. He was bent all the time and got a big fat pay cheque each and every week for it.

Cozy lied. 'The weed you have as evidence isn't the weed I sold him. And your shit-for-brains stool pigeon there asked for it. I wasn't going round advertising dope for sale.'

The young man was ordered in no uncertain terms to shut up by the beak, as the prosecutor had a piss fit about his interrupting.

The judge fumed. 'Our great state does not support entrapment laws!'

Cozy thought, It was worth a crack.

The whole courtroom knew they were sunk. The boys, they knew it. We're fucked. Maybe they should have run away? Interstate crossed their minds a thousand times these last weeks. But no one could run forever, so here they were. Their luck took a heavy nosedive into fresh, hot, custard-like camel shit early in the court's sitting. Every other case was some bastard running amok from Tribute. The judge noticed a pattern. He was none too happy by the time Bugs's case finally came before him, for the last time. The boys had drained dry all the conditional bail they could milk. He told the busy courtroom he would make an example of these three to deter any further hooliganism and tomfoolery within Tribute's community.

Bugs was called first for sentencing.

'I have a good, kind, generous friend in the reverend of your former church and orphanage. Many sad, disturbing tales of you and your friends' unruly, larrikin-like behaviour, and the never-ending limits you all pushed him to, have crossed our dinner table. Keep in mind this is a man of God. A noble, educated gentleman. The man, by the way, you owe your very life. And still you, every one of you, for years sought out ways to madden him and cause him grief. I have

come to know the great man on a personal level, and his God, his church, his community, including myself, are forever thankful for his kindness of heart, his endless devotion and warmth. We dread to think of any person in our society provoking a pious servant of the good book, let alone our wonderful, great reverend.'

The judge counted off time for each of Bugs's hundred and fifty or so charges. Amounting to around four years. Then Kenny was called as Bugs was handcuffed and escorted in a dream to the police watch house. Kenny stood awkwardly silent. The machine-gun-venom, mathematical additions saw him with a month less than Bugs.

Out of character, Kenny whispered, 'Mother-fucker.'

Cozy was next, and braced for his name. Evie and he had a tear or two in their eyes, watching Kenny, shoulders slumped, quietly sobbing, led away. She squeezed Cozy's hand tightly, stared deeply into him for a second. His jaw slack with regret, Cozy stood up before his name and case number were called and whispered with surprise and disbelief to Evie, 'Did you hear what he said about Rev? Fuck it. See you, mate.'

He kissed her cheek and hugged her. 'We'll be okay, Evie. Try not worry.' She was a good stick. Cozy promised her, and he lied, 'Evie, jail always sounds worse than it really is.'

'You're a lousy liar, Cozy.'

The bailiff became pissed, but Cozy ignored him. What could they do? Lock him up? He sauntered to the dock where Kenny had just been sentenced. The judge grinned. He yelled and spat about his having no respect in his courtroom, his towns, and none in general. He gave Cozy time for busting his probation orders. So he faced again the charges applied when he dragged Sarge's arse off in the hardtop. Impatient, Cozy looked as if he needed to be somewhere else, and was disinterested in what the retard had to say. He wondered, Where the fuck was this arsehole

Tribute © Robert Lee Johnston 2016
Email: tributerobertleejohnston@gmail.com

when Syd and his slut lived in 'his town'? Under 'his rule'? Fucking nowhere's where!'

Cozy got just over four years.

He only came to when the judge asked if he had anything to say for himself, as he had asked the others. At first Cozy was in too much shock to say a word. But he'd heard him ask the question twice now, and knew his turn was coming. The young fella cleared his head and asked curiously, 'All this for some pot? Shit, man. I'm a criminal cos I smoke weed?'

Evie winced and squirmed. She kicked the seat in front of her to distract Cozy and shut him up.

'You never asked once why we all smoke, and you sentencing me to however long you just did—I don't know, I lost bloody count—isn't going to change a fucking thing. I'll smoke in your prisons, in your watch houses, in your towns, and when I get out, just to spite you and your stupid, prehistoric laws. You could've sent me away for fucking life, I would've told you the same thing. You dinosaur. Why don't you all fucking grow up and open your eyes? Smoking weed is the smallest, most inconsequential, trivial problem Tribute has. You and your pigs have got fuck all else to do and have to appear busy, right? And you lazy, shyster bastards, to look busy pick all the low-hanging fruit. Those two boys you just locked up ain't angels. But they barely hurt a fly their whole lives, and you send them to jail for that long. Fuck it, arsehole, do what you got to do. Just know this. I was never accepted. We, were never accepted by your society and its shitty rules, ever. Hey, judge, what if I don't believe in that Bible there I had to swear on? What if I believe it's a joke, Rev's a joke? The crap that goes on in your God's name, in that book, and behind its spine is the cruellest joke. What if I told you your Almighty God, made me do it? Jesus spoke to me? Halle-fucking-lujah. Does that count? That sad fantasy, it's just hilariously awesome fiction to me. I'll never accept that comedic fantasy novel or my punishment, or that the

Tribute © Robert Lee Johnston 2016
Email: tributerobertleejohnston@gmail.com

power received by you through it is holy or just. Or that jury youse handpicked as my peers. If my peers, my kind of people had been sitting there in those jurors' fucking chairs … this sentencing us years, heaped upon fucking years, would never be happening. You're all blind sheep.'

Cozy wanted to rip his shirt off and show them all just how blind they were and prove how friendly and warm Rev and his community could truly be.

'Oh yeah, I almost forgot, judge. You're a faggot. And both you and your precious, child-slaver mate, Reverend, can go forever fuck yourselves.'

The judge fumed. He asked if Cozy's two young friends were of the same opinion.

'What? That you're both faggots? Fucking oath they are.'

Evie had had enough. She screamed at Cozy. 'COZY, WILL YOU PLEASE SHUT UP. YOU'RE MAKING THINGS SO MUCH WORSE. JUST SHUT YOUR MOUTH.' She cried uncontrollably. 'Stop provoking him, please Cozy.'

Hurting poor Evie stung Cozy. He became so angry he ripped his shirt buttons and tore his shirt off. He turned his back to the jury and crowd. There was a sharp intake of breath and 'Oh, my God'. People shifted in uncomfortable pews. Cozy turned slowly, revealing all to the prosecutor and judge. A standing, gobsmacked police prosecutor sat heavily, muted.

'Here is your Almighty God. Here's evidence of your precious rev's devotion and warmth. Ask your great, powerful friend Rev how much he has been paid for our grief. My blood. My carnage. Rev's not GREAT; he's a rodent, an animal. He's weak. That sad excuse of a man couldn't pull a greasy fucking stick out of a dog's arse.'

The judge turned his head in disbelief and yelled for Cozy's shirt to be replaced, and for instant silence.

Tribute © Robert Lee Johnston 2016
Email: tributerobertleejohnston@gmail.com

A thunderous, unintimidated growl escape Cozy's mouth. 'Fucking look at it, you blind haven for paedophiles, pimps and child-slavers.'

The judge demanded the defendant be silenced and, if necessary, restrained and gagged. He demanded Evie be quiet and control her outbursts. Sarge, out of uniform, moved to sit beside Evie. He felt he had lived in a box. He was in tears of shock when the penny suddenly dropped. He had never seen Cozy's upper body unclothed until this point.

He was fired up as the thin walls of his world broke down around him. He loudly interrupted, demanding the judge give him warrants to investigate these gruesome accusations.

He apologised to Cozy, shaking his head in empathy and shame. 'I'm sorry, Cozy, I couldn't, didn't, see. I ... I'm ... I'm so bloody sorry, mate.'

Once the young man was restrained, clothed, gagged and handcuffed to his dock, the court made amendments to all three of their records.

'It's a pity, young Cozy, you're not as wise minded as your lady friend. Very serious allegations have been made against our reverend, and the court shall investigate and deal with those complaints in a timely fashion. However, this action you have chosen, Cozy, will have no bearing on the court, or the crimes you have previously committed. The Law's focus for the moment, young man, is upon your sentencing. Therefore I propose it be forever noted and recorded on all three of your criminal histories that if an officer of the Law comes into contact with you or your two co-operatives, background checks will reveal the following: At all times it is highly likely this person will have large quantities of drugs in his possession.'

Cozy was taken away resisting, and grunted through his gag, 'Yu og.'

'Three more months for that outburst.'

Tribute © Robert Lee Johnston 2016
Email: tributerobertleejohnston@gmail.com

Cozy went down fighting. He had got a few shots in, but all was lost. He tried to apologise to Evie as he was carted off. 'I orry Errie.' She was a burning wreck and Cozy felt terrible for upsetting her. Sarge was abashed, shattered by confusion and guilt. Sarge never believed a word Cozy breathed his whole life, but right here, right then, he felt the truth as if the scars were his own.

When he boxed, he always wore a shirt.

Sarge's mind raced to young Jen. The ruin of her tiny body. Then little John Henry, and all the befores and in-betweens. Sarge craved a fresh, enlightened audience with Tribute's great, illusory reverend.

Rev was heavily investigated and died soon after it started. Cozy never found out how. He figured stroke. Perhaps a guilty conscience, or lack thereof, assisted. Six months later Deidre died. The postal worker that delivered the mail from her overflowing PO box got a whiff as maggots hatched and ate into Deidre's swollen, fly-blown, putrefied orifices. Sarge was called to take care of her gassy, almost burst carcass. She was on her belly, and had, in her dying moments, rolled off her filthy sofa. Sarge, approaching, couldn't help but notice, Deidre's all behind, like Barney's bull. And, on inspection for his paperwork, Sarge discovered two birth certificates in a drawer, revealing that Syd and Deidre where not husband and wife. They were, in fact, first cousins.

Sarge found other wretched things in that decrepit, hellish house. Hidden carelessly in a dark, window-less bedroom, inside a bedside-table drawer, next to a dirty bed, was an envelope, filthy, fat and full. It contained well-fingered photos of all the kids. Many, many polaroids of each of them.

No older than ten. Tied to furniture and to each other. And being molested by both Syd and Deidre, and the odd local here and there he recognised. The high school headmaster caught his eye. Bugs and Cozy would never give

Tribute © Robert Lee Johnston 2016
Email: tributerobertleejohnston@gmail.com

Sarge the name of who had whipped them. He wasn't surprised. The boys never gave anyone up, ever. The mystery was now solved. There were pictures of Bugs's back, ripped and bleeding still, while Syd fucked him from behind. Bugs was lashed into a foetal position. Then a picture of Cozy, unaware of the camera. Though Sarge couldn't see his face in this photograph, the boy's long, blond hair made him easily recognisable. His back was freshly ripped, the slices sharp, deep, and swollen red with anger. In the foreground, Jenny was tied with a rope, her legs spread wide. Her eyes tightly closed. And a happy, smiling, drooling Syd, inside her fragile body, and Deidre on all fours, happy as a rat with a gold tooth, with a thick cucumber being shoved up her arse by Cozy. There were photographs of Kenny, John Henry and Evie. Sarge's guts churned and he vomited in that septic house.

His mind raced to the last time he was here, Syd's accident, and how calm and relieved Cozy and Jen had been. How removed Cozy had seemed. Sarge looked back in his memory. He compared this to when he saw Cozy at Pops' death. Was Syd's accident an accident? All the guilty were dead. He spent no time wondering. If Cozy killed Syd, Sarge decided he couldn't blame the kid. Syd's death to all others, excepting Sarge and his god, was an accident. Happens a hell of a lot round here.

Sarge had one other thought. It aired out as he was leaving the house of pain that was Syd and Deidre's home of children's misery. The photos, they would serve no good. Not to the kids. Not to the Law, Tribute, or himself. The polaroids were the first photos anyone, now alive, other than him, had ever seen of them all together. Sarge realised that simple thing. The fact that there was no photographic history of his colonial kids, other than these sad examples. More important than that, he cried out hopelessly, with love, guilt, selfless disgust, and tender, tender, respect for the dead, and their living tribe of siblings.

Tribute © Robert Lee Johnston 2016
Email: tributerobertleejohnston@gmail.com

He burnt the envelope and all of the forty or so, glossy, life-altering polaroids. The packs secrets, good and bad, would die with Sarge. Forever unspoken. Watching the fire eat the pictures, and the images on them crumbling and disappearing into ash, he told the house owners' souls, 'Burn in hell, you inbred fuckers.'

The remnants of Tribute's humiliated orphanage fast closed down. The mortified, shell-shocked regular churchgoers left to be preached at elsewhere.

Only the church had any idea where the remaining youngsters were sent.

No doubt to ignominy.

CHAPTER TWENTY: FREEDOM AIN'T FREE.

Cozy, sixty-six kilos, a skinny, buck-kneed welterweight. Kenny fifty-five kilos soaking wet. Bugs, the largest, weighed in at around seventy-five kilos on the prison scales.

The young men decided to hit the gym to pass some time and get in shape. At least try to put some weight on. No fighter ever scared Cozy as much as the place they were in. A fighter has to assume that everyone can be beaten, that he can win, that there is a counter for every attack. It was obvious to Cozy that he would have little to no control. He knew this slow-rolling, end-for-end accident would get worse before it got better.

The three boys hadn't had much freedom after leaving the orphanage. Two and a bit wonderful, heady, fast years. It didn't take long for them to fuck it all up. Cozy reluctantly began to accept his fate and misfortune to better deal with the finality and traumas of prison. He had to compartmentalise and compress his emotions. His natural survival instincts were usually pretty accurate. Cozy would trust, absolutely, his gut in here.

He wished to feel clean again. He felt as if he was being punished for killing Syd, and for every other bad deed. He actually felt a bit better when he thought that. If this time was for Syd, in any way, shape or form, he'd do it standing on his head, with a big, fat, cheesy smile.

That toothless fucker deserved it.

And Cozy would do it a million times over again. For Jen alone. Cozy wished he hadn't hurt Evie. Cozy hated hurting her.

Similarities between the orphanage and prison were soon obvious. Religious snipers all over, sexual predators everywhere, and no shortage of brutal, mindless violence. The three stoners tried keeping their heads down, they truly did. But three young roosters tended to stand out amongst those world-weary faces. And the prize of three young scalps was irresistible to particular predatory minds, the sorts of minds that challenge your gag reflexes. All sorts of groups formed. Dopers usually hung around dopers, junkies around junkies, rapist fucks around rapist fucks, and so on.

It was impossible to pick the crimes people had committed by the way they looked. The kindest-looking bloke was, more often than not, the most savage. Murderers and kid tamperers didn't have a distinguishable look. No cover-judging ever worked in any prison.

Lots of violent, angry men in one broiler, with all the combined pressures of inner and outer lives. Each man tossed into a crispy stir-fry of intense heat and turmoil. Some days the boys wanted to kill every fucker close by just so they could breathe and relax, for one second. Other days the bloke next to them was going through the same thought process. Put any man in a cage long enough and his world will warp. His mind will go to some fucked-up, shitty places. And, like tripping on acid, now and again a bloke can stay lost in its warped, twisted folds.

From day one, minute one, they had found trouble. Some fuck walking by Cozy bummed a durry while they were

Tribute © Robert Lee Johnston 2016
Email: tributerobertleejohnston@gmail.com

being held in a processing cell, looking into the belly of the jail. Brunk, a largish blackfella grabbed the packet of White Ox offered to him by Cozy and took half the tobacco as if it was his. Cozy turned to Bugs, a little stunned by the blatantness of the gutchy thief. Bugs's soon-to-be-cut hair sprang forth and overflowed like a badly poured beer. He shook his head and, without words, his eyes screamed loud to let it go and forget it. The fresh inmates were told by Brunk not to confuse him with Brunker or Bronc, two other hard inmates he hated. Cozy hadn't met those other two blokes yet to form an opinion, but he already hated this fella.

'Never bum another cigarette of me, Brunk. You done your dash with me, bloke.'

He laughed at Cozy, and a bit of spittle flew through the prison bars, landing on Cozy's neck. It was the most ridiculous, high-pitched laugh the boys had ever heard.

Like a bird call. IH IH IH!

Brunk stared through the bars at the teenager. 'I'll remember you, you big-mouth white cunt.' Then he casually strode off.

'What the fuck are you doing, Cozy?' Bugs was agitated and annoyed with Cozy and lost it. 'Why didn't you just fuck up? Just let him have the fucking tobacco! Fuck it, man. Between the three of us we got plenty to smoke.'

'Bugs, we're swimming with hungry, frenzied, starving fucking sharks here, mate. You think that fuckery isn't telling all his mates, right now, how easily he's walked all over me. Discrediting me. I don't care if his name is Billy Bob, Brunk, Bruce, Bronc, or fucking Beelzebub. He's just a man. Hey, if he wanted your butt cheeks, Bugs, would you have handed them over and told me, "It's all right, Cozy. Don't worry, we got two others"?'

'You fucking smart arse. So you admit we're in a fucking shark pond do you, Cozy?' He was pissed and didn't let his litter brother answer. 'You're a fuckhead at times, mate.'

'Me?'

'Yeah fucking you. You just couldn't shut your mouth and let it ride. As usual. We got to cause little to no waves, bring no attention to ourselves. Then the first, the very first, fuck you meet, you make enemies of. For us two as well.' It was getting loud in their little holding cell. 'Cozy, I'll pay you twenty bucks a minute once we get out if you shut your cunting mouth for a bit. Just fuck up, man.'

'You're fucking joking me, right?'

'Fer fuck's sake, Cozy! No, I'm not joking one fucking bit!' Poor Bugs nearly blew a vein in his eye. 'Fuck knows what that big, evil bastard has done to end up here. Do you know, Cozy? No, you don't. For all we know he's the heaviest heavy in here to the back-of-Bourke. And you go and antagonise him. You shit me to tears at times.'

'Where do you think we are, Bro-Jack? What the fuck do you think is going to happen in here? There's no sanctuary here, Bugs. If it wasn't that caveman, missing-link-looking, ugly mother fucker, it would've been another. Hey, Bugs, guess fucking what?'

'Fucking what!'

'I bet we meet ten other degenerates just like him today alone. You better fast get fucking used to it, bloke.'

'Fuck you, Cozy. We won't meet any if you keep your fucking mouth shut. And pull your fucking head in. I'm sick of hearing your voice! Failure is an orphan, Cozy; success has many families.'*

'What? HA. Yeah, tell anyone that fucks with you that. See how that pans out for you. You idiot. Fuck you, Bugs. Did you read that on a public toilet wall, while some fags rogered you or something? Did you? You're a coward. Always have been. Look how yellow-feathered he is, Kenny. So if Brunk comes back and flops his cock out through the bars, Bugs, and tells you, "Liven up, white boy, and kiss me where it smells funny!" What? You just going tell him your little quote, fall on both knees, and be skull fucked by a pre-

Tribute © Robert Lee Johnston 2016
Email: tributerobertleejohnston@gmail.com

historic rock ape? Once all his mates get a sniff of your bleeding, fresh arsehole, and know they can throw a leg over you, they'll all want to shag you. Just to hear your wise, sagely words.

Bugs let go a thunderous growl. 'You calling me faggot and coward, Cozy?'

'Didn't call you faggot, Bugs. I called the ten back-biting bastards that fucked you, fags.'

They were both up and face to face.

'Go on, say that again, fuckface.'

'Righto, you cock-sucking, poofter-rooted coward. You couldn't go two rounds in a revolving fucking door. Go on, throw a punch. Please, Bugs. Just one.'

'I'll belt the living fucking suitcase out of you, Cozy, once I start!'

They were about to unleash when Kenny moaned loudly. 'Aaahh, stop it, fuck youse. Fucking Jesus. We're supposed to stick together in here and watch each other's backs. The first sign of trouble, and you two want to fight each other. Settle the fuck down the pair of you. I see both your points. You're both right, but you're both wrong. This isn't normal, this place. It's all wrong, all back to front. And you pair, right now, are scaring me.'

'Don't call me coward, Cozy.'

Cozy took their advice and shut his mouth.

Turns out Brunk was one of the three heaviest inmates locked down in the joint. A constant tension and instant hatred between Brunk and Cozy would relieve many an inmate's slow day. A bloke can't dice any inmate for long in prison.

Their first week was interesting, if not so frightening.

The first visit to the gym ended in total failure. They walked in and casually checked out the rusty old gym gear. They basically just tyre kicked. It was the first day they'd had the courage to leave their cells.

Tribute © Robert Lee Johnston 2016
Email: tributerobertleejohnston@gmail.com

Four big blokes were training together amongst the small crowd. Compared to the skinny teenagers these men were huge. They checked out the kids, discussed something and then casually and terrifyingly shadowed them until cornered. They were in the boys' faces, weighing them up. Far too close.

One of them asked Bugs, 'Are you that Cozy cunt?'

Kenny was on Cozy's left, Bugs on his right. Both were silent under the weight. This was no place for technical rhetoric.

'Nah, that's me. I'm Cozy.'

Their gazes fell on Cozy as he took a long, slow, frightened breath. Readying all his muscles, bones and flesh for the colossal hiding they were about to humbly receive. Bugs and Kenny knew this was not tenable. The bullock-team of man-mountain towering over the three of them appeared homicidal. It was practically suicide to contemplate a confrontation.

Still, Cozy was thinking, my mates are by my side, and the three of us will at least have a fair old crack. No words were used for a painful eternity, and the big fellas, in no hurry, let the situation sink in. Cozy noticed movement in his peripheral. He was trying hard not to break eye contact. Bugs had slipped away far to his right.

He left me.

The big fella held the young man's gaze and saw him cut. A movement to Cozy's left and Kenny was gone. Cozy tried to hold his gaze but blinked in shock at being abandoned and left to fight a surly crash of human rhino.

I'm alone.

They closed ranks on him. He was trapped and already heavily wounded, though not a single punch had been thrown. He quickly summed up the other three and returned his eyes to the biggest bloke, the same bloke who'd asked the question. Cozy nodded reluctantly and accepted the challenge. His hands were clenched by his side.

Tribute © Robert Lee Johnston 2016
Email: tributerobertleejohnston@gmail.com

If he was going to fall he was taking the biggest fella with him. His eyes focussed, envy green. Brutes verses Warrior.

The giant inmate put his mouth close to Cozy's ear. Cozy was about to head-butt him and drive the next biggest fella with a straight right hand and break his scrap-iron jaw. He was seeing it before doing it, visualising every step and counter.

'There it is. That's the face, the Cozy, the eyes I remember. You got no mates in here, Cozy. They didn't last ten seconds, that pair. How long you known them pelicans?' He moved away slightly and paused.

Cozy was completely confused as the big bloke's eyes softened.

'I'm Brunker. I met you once or twice in the city when you were a kid.' Brunker smiled. 'I was a coach for a Sydney boxing club. Bernie trained me. You fought against some of my boys a couple of times, here and there.'

'Holy fuck! I nearly fell over, Jack. Right? Your first name's Jack? And one of your sons' name's Geoff?'

'Yeah, you recognise me now?'

Cozy's chest relaxed as he exhaled his demon, smiling large with relief.

'I do, man. Not until you said, but. No hair, long time, you know.'

Cozy extended a hand.

'I thought it was you, Cozy. Thought I'd show you how things really are in here. Sorry for scaring you like that. Those mates of yours, they couldn't run the guts for a slow butcher.'

'Fuck. Give me a sec. Me arsehole, it near caved in then, Jack.'

'Yeah, Cozy. Ha ha! You weren't looking real flash, mate. You didn't look fit to fuck there for a bit.'

They laughed, hugged extra hard, and slapped each other's backs.

Tribute © Robert Lee Johnston 2016
Email: tributerobertleejohnston@gmail.com

'Not wrong. I felt a bit green. Good to see you though. Bar the immediate surroundings.'

Cozy was so relieved. Cozy's old friend introduced him to his coes, and, when Cozy's two blokes saw them all laughing and joking, they sheepishly crawled back to work out what had just bloody happened.

Shamelessly, Cozy introduced them to a cold, unimpressed mob.

'Fuck, boys, you got to see this kid fight. He's a natural born, living, breathing, fucking thrashing machine. He gave a few of me boys a touch up and a boxing lesson here and there. Even made my son and a couple of them quit.'

Cozy wasn't enjoying the praise. The other three monsters looked hard and all over the youngster for traces of ability and saw, nought, zero. They laughed, thinking Jack was pulling their leg. Cozy smiled politely.

'I got a little boxing club in here, Cozy. If you want to join up, it helps pass time.'

'I had no idea. Fuck yeah, Jack, count me in. I'm still finding me feet here. How exactly do I join?'

Jack explained. They talked coaches, Bernie, fighters, fights. Jack said if anyone fucked with him to come see him. He wouldn't leave Cozy strung out to hang.

'You boys want to join too, I reckon.' He glanced hollow at Bugs and Kenny. 'You're built like robbers' dogs, and it'll put some starch in your bones. You're both going to fucking need it in here. Cozy can't fight all your battles.'

When the big fellas left, Bugs couldn't look his blood brother in the eye.

'I'm fucking sorry, Cozy.' Bugs was disgusted with himself. 'I'm ashamed. I just didn't know what to do, man. I panicked. How fucking big are they, man? Bloody giants all of them. How big were that bloke's thighs? Fucking human tree stumps they were!'

Kenny wasn't embarrassed one bit.

'Fuck that, fuck this, and fuck them blokes. Holy shit, man! I was thinking, hoping, you'd be right behind me, Cozy. I imagined some horrible, inmate orgy, teenage, rape-fest, and had to leg it. That was fucking scary, man. So fucking scary. Man, I shat myself and nearly had a fucking heart attack as well. Fuck them. Fuck the gym! And definitely, fuck the fucking boxing club, brothers. I'm going to the library and get me some books, and lock my arse up safe and sound in my fucking cell. Fuck this place! Fuck them big, iron-eating monsters! Fuck this whole fucking place, man!'

Kenny was rattled and did just what he stated. The boys never saw him in the hall where the boxing ring and gym gear was found. Kenny accepted work at the mechanic shop and honed his skills every day. The blokes around him there were all good guys. When he wasn't there, he was always in his cell, fart-arsing around, reading books from the prison's well-stocked library, studying all sorts of things. He studied soils, rocks, prospecting minerals. How to find gold, identifying tree species and different bush tucker; outback survival; and especially maps. He was doing his apprenticeship while doing time. Three or four years of patient studies to perfect his trade.

'Professional Crop Grower.'

Kenny knew average rainfalls in each of his top-ten chosen areas since recording began. He knew exactly when the seasons turned, and how many days' sunshine in his allotted grow time. Where the water was, and if and when the rivers and creeks ran dry. He knew all the local wildlife of each area on his wish list, the bush medicines and food the areas supplied. He knew the exact distances to the nearest farms, stations or traditional land owners and surveyed maps to find access that was almost impossible to follow. He investigated the aerial activity around his choice selections, making sure his big, fat crop wasn't going to be under an interstate flight path or found by some nosey station owner's private chopper while mustering. The others spent

Tribute © Robert Lee Johnston 2016
Email: tributerobertleejohnston@gmail.com

time with him, pouring over maps and old stock routes. Dreaming of the perfect place. Bugs and Cozy knew it kept Kenny sane and his mind occupied.

They met a true to life Blow-Job-Bob. He was the ugliest, hairiest, red-headed son of a bitch they ever saw. But every visit, every damn time, a different hot, scantily-clad honey would come to see him. Looks or prettiness are, of course, based on individual personal taste. The boys will testify that a year or two without women can make a three look like a ten. If the boys were lucky enough to have a visitor when he was getting comforted they would clamber as close as possible to him, just to perve on his goddess of the day. After a while they asked him how come all these girls visited him.

He stuck his tongue out and nearly licked the back of his ear with it. 'Once I go down on them girlies, or they see or hear about this and my cock, they always want more.'

He wagged it, like stroking a wall with a paint roller, flattening out the tip.

'Say no more, Bob,' Bugs said, 'say no more.' They understood.

Bob was ridiculously well hung and never wore clothes once back in his unit. Bugs reckoned Bob must have eaten a cargo ship of carrots. Serving a lengthy sentence and fearless of nudity, Bob, a lifer, was always naked except when he worked the laundry each day. Screws gave up trying to dress him years ago. His dick was easily four Coke can's long and a can wide. His favourite trick was to sneak up without a stitch on behind some poor bastard, sitting down reading or whatever, and say, 'Mate, can you blow some air through this for me?'

As his victim turned around, he'd smack them, dumbfounded and shocked, in the face repeatedly with his fire-hose dick. Bob was not at all gay, just really strange.

Bob's female visitors were revered because, when they could, when the screws were preoccupied, they gave him

Tribute © Robert Lee Johnston 2016
Email: tributerobertleejohnston@gmail.com

hand jobs. Now and then, to everyone's surprise, they went down on him. Once, when he was beaten up by some bloke for being a fuckwit, he received private infirmary visits for weeks. His attacker was soon bashed and a handsome bounty was placed on the seats nearest to Bob's visitor table. The strangest sentence the boys ever heard in prison was: 'Nobody is to go near, or fuck with, Blow-Job-Bob.'

It came from the very top down, that message. Top ranked inmates and screws alike. Turns out the screws loved patting down all Bob's lovelies as much as criminals liked perving on them. Bob, consequently, pushed everyone's boundaries, instinctively knowing that if anyone hurt him he would get private visits for a week or two, and a chance to exercise his hugely endowed tongue. The holes his removed piercings left were as big as Kenny's ear. It was a Neolithic creature's, or Jabba-The-Hutt's, tongue. Like some huge dog's, it barely fit in his too-small mouth, and he could catch on the wing anything from small dragonflies to low-flying, fully-grown wedge-tailed eagles with that thing.

A couple of times a year someone would totally snap and get sick of him being above the law, so to speak, and belt his dumb arse and cheeky, repugnantly ugly head. If not, he'd often throw himself off something and do enough physical damage to require him to be held in the infirmary. The boys loved to watch those moments and always booked a ring-side seat. Call them cruel, but it was some funny, highly entertaining shit watching the fat, freckly fuck burn, break, and bloody himself on purpose. He was at heart a total chicken shit, so it often took a few attempts to perform the coup de grâce. To loud applause, he'd climb prison bars. Bugs likened it to watching King Kong trying to scale a greasy pole. Bob would fling himself off from a great height, hopeful of snapping something when he met the hard, cold concrete. Sometimes only to bounce. How the boys laughed when the first go only hurt, winded or bruised him, and did fuck-all serious damage. Back up he would limp, moan and

Tribute © Robert Lee Johnston 2016
Email: tributerobertleejohnston@gmail.com

climb. They would yell and chant, watching out for kill-joy screws.

'We wanna see a casualty.' Or, 'Ya pretty to watch, mate. Can ya twist, man? A somersault or something would be cool. Climb a bit higher, Bob, and this time aim for your face.'

Bob ran fast as he could up unsupported ladders, as high as possible until it lost balance and went tits up. They could have watched him do his thing all day long. The boys' all-time favourite was the tennis courts. The umpire's chair was soon banned and removed forever, because Bob leapt off it so often. He'd climb his huge, plumber's-cracked arse, with angry screws screaming at him, to the top of the tall courts' fence and swan dive, crunching ingloriously into the fake-turfed concrete tennis court deck. It sometimes worked a little too well, and Cozy would give him a soft kick in the guts to make sure he hadn't killed himself. The boys soon learned if you pressed hard on Bob's fat guts with a foot for about a minute, when he was knocked out, he'd shit his pants, every time. Sometimes the very act of shitting or the sharp stink woke him up and brought him around. He'd feel around his pants, dazed, not knowing the boys or who and where he was, and ask them all, confused, while sniffing his mucky fingers, 'What's the deal with me shitting myself?' The friction burn from the fake, rough turf and landing on his head would always last a fair while. Weeks later, the scab site still had the power to make the three collapse in fits of laughter.

Every inmate rioted and shat bolt cutters when a busty set of hot, leggy Chinese twins showed up one day. Everyone wondered how he juggled all these goings on from a prison cell. Surely one day he'd mix up schedules or names and two would meet? Never, ever happened while they were in there. The young fellas loved Bob's visitors. Every one of them.

Tribute © Robert Lee Johnston 2016
Email: tributerobertleejohnston@gmail.com

Bugs and Brunker, from day one, never got on. So Bugs never boxed, but every other day he and Cozy worked out. On the other days the three of them would kick a footy about, have a hit of tennis, or walk and jog for an hour. Bugs loved all the drug guys and wanted to know all they knew, even the junkies. Cozy couldn't handle the smack heads. It wasn't the drug, it was the people. They all seemed slippery and shark eyed to him. They seemed to want pity and moaned more than other drug users. The pharmaceutical blokes were compendiums of every known high there was. The boys had never heard of such things. Jail was pharmageddon, and Bugs would remember forever every recipe he learned. His apprenticeship was a little different to Kenny's, but no less complicated. It seemed to him a new universe full of wonder to explore. 'Professional Drug Consumer.'

Cozy, his trade would be set about steel and flying leather, in the gym and boxing. Within twelve months he had put on twenty kilos. He boxed three times a week, read a lot of fiction and a lot of biographies, but his flighty mind was hard to distract. Cozy hated the place so much. He hated the smell, the food and the screws. Those head-fucking screws, and their pissy little, ever-changing rules. Mostly he hated the sick, sly sheep that inhabit such places. So punching and lifting made him too tired to fight or care. Then some fool would cause him to fight, and he could again harness unbridled fury. Cozy got beat lots and lots. King hit, ganged up on. It didn't really matter to him. He always felt better after. Cozy's trade, his apprenticeship, was physically testing compared to the others' chosen fields, and not so complicated.

He secured a Baccalaureate in Bloodshed and an Addiction to Hatred.

Being an Aussie prison, the population was sixty to seventy percent indigenous. White fellas were the minority. In some cases for the first time ever in their whole, ignorant

Tribute © Robert Lee Johnston 2016
Email: tributerobertleejohnston@gmail.com

lives. The boys soon learned that bad people came in all colours, white, black, yellow and red. Grab a globe and spin it or throw a dart at a map of the world. Wherever that globe stops or the dart lands the boys could guarantee with a hundred percent certainty that some bad fuckers lived there. They are everywhere. The three got on fine with the majority of the inmates. Aboriginal men were not new to them at all and, of course, it helped that some were related to people they knew from Tribute.

Brunk and Cozy met again, this time without bars separating them. Cozy was with Bugs in his kitchen, the vegetable kitchen. Cozy was working the meat kitchen in the opposite unit and had some time to kill so he was sitting there talking shit: sort of daydreaming, staring into nothing. Cozy snapped to for a moment when Brunk walked past into his line of sight. Cozy noticed a shitty, liquorice-green, homemade tattoo of a ninja throwing star. It was terrible, easily the shittiest looking tattoo he had ever seen. Cozy had to look away as he smiled to himself at seeing the worst, cheesiest tattoo ever. Being on a supposed hard bastard made it all the funnier. Cozy looked at his feet, and suddenly Brunk was right in front of him, his hands tense and fingers twitching by his side like those of a gunslinger

'What the fuck are you looking at!'

Brunk had seen Cozy's look of contempt. Cozy shat because he was so suddenly in his face.

'Nothing. I was just admiring your tattoo.' Cozy couldn't keep a straight face at his lie.

Bugs wondered, What the fuck is going on? He looked at the ridiculous, jailhouse tattoos and back at Cozy. He had missed the start of it all.

'You want to sort this out in the yard, Cozy? C'mon. You want to stare? Come and stare at me in the yard. See what fucking happens.'

He was trying it on, standing over Cozy, his face too close, his breath too vile and thick for Cozy's liking. He was a

Tribute © Robert Lee Johnston 2016
Email: tributerobertleejohnston@gmail.com

solid, burly fella, known for his power and toughness. The teenager was feeling pretty fit, fairly sharp, and thought, Fuck it. He has got a good head for beating and, after all, man, what else is there for an outcast kid to do in here?

'Righto. No worries, fuckface. I really, really wanna see what happens too.'

Bugs's eyes were bugging out. He had a forty-litre steaming pot full of spuds on the ground and a giant spud masher in his hand, shaking his number-one shaved head at his friend. It was too late.

Bugs asked, 'Cozy, the fuck, man! What? What's happening, bro?'

Cozy gave him a wink, got up, and locked eyes on Brunk. His six foot two was now only two inches taller than Cozy. His hundred-five or ten, against Cozy's new eighty-five kilos. Cozy was the heaviest he'd ever been, though he had tried hard to keep a welterweight's footwork. Brunk led the way.

Cozy thought, If this fella gets hold of me, he will tear me in half. I got to keep him away. Keep moving and make him, force him, to attack.

Cozy shoved the brute hard in the back and taunted him on the way out to the unit's lightly populated caged yard, to try to make him mad.

'Hurry the fuck up. I only got a minute to mop this fucking yard with you.'

Brunk took his shirt off, and when he shaped up, Cozy panicked. Thirteen long years in jail can harden a man. Brunk's hands were loose, his elbows and shoulders tight. He scrunched side on into his bent-kneed stance. Brunk revealed no easy targets as Cozy read his little warm up. A shadow-boxing display revealed a sweet technique and a dangerous, confident style.

His multiple traditional scars, long ago cut in and filled out with ash to thicken the blackened tissue, looked impressive. He saw the look of surprise on Cozy's face.

Tribute © Robert Lee Johnston 2016
Email: tributerobertleejohnston@gmail.com

'What! You think you're the only one who knows pain and how to box?'

His English was perfectly refined. He spoke clearly, his pronunciation better than most highly educated white men.

'My coach used to fight your pathetic Bernie. I know every trick you got, Cozy.'

'I reckon we'll soon see. Old coaches and old men won't win fights here.'

They fought, hard.

Cozy couldn't shake the thought that Brunk knew his styles, and he stupidly double guessed himself. Brunk attacked and fake ripped into the body with a low right hand before throwing a bog-standard stiff jab into the young man's face. It stung Cozy. The oldest trick in the book and he fell for it. The young bloke wasn't going to make that same mistake twice. He saw the body shot coming, then the jab. Cozy knew it was coming. Brunk couldn't resist trying the same move again as Cozy placed himself squarely in the same zone where he'd successfully been tagged. The teen slipped the jab and dropped to his left. Rising quickly, he drove a solid left hook into Brunk's rib cage. Cozy heard the wind rush out of him. He knew it hurt. Cozy kept his feet alive. Brunk's head movement and shoulders were elusive, his feet heavy but brilliant. He feigned a heavy right hand, but instead doubled up his left hook, one low, one high. The high one Cozy misjudged. He just managed to get his chin out of the way. The breeze that came off it was cool and strong. Cozy thought, Shit, I was lucky then. If that had a landed?

It was a well-rehearsed, effortless left hook. Cozy attacked his ribs again, the very same spot, Brunk took a knee for a second, and Cozy backed up and let him rise in his own time. He threw the routine jab again, and, as Cozy easily slipped it, he fired a stiff right into Cozy's head. As it landed the teenager dropped his forehead into the punch, protecting his face. Cozy went down when his head recoiled.

Tribute © Robert Lee Johnston 2016
Email: tributerobertleejohnston@gmail.com

Brunk gave him some space, rubbing his hurt knuckles, and let the boy get up. Cozy had been thumped. A small crowd was gathering. One more bloody time each they went down, until at last, thank Christ, some screws showed up and broke them up.

Brunk was a tough, skilful fighter. And that wouldn't be their last bout. After they got out of the detention unit, two weeks later, Bugs recalled what it looked like from where he was standing and told him, 'You hit Brunk so hard to the body that I got a fucking haemorrhoid.' After, of course, the boys asked how their old friend was doing. Cozy was still busted up and had lost a tooth. When they saw Brunk around he was in no better shape.

Cozy told the boys, 'Brunk, that bastard, can fight. Round two should be good, I reckon.'

The young fellas never involved Jack, or anyone else, in any battles. It wasn't the done thing. They had to fight their own battles and do their own time. They never joined any of the gangs or weird groups and kept to themselves, with a couple of cool people thrown in. Not everyone in prison was a bad bloke. Sometimes a great bloke could be in the wrong place at the wrong time. Happens more than people suspect. There are honourable inmates, like when, for instance, some fuckwit is beating a woman in public, so a good man breaks it up and ends up in here, for accidentally killing, or hurting, the woman-bashing idiot. Now and then people who shouldn't be there were there. The few who actually admitted they deserved jail were rare. The three boys were guilty. They knew it and didn't fight it. Many others were, in their own guiltless opinion, innocent. 'Jail,' Bugs told the boys, 'would be fucking empty if an inmate's word was gospel.'

Mostly they were guilty. Maybe one or two a decade were there by mistake. The youngsters were flat out finding someone who admitted they deserved jail.

Tribute © Robert Lee Johnston 2016
Email: tributerobertleejohnston@gmail.com

Bugs was allowed, after some time, to have a guitar with nylon strings. Prisoners can't have steel strings; they're too great a hanging tool. He was getting deadly at it. Now and then he'd make the boys laugh, sitting in his cell strumming away. He'd sing about living amongst rapists, murderers, and dirty-deed doers, or herald a bad day with a blues riff.

> *Cozy and Brunk fought.*
> *Nah nahna nah na*
> *Two weeks in the DU.*
> *Nah nahna nah na*
> *What's this poor boy to do?*
> *Nah nahna nah na*
> *But to jerk off, non-stop, in his room!*
> *Nah nahna. Ha Ha Ha!*

Bugs had a secret. A painful, sweaty, embarrassing one. He'd rooted some chick a couple of nights before sentencing. The boys were cashing in on as much pussy as they could, as men do when they're going away for a bit. He met a girl whose claim to fame was she could fit a whole grease-gun cartridge in her mouth. Bugs was keen to see. His naked knees became human plough shares working over her front yard, that night. Turns out the honey trap was diseased, rotten and sickly.

After being detained the boys were kept in Tribute's old crappy watch house for a month and a half. No hot water. Baked beans and cold fried egg for breakfast each day. Not to mention the lice-ridden and piss-, vomit- and cum-stained—and God knows what else—mattresses they had to sleep on. Drunks, loud fuckwits, and bright fluorescent lights at all times ensured no sleep. It's a tactic used to make the prison they finally arrive at seem like luxury. Oddly enough it works a treat. The judge also wanted to make a point. The lads were fairly sick and scurvy-ish on arrival at real prison. They stank, and looked and felt hairy

and dirty. Each had worn the same clothes every day for the whole duration. Boils and tropical sores plagued them, but once in the prison and deloused, they all received doses of hygiene and better food.

All the above symptoms faded fast. All except those of stoically shamed Bugs. For six long months he was sure he had pox, the clap, or maybe even the herp. His balls had rotted in the watch house with a tropical rash that ate into layer upon layer of sensitive, thin skin from his sack to his ring, and all the semi-moist flesh in between. He revealed nothing to anyone and tried everything to get rid of it: baby powder, soap, aftershave, metho. How the hell he got metho in jail the boys could never properly figure. He gave it all a go. The blame was on Sarge. He was sick to death of seeing Bugs's ball bag hanging out in the watch house and so forced Bugs to wear underwear. The first pair of jocks Cozy or Kenny had ever seen the bastard own. Those jocks were wet with sweat the whole time and bacterial fun-guys soon took hold. Bugs's balls were always itchy and irritated. Shamelessly, mid-sentence or conversation, Bugs would furiously scratch his plums, leaving nowhere else in the wide old world to look.

Kenny told Cozy, 'His scrotum was like the Mona Lisa's eyes.'

Kenny and Cozy thought he surely had crabs. Finally, after six long months of mind and bodily torture, he buckled. 'Fucking hell, boys. I think I caught the herp off one of those sluts I fucked.'

Bugs pulled a defeated face and shifted his shorts across. His nuts were huge, swollen and angry. A red, purulent, weeping matrix of itchy rash and leaking pustules.

Kenny yelped, 'HOLY TITTY FUCK.'

Cozy and Kenny both oohed and aahed at the sickly carnage presented to them.

Bugs, doe-eyed, asked them, 'What do youse reckon? Every time I crack a fat it nearly rips me apart. I poured

everything on the bastard. It won't die. Aftershave and Dettol burnt like fuck.'

Wide eyed, they both sat up in sympathy pains.

Kenny told Bugs, 'You got it bad.'

'I'll track the bitch down and brand an H for herpes on her forehead. Then I'll kick the rotten, diseased bitch right in her infected ovaries. I got to see the unit doc this arvo cos it's driving me nuts, nuts. You know? The itchiness, man. It's making me mental, fucking dirty slut.'

The boys laughed at his ovary and driving-me-nuts riffs. And at how no responsibility for catching pox was his. It was all her fault. They agreed, once Bugs was gone to see the doc, that his leaking ball sack looked bloody painful. Fucking horrible, with those peeling, red-raw, bloody scabs. Cozy and Kenny gagged. They didn't want to imagine how terrible it must've stunk. But both couldn't help but wonder and squirm out loud about it.

They sang to Bugs later a version of the VB song from the ad: 'You can get it pulling a plough. You can get it rooting a sow. Matter of fact, he's got it now.'

That, or some necrotic spider bit him fair on the nads.

Turns out it was jungle/jock rot, and topical cream worked from the moment Bugs applied and repeated, instantly relieving his discomfort. Within a few days it was gone, along with his worry.

Bugs reckoned to both the boys with a relieved grin, 'I fucking suffered for ages thinking I had gonorrhoea, or was syphilitic. Too shamed to tell you blokes or anyone. Then after all that shame and pain, all that sleep deprivation and worry, one visit to the doc and he gives me a tiny tube of cream and it's gone. GONE. I thought I was fucking dying, man.'

Bugs, gracious in victory, forgave his dirty slut.

'Fucking never wearing jocks again. That pair Sarge give us? Nearly bloody killed me, boys!'

Tribute © Robert Lee Johnston 2016
Email: tributerobertleejohnston@gmail.com

Two years in prison sent the boys bat-shit crazy. Bricks, lime, bars, mortar and time got inside their minds. Watching their backs each day induced regular panic attacks.

The devil dwelt there. Tyranny lived in each man's soul, tormenting every dream. Crushing men and spirit under foot.

Cozy told himself many times a mantra while locked down in the DU's darkened isolation:

Let me stay the coward in me.

Let me stay sane.

Man, one more year.

My prison home.

Anonymous quote

Tribute © Robert Lee Johnston 2016
Email: tributerobertleejohnston@gmail.com

CHAPTER TWENTY-ONE: PINK LACE

Lacey had been blue and down since the boys had been locked up.

They asked him not to visit and it really hurt him. Visitors get recorded by the jail and police which attracts heat none of them needed. Lacey worried for them all the time and tried to keep his mind busy.

Other than smoking pot, he lay off the acid, speed and pills for a spell. He was even slowing his drinking down to half a bottle a day. Lacey had steered clear of chemicals and substances. Except one. The coke. To him it was divine, clean and clear. He could still perform all the farm asked of him. The potent lines rendered him fully functional. The bag bequeathed to him to sell was mammoth, and the premium-quality powder far too lovely to be left alone. Selling little bits and pieces here and there meant he had someone to get high with. The town had no clue it belonged to the boys, and their being in jail removed them from the picture.

Pinky had been scoring some weed from Lacey. He noticed Lacey at the pub, drinking alone a lot more often the

Tribute © Robert Lee Johnston 2016
Email: tributerobertleejohnston@gmail.com

last few months. Until recently, Lacey had been partying hard, spending a lot of time drinking and smoking with the three lads, until prison beckoned.

Pinky was helping an old mate move fresh into the area, after a messy ending in their home state. Pinky was a gifted trouble diviner. He could sense the hidden; your secrets, the dark. He could tell by looking at you what drug you enjoyed; could estimate your worth and if your crop was a hundred strong or a handful of fatties. Pinky decided he'd stay in Tribute for a while and keep an ear to the ground, listening out for large, safe, easy jobs or, at the very least, for a few nice crops to pilfer. He saw firsthand how tranquil and soft the dope growers were around here. Passive, relaxed, non-aggressive, Bob Marley-loving, tree-hugging hippies.

He recalled the last job and the mess it became. No way could he go back to his home state, probably ever. A woman screaming and bleeding in his car's back seat as his boys pistol-whipped her. Her big, bloody mouth stirred up the boys, and somehow it got aggressive, sinister, and sexual. Her junkie husband, bound and beaten, in the boot, had Pinky in a calm panic of anticipation. The amount of cash and smack promised from the job was a lie. It all went to shit. Risks were taken. Pinky snapped, blew a circuit breaker. Tempers flared, voices were raised. Bodies disposed of. Pinky found killing the noisy, skanky-looking bitch and shutting her up satisfying. Nothing at all like he imagined. He played like a blooded lion cub with a fatally wounded piglet, with her scared, doomed, dreadlocked man. Pinky discovered a sweet taste for torture, and being the cause of terror and finality. He felt he absorbed his victim's divine powers. Pinky cut deeply into the skin of his victims to release maximum energy. His favourite part of the gruesome, dragged-out process was 'defacing' and removing teeth and fingers from the bodies. The boys in his little operation noted his transformation. They sickened at the

Tribute © Robert Lee Johnston 2016
Email: tributerobertleejohnston@gmail.com

strength of his demonic possession, the normality and easy going comfort of his debasement. Pinky found himself plotting more and more situations and jobs where death would be the ultimate outcome. He promised himself to not hurry next time and to savour every second.

All the work he had put into his home city had paid off. All the opportunities, connections and haunts were his to exploit. He never had to go far from home to find prey. Time to start again. Tribute and its small-time towns had never seen the likes of him and his boys. Perhaps down south a bit might provide a better base. He would do an annual visit to the Tributes of the world when all those hippies' fat crops were ready to harvest.

He told his friend, 'The hippy chicks round here look like they could use a decent fucking, and a real man rooting them for a change. Their men, shit, all look like badly clothed, dirtier versions of Cat Stevens. There's little or no resistance here. Not one of these fuckers will risk their children, or his or her beaded, peace-loving neck for a hill of dope. It's amazing how fast these fucking cowards give up their crops. It may not be as lucrative here as back home. But I'm sure a decent living can be made with a bit of elbow grease.'

Out of the blue, out back in the Middy pub's beer garden, Lacey offered him a line after sharing a fat joint. Pinky's eyes grew when he tasted the coke. 'That's fantastic coke! How much is it? Is there any around to buy, mate?'

Pinky, straight off the bat, seemed all right to Lacey. He was a similar age, had a dry sense of humour and came across as staunch and straight shooting. So Lacey gave him a couple of points. 'There's a bit about.'

Pinky now made it a priority to know Lacey closely. For a few months he dropped in now and then, unannounced, to just hang out, joke, smoke and score dope and coke. He never revealed his true intent. Casing the joint. He cunningly avoided questions, and let the gear speak through the man.

Tribute © *Robert Lee Johnston 2016*
Email: tributerobertleejohnston@gmail.com

Lacey was smart enough to not mention names, bent enough not to notice all he spoke, and lonely enough to say it all over time. Pinky played patiently, knowing in his gut that this was something bigger than a few plants. His visiting became regular and arranged, and each time coke appeared. Pinky even helped out now and then on the farm and loved the idea of no visible neighbours. He let Lacey befriend him and figured after a while that the boys were Lacey's secret. It was a game to Pinky, a huge jigsaw puzzle, and eventually he grew bored, impatient, and dangerously covetous. He wanted all Lacey's coke, all his smoke and all the owners' names. He tried asking him straight out one day. Lacey baulked at telling him. 'Pinky, no one needs to know any names, mate. I'd never mention names, man.'

All that day they had been drinking. All that day Pinky gnawed away, trying to confirm the clues. An awful power took him over. Pinky attacked and beat stubborn Lacey with closed, frustrated fists. He tied him, knocked out, to a chair. Woke him, questioned and tortured him at length with power tools and boiling water. Lacey gave Pinky toes, scalding tears, blood, teeth, fingers, cash, the coke. And not a single name.

Lacey gave him directions to his crop. 'Take it all, man.'

Pinky would take it all, but the cocaine called repeatedly to Pinky. The money it could bring begged his very soul. The wanting, need and hunger grew. He wanted to know how much coke his source had.

In anger, he stole one more important thing. Pinky fired Lacey's own rifle into the man's back. Pinky found a can of fuel and doused the firewood beside Lacey's pot-belly stove and torched the joint. Lit it up. Pinky drove Lacey's four-wheel drive, unobserved, to the patch, and with a cane-knife harvested every bud Lacey had grown while his torn body and his fine wooden house burned nightmare-orange.

Lacey wouldn't give anyone up. Pinky suspected the coke owners must be personally close to him. He always

Tribute © Robert Lee Johnston 2016
Email: tributerobertleejohnston@gmail.com

talked about those kids. Lacey seemed to trust them. The funeral might lure the powder owners out. If not, he would return to Tribute when the little shits get set free. And see for himself if the hot spring of cocaine he magically divined flowed once more when the boys were emancipated and their extremely short-lived liberation renewed.

He would watch Tribute from afar, smoke, snort and sell the pot and coke he had freely accumulated, bum around and then find: The Source. The kilos of powder he stole from Lacey would fund him easily a few years, so he settled in for a long-playing strategy. He waited as impatiently as the three boys for their release. In further proof of his theory, Pinky noticed the local coke scene had died and burnt out with Lacey.

Lacey's six-week pregnant lady found the smouldering remnants of the house and his charred body four days later when he hadn't been in touch. Detectives soon found evidence of foul play. The next day they visited his three young friends, locked in their cages, all three in separate special interrogation cells with the ability to record the interviews. First thing in the morning.

A tired, cranky Cozy saw the two detectives and teased them. 'This had better be fucking good, ladies. Aerobics Oz Style is on the fucking telly, and you two closeted trannies are keeping me from my girls.'

One told him, 'Your drug-dealing, scumbag, dropkick of a mate's been murdered.'

Cozy was awake now. 'What? You're going to have to be a little more specific, you semi-hard, sad, wasted flog. Cos in your eyes, all me mates are drug-dealing, scumbag, dropkicks, you pus ridden fucking toe-rags.'

'Still got your big mouth, even in here, eh, Cozy?'

'Fuck the pair of you. Faggots fuck. How's your fucking form? Who the fuck tells a bloke a mate's died like that. Who was it, you fuck?'

Tribute © Robert Lee Johnston 2016
Email: tributerobertleejohnston@gmail.com

'Lacey. He's been shot, and he was tortured beforehand.'

'Jesus fucking Christ! Lacey?'

'Cozy, do you know who could have done this?'

'You … You're kidding? You're like dingoes, you pack of dogs. There's never one around when you fucking need it.' Cozy pleaded, 'Where the fuck were you blokes? You're like flies on shit if some poor bastard wants to smoke a spliff on Friday night. Murder some poor fuck and youse turn to water and turn to the very same spliff smokers you fucked over for answers. You're fucking useless, you mob.'

'So, you don't know?'

'I'm in jail, you morons. How the fuck would I know? You're the fucking detectives. It wasn't me or them two blokes. Now, cheers, and if that's it, fuck off!'

The detectives had no idea who had done it. The boys had no idea who had done it. Lacey was buried six or seven months into their sentence. They never saw him again. They hated themselves, because if one of them had 'given him up' he would be beside the three. In prison. Still alive. That wasn't their way, and their way felt all wrong right there in hopeless, empty, cold cells. Cozy decided he would never tell the boys who Lacey had really found and handed in. All three of them could forever share his story, true or not.

Pinky had gotten away cleanly with murder. Pinky's low profile around Tribute, and the shutting down of the operation that had landed all the lads in jail, left Lacey without any narks and cops watching or recording his every coming and going.

The boys wanted answers and tried to guess or figure who they knew that could, would, and wanted to kill Lacey. No name came to their dumb-struck minds.

But they knew the drum was to blame.

Tribute © Robert Lee Johnston 2016
Email: tributerobertleejohnston@gmail.com

CHAPTER TWENTY-TWO: "BUFFALO SOLDIER"

Bob Marley – Song Title

Lacey had bought the boys a brace of bikes.

Bugs's twin-cylinder bike finally burst into life after kicking away a bunch of times. He was pulling a fighting face at Cozy, through his beaten, black, open-faced helmet.

Between kicks he'd engaged the choke, pushed it back in, fiddled with the throttle and checked that the fuel cock was turned to on. Sweat beaded down his face. It was a great little bout. He smiled at his brothers when, victoriously, she finally burst to life. Cozy grinned inwardly at him and effortlessly thumbed the starter on his Kwakka's handlebars, and then pretended to wipe sweat off his brow.

Bugs shook his head. 'Boo, bro. It ain't a real bike if it ain't got a kicker.'

He took off in a haze of spent gasses, trumpeting exhausts, and a smoking rear tyre, having, of course, the last word, and gave Cozy no chance to respond. The two boys on their bikes were right behind him.

Tribute © Robert Lee Johnston 2016
Email: tributerobertleejohnston@gmail.com

For years they had planned today. This very ride, while the world happily spun without them in their shared, suspended animation, earning their thirty cents each day. The sun, the air and they themselves were just how they had envisioned and dreamt it. Lacey had the bikes lying around and his lady gave them to the boys as payment for the promised holiday. Bugs had an old Sporty. Cozy and Kenny had Kwacca nines, oldies but goodies. Lacey had reconditioned every bit on them. The boys kept getting in trouble while imprisoned: contraband, drugs, alcohol, fighting; the list was long and varied. The three couldn't jump parole, because parole was denied. They had lost any good behaviour earned, and did all their time, released with remissions and no authorities telling them what to do, where to be, and what pot to piss in. That was most important: no random parole drug testing for each of them to fail dismally.

They were free completely once more.

They had dreamt of days like this. They were fulfilling promises made while locked down. They couldn't believe they were actually doing it. Everything smelt fresher, looked more colourful, and felt so fast. The long-incubated plan involved their favourite forest mountain-range ride. Three hundred or so steep corners of varying degree and camber. Up or down, it was both fun and challenging. Anyone could go fast in a straight line. Around here, individual mettle and ball circumference was tested by the pace at which you attacked corners. Truck wrecks, old bike carcasses; Simon's old Torana, written-off four wheel drives, and all sorts of busted-up vehicles were strewn over the hillside. In the gullies. Or perched precariously in the trees, unable to be recovered because of the deep ravines and steep, impenetrable mountain sides.

Countless one-vehicle accidents earned the road a begrudging, healthy respect from every local, each of whom had had at least one unforgettable incident on the twisting

range. Tourists often came unstuck on the very first tight right-hander. The brutal deceleration from a hundred to thirty klicks must be strictly adhered to. If you were racing you could hit a hundred and fifty here and there, and guarantee your passengers wouldn't say boo. They would be far too busy trying not to shit themselves or distract the driver. Most newcomers to the road spewed up once motion sickness kicked in.

The boys had known this road and every corner since they were kids. They would take their pushies down it; go-carts, skate boards, shopping trolleys. Shit, if it had wheels the kids threw it down there. Kenny was the best rider amongst them. Since he was a kid he could wheel-stand any bike, pedalled or motorised, all day long, for kilometres. He could get on a rusty bails gate and make it wheel-stand. Cozy always tried to emulate his smooth style, but today all of them would take it easy. Rusty and out of practice, they hadn't been down the range for yonks. Cozy was watching the road, concentrating hard, when Kenny frightened the crap out of him, shooting under Cozy at speed. So fast Cozy nearly leapt off his bike with fright. He was on his back wheel, going around a mild corner, showing off, with both his feet in the air, waving at Cozy with his right boot. Kenny never took his eyes off him, nodding his helmet the whole time, steering by what appeared to be perfect memory.

Various beaches and pubs were on the cards today as they pulled up at a lookout and sparked up a tasty joint.

Cozy asked Bugs, 'Did you see what Kenny was doing? Did you see that shit?'

The first major stop, since the sun was shining, was a large, fresh-water swimming hole. Good for a perv, a chance to get out of hot, heavy jackets, and have a relaxing session. For the rest of the day they cruised beaches, checked out pretty women, teased each other, laughed, and carried on like pork chops. It was the first time they had all been together outside of prison. They discussed the pen, yarns,

Tribute © Robert Lee Johnston 2016
Email: tributerobertleejohnston@gmail.com

jokes, inmates, shits of screws, and good-bad experiences. Tears were shed and anger expelled. Cozy caught up on all the local shite he hadn't heard, since they had been out in his absence. They were glad to be together once more. No amount of lovely honeys in bright, tight bikinis could stop their minds and stomachs from turning to food and drink. Real food. Tasty, real alcohol, that wasn't made in some alcoholic inmate's toilet or, even worse, made from stashed, fermenting water melons, soiled with Fruit Box poppas.

Cozy was craving. 'Fuck, I could murder a T-bone steak and some Wild Turkey, boys.'

Inmates don't get T-bone in prison. The bone makes a perfect shank.

'Well, let's kill some T-bone!' Kenny smiled. 'And ravage a drink!'

'Gobble, gobble,' Bugs tastily admitted, licking his lips.

They stumbled out of one of those all-you-can-eat joints and marvelled at how they could make a buck when three, young, hungry-gutted stoners ate everything in sight, even securing fruit for later.

Cozy missed freedom and its sweet touch, these boys, on these sorts of days. An after-eats bunger hit the spot. A beach pub with lots of friendly, smiling lovelies swimming about and getting sun made for good viewing and an enjoyable day. They discussed and chewed the fat about their futures at length.

Kenny, defiant, was going full steam ahead with growing the huge crop he had dreamt about all through his lagging. Bugs and Cozy needed some space. They loved the new freedom but needed time to adjust and recover, time to purge some anger. Kenny knew one place that could heal all and perhaps ease the boys' minds. The jungle. They knew a river, wild and remote, with absolute freedom. They would sell the bikes to stock up and get a half-decent four-wheel drive. They found a fine spot, a million miles from anyone, within Australia's deep north. They left the truck, taking all

supplies in on foot. Several trips were needed which they did once a day. It took three hours to get to the new, rudely constructed camp from where the boys stashed the truck, and it was a two-day dirt-track drive to any form of civilisation. A beautiful, fresh-water river fed into the mighty Pacific. The river was close enough to the camp to access, and far enough away to stay safe from the massive crocs. Fifty metres was the trusted Aussie norm. Apparently croc's get to forty-nine metres and can't be bothered to take another step. They decided, 'Fuck that bullshit. A hundred must be twice as safe, eh?'

In preparation they had brought shitloads of rice, a rifle, and some seeds for vegies. The rest would be hunted and gathered.

Bugs had packed his old camping guitar and a pack of cards for entertainment. But no jocks. The boys stashed two clean, empty paint tins full of coke, hoping it would be enough. And a couple of fat pounds to see their lungs through until the crop started producing. Most importantly they brought along a radio and some batteries in the hope that they could access a radio station. The only one they could find was from New Guinea. They had packed shovels, pickaxes, hoes, and a hand-operated rotary hoe. Three best mates, sharing life, nature and freedom. Bloody perfect. In no time they had a waterproof camp and had cleared enough scrub to be comfortable. Then they started clearing the crop site, with the help of good hard work and lots of alcohol. Fishing and hunting they did in their down time. The recovering recidivists had the whole coastline to themselves.

Cozy had brought tonnes of salami, cordials, gravy powder and sauces. Along with a recurve bow, and all the arrows and accessories it needed. Their first hurdle was the discovery that only one mozzie net had been packed. They drew straws for it. Cozy secured the mozzie net. Life was peachy for him. Loads of parrots, fish, wildlife, and a mozzie-free sleep every night didn't hurt one little bit.

Tribute © Robert Lee Johnston 2016
Email: tributerobertleejohnston@gmail.com

Along the coast there were barramundi and mangrove jack to fish. Crabs and plump, young, succulent oysters were plentiful. The wild boar and bulls were healthy, fat buggers. So the boys chowed down on those now and then to satisfy pork and beef cravings. Compared to prison they were eating like kings. They wisely rationed tobacco, tea, coffee, and sugar, and, most importantly, the many cases of spirits that had to see them through.

The boys preferred to hunt pigs with the bow. On one occasion the rifle came out and got a thorough work out. Thirty pigs had meandered into camp, raiding it en masse at a dark three or so in the morning. They destroyed everything in the pitch-black night. The drunk, sleeping boys were alarmed at first, waking up to panicked, chaotic pigs, squealing their lungs out, grunting and shit fighting. The pigs went every-which-way in fright as Kenny let two shots rip into the air, through the roof, from his thirty-thirty.

Their only link to society was their trusty little radio. They soon nicknamed the station 'the gluck-gluck channel'. Transmitting in pidgin, the boys only ever understood one out of every five or so words. 'Gluck gluck gluck, rain, eh. Gluck gluck gluck, lots, eh.'

They endured bad reception, and hours of sizzling-bacon-sounding, crackling entertainment, trying to figure out the latest news. The best part was they loved Bob Marley up there, so 'Buffalo Soldier', 'Exodus', and 'Get up, Stand up' were often played.

Within three months, their card playing/cheating and hunting skills were greatly refined. As were their beards, and musky body odour. They bathed in a croc-free, crystal-clean stream every day. But they had forgotten soap, which made it hard to shift the fish oils, animal oils, and stubborn fats that had slowly built up. They felt and smelt like cavemen of modernity.

They never went short of damper, fish or meat. Bugs and Cozy decided to hunt a mickey bull, a clean skin the two

Tribute © Robert Lee Johnston 2016
Email: tributerobertleejohnston@gmail.com

had seen around. A freakishly big bull, untainted by humans, mad and powerful. The lads could almost taste the thick, fresh steaks. They stalked and tracked him for three days. Though now and then the feisty big fella, he hunted them. He chased them both up trees within the scrub. Sometimes they panicked, with no choice but to dive, scared shitless, into heavily croc-infested waters. With Mickey bellowing, huffing, and crashing through the bush behind them. He stared them down from the bank, waiting for a croc to finish them off. The boys figured it was a pretty fair fight, and the bull seemed up for it and relished the challenge. Cozy was up for the challenge of putting some relish on Mickey. A bit of gravy and damper would be just lovely, he thought.

Mickey protected his territory more like a bull lion than a lone bull. Two arrows were lodged painfully into him, one from each of the hunters. Cozy's next was a clean lung-shot. It seemed to take hours for him to drop, weak enough for them to cut the big fella's throat and put him out of his misery. He was out to kill them, Mickey was. Right to the kicking, thrashing end. Bugs and Cozy felt worthy and vindicated. Alas, they could only carry and store safely so much meat. It was a shame, and morally embarrassing, to leave so much of their fine, brave adversary there on the dusty earth. They both, in their own way, thanked Mickey for the hunt, the fight, and the fresh food he provided. And for the mighty fine challenge he delivered. The mallee scrub fed humbly on the rest of him. Later, back at the camp, with content stomachs full of sweet, tender, juicy red meat, all three respectfully thanked the god of hunting, the god of great bulls, for the beef from their warrior beast.

Slowly but surely the camp ran out of fishing tackle, bullets and arrows. The pork and beef diet was getting old and boring. Fish was again back on the menu.

They had two hooks left, a large one and a tiny one. Thank God they were alone, because three lads tiptoeing and skipping through the tulips, catching insects to bait up

Tribute © Robert Lee Johnston 2016
Email: tributerobertleejohnston@gmail.com

the small hook to catch a small fish to put on the big hook, must've looked strange. They put the tiny critters into their pockets and made their way to the river. Kenny had a busted pump to fettle, so stayed behind. When Cozy and Bugs arrived at the choicest fishing hole there was, on the other side of their thin, brown estuarine river, a five-and-a-half-metre croc.

'Jesus Christ!' two scruffy-beards whispered when they saw just how big he was. His head looked like a lumpy, forty-four-gallon drum. With lots of bloody big yellow teeth in it. He was a giant snappy-saurous, and judging from the huge gash and large scars on his head, he'd been getting hit with a propeller.

Both could plainly see blood pooled around his head from what looked like a fatal cut. It looked as though he just managed to crawl up the bank, only to drop dead. To be sure he was dead, Cozy threw heavy river stones and wet branches at him, clocking him in the head a couple of times. No reaction, no movement. Didn't even blink.

'Poor bastard. He's fucked,' Cozy mumbled through his unkempt beard. Bugs moaned about the wasted meat and leather. Seeing he was out of commission, they set about catching lunch.

Bugs put an insect on the small hook and caught a little mullet to cut up for bait. He then tied and baited the larger hook. He threw it into the deep hole, immediately getting bites.

'Hey. A couple of little bites.' Then, 'Shit! I'm snagged. Last hook, bro.'

They drew straws to see who was going in to fish it out. Bugs keenly searched his opponent's face for any hint of which straw to pick. He chose and shook his head. 'Arghh, be fucked. How do you keep doing that? I don't think I have ever won this bloody game once.'

Bugs took off his shirt and eyeballed the dead croc for a second, and then his short straw. He smiled sarcastically at

Tribute © Robert Lee Johnston 2016
Email: tributerobertleejohnston@gmail.com

Cozy and threw another decent, fist-sized rock at the croc, just to be sure. Shaking his head, he called Cozy a 'lucky, arsy bastard. Fuck it! I don't want to get my shorts wet.'

He dove naked into the deep, murky hole. The croc lay motionless. Bugs surfaced and took a deep breath, duck-dived, flashing his white arse, and kicked himself under. That big, old-man-emu bull croc just exploded into furious life. Bigger than life. He propelled his huge, killing body with great effort into the water. He was, all of a sudden, very much alive. It was a hell of a thing for Cozy to witness, to see that much beastie airborne. That much animal desperate to live, desperate to catch, desperate to kill. Cozy struggled to find his tongue to yell, 'BUHOFUCSHIARGGHHJESGITYAOUTUGS!'

Something like that. He was metaphorically shitting one of those, big, fat, rectangular clay house bricks. The dirty mongrel had been playing dead. The big fella was hunting. Hunting Bugs. For a second, Bugs had assumed his mate had dived in to help him when he heard the water's surface break. Then he thought, That splash, man, it's a lot heavier than Cozy! Bugs, panicking, surfaced as fast as he could.

Cozy was wondering, What the fuck to do? He bellowed, throwing a rock or two into the water, trying to distract the desperate, hungry brute. 'Ah shit. I'm going to have to go in.'

As Cozy was about to dive in and distract the great beast, Bugs appeared. Breaking the water's surface, he was climbing an imaginary ladder. More dolphin than human. He filled his lungs with air as the first giant wave from the croc's ripples went over his head. His eyes widened as water surged over him. He thought it was the monster's mouth opening up, and he didn't want to look back to see.

'FUCKING HURRY UP, MAN. MOVE YOUR ARSE. MOVE IT, MATE.'

Tribute © Robert Lee Johnston 2016
Email: tributerobertleejohnston@gmail.com

Cozy ran on the spot, air swimming with both arms, head down. The croc surfaced. He generated speed using his tail and his feet. His whole body wriggled. The old fella was atop the water like a little frilled-neck lizard running across a puddle. Except this lizard wasn't little, didn't have a frill, and this wasn't a puddle. The desperately injured, starving bull gained quickly on Bugs. Bugs's muscles, and each and every one of his many sphincters, started fast-twitching and straining all at once. The second and third smaller ripples moved across Bugs's body, over his head. The bank he was frantically swimming for wasn't steep or large. In one Olympian effort he somehow shot out of the water, commando rolled as he hit the ground, and then got up running, all in one fluid, in-the-nuddy movement. Cozy was desperately watching all this, gauging speed, distance and all possible outcomes. Planning in panic how to get Bugs's nude, freshly ripped arsehole out of the croc's mouth and to a doctor.

Bug-A-Lugs was out.

Cozy's planning ceased.

'You beat a bull croc. You fucking beat a bull croc!'

They both legged it. They didn't know where. Just fast as they could, and never looking back. They figured pork and beef weren't that boring after all. They hugged best mates' hugs. You know the ones: when you're safe, after one of you nearly gets eaten alive by a modern-day dinosaur.

All Bugs could ask, puffing, was, 'Holy fuck, man, did that just happen? Shit. Is all of me here?'

He and his mate patted and checked. His naked limbs and digits were still intact. Relieved and happy to be alive, he said, 'That cunning bastard.'

'That was legendary swimming, man. JEEZ-US. I thought I lost you, Bro-nads. Thank fucking whoever, that hungry-gutted, greedy bastard wasn't already under the water when you jumped in.'

Tribute © Robert Lee Johnston 2016
Email: tributerobertleejohnston@gmail.com

They laughed nervously with relief. They had been lucky and stupidly naive.

Bugs had an idea. 'We should write a book about all this crap. No, man, I got a better idea. We should write half a book each and join them together. You know, see what the other sees. I might have thought I looked cool as cool can be one time, while you saw nothing cool, no coolness, no cucumber. You know what I mean?' He was excited. 'But it's got to be something brilliant, universal. Nothing gammon, you know what I mean, eh?'

Cozy smiled. He knew what he meant. He got it.

They promised each other to write half an awesome book each.

Arriving back at camp, where Kenny was fixing the pump, Bugs mimed, with much noise and vivid animation, what had just happened.

'Fuck you Mary Lou!' exclaimed Kenny. 'What the fuck are you doing swimming with a big old lizard just laying there?'

The rest of the time there passed uneventfully. The whole trip they spoke at length about John Henry, Stirrup, Jen and Lacey. They shared stories, unknown or forgotten, from different perspectives. They discovered a lot about their dear, departed friends, sharing their individual stories and memories. Fresh, hot tears were shed, when something hit home hard.

They hoped Evie was okay down south. When the boys got incarcerated she decided to split. Cozy was glad they got locked up. It gave her the space she needed, and an excuse to get out. Evie loved them all and hated going, but she knew they were tragically broken, and their futures were looking wasted. She needed to get away from them, and from Tribute. The deaths of John Henry and Jen were so rapid fire that her grieving for Henry was interrupted by Jen's death. The three boys getting tossed in jail, and then Lacey getting murdered, pushed her over the ragged edge.

Evie visit them all once a month. It was terribly painful for her. When she left the prison she was completely alone, all the time. The boys at least had each other. As she sat in the courtroom that day in the midst of her boys, part of her snapped and was forever destroyed. She knew Cozy would say something to the judge, and try as usual to be blameless, unaccountable and irresponsible. She was tired of the boys living in a vengeful state and blaming everyone else for their calamities. Her heart wasn't like theirs, but the brothers were rubbing off on her. She didn't want the world to win and beat her, as it had done Jen and the boys.

She thought how ashamed Henry would be, if he were alive to witness that day in court. She often wondered if he would have been right there with the boys in that dock, and locked in that hellish prison. Evie knew in her heart of hearts that he would not have. If her Henry had been around, he would have provided the common sense those three boys lacked. Revenge and hatred had distorted all their minds. They never once fought it. She thought, If they put the same effort they put into growing and selling dope into forgiving or moving on, they would be the most brilliant young men. But in her heart she knew the three would never change. Like the scars on Bugs's and Cozy's backs, the rips and hurt cut too deeply. Just like carnage on their skin, Evie could see the trauma inside them. It was even messier than the mangled roadmaps of torture splayed out over their bodies. Evie sent all three a letter, saying she needed to get out and go to university. If they wanted to follow her they could stay with her, anytime. She let them know how much she loved them, and wished them luck when they got out. She asked them to wish her luck, and apologised for not saying goodbye in person. 'It would be far too hard, boys. You know? I'll see you lot soon enough.'

One of them never saw Evie again. The boys felt sad and lost when reading her letter. Part of Cozy rejoiced and smiled for her. Evie was the toughest and most determined

of them all. Evie would become a no-nonsense human being, a proper person. An unaffected, sweet, powerful woman who was still capable of loving and, most importantly, of being loved. Cozy knew it. They all did. Evie couldn't watch another of them die.

After that trip away the three of them would never know freedom like that again. Best mates surviving off the land. Cozy smiled at the memories and lessons that wild river had bestowed on them. If there was a Bugs, Kenny, and Cozy heaven, and they hoped there was, it was there.

Tribute © Robert Lee Johnston 2016
Email: tributerobertleejohnston@gmail.com

CHAPTER TWENTY-THREE: MATHILDA MY

DARLING

She purposely looked into Cozy's eyes and gently held her gaze there.

Instantly he felt visible to her. There was an awkward moment when she tried to look beyond his eyes into him. Cozy looked over a shoulder, half expecting her large, handsome boyfriend to be standing impatiently behind him. No one was there, except the many customers eating their counter-meal lunches. Both had finished theirs already, and when he looked back to her she smiled knowingly. She seemed to know what he was thinking.

'You know your eyes turn bright green when you're nervous?'

He smiled freely and without inhibition. 'I know. It's weird, eh? They change colour depending on my mood.'

She bit her lip. 'They're changing as I watch them! Turning bluey-green and getting bluer.'

'So strange, right?'

'No! Not at all. It's wonderful. I've never seen eyes do that before. I like them. They're hypnotising me.'

'Ha, I'd need to know your name to do that.'

When she laughed, she got even cuter.

'I'm Mathilda. Do I hypnotise you?'

Cozy nodded and thought, God, even her name's cute.

'G'day, Mathilda. I been under your spell since you walked in and sat with your lunch at my table.'

She spoke like a ghostly magician. 'Tell me your name.' Then she returned to her normal voice. 'Since I have you in my power.'

'I'm Cozy.'

'What was that?'

'My name's Cozy.'

'Cozy?'

'Yep. I'm Cozy.'

'What's your last name, Cozy?'

'It's a silly one.'

'Go on, don't be shy.'

'Withazed.'

'Cozy—Withershead?'

'Nah, "with a zed".'

'Oh, Cozy Withazed.'

'Yep, that's me.'

'Pleased to meet you, Cozy Withazed. You have the most amazing, friendly eyes I've ever seen!'

He shook her hand. 'Good to meet you, Mathilda.' Her hand was cool, small and strong. It looked fragile in Cozy's busted, clumsy paw.

'I can usually read people. You know, if they're good or bad? By looking into their eyes. Yours, Cozy, stop me from seeing too deeply with those colour changes. They distract me. I can't see what's going on behind them. It's like peacock feathers or an opal in the sun. The colour draws your eye to an illusion while something's … hidden. Oh, I'm sorry, Cozy! I don't mean to be rude. I've had a few wines

Tribute © Robert Lee Johnston 2016
Email: tributerobertleejohnston@gmail.com

and tend to think out loud and yammer on when I'm a bit pissed!'

Cozy smiled awkwardly.

'I'm curious, Cozy.'

'About what?'

'Just, what they have seen to be able to do that.'

He had to break eye contact. He hadn't ever thought of it that way before. He was lost in thought, a little anxious. Cozy suddenly felt ugly under her gaze.

'Hey!' She distracted Cozy with a sweet tone, putting her hand on his arm. 'I didn't mean no harm, Cozy.' She punched his arm, grinning. 'Shit, you should see your eyes. Green like a jade jungle they are now.'

She moved closer to admire them. Cozy was thinking, Shit! She smells good as well.

She leaned in, her tiny hand on his chest, and whispered in his ear, 'Cozy?'

'Yeah.'

'What colour do your eyes change to when you're about to cum?'

Holy shit. He was too dumb founded and surprised to answer.

'I could guess. I bet blue, bright blue. Don't tell me. I want to find out for myself.'

Her hand, resting on Cozy's chest, fit perfectly. She told him, 'Wait here a sec.'

She made her way to the bar, borrowed a pen and a coaster. Cozy noticed her light gait, the way she walked. She moved effortlessly, smoothly and gracefully.

He was telling himself, My God, she's fucking hot, smart, bright, funny. And she smells great. Do not fuck this up, Cozy. Be cool. You're cool. You're cool. Be cool. Cozy was spinning. She returned the borrowed pen, thanked the barmaid and playfully made her way to the table they shared. It was dazzling, mother nature in her finest form. Like watching a greyhound run freely, witnessing a nimble

Tribute © Robert Lee Johnston 2016
Email: tributerobertleejohnston@gmail.com

creature do what it was born to do. His mind froze once more. You're cool, you're cool, he reminded himself as she got closer.

'Do you live around here, Cozy?'

'Yeah, Mathilda.'

'Call me, Tilly.'

'Okay. Not far from here.' He pointed. 'That way.'

She nodded. 'Perfect. Here's my number and my name, in case you forget it.'

Cozy was physically unresponsive, still frozen solid. The handwriting on the coaster was beautiful, with love hearts for full stops and the dots on her i's.

'If you want it, that is? If you're not interested, or have a girl, I get it.'

'No way.' Smiling, he finally found his tongue. 'I was just hypnotised still a bit is all, Tilly. Brilliant.'

'Well, I got to run, Cozy. I'm so, so glad we met.'

Cozy stood and shook her hand, and walked her from the shared table to the footpath. 'Yeah, I'm glad too, Tilly.'

As she walked off she turned around and smiled. 'You better ring, Cozy. You said you would.'

'I will, Tilly, I promise. Catch you later.'

Cozy waved like a princess in a parade. What the fuck just happened? All day he could smell her. Her smile was honest and light and, Jesus, her body was sweet. She was so free and comfortable. She reminded Cozy of when Jim Morrison told a massive LA crowd, 'I'm gonna get my kicks, before the whole shithouse goes up in flames.' Mathilda, Tilly, looked like that sentence sounded. Perfect. He struggled to fill his mind with anything other than her. He went to training later and had no rhythm or timing. He wasn't present or in the now, and got belted a few times when sparring with Bernie.

'I need the night off, Bernie! I'm off tap. Not feeling it.'

'Righto, no worries, Cozy. Be good, son.'

He got to a phone and called.

Tribute © Robert Lee Johnston 2016
Email: tributerobertleejohnston@gmail.com

'I was just thinking about you, Cozy.'

'Hey, Mathilda. How's your night going?'

'Better now. I was bored, hoping you'd ring me.'

'I sort of had to call you. My head's been all over the shop since I met you earlier today.'

'It's nice to know you noticed. I'll give you my address. Come around.'

She opened the door. 'Hey, Cozy, come in. What have you been up to today?'

'I just knocked off boxing training.'

'You box?'

'Yep.'

'For how long, or did you just start this arvo?'

'Yeah, nah, since I was six or seven or so.'

'So young?'

'I guess. I figured, if I start young, I can retire early.'

'Oh, I see.'

'Is that bad? Did I just put you off me?'

She purred. 'You didn't put nothing off. In fact, you switched something on. Do you run a lot?'

'Sure do. Sixty kilometres every week.'

'Cool. I go for a run each day, maybe five klicks, if it's not raining. I used to run competition for the state, in high school.'

'That explains your legs. You kind of get used to running in the rain around here.'

'You should join me, Cozy, for a rainy run one day.'

'Righto. But you'll have to promise to go easy on me.'

'Ha, good luck with that! I'm a competitive bitch. Ha ha ha! I'm not above tripping, hair pulling or eye gouging and cat fighting. That's how I won all my races, you know.'

They cracked up laughing as she mimed scratching eyes out and head-locking some poor bitch. Or Cozy.

'You'd be right at home in the ring then I reckon, Mathilda.'

'Do you compete, Cozy?'

Tribute © Robert Lee Johnston 2016
Email: tributerobertleejohnston@gmail.com

'Yeah, I got a home fight on this weekend.'

'You look too friendly to be a boxer. And your face ain't all busted up.'

'I'm just lucky I suppose.'

'Aren't you afraid of getting hurt, or losing?'

'I like losing, Tilly.'

'What? I hate losing.'

'Everyone loses. Everything gets lost eventually, right? I'm just preparing for then, now.'

That caught her by surprise.

'Well, what are you scared of then?'

'You.'

She laughed. 'No, seriously.'

'I'm serious. Pretty women like you frighten the fuck out of me.'

She innocently batted her eyelids while fanning her face. 'Me? But I'm so fragile and helpless.' Then she hissed, exposing her claws.

Cozy got a laugh out of that. 'It's spunk and innocence I'm afraid of.'

'And so you should be, cos I'm going to tear you up, Cozy.' Her smile broadened. 'Maybe I could go and watch the fights this weekend. I hear there's a cute blondie fighting. Do you know him?'

Fuck she's funny, Cozy thought.

She asked Cozy, 'Why is it that old boxers are called punch-drunk bums, and old martial artists are called masters?'

'Cos they never get hit. Mostly they don't hop into a ring. Fighting is a young man's game. It's easy to be an old master, when you only have to break a board. It hurts more when it's a jaw that's getting broke.'

She sat beside him on her lounge, handing him an icy bourbon.

'What are you doing in Tribute, Mathilda?'

Tribute © Robert Lee Johnston 2016
Email: tributerobertleejohnston@gmail.com

'I'm studying to be a vet. And the farms up here have all the animals I love to work with.'

Cozy was impressed. John Henry wanted the same. She was cute, cool, funny and smart.

'I love it here. I love the rain, so I'm staying awhile.'

'Are you good at being a vet?'

'I suppose. I'd like to think so.'

'I'd have to ask the animals, right? Lucky for you they can't talk, or dob you in and complain too much, eh? After you doctor them.'

She raised her eyebrows high and smacked his leg. 'Oh, you cheeky bugger.' She made two fingers into a pair of scissors. 'I'll doctor you!'

She looked to Cozy like a rare, exotic orchid flowering in a barren field of ash.

'I'm glad you're here, Cozy. I don't really know anyone in this town.'

'Lucky for you. I kind of, sort of, know them all.'

'I've seen you with a bloke around town, with long, messy afro hair once or twice.'

'Oh yeah that's me mate, Bugs.'

She blinked exactly three times. 'Go on. How come you call him Bugs?'

'Everyone calls him Bugs here. I can hardly think of his real name. Not many know it.'

'Why Bugs?'

'Well, righto. Shit. Hmm. When we were little kids, tiny fellas, we worked on this farm, and the bloke that owned it used to get us to help him out, fencing and shit like that. We would, of course, piss outside in the paddock when we needed to go. One day this old fella, he pulled this thing out of his shorts and it was as big as our thighs. We both just stood there shocked, looking at his humungous knob. Bugs, asked him, "How'd you get …? How come your dick's so big?"'

Mathilda smiled in anticipation.

'"Truth is, boys," he said, "you got to eat lots of carrots. Every bloody day. The more carrots you eat the bigger your hammer will get. Eat plenty of carrots, boys."

'Bugs believed him for years.'

Mathilda laughed.

'So from that day forwards, till he was fourteen or fifteen, every time you saw him he had a carrot in his hand, pockets or school bag. He chewed on them all day, every day checking to see how much his knob had grown. For years his skin turned a deep orange.

'One day some bloke asked him, "Who the hell are you? Bugs bloody bunny with all your carrots!"

'He was five or six then, I think. And Bugs it's been from that day forward.'

That night Cozy and Mathilda got drunk together and slept in Mathilda's bed. They only kissed and sweet stuff like that. When Cozy left, she told him she would see him at the fights.

***

Tilly saw Bugs sitting in the crowd with a few spare chairs around him and extended her hand, a drink in the other.

'Hi, I'm Mathilda. A friend of Cozy.'

'G'day, Mathilda, I'm Bugs. Grab a seat. I've heard all about you.'

Kenny came back from the bar and pulled up a stump next to Bugs, his long black dreads hiding his face.

'Kenny, Mathilda. Mathilda, Kenny.'

They shook hands across Bugs.

'Call me Tilly. Good to meet you both.'

'You too. Is this the first time you've seen Cozy fight?'

'Yes, my first fight ever.'

'Well, you're in for a treat tonight, mate.'

Tribute © Robert Lee Johnston 2016
Email: tributerobertleejohnston@gmail.com

'It's a big crowd. Will Cozy be okay?'

Bugs choked on his JD. Kenny looked at Bugs. 'I never heard those two words in the same sentence when it comes to Cozy. I've known him since I was a pup. Cozy okay? Ha ha! He'll be all right.'

'He seems a little too nice, to be a fighter.'

Bugs nodded thoughtfully. 'Cozy'll be all right, you'll see.'

The crowd was anxious and getting louder.

'Are you all relatives?

'No, none of us have relatives,' Bugs explained. 'Here he comes.'

Everyone clapped Cozy's opponent as he made his way into the ring. Kenny yelled over the crowd to them both, 'This bloke's supposed to be good. An interstate champ. Cozy's going to love that.'

Mathilda was a bit off balance. She asked Bugs, 'You're all orphans, then?'

'Yeah, we're all orphans.'

'Cozy didn't mention that. And why did Kenny say Cozy would love that?'

'Cozy hates easy fights. For some reason good fighters make him feel worthy. He reckons it's no fun at all to take on false-hearted fighters.'

The noise after the bell rang was tremendous. Mathilda smiled at the sound and spectacle. She relaxed her distracted mind and decided to enjoy her newfound company.

'Fuck me dead, Bugs!' Kenny sucked in a breath as Cozy's opponent attacked. 'Fucking into him, mate. This bloke looks dangerous.'

Kenny was loud, Mathilda thought, but couldn't help laughing at his casual outbursts. When the bell rang they were all yelling Cozy's name and shouting. She exhaled, shaking her head after taking a mouthful of her JD, and joined Kenny's mood. 'Fuck!'

Tribute © *Robert Lee Johnston 2016*
Email: tributerobertleejohnston@gmail.com

Kenny nudged her across Bugs. 'Pretty good, eh?'

She grinned and nodded. She hadn't paid attention to fighting or fighters before. Cozy's eyes were now much meaner. Both fighters looked as though they knew what they were doing. She noticed how their feet were dancing and light on the sprung canvas. How smooth they looked, and how effortlessly their hands fired heavy lightning. It was polished. Russian ballet at its finest. Except that when those punches landed the sound echoed around the old wooden town hall. The sweetness of movement turned into savagery of an ancient kind.

Bugs yelled out, 'What a fight, man!'

Cozy's shoulders and torso were one, like a golfer's swing. Gloves whizzed past his head, half a dozen at a time, but his poor opponent couldn't land any cleanly or make solid contact. Every miss gave Cozy an opening. He was like a hungry vulture, greedily picking at the eyes, lips and choicest cuts of the still-breathing carcass. It was both brutal and delicate. She couldn't hear the crowd or other noises. Every part of her was in the fight.

The bell rang.

Her hearing jolted back and her muscles relaxed. The boys were on their feet, confident in their old friend. Mathilda yelled over the crowd to Bugs and Kenny, 'I don't want to blink. Cozy's a menace, isn't he?'

The boys laughed, and Bugs yelled toward the ring, 'You're a fucking menace, brother!'

The crowd, pissed as farts, saw the fight was a dead cert, and started chanting things like: Bore-it-up-'em, Typhoid Cozy! Ave-a-go-ya mug! You dirty grub! You're rat-shit! Knock him the fuck out, Cozy!

They were going rank, a rowdy gang of drunken corellas.

Mathilda thought out loud, 'They love him.'

In his corner she caught a glimpse of something not right, something raw. The shirt he was wearing was torn off

one shoulder, exposing half his back. It was tangling Cozy up so he quickly ripped it off and grabbed a towel from his coach to drape over his shoulders. Tilly got a second, focused look and struggled to make it out. She covered her mouth with her hand. She felt sick. The fight was over, and Cozy was now helping his opposite number off the canvas and walking him back to his corner.

Kenny, seeing her revulsion, explained, 'He's a bullwhip boy. He should be dead a hundred times over.'

'A what? But he's so sweet, happy. So easy going.'

'Cozy's fairly unaffected by it all,' Bugs said, 'cos he takes it all into that ring with him. He punishes the blokes he fights for it all. It's Cozy's boxing ring and he almost dares people to get in there with him.'

That was what his eyes hid. They were a maze to ... She couldn't imagine where. They're a sexy distraction, hiding what lies behind them.

'That's why his eyes change.' She had thought aloud again.

Bugs smiled. 'Yeah. His eyes are fucked up, man.'

'They're gorgeous, Bugs.'

He smiled and teased her. 'Yeah, but still fucked up.'

She was relaxing again.

Kenny shouted them, and fetched Bugs and Tilly another drink. Every time she closed her eyes she could see Cozy's ripped up back and neck. It was like when she'd looked out of a bright, sunny window and the image stayed tattooed in purple on the back of her closed eyelids. Her drink suddenly contained meaty bones. Her stomach turned.

'Do you boys smoke weed at all?'

They grinned.

'Just a little bit.' Kenny nodded his head, smiling approvingly. 'Let's burn one down, my friends.'

They went outside, behind the crowded hall, under a tree. The noise faded in the shadows when the lighter

Tribute © Robert Lee Johnston 2016
Email: tributerobertleejohnston@gmail.com

flashed. It was a yummy joint and it took away her nausea and cleared her mind.

'Thanks for the smoke, boys.' She passed it on. 'I needed that.' She tried to ask, 'How did ...? What was ...? Shit!' She didn't know where to start. 'How come he's called Cozy?'

Bugs explained. 'That's what they called him when he was found. Someone said he looked comfortable and cosy, and they decided that name was good as any.'

'And his last name?'

'His last name? It was just a misunderstanding with his paperwork.'

'Okay. He was found? Where did they find him?'

'In the jungle around here. On a path tourists use next to a waterfall.'

'Seriously?'

'Yeah. He was covered in the mulch, dirt, leeches and shit, laughing and giggling, left to starve and die.' Bugs passed the joint to Kenny. 'All the pigs and snakes and shit that would eat any baby. How long he was there only his mother knows. Some say an hour or two, some say days. The local abbos reckon the jungle's his mother, gave birth to him.'

It was all too much at once for her to comprehend or believe. She felt slightly ashamed of herself for not knowing.

Kenny passed the joint to her. He could see her discomfort. 'He's okay, but.' She shook her head as she exhaled the sweet smoke. She needed to confirm what she had heard.

'So you're all orphans?'

The boys agreed.

'Are you adopted?'

They both confessed no.

'Is Cozy adopted?'

Again no.

'How come?'

Tribute © Robert Lee Johnston 2016
Email: tributerobertleejohnston@gmail.com

She passed the roach to Bugs. He shook his head and told her to throw it. 'We got too old, eh. They all wanted newer models.'

'And you two have scars too?'

'Kenny dipped out, and me, yeah. Not nearly half as many as Cozy's got though. The fella that did it to us hated or, I suppose, loved how Cozy refused to bend or buckle. I folded pretty fast and never did offer much in the way of entertainment for the bloke. Cozy tells people all the time we had the same punishment. Truth is, I only got a few. He just hates, I mean, really fucking hates the fact I got them and not him. One of my lashes hurts him worse than a hundred of his. Cozy gets guilty cos he couldn't stop it from happening to me. He's got a protective streak, a sacrificial soul. Cozy himself don't mind pain. He gets torn up inside and can't bear seeing people he cares about hurting. That tortures him more than anything else.'

Kenny cut off any further response. 'Let's go inside, get some more drinks.'

They trundled off as Bugs caught their attention. 'Uh oh.' He flashed a grin. 'Stoned again.'

Bugs grabbed some drinks from the busy bar and the other two found their seats. Cozy's two trophies were sitting in one of them, alone and unattended.

'Another couple for the shed.' Kenny placed them on the ground.

Mathilda asked, 'What did you say?'

Bugs turned up with drinks. 'Shit they're nice ones, eh. It's a bloody monster that big one. He must've won fight of the night as well.'

'Has Cozy got a few?'

'Just a couple,' Kenny lied.

The shed housed far too many trophies and medallions to count. Only one stayed in the house. Cozy's very first fight-of-the-night trophy.

Tribute © *Robert Lee Johnston 2016*
Email: tributerobertleejohnston@gmail.com

Cozy joined his tribe. The boys slapped his back and hugged him to congratulate him. Mathilda kissed a shocked Cozy softly, right on swollen lips, and put her hands around his neck. Her lips tasted great. She came close and whispered, 'Hello, stranger.'

She winked at Cozy and offered him a sip of her drink. She wore a mini skirt and her long, hot, athletic legs revealed a tattoo, purple and azure. Half a dozen jelly fish gripped her thigh like the choker around her neck. They started at her ribs, but Cozy hadn't seen that part yet. Blueish tentacles explored her leg. It was the best tattoo Cozy had ever seen on a woman. Delicate, feminine. But deadly wicked, and dangerous at the same time. He reckoned it made her sexier.

He had to shift his thoughts. 'I'll just be a second.' Cozy went and fetched a drink and sat amongst them.

They chinked cups. 'He nearly fucked me.'

Everyone repeated the toast. 'He nearly fucked me.'

Cozy's opponent and his girl came over later, when his concussion had eased, and shared a drink with them. Cozy invited them for a session outside, where Cozy told him he was a good fighter.

'You won easily, Cozy. Your feet, man. I couldn't catch you. You kept cutting me off. And that fucking left hand of yours. Fuck! Knocked me clean out. I'm still sore. Have you thought of ever going pro, Cozy?'

'Yeah. Nah. Fuck that. I like fighting all you strangers. Pros do too much homework on you and make the fight stale. I just want to fight.'

He was perplexed. 'You mean you haven't watched or studied any of my fights?'

'Nah. Till tonight, I never heard of you.'

He was in shock. Then he saw some stray kids running round, playing with Cozy's trophies. 'Hey! Those kids there got your trophies.'

Tribute © Robert Lee Johnston 2016
Email: tributerobertleejohnston@gmail.com

'Yeah. I give them to the young fellas who lost their fights They'll be right.'

He realised what Cozy had said, before the kids caught his attention, and choked on his drink. 'Hang on. What? I watched every fight of yours I could get my hands on.'

'Watching you fight would ruin the surprise for me.'

'Do you even know what us amateurs and all our coaches call you? "The journeyman to the pro show." If anyone can beat you in your division, they are then, and only then, ready to turn pro.'

'True? I didn't know.' Cozy was proud to hear that. 'Did it help you? Watching my fights.'

The beaten fighter shook his beaten head. 'Fuck no! You fought completely fucking different to them, and changed your style to adapt to me. I got confused in there and just couldn't keep up with all the changes!'

'Fuck the videos. I knew your style within thirty seconds. A minute into it, I found your weaknesses and exploited them for the rest.'

He looked hurt. 'But you weren't even looking at me or my hands. You were looking at the ground. How did you slip my punches?'

'Your feet, dude. They give you up every time.'

'My fucking feet! You're kidding me?'

'It's just something I learned. And I didn't slip all of them, man. You tagged me plenty. That's a great right hand you got. A great fight, man. A real cracker. One of the best I had. You keep on training hard and you'll eat us all up.'

'Cheers, mate. But what about you, Cozy? How far do you want to go? You don't want to turn pro. You obviously don't give a shit about the trophies. I wouldn't let all those kids run around with any of mine. What do you want from this game, man?'

'I just want to hurt people.' He shrugged. 'It's the only thing I'm any good at.'

'I noticed that. How many fights you had, Cozy?'

Tribute © Robert Lee Johnston 2016
Email: tributerobertleejohnston@gmail.com

He looked at the boys, shrugging his shoulders. 'I don't know. Never really kept count. A couple of hundred, I guess?'

'And how many you lose?'

'Shit. I don't rightly know. Maybe thirty or forty. I lost twelve in a bloody row, once.'

They chuckle nervously at the thought of a losing streak. The yips.

'You been knocked out?'

'Not yet. Nearly, I think. Plenty of concussions but.'

'Fucking concussions. Mate, I hate them. Makes me spew every fucking time. I've had fifty fights, and thought I was experienced and knew it all. Fucking hell, no wonder I couldn't catch you. Couple of hundred! That's why you look so clean and uncut; no one catches you flush.'

'You're wrong man, so wrong. I'm cut. I'm beatable. Everyone's beatable. You could've won tonight. You just made the same mistake twice, is all.'

'What mistake?'

'You really want to know?'

'Hell yeah, I really want to know. Ha ha! What did you see?'

'It's simple really. Every time you throw a combo over four punches, you lose balance and rush your feet. They come together under your shoulders to try to regain your balance on punch five.'

'You picked my fault in two moves?'

'No. I saw the first time you did it.'

'What!'

'So I sucked you in to do it once more. I was surprised when you did it again. When I realised it wasn't a bluff, I pounced on you, brother.'

'Shit! Really? Arghh, man! Well, what are your weaknesses?'

'I'm not telling you that, fuck ya. You watched my tapes. You tell me.'

Tribute © Robert Lee Johnston 2016
Email: tributerobertleejohnston@gmail.com

'Well, my plan was to Roberto Duran you. You know, try and force you to brawl. And get sloppy.'

Cozy smiled inwardly. Silly move. He loved those fights, and that particular fighter.

'But you seemed to like it a little too much, so I tried boxing you. And got seriously out-boxed. Then I bounced, lost somewhere in between my two plans.'

'Watch my fights, mate. My feet, you watch them close. They'll show every mistake I make.'

Kenny gasped. 'You're telling him how to beat you. You're fucking mad, Cozy.'

Mathilda smiled to herself. Cozy truly wasn't worried about losing. The highly ranked fighter thanked the mob for everything, and all bid each other goodbye.

'It was good to meet youse.' Cozy wished him luck, and the fighters hugged.

When he was gone, Cozy told Tilly and the boys, 'Cool kid. Soon to be a great fighter.'

Tribute © Robert Lee Johnston 2016
Email: tributerobertleejohnston@gmail.com

CHAPTER TWENTY-FOUR: TO KILL A KILLER

The weed scene, locally, had become pretty ordinary of late. The unseasonal early rains had soured and moulded crops.

Everyone's girls were doing it pretty tough this year.

'Fuck.' Bugs choked, coughed and moaned. After exhaling his second cone of shit, his eyes furrowed as he picked the sack up and sniffed at the shithouse contents. 'Absolute fucking rubbish!'

Cozy and Kenny grinned in sympathy as he tossed it on the table.

'It's devil's cabbage!' He emphasised the last two words, making the boys belly chuckle at the disgusted look on his face.

'Better than nothing, BUG-A-LUGS,' Kenny shouted, and then repeated quietly, a hint of transient melancholy in his voice, 'Better than bloody nothing.'

'Fuck it, three in a row might work.'

'You're a sucker for punishment,' said Cozy.

Tribute © Robert Lee Johnston 2016
Email: tributerobertleejohnston@gmail.com

Bugs picked through the seedy, sadly cured, badly manicured, amateur excuse of a smoke for cone number three. He shook his head in obvious heartbreak.

'Got to drink lots of piss!' Kenny was loud. 'Otherwise, you'll get fuck all out of it.'

The table had gathered the usual paraphernalia. Each had piled a stack of the better buds in front of them. Cheap, rotgut bourbon filled their glasses. Bilge water really. Even with a bottle or two of Coke to mix in. Bugs took a great swill from his large glass, after coughing up a lung again, to drown out the foulness. Bowie finished, and Sky Hooks was the current choice.

Kenny asked Cozy, 'What are you doing later on?'

'Fuck all. Why?'

'You wanna come for a drive?'

'Where are you two off to?'

'To see old mate.'

'Who?'

'You don't know the bloke, Bugs. Cozy does.'

Cozy didn't know who, or what the fuck, he was on about. Kenny knew Bugs couldn't stand not knowing every single person they knew and every connection of theirs, while revealing none of his own. Even if the boys knew the person or the weed, he'd deny it, often dropping them off on the side of some road, on the way to some fella's place they all knew well.

He always reckoned, 'It's some new bloke. You two don't know him.'

'Bullshit!'

He thrived on it. Being the bloke that knew everyone appealed to Bugs. Cozy was trying to figure out who Kenny was talking about, while packing a cone. When Kenny winked at Cozy, the wink told him, We sucked this prick right in. Suck it, Bugs!

Cozy smiled to himself as it dawned. Bugs grew more and more anxious about their newfound fictional friend. It

was raining out and Cozy figured Kenny was bored, and Bugs was, after all, so much fun to take the piss out of.

Cozy paved the path a little thicker. 'That fella we met at the pub? With those filthy noggins? They were nice joints he blew us out with that night, eh? Shit, pity we bought this crap first. I would've bought that in a heartbeat if I hadn't done me dough.'

'Was it Vaughan?' Kenny lied through gritted teeth.

'Yeah, Vaughan rings a bell, mate.'

Bugs's animated bug eyes were on them. 'Who's this fucking Vaughan? I ain't heard of no Vaughan! You boys holding out on me? Boo!' Bugs grabbed the shitty bag of weed and, holding it up, made one hand into a pistol and pointed it at the bag of shitty dope. 'Tell me, or the gunja gits it.'

The boys were grinning inside. Bugs was pale.

'He's all right, I guess. I only met him the one time. Vaughan seemed okay to me. Cool lad.'

Kenny chimed in, lying, 'Man, I saw him at the butcher's a couple of days ago.'

'Oh yeah,' Cozy replied.

Kenny acted as though he'd just been smacked in the head by a steel pipe. 'Shit! I clean forgot. Now I remember, but. He had some sweet, sticky elbows of that yummy gear for sale. I just bloody remembered!'

Bugs nearly choked. 'What! I'm puffing on this crap while juicy, fat nugs and this Vaughan dude are out there? Just waiting for us?' He paused, got up and pretended he had a whip, simulating cracking in one hand, using his voice twice to imitate the crack. The other steering a dog sled. 'GO. GIT NOW. FASTER. MUSH, MUSH. FUCKING MUSH, YOU LAZY BASTARDS! AAAAGH.'

Kenny had started laughing, keeping it low down, and getting progressively louder in pitch and tone as it went on. 'You fell for it! I was just gammon you, Bro-Jack.'

Cozy was laughing as Bugs's brilliant, speedy rollercoaster, dipped and surged. He looked at Cozy and then Kenny, searching eyes for confirmation. Finding none. Then he cackled like a witch at midnight at their cheek. 'You cold, heartless bastards. You gammon bastards!'

He was hoping they had double-bluffed him.

Kenny saw the look and shook his head hysterically. 'No man!' He sharply extinguished any hope.

Bugs drew in a massive breath and admitted, 'You two fucking got me.'

Cozy flashed the lighter and grinning, lifted his bucket-bong of wretch. 'Fucking oath we did.'

Bugs asked Kenny, 'Can you give me a lift to the Middy?'

'Yeah, no worries. I'm a bit thirsty to. My tongue's so dry I'd lick pus out of a gangrenous camel toe.'

Once Kenny's four-door took off, Cozy knew he'd have an hour or so to himself. They'll bump into someone, for sure, he thought.

Cozy was still a bit sore from the weekend's fight. He lay on his bed and a tinge of despair lay with him. He was tired of boxing and fighting. He felt tight in his own skin. No family, no past, no future, no education, no secure career prospects. Uncertainty and fear riddled him. The only places he felt at ease, other than the jungle, were boxing rings, or seedy, low-down, shady joints. Cozy was sick to the guts of these dingy holes. Sick to death of his body. Sick of its scars, pains and aches. He wanted peace. Just a bit of it, a tiny taste. Cozy also wanted a shot at normality, despite it all.

Mathilda was visiting her home city to drop in on family and to celebrate her success for passing this year's final exams and graduating. Tilly and Cozy had bonded fast. Cozy could let his guard down around her. Mathilda learned all about Cozy's youth. Sensing her kindness, he confessed everything to her. She never again considered his scars ugly. She accepted them as part of Cozy and even as somehow

Tribute © Robert Lee Johnston 2016
Email: tributerobertleejohnston@gmail.com

part of herself. Mathilda wasn't ready for kids so his inability to be a father was not a problem. Neither she nor Cozy applied pressure to get serious too quickly. They simply enjoyed an effortlessly wonderful collusion of heart and mind.

Cozy panicked now and then. He was not used to the emotions Mathilda showed him, or gently drew out of him. Falling in love was a frightening prospect, like walking a tightrope blindfolded, each blind, shaky step unsure. Love and its mystery confounded him and tested his ability to trust and be trusted. He knew nothing of love and would follow Tilly's lead, until he learned some chops.

Mathilda could shape affection and feeling from their atmosphere. She bathed Cozy in tenderness and exuded joy. Some days Cozy couldn't figure her out. He couldn't understand how she was raised. Where she came from, her belief in family support and infinite love, were difficult for the orphan to share.

To general observers or casual passers-by, the boys' lives seem self-inflicted. 'You had choices, mate' or 'There are other ways' left the lads dumbstruck at times.

Bugs asked the other two all the time, 'How do you answer that shit, man? There was no choices. No plan B or a getaway map.' Sweet girls didn't fancy this hardness. They wanted affection and soft attentions. The scars made it easy for girls and people in general to leave; it gave them a plausible excuse.

Restless, Cozy wanted out of the house with all the heavy rain about. The scrub would be empty and a couple of bodgy shelters would keep him dry. He found a few things along with some weed and a magazine, shoved it all in a garbage bag and ran the two klicks or so through the jungle to the empty shelter. He took off wet clothes and retrieved a stash of dope and the bucket he bought along with fresh dry clothes in it. He lay there for a bit as the bucket filled from the corrugations off the roof. Thinking and feeling pretty

rotten right to his core. His breathing was shallow and slightly pained.

He wondered, Could I stop fighting?

Then asked the forest, 'Who would I be without it? Does a fighter ever really stop? And would Mathilda like that bloke? A quitter.'

He cupped both hands under the water running into the bucket and drank deeply from his palms. The naturally chilled water always tasted sweeter in the rainforest. Then he sat the bucket on a table and organised a session. He panicked for a second when he couldn't find his lighter. Finally, after much swearing, he found it and smoked some sweet buds he'd stashed away for just these occasions, much superior to that shit they were choking on earlier. He savoured the sweet, nutty taste. The tannins pleased his fussy tongue. He reluctantly blew out the tasty cloud and repeated this a few more times. He lay on a table, dry and high, feeling vulnerable and weak. He was sick of his lifestyle, sick of hurting people. He read his magazine till he tired of it. His broken body slept on the table as his mind fidgeted and fussed, as loud as the rain on the tin roof. He tried to dream of a better place. A couple of hours later he woke and drank some more of that crystal rainwater and then had a few more buckets. He was thankful he'd packed a couple of mozzie coils, although they broke in transit. He lit the busted-arse shards to keep the hungry swarms at bay. Being here now, alone, was perfect. Scrub turkeys, pythons, tree snakes, mad crazy parrots, and forest birds went about their business unfazed by the downpour. Lizards bolted and then stopped on a dime, with brightly coloured tongues licking droplets from their faces. Huge spiders and their webs dripped, their web's invisibility foiled by the storm water. Poor things were soaked solidly. All the while teased and tortured by the rapid stimulation of their webs.

If Cozy were to kick a tree, he would quickly drown in wet possums, bandicoots and soaked tree kangaroos. The

Tribute © Robert Lee Johnston 2016
Email: tributerobertleejohnston@gmail.com

floor of this jungle was his crib, his nursery. She was, after all, the closest thing he had to a mother. His loving mother responded by wailing, as storm winds tore through her canopy. A truly ferocious wail, strong and uncompromising, stoic and proud, shifted the weight of all the old originals. The jungle was, for a moment, a single moving entity, dancing and swaying an ancient, elaborate indigenous dance. Leaves struck loose, falling like a confetti sun shower. A gentle rain of green flashes, yellows, browns and reds. She moved gracefully and was ruffled like a fine dress on a woman's body. A chorus of creaking timbers sounded earthy and reminded Cozy of a stiff leather jacket, complaining about movement. Cymbals clashed in the form of lightning and thunder. Broken and breaking branches accentuated the musicality as they snapped and crashed. The sound mesmerised Cozy. The sight hypnotised him so powerfully that strange tears of hot happiness ran down his face.

Cozy remembered Pops' words to him as a young boy. With his all-knowing, toothless smile he said, 'If you listen proper like, you'll hear her talkin to you.'

Cozy was listening. She was singing, howling, shrieking, raising goosebumps on his skin.

She's upset that I'm unhappy. She's showing me she was here and there is nothing to fear. She's with me and won't forget me.

Cozy thought of the secrets Pops taught him and yelled into the forest, against the howling winds, 'I love you, old man.'

Tears flowed. He took off his dry clothes and stepped naked, crisp and clean into the strongest smelling rain he had ever smelt. It was energising. It brought out the innocent and unguarded kid in him. The sweet water washed tears into his jungle's earth, binding them ever deeper. Cozy stepped back under cover as hungry mozzies tore into him. He used the webbing between thumb and

Tribute © Robert Lee Johnston 2016
Email: tributerobertleejohnston@gmail.com

forefinger like a squeegee to dry his body and then shook his head of long hair like some punk headbanger, or one of those shampoo add models. Maybe not as gracefully.

It was about 4.30 pm and he had another hour of daylight. Cozy loved it here, and understood Pops perfectly. 'Dis is da only place I can breathe proper, eh. No fuckin coppers in ere, no arseholes. Eberyting you be needin be ere, Cozy.' He was correct. Not many ventured in here without company or a guide. So only the jungle-savvy, cooler sort of people came here. Arseholes couldn't stand jungle.

Cozy enjoyed some more cones and watched his forest. He put his dry clothes back on and sat there wondering and watching. His mind wandered to John Henry and Stirrup and the mischief that blue dog would have created if he was here now, shaking mud and shit all over everything and everyone. Henry loved the bush and doing just this sort of thing. He wondered again if God would be pissed at him for burying Stirrup with his master. 'Fuck him, anyway. That boy needed his dog. He'd just have to be fucking cool.'

Cozy missed Henry and his Stirrup. Together they'd hung out here a million times. Their names were still carved deeply into buttresses as high as the kids could reach, no older than five or six, with stolen pocket knives. Those with golden tips on the black handles and a small eagle stamped on the blade. The same knives the mob, girls and boys, cut still-scarred hands with, swearing blood brotherhood and sisterhood forever. The boys had easily a hundred of those newsagent knives and carved their names on every tree in this poor forest as they blazed a million trails.

The last hour simply flew by. Cozy figured it was time to go, so he put back on his clingy, wet, cold clothes and legged it home to an empty house for a hot shower. He was relieved he didn't have to explain where he'd been. The boys would've found someone with decent weed. Cozy kicked back in front of the telly having the odd bucket. He was hungry, fixing to get up and eat something, when the

Tribute © Robert Lee Johnston 2016
Email: tributerobertleejohnston@gmail.com

news came on. The day's top story was about a fisherman finding three barrels of cocaine washed ashore on a stretch of coastline close to where theirs was found. Cozy was gobsmacked. Three more! Fuck me dead! We should've kept looking.

The pigs looked very pleased with themselves and bragged how this would put a dint in things. A fisherman discovered the drums, investigated and then rang the cops.

'What a fuckhead.'

Cozy was stunned. He rang the Middle Pub and asked for Bugs. 'Did you blokes see the news yet?'

'Nah, just playing a game of sticks. Why? What's happened, man?'

'Three barrels just got found up north.'

Cozy left it at that and hung up, knowing they'd be flat out home. He heard Kenny kill the motor, doors slam and both their footsteps running heavily up the stairs. They crashed through the door soaked.

'WHAT THE FUCK,' Kenny shouted excitedly.

'Cops got three more around where we stopped looking.'

Kenny was gutted. 'Awwww! Fuck me dead.'

'Seriously?' Bugs asked softly.

'Yeah, mate.' Cozy teased about the fisherman ringing the pigs.

Kenny blurted out too loud, 'What the fuck? Called the cops? What a cockhead.'

Bugs looked at them both solemnly. 'Fuck, man. Everyone will know.' He nervously ran his hand through his moppy, muppet hair.

Cozy disagreed. 'No, man. They can think they know. They don't and won't know shit unless we tell them. Those cops did us a favour, boys.'

'How so, man?' Bugs was curious.

Tribute © Robert Lee Johnston 2016
Email: tributerobertleejohnston@gmail.com

'Well, no bastard will ever taste it, or be able to compare it to ours. Once the filth burn the evidence, ours is just a another sack of coke.'

Bugs wasn't buying it. 'I think we should shut shop for a bit, just until the heat dies down.'

They all agreed.

The cops were a step ahead of the boys. They had, in fact, tested their coke when some fool farther down the line got himself busted. When they tested the barrels against his, it was a perfect match. The drug squad were positive there was a local connection, and applied some pressure to the aforementioned fool. Luckily for the three young fellas he was lots of people and connections away from them, and knew fuck all anyway. That didn't stop the police's heads or their hard-ons growing bigger. And they figured whoever had it could have countless barrels. That made those hero, drug-squad detectives very erect, wet, and extremely toey.

'We should go north with metal detectors. And find more.' Kenny wasn't thinking.

'Fuck you, Jack!' Bugs cut in. 'The joint will be red fucking hot at the moment, a fucking federalley fest. Those pigs and every bloke and his dog will search for miles up there and that whole coastline will be turned inside out.' Though he added, 'Man, three more barrels. Shit. We could've cleaned up.'

Cozy jumped in. 'Fuck that. Stashing one barrel, even getting it off the beach, was worry enough. Imagine moving four of them?'

'We would've managed, figured it out. We would've thought of something, Cozy. You, me and Bugs, we couldn't've, wouldn't've, walked away from that. Just on principle alone, man. In fact, I bet that fucking fisherman is full of shit and has half a dozen drums sitting in his old nana's bloody lounge room right now. We wouldn't've left them I reckon, bloke. Even if we were ninety-six and crippled.'

Tribute © Robert Lee Johnston 2016
Email: tributerobertleejohnston@gmail.com

They all laughed because Kenny was probably right. They tried to calculate how much the pigs' score would be worth. The end result, after much deliberating and out-loud long division: A fucking butt load!

***

The news made its way to every house in the country, including Pinky's. Then the final part of his jigsaw puzzle fell into place. He knew in his guts it was those three lads. They had found a barrel. Maybe more. His incubated plan started to hatch.

'Clever little fuckers. They never told no one. Not one word.'

Pinky respected bitten tongues, and knew the jail birds would never involve the police.

'Hang on to your butt cheeks, you little shits. Things are going to get rough.'

He dialled four mates' numbers. 'It's time. I was headed up Tribute anyway for a look see. But I'm sure now. Two days, meet me in Tribute. We got some kids to sort out.'

***

Kenny was singled out. They caught him alone, pulled a gun on him, and threw him in their car and beat the living tripe out of him.

'They wanted to know where you two were,' Kenny said later. 'I said I don't know. And They drove me here. One of them drove my fucking car, after they stole my keys. Here to our own fucking house no less. And tied me to that fucking chair. That was when Bugs came home. He opened the door to a couple of strangers, and me gagged and tied up. Before he could react he was king hit and smacked hard

Tribute © Robert Lee Johnston 2016
Email: tributerobertleejohnston@gmail.com

about the head, dragged down and beat some more, and then tied to a chair.'

Bugs continued on, 'They questioned both of us about the coke and where you were. While they flogged us with that piece of fucking poly-pipe.'

'Two down. One little fucker to go!' Pinky had looked over his fresh capture. 'Watch this last one. He's a cut snake.'

Cozy was in the scrub again. He woke to darkness and starving mozzies. The mozzie coils had all burnt out. He walked back to the cheap, rented, three-bedroom farm house in no particular hurry, other than outrunning the mozzies.

The boys loved having no visible neighbours to bother them. The road ended at the jungle. There was no property past their rented farm house. Cozy arrived through the backyard. The lights were on and Kenny's four-door in the yard, so the boys must be home. Walking under the two-storey Queenslander, where the hardtop was parked with its windows open, Cozy reached in and grabbed some dirty training shirts that needed washing. There was no music or sound coming from the telly upstairs. One or the other was usually always going. He guessed they just got home.

Cozy heard footsteps above him. Not just any footsteps. These were heavy, really heavy. The floor boards complained. Easily a hundred kilos. Much more than Bugs's eighty or Kenny's seventy-two. Cozy heard a voice he didn't recognise. He stopped dead in his tracks, surrounded by darkness. His senses tuned sharp. Maybe they invited someone from the Middy home for a smoke, or a poke? She must be a bloody biggun. Imagining an angry, hungry hippo, Cozy smiled. He waited for something, anything, all senses now focused. He couldn't make out words. Then another strange male voice, and more laughter that was trying not to be heard. But no laughter from the voices he knew. Something dripped, sticky and heavy, onto Cozy's head,

Tribute © Robert Lee Johnston 2016
Email: tributerobertleejohnston@gmail.com

through a gap in the floorboards, and even in the dark he knew what it was. He was born in it, raised by it, lived for it, fought amongst it, and spilt litres of it. Cozy knew the instant that syrupy warmth hit his head. It was blood. He could smell it. My friends' blood? He panicked in thought for a second and then came to. Dropping his shirts, he crept to the corner where some garden tools were kept. He fumbled around as quietly as possible for a brand-new hickory pick axe handle as long as his leg and as thick as his arm. The boys hadn't got around to attaching the pick axe yet.

Thank fuck.

Cozy raced out into the yard, now armed in the gentle moonlight. He confirmed it was, in fact, blood dripping down his face. Cozy was shaking, though without a trace of fear. Cozy heard the crack of bone on bone, and the chunky thud of impact, and then Bugs moaned in pain.

What to do, what to do? Fuck it.

Cozy kept to the darkness and crept on tiptoes up the stairs, avoiding the creaky ones. He stood silently at the door, pick handle in hand, not really knowing what to expect on the other side.

'Fuck it. Here goes.'

Cozy bashed the door hard three times while yelling, 'POLICE!'

It was a low-down, shitty thing to do, but it was all he could come up with. He kicked the farm-house, piss-ant back door open when he heard panic inside. Opening up both barrels, he smashed the pick handle into some bloke's face, clean peeled his top lip off his face before he went down screaming.

Bugs and Kenny sat bolt upright, their eyes wide. They were grunting at Cozy through their taped mouths. 'Ill de unts!'

A second bloke tried to rush Cozy. Cozy smashed him with an overhead blow across his shoulder, pile-driving him into the floor, and then drove the thick, wooden tip deeply

into his guts. Cozy didn't know his face. The last he didn't recognise either.

'Who the fuck are you blokes?'

A big bloke was backed into the corner with a truncheon-sized piece of poly-pipe that he had been smacking the boys' faces with. He looked desperately towards the kitchen sink. Cozy followed his gaze. He had left his .38 pistol near the kettle. Cozy made his way to it. 'Guns? You fucking low life.'

The stranger wanted it badly. Up to now the boys had only ever held rifles, and this tiny pistola felt heavy and dependable in Cozy's hand. Though a snub, it felt huge. Cozy flicked the safety off and pointed it at him. His face and arsehole both caved in. He looked to his fallen mates for back up, but there was nothing going there. He knew he was fucked. Cozy held the pistol level at his face from the other side of the room.

'How you like that, mate? How soft is he, boys? Brings a piece like some fucking seppo gangster. You're in Australia now, mother fucker. Not yankee fucking land, Jessie fucking James. I'm going to put this piece of shit down and pick up where the first fleet left off.'

Bugs was frantic, hopping and rocking in his chair to gain his brother's attention. Cozy leaned the weighty pick handle against the table beside Bugs. The hand gun, for now, was still trained on the big fella.

'I hear you, brother.' Cozy kept an eye on his trapped prey, found a knife on the table and cut Bugs's arm free with one hand, leaving him the knife to free themselves. As he aimed the business end of the snub at the stranger, he put his other hand on Bugs's head, and then Kenny's. 'I'm sorry, boys.'

They were soon unrestrained and angrily kicking the shit out of the two that were grounded.

'Let's just talk, boys,' the trapped, fat one pleaded. 'I'm sure I got something you want, something you need.'

Tribute © Robert Lee Johnston 2016
Email: tributerobertleejohnston@gmail.com

He knew he was in the shit. They all knew it. They were fucked, Cozy wanted them to know. 'Youse are all fucked.'

**

'I'm sorry, Cozy. I'm sorry, Bugs. They wanted to know where you two were.'

Kenny recited his story. 'He's Pinky! His name's Pinky! I met him once. I saw him around the Middy for a bit. Fucking years ago.' Kenny went on to Pinky, 'Yeah you got something I need, Pinky, you cowardly fuck. I need you to shut your fucking mouth.'

Sweating with old fear, Bugs stared at Pinky. 'You got a proper sour dose coming. You will catch your death in this cold.'

Bugs hadn't finished his sentence before Cozy attacked Pinky, swinging hard at his ribs. When Pinky dropped his elbow to protect his body, it smashed. Cozy swung again into the very same spot. This time he lifted his injured arm. The axe handle chopped him deep, under his arm pit, shattering ribs. He dropped, winded.

'You still want to hurt us, fucker?' Bugs had the pistol and was in shock, pointing it at Pinky's head. 'I should shoot you. I should fucking shoot you! Hey, boys, I bet this maggot spent hours in front of his faggot reflection with this very gun. Talking tough to himself, you know, pointing it, posing, and drawing it, like Billy the fucking Kid, talking all sorts of hard-man talk. Did you lower your voice when you spoke tough to yourself, Pinky? Make deals with yourself? I bet you were calm. Real strong and brave.'

Bugs was rock steady as he tried not to pull the trigger. Pinky's hands were in front of his face protecting himself from the blast. Bugs was way beyond the brink. He whispered menacingly, 'I ain't using no gun on you. And I don't need no mirror to scare anyone.'

Tribute © Robert Lee Johnston 2016
Email: tributerobertleejohnston@gmail.com

Cozy hammered the handle into Pinky's thigh while he was down, and then flogged the man's knees, shins and hip bones. His hand found the ground for purchase. Cozy smashed that as well, so hard the pick-axe handle bounced off the hardwood floor. Pinky would never pull a trigger again with those fingers.

'You're going bloody nowhere, mate.' Then Cozy picked up the lip he had torn off the other man and placed it like a trophy on the table. Pinky passed out, and the dripping blood off Cozy's friends seeping through the floor now ran with his enemy's. The boys rearranged the seating.

When the men awoke, bound but not gagged, they realised their fate. The boys acted as though they weren't there at all and sat at the table smoking cones, snorting fat lines, and drinking. In the meantime, they had shown Cozy their various injuries. Two of the liberty-less were awake now. The boys never so much as looked at them.

Cozy asked Kenny, 'Is this all of them?' He noticed some eye contact between Pinky and his mate and turned back to Kenny. 'Is there a driver, mate?'

Kenny answered after exhaling his shaky cone, 'Yep, there's one more out there down the road, waiting for these fuckers to finish. In a newish Ford.'

'Two-door?' Cozy asked.

'Nah, four-door.'

'Okay, okay. Kenny can you go have a Captain Cook and grab four star pickets from the shed after your cones? Grab some fuel too, bloke.'

Kenny took off to raid the shed. Bugs was itching for revenge. 'Let's just go out there, put the fucking gun to his head, and skull drag the piece of shit in here!'

Cozy shook his head, encouraging Bugs with a sadistic grin. 'That's too easy, man. Yeah, we could do that, but I got a better idea. They wanted to burn us. Let's burn them back. A trial by fire. If he's innocent his God'll save him, right?'

They smiled like chicken thieves.

Bugs replied, 'Burning a fucker, man, that takes balls. Heh, heh. We'll leave it in God's good hands.'

Bugs and Cozy heard the men take a collective breath. Cozy thought of losing Tilly. What would have happened if Mathilda had walked through the door. He wasn't happy. Cozy saw Pinky trying to free his hand. 'Go on, fuckface, move that maggot fucking hand once more, Pinky. I'll hack it off, then deep fry and eat your crunchy, fishy fucking fingers.'

'Fucking stay still.' Bugs snarled thunder. He trained his stare onto Pinky and moved within inches of his face. Then he found the cigarette lighter in his pocket. Bugs lit it under Pinky's bulbous nose. Every time it came close to his skin, Pinky winced away. Bugs grabbed the index finger of Pinky's unbroken hand. 'Stay still, or I'll snap it.'

Pinky held his nerve and kept his head still as the lighter ignited under his nostrils. The smell of burning hair was sharp in Pinky's nose. When he eventually flinched from the Bic's flame, Bugs snapped his finger clean, like a stick of chalk. Pinky screamed and moaned. Kenny returned, leaving four star pickets and a three-quarter-full jerry can downstairs. He joined the rest for a few cones as they planned and plotted out loud. The captives didn't like hearing the many various ideas proposed.

Their games were chosen. They moved quietly through the dark to the car parked fifty metres or so from the driveway. The Fairlane's stereo played Fleetwood Mac, just loud enough, helping cover any unwanted noise the boys made.

Bugs opened the Fairlane door quietly and quickly. Kenny, bottled lightning, stole the keys from the ignition, killing the tunes and locking the steering wheel. Kenny stood out of the way, and Cozy threw fuel over the driver and helm, as if he was throwing water over a fire. Bugs slammed the door as Kenny wedged the last star picket into the

Tribute © Robert Lee Johnston 2016
Email: tributerobertleejohnston@gmail.com

ground tightly under the door's handle. The other boys had silently done the same to all three doors.

The occupant had awoken, yelling 'Fuck yas!' to a face full of petrol. Bewildered, he heard the door slam. He wiped his eyes and dripping face. His eyes burnt with petrol. He tried opening his door, and then tried the passenger door. He fumbled around the ignition, looking for his keys. No keys. He decided to leg it, leaping into the back seat like an ambushed gazelle and trying those doors.

He was defenceless, powerless and trapped.

Cozy was on the bonnet as Kenny fired up the hardtop under the house. They had all the time in the world. Cozy had covered the driver in at least two litres of fuel. He poured the remaining petrol all over the Fairlane, walking backwards over the bonnet to the boot. Kenny backed up the two-door as the Ford's occupant panicked. Bugs hooked a five metre chain to both cars. Cozy yelled, 'Kenny! This fucker will leave it in gear or brake for a bit. Drag this piece of shit to the dump.'

The driver was wide awake now. No ignition meant no power windows, so he tried punching his way out. Cozy lit a lighter and the driver shat himself. Cozy added fire to the accelerant coating the bonnet and it WOOFED.

Cozy yelled over the hardtop's anxious motor. 'Not yet, Kenny. Not yet, mate. Wait up.'

The petrol ignited, at once sucking the oxygen out of the car. The boys waited calmly, until the flames were inside, and old mate was well and truly rooted. The fire malicious and lively. He had some vigour this one. He twisted and battled, trying to evade the orange-blue flames scourging him. The three boys waited until he ceased.

Bugs smacked the back of the hardtop. 'Go!'

Kenny nailed it, dragging an out-of-control fiery chariot into the night. Bugs and Cozy watched in awe until it was gone from sight.

'The stink, man.' Bugs choked. 'It's fucking rotten.'

Tribute © Robert Lee Johnston 2016
Email: tributerobertleejohnston@gmail.com

Pinky was terrified. Not for his mates, but for his stupid self. He knew these boys were a little wild but could never have imagined this. That these kids were capable of murder. And when the door opened he knew he'd never see another open. Bugs sat on the table, nuts out, free balling, and told him, 'You boys might need a new driver, me thinks.'

Cozy and Bugs sat and looked their hostages over for a time.

'Bugs?'

'Yep?'

'Have you thought much lately about who murdered Lacey?'

He looked in Cozy's eyes, and both turned to Pinky. Pinky looked away quickly. Bugs looked back to his friend, his brow furrowed. Bugs was demure, almost opiate. Calm as a robbed monk he said, 'I'm fucking thinking it now, Cozy.'

'Me too, Bugs.'

'Mayhap we need to chat to our cold-blooded friend?'

Bugs bled out one of the other men. Loudly. Slowly. He sliced the man's wrist vertically and bled him, tied to a chair, into the emptied bong bucket. Neither of the boys asked a single question.

'They were going to kill us all.' He looked Cozy's way, bloodied knife in hand. 'If you hadn't shown up, man, when you did, the way you did, bro, us two, me and Kenny, we'd be rooted. Any other way, man, the three of us might be dead.'

Meanwhile Kenny, looking piratical, skull-dragged a flaming, out-of-control, ghostly, infernal missile into the dark, black night. He was sure the Fairlane would roll once it started tank slapping. Being a weeknight and 3 am in Tribute, not a soul stirred. Especially not the Ford driver. Thankfully, Kenny had not been able to hear all the burning man's screams. In his rear-view he could see fire, slicked back around the body of the car like long, angry, orange hair

Tribute © Robert Lee Johnston 2016
Email: tributerobertleejohnston@gmail.com

in the wind. It looked like some fiendish, abominable creature chasing him.

'FUCK ME DEAD,' he yelled. 'IT'S A FUCKING AFTERBURNER!'

Ten klicks away, Kenny and his deep-fried mate came to a slow stop. He unhooked the chain, stood back and watched the Ford burn for a bit. It was a demonic spectacle. Kenny screamed in fright as tyres exploded.

'FUCK YOU, CUNT. FUCK YOU. YA FUCKED UP!

Bugs had reminded him before he left home 'not to panic. No burnouts near where you dump him, mate. No speeding home, crashing, or any dumb shit. Okay, brother?'

Slowly Kenny left. He started crying at the thought of what was going on. The poly-pipe had triggered potent memories of Syd and his toe-jam peers. Then the shock of seeing Cozy crashing through the door. Then hope. The feeling was like no other he had ever felt, silently hoping Cozy would get the better of them and not be overpowered. Kenny was completely spent. This revenge didn't taste sweet. He pulled to a stop on that empty old road, opened the door, leaned out and spewed his guts up. He could still see it all in his mind's eye, in the mirrors. That dude, trying to kick and punch the windows out and open those wedged doors. Burning alive. He saw clearly the fireworks as flames discovered their way inside the cab. The petrol over him igniting instantly when it found access. Melting flesh still burned in Kenny's nostrils, burning hair and rubber still stung his senses.

He assured himself, 'They fucking deserved it. All of them.'

Pinky, his coes, Syd, their kind, his caterpillar larva of a missus. Prison, inmates and that rock-spider Rev. That fucking Rev.

All those fuckers melded into one identity: Pinky.

'They tried fucking killing me, killing us. Fuck, they almost did it.'

Tribute © Robert Lee Johnston 2016
Email: tributerobertleejohnston@gmail.com

The shocking image of Jen's body, headless, came to mind, in a deep, still, crimson lake of blood, around her shoulders where her bright hair should be. Lacey being tortured and murdered. The whip tearing chunks of beef off Bugs's and Cozy's backs. He was nine years old again. The bunker was too deep to climb out of, the walls too steep to gain purchase. He wanted all his enemies to stop breathing, to be dead. He sucked in a couple of skinny breaths, spat the foulness out his window, and reached over and opened the glove box, knowing some Acca Dacca albums were in there. He put in the first one he found and smiled to himself, nodding as Bon let off a yell. "Problem Child!"*

'You said it, Bon! You fucking know it, every time.'

He hardened to become as steely and rock solid as Malcolm's rhythm guitar. He suddenly ached to spawn as much torture as Angus caused his smoking Marshals. It was time to put an end to feeling this way. He joined Bon in song, singing out with a new-found lust for the taking of life, a lust for revenge and suffering.

"Problem Child!"*

He tossed the Fairlane's keys far into a large, rested, long-grassed paddock and took off calmly, without any wheel spin. The raspy motor idled innocently as if nothing had ever happened.

Problem Child, AC/DC – Song Title

CHAPTER TWENTY-FIVE: "TRUTH, MEET WRATH."

'TRUTH'
Truth never comes into the world but like a bastard.
To the ignominy of him that bought her forth.

John Milton

'WRATH'
I am wrath, I had neither father nor mother:
I leapt out of a lion's mouth scarce half an hour old;
And ever since I have run up and down the world with this case of
rapiers,
Wounding myself when I had nobody to fight withal.

Christopher Marlowe

Bugs had a similar rush of emotions to Kenny. The way this world had treated him, the cops, jail, his ridiculous foster parents, being abandoned in the first place. A sick part of him, secretly buried away, wanted to kill someone. Cozy had done it, and it always sat crooked with Bugs that he'd never had the balls to do it before him. The boys could hear the coupe's fruity, cranky motor pull into the drive.

'You know, Cozy, we'd be fucking dead like that bastard there. Bled out like fucking pigs.'

The motor died.

'You know it. The thought had crossed my mind.'

Bugs then turned to the men. 'You dopey rat-bastards. What, youse think you can come here murder us? Then what? Walk away? Fuck youse. Ballsy fucking effort but.' He paused. 'All this for some coke? I bet. Well, I know I would! I reckon you would've been keeping low around here, seeing as you fucks-for-the-dogs were going to be doing a spot of killing. None of you would want any pigs, or too many nosey locals, seeing you blokes, or noticing you about. No waves, no witnesses, like you're invisible. Guess what, Pinky? I can see you twenty-twenty now, mother fucker. I can see you so fucking clearly, you snake in the grass. You fucking death adders. You thrived like a trapdoor spider on invisibility. We'll be doing the world a big, juicy favour squishing you. I bet the cops would hardly fucking miss you or even bloody care. I bet they know your form. I reckon you're the sort of fuckers who'd spook them. You're a fucking burnt-out, sloppy, end-of-the-road standover merchant.' Bugs became sentimental for a second. 'Just like all those slippery serpents before you. I can bet the whole fucking farm, you mob hardly told a sausage. Cos you're fucking greedy bastards, aren't you? You wouldn't want the coke split too many ways. Or blokes would do this very same thing to you. Nah, you poofters are here on a mission. Almost on the lam. Lying low. No one knows you're here, do they? Your hands,

Tribute © *Robert Lee Johnston 2016*
Email: tributerobertleejohnston@gmail.com

Pinky, they just slipped off the tiller for a sec is all, old mate. That's all we ever need.'

'Are you hurt, Bugs'

'Fucking oath I am. Hurting bad from a lifetime of dealing with these unimaginative, black-hearted arseholes.'

His forehead was swelling where he'd ducked into punches. His face was bright red, a welt or three coming up after being whacked with poly-pipe. His Dylan shirt was bloody and torn.

'But it's easing every second, Cozy, knowing this fuck is getting put down and hurt and has breathed his last.'

'He's a snake-eyed fuck isn't he, Bugs? Reckon he's fucked plenty of good people over. He's just like Syd, this one, except he gets off on ambushing blokes with guns, not whips.'

Bugs snarled. 'This prick's done it before, mate.'

'You think?'

Kenny delaminated and shred apart as he came through the door. He made eye contact with both his brothers. He hardened and grinned like an evil, blood-soaked clown when he saw all the carnage. He and Bugs were both fairly busted up. Kenny's lips were split and really messy, his nose broken and his eyes blackening and swelling. His shirt was also covered in his own blood. He'd been crying and looked a bit rattled. The boys hugged their little brother and patted his back.

'You okay?'

'Nah, boys, this shit is crazy, and too fucking close to home. I got the orphanage on my mind and can't fucking shake it. I don't want to. I'm going to ride it out and get this shit off my liver.'

He noticed Pinky and one of his five eighths were still alive amongst the carnage.

'It's going to get fucking messy around here.'

Tribute © Robert Lee Johnston 2016
Email: tributerobertleejohnston@gmail.com

Kenny let go of the boys and walked Pinky's way. He was incandescent and unloaded a quickstep, resentful right hand into his face. Crunch. 'YOU'RE DEAD.'

They tried to un-ruffle and smoked some sweet cones. With a dead bloke sitting slumped at the table. The boys went through their wallets. Terrance was the joker whose lip Cozy had torn off. He now jokingly spoke with it, moving the soft flesh like a puppet. John was the dead one, whom Bugs bled into the bucket after hacking his wrist. Cozy removed the thruster—an empty two-litre plastic milk bottle with its bottom cut out, and a cone piece shot through the bottle's lid—out of the bucket and threw the water off the top landing. Bugs and Cozy watched John's life blood drain into the yellow bucket under his left hand. Bloody, red, warm bubbles formed fresh on top, like red rapids' foam. Bugs shifted the three-quarter-full bucket onto the table and put the thruster back in after adding a little water. Cozy smoked a crimson cone. An ox-blood-red, dripping bong. Thick claret slid ghoulishly down the two-litre milk container, leaving smears, bubbles and stains where it had already congealed. Cozy felt like some ancient warrior drinking the blood of his freshly vanquished rivals. John's blood dripped from Cozy's hair, down his face. He looked and felt amazing. They sat smoking, all three bloodied, Bugs and Kenny beaten up and still dripping oil. Cozy looked at Pinky as he toked. His and Terrance's eyes were wide. Terry, with his top lip missing, smiled like a fool or some evil comic-book character. They smoked from that garish bucket. The blood gave a lot better suction and much more resistance. Fresh, frightened blood was so much more viscous than water. Bugs exhaled the thick smoke and wiped his mouth with its bloody milk moustache on his already stained forearm. Kenny cut up some lines, three fat, thick, long lines, tainted red from the surrounds and his hands.

'All that for some coke, eh?' Bugs snorted, casting a pitiful glance their way. He inhaled his line. 'Thank fuck it's

Tribute © *Robert Lee Johnston 2016*
Email: tributerobertleejohnston@gmail.com

good coke, man. You'd feel pretty fucking shitty and stupid if you died over epsom salts, or some fucking baking powder.'

Cozy belly chuckled. Bugs felt stronger. Kenny jumped into his and Cozy followed. Kenny's line was divine, and when he rose he looked focused and clear. Cozy broke out some spirits and some tunes, choosing 'Frank's Wild Years'. He thought, A great album to kill to. It just feels right.

The young fellas ignored the hostages for an hour or so, preparing themselves for the grand finale. Cozy imagined life without ever being with Mathilda, or ever seeing Evie again. Bugs distracted them with a great Churchill impersonation.

'Never before has the courage of so few been so important.'

Two smiles broadened, as Bugs's lips stiffened and curled like the great Winston himself. They threw their heads back, laughing.

'We will fight them in our town. We will burn them in their car. We will cut the maggots up, and gut them in our house. Never in the field of conflict, was so much owed to so few. For them … we shall … be … victorious.'

Bugs bowed his head solemnly with raised fist. He even cracked himself up.

'Stop it!' Kenny begged, almost in tears.

Bugs spoke seriously. 'We got to be exacting, man. And exactly right. Completely careful, every step from here, boys. No shortcuts or panicking. Man, we have to kill these two fucks, clean this shit hole, and git rid of their carcasses.'

Bugs was wiggling a loosened front tooth when Kenny asked, 'How many blokes you reckon he's killed before? You reckon?' Kenny was thinking out loud. 'Was he around when Lacey Knickers got burned?'

'We was just fucking talking about that,' Cozy admitted.

They felt the fit, and all gazed at Pinky.

'Blind fucking Freddy can see it!' Bugs spat.

'Those shark eyes, I've seen them before, before Lacey was killed.'

'I can't recall. I haven't seen any of those faces. Until now,' Cozy said.

'Neither can I,' Bugs admitted.

'I'm fucking positive. I know it, boys. I fucking know it!' Kenny assured them. 'Righto, let's hear what he knows!'

In the background Tom Waits sang and growled his heart out. Bugs lit a gas hot plate on the stove and rested the blade of the biggest knife they owned over the flame.

Cozy watched on as Kenny threatened them matter-of-factly.

'Whether you talk or not, you're fucking dead, you pair. You jokers fucked with a man and his mates. No one comes back from that, not fucking ever. It ain't going to be pleasant the way you pair die.' Kenny let it all out. 'And it's going to FUCKING HURT.' He calmed himself. 'A fuck of a lot, for a fuck of a long time. We got no neighbours, no plans, lots of drugs, and absolutely no fucking hurry.'

They cut up some fresh lines and smoked some of Cozy's good stash. The other two boys pulled out their secret stashes as well. Without warning Bugs grabbed his knife off the flame, with its seven-inch, glowing-orange blade. He approached Terry and without fuss drove the tip, slowly and completely into old mate's fleshy, upper thigh. He twisted the blade three-sixty degrees, as the steel sizzled and spat in anger. Poor Terrance didn't like it much. He squealed, grunted, pissed, shit, and spewed all at the same time. Smiling his foolish, lipless grin. Bugs didn't remove the red-hot shiv.

'We can't do any time for these low lives, boys. I ain't doing no life sentence for these sacks of crap.'

Cozy imagined being one of those sad inmates with a girl on the outside. The worry, shame, and pain for him and Tilly. The torture of distance would kill any future together.

Tribute © Robert Lee Johnston 2016
Email: tributerobertleejohnston@gmail.com

He had to protect her from that scenario. He knew none of the captives could live or ever be found.

Until he passed out, Terrance's eyes were painfully open. He pulled faces, trying to remove the blade telepathically from his leg. Pinky's heartrate went up just a tad. Bugs opened the cutlery drawer and placed the second biggest slicer, a thin, six-inch boning knife, over the flame. Then he joined his friends sitting at the table, as poor Terrance passed out in a thick mist of his own smoking flesh. Cozy poured drinks into red-raw, bloody-fingerprinted glasses, and they commented to each other how soft this triad was and laughed at how pitiful they appeared.

Kenny asked Pinky, 'Did you think you were fucking hard? Look at you all, moaning, squealing, and screaming, like some bitch who broke a nail. You fucking poofters.'

'Fucking cowards!' Pinky told him.

Kenny fired up. 'US? COWARDS? You thief-in-the-night. Fucking VULTURE.'

'Fuck you, man.' Bugs had never liked the word coward. 'We may have to assert the truth a little tougher, you blokes. If there's a hell, fellas … and it's what we're lead to believe. Well us boys, we got one-way tickets and the greatest back-stage pass ever. To witness the freakiest of bloody freak shows. Whether we like it or not. But fuck it. We'll be together.'

He got up, smiling weirdly, grabbed his second blade and made his way to Pinky's chair.

'No! No!' Pinky panicked and pleaded.

Bugs spoke deeply. 'Shut your guts and take what's owed.'

The red-hot steel welded into flesh with even more smoke and heat than the first on Terry. Pinky screamed for a while and then bit down on his breath when he realised the boys were laughing at him.

'Good girl,' Cozy tormented with Terrance's folded lip speaking in his fingers. 'Be strong now, little one.'

Tribute © Robert Lee Johnston 2016
Email: tributerobertleejohnston@gmail.com

Bugs rotated the handle to make it sting a bit more. He looked back at the other two in excitement, his eyes bright and wide. 'Look. Fuck-all blood hardly, eh.'

Kenny reckoned, 'Clever, dude.'

'Yeah, it cauterises and don't bleed fuck-all. I read it some fucking where.'

'Bravo, Bugs, bravo.' Cozy was truly impressed.

Pinky not so much. Breathing hard and moaning and annoying Kenny to no end.

'Stop your fucking whinging, you gutchy flog. You're driving me up the wall.' Kenny held eye contact with Pinky, shaking his head. 'Not much fun, eh? Can you just shut your misery guts and die properly?'

Pinky's eyes were drawn fearfully towards Bugs going for his third knife. Bugs looked back at him.

'Oh, don't worry, Pinky, ole cock, we won't run out anytime soon.' Bugs smiled a wolverine's grin. 'We got plenty of silverware. But now it's time to get a bit meaner, mate. We was barely sparring light up to now.'

Number three chopper was over the flame and Bugs back in his chair. All three sat in relative silence as this knife heated up. Pinky's right leg was hurting and burning. The rest of his body wanted to go away from this place. His brain was clicking over, calculating all types of plans and ideas. Nothing solid could form with the sharpened agony piercing his thigh and mind. His train of thought was arrested when Kenny broke the silence.

'Cozy, you know how to tie a noose, eh?'

'Fucking oath I do.'

'Cool.'

Kenny walked casually back down to the shed and grabbed a spool of rope. Back up the stairs he threw it to Cozy. He got to work tying the knot, thinking, Where will we hang this fuck from?

They had plenty of time to think of something. Bugs got up nonchalantly and drove the next blade home into Pinky's

Tribute © Robert Lee Johnston 2016
Email: tributerobertleejohnston@gmail.com

left thigh, again twisting it around completely and leaving it there. He repeated with another on the hotplate. Pinky was really hurting now. He was bunny hopping in his chair as an overload of agony ambushed every cell of his skin. He swore loudly. Cozy was almost done with the rope.

Bugs asked Pinky sedately, 'Did you kill our mate?'

'I didn't kill no bastard. Fucking wasn't me!'

Kenny yelled, 'BULLSHIT.'

'I swear it wasn't me. On my kid's life.'

Cozy got pissed at that. 'Shut up, you dog. Your kids? You slimy rat. Your kids, your fucking wife, your granny. Even your dear old, fairy fucking godmother can't save your arse now.' Cozy looked in disbelief at his old mates and laughed in contempt. 'He tried pulling the "my kids" card on us, or "my poor, dear old, helpless nanna". Reckons we might feel sorry for him. Ha! No mercy for you.'

'No fucking quarter.' Bugs was happy. He had always wanted to say that phrase and felt pleased with himself for coming up with it at such an appropriate time.

Cozy told Pinky, 'You should've thought of that, you murdering fuck, before you left Lacey's unborn kid without a dad, or his girl alone. I bet you blokes showed him the same mercies we're granting you. I know he would've tried to convince you not to kill him. You could've taken all his weed, all his coke, all his money. As long as you left him and his alone.'

Bugs got up, annoyed. 'Fuck this.'

He fetched the fourth knife and jammed it close to the last. Pinky is looking like a human knife storage system, he thought.

A combination of screaming and laughter woke poor Terrance up.

Cozy asked him, 'How did you sleep, princess?' as if talking to a four-year-old girl. He could see Terrance's memory kick into gear, the sickly moment reality dropped unbelievably back into its place.

Tribute © Robert Lee Johnston 2016
Email: tributerobertleejohnston@gmail.com

'Wakey wakey.' Kenny's face was churlish. 'I'm going to cut you, snaky.'

Cozy, with Terrance's lip as his finger puppet laughed: Ha ha ha.

Terrance's day was rapidly going from bad to worse. He started begging, crying and sobbing all at once. It was shamefully embarrassing, and hard to witness. He pleaded, puppy-eyed, 'Sorry, I'm so sorry,' over and over.

'SHUT UP, FUCK FACE.' Kenny was disgusted. 'No fucking moral fibre or balls, these so-called gangsters. Me and Bugs sat there quietly, prepared to die, like real men. You lost! And look at you, you pavlova, wine, and cheese eating maggot. Shut up and die properly without the whimpering, for fuck's sake. I've had enough of this sooky pair of faggots, boys.'

Kenny went to the cutlery drawer, searching for a razor-sharp paring knife he knew was there. Once tooled up, and to the surprise of the others, he sliced Terry's long, scrawny neck as if he was sharpening a dull blade on steel. Over and over, while holding a fistful of Terrance's fringe, reefing it back and exposing his throat to be sure. Blood arced away from the shifty, still-living dead man all over Kenny. His carotid beat to his heart's arterial rhythm for the first few powerful spurts.

Kenny yelled all the while. 'SHUT UP. SHUT UP. SHUT THE FUCK UP AND DIE PROPERLY. FAGGOT FUCK FOR THE DOGS.'

Kenny lost it for a minute. When he came back, the feeling scared and shook him a little. Bugs smiled for Kenny and told him, 'No more dreams for him.'

All that the boys had suffered would come to a head. Their whole lives led to this perfectly rooted sequence of events. The depravity society had bestowed on them was being blown out under magnified pressure. They were killers born and dangerously alive. For a moment they were

reduced and decocted to the lowly depths of their antagonists. They just lost the plot for a moment.

Terrance, criminal, tall, and terminally skinny did, after a moment in fact, totally shut the fuck up. He bled heavily from his neck with his misplaced, wretched, perpetual smile. Pinky was pale and shaking. Bugs's knife glowed in fiery angst, like the red heat inside the boys. They sat quietly for a time.

The boys killing felt nirvana-like. They were housed within blood alley in a state of pleasurable annihilation. The boys looked devil hot and so lawlessly sexy.

Then Cozy asked once more, 'It was you that killed Lacey?'

Pinky was going to tell them to get fucked again. Then he grimaced in pain, finality and defeat. What have I got to lose? Nothing! He breathed deeply. Fuck it!

'Yeah, I killed your fucking hippy mate.'

The boys inhaled and leaned back in their chairs. Shock, silence, and a smoky, dank vacuum hung in the air for a minute or so. The news soaked into the boys' minds like shit into sugar.

'I fucking knew it,' Kenny whispered. 'I fucking knew it.'

Bewildered, hot tears burned down Cozy's face.

'Man, why?' Bugs asked. 'Why? He was a good bloke, he hurt no bastard, had a pregnant missus, a house, farm. He took care of us. Lacey hurt no bastard.'

'Don't you three fucking get it? You really are dead shits, aren't you? Cos he had your coke and he wouldn't give you up.' Pinky wanted the agony over with. 'End of story, no mystery. Nothing personal. I wanted your coke. He wouldn't give you young fellas up. So his fucking fault, really.' He laughed loudly and deeply with as much contempt and defiance as he could muster. 'You three reckon I'm the only drug-fucked scum that's going to fuck with you and try to rob you? You boys got a forty-four-gallon drum of coke. People notice that sort of shit. All sorts of people. Specially

Tribute © Robert Lee Johnston 2016
Email: tributerobertleejohnston@gmail.com

people like me.' He smiled. 'Millions of dollars worth. Millions more if you found two or three. How many did youse find?' He rallied. 'I know how to get rid of it fast. I can unload it all for you blokes, every last speck. If not, good luck. Ha ha ha! You three poxy amateurs selling all that coke.' He paused. 'That's a shitload of paranoia to be sitting on for any length of time.'

Kenny laughed. 'You think we're that stupid, you cock-munching bottom-dweller? What do you think? We keep it here? No one's that fucking stupid.'

Pinky was bull-shitting for his life, stalling the boys with one final hope. 'No one would keep that amount close. You blokes got a stash spot, haven't you?'

He was like Bugs. Pinky had to know everything about everything.

'You'll be raising eyebrows wherever you go. Attracting the bully-man or the next fucker like me. Now, hurry up and fucking kill me, you fucking nobodies. You lot got fucking lucky tonight. You lot should be in these seats. You blokes think I haven't got mates?'

Cozy stopped him there. 'Yeah, I reckon you got mates. But I don't reckon they're your friends. Or will give a fat rat's arse when your final, bloody crunch comes. I don't reckon you know what a true mate is. Just so happens you come across us mob. We might not look it, but we're the real deal, Jack. I don't reckon any of your mates are worth a pinch of frog shit on a cold winter's night, or give two fucks if you're dumb, delinquent arse isn't around. I'll take, we'll take, whatever your mates throw at me, Pinky, at us. After tonight … Well, I'm guessing us boys got it coming. I ain't going nowhere. Your so-called mates won't have to look too hard or far for your revenge.'

Pinky was looking right at Cozy, hating him. He continued where he left off, unfazed. 'Begging for your lives like your fucking mate.' He paused for affect. 'Your mate, Lacey, he begged.' He looked at Cozy. 'Boyo.'

Tribute © Robert Lee Johnston 2016
Email: tributerobertleejohnston@gmail.com

'You didn't just call me "Boyo" then, did you? Did he? Did you?' Cozy looked to the boys. 'Did he?'

They nodded. Cozy shook his head, smiling. 'No one alive calls me that. Righto, shit for brains, no worries.'

Cozy took a deep, angry breath. Holding it a second. Revelling in his addiction to anger. His hand found the handle of the pick axe on the table, his eyes never leaving Pinky's. Kenny put some AC/DC on the stereo. 'Hell ain't a bad place to be,'* screamed out.

'Perfect,' Kenny whispered.

Bugs took his hot knife from the stove, his messenger of pain in his bloody hand. He told Bon and all and sundry, 'Well, we'll soon see, eh, Pinky? Sit back, relax, and enjoy the show. In my experience, things will work out, just as they should … for you.'

Then all three of them were mobile.

Cozy admitted, 'I'm really going to fucking enjoy this.'

It was a blood-maddened frenzy.

Cozy attacked. Bugs stabbed. Kenny sliced.

Cozy got behind the chair with his pickaxe handle and belted Pinky's back, neck, head and shoulders, as Kenny ripped and swung. Pinky was pulpy, crying, and screaming nonsense. The young blokes saw different things at different times: Syd, his Deidre, Rev. The whip, and all who trespassed against them. It was like Cozy's dingo, King Louis, welcoming an old enemy into a hot trap. Cozy dropped his pick handle and grabbed the noose. The boys dragged Pinky, tied in his chair, to a bedroom. Cozy strung the noose around Pinky's neck and threw the coiled rope over the open door. Bugs and Cozy pulled the rope and, from the other side of the door, heaved his heavy, seated body up. Kenny pulled one of the many blades out of Pinky's thighs and stabbed him over and over in the guts and chest. Pinky struggled against the rough rope. Kenny saw the strain in Pinky's neck muscles and instinctively started stabbing there. He watched the man's eyes slowing dying. Pinky's elevated heart rate

sprayed and squirted blood as if from a burst hydraulic hose, creating a thick mist of blood. The two pulling on the rope dropped Pinky, still in his chair. It crashed and smashed on impact as they came around the door to join Kenny in watching Pinky die. Bathing in the waterfall spray of claret, Bugs kept on punching and elbowing him till his mind found its way to a tale. The story of a powerful Japanese emperor, flogging the ocean with whips, pitching oil and fuel into it, burning it. Punishing the sea for sinking his nation's great fleet. Doing no harm at all to his enemy. Bugs, like the emperor of old, stopped.

There was only so much damage three hell raisers could do.

Kenny told them in a serene state, 'We're not fucking serial killers, boys. We don't leave evidence. Promise, not a single fucking clue, or any bloody calling cards, okay?'

The bodies were rolled in ripped-up bedroom carpets. Cozy gave Pinky his pistol back, and Terrance his lip. They used some black builder's plastic to wrap the carpet and duct-taped the big, human cigars securely. They dragged them downstairs, thump thump thump, and carelessly chucked the carcasses onto the bonnet of the two-door. Then they slowly drove them to the scrub from which Cozy had walked back earlier, with Kenny sitting on the bonnet, holding the wrapped corpses so they wouldn't roll off. The boys fashioned a stretcher of sorts with the rope from around Pinky's neck and a few sturdy branches. Cozy knew a piece of jungle where no one ever went, with deep, vertical, gold-mine shafts. Even the local blackfellas didn't like that part of the scrub because of all the hidden pits.

Beside a black, hard-to-access, overgrown, deep and craggy shaft lives a golden penda, now huge and extremely well fertilised, growing happily amongst the thick evergreen.

They, all three of them, would be lost from this world forever. Never, ever found. They fell awkwardly, clumsily, disappearing for an eternity into that deep, dark abyss.

Tribute © Robert Lee Johnston 2016
Email: tributerobertleejohnston@gmail.com

Instead of saying any final words over the dead, Cozy hummed a few bars of a Tom Waits song and sang, 'You gotta help me keep the devil ...' He paused and the others joined him: 'Way down in the hole.' *

Cozy, here in Australia's own deep north, in this forest, could make them, himself, his friends, his enemies, anything he wanted, invisible. Make things disappear from sight, and the now. It was his jungle. Cozy's mother would protect her white first-born and his beloved friends. In time, she would cover their tracks and reveal nothing. Tell no one. Keeping her son's deepest, joyless secrets, and forgiving his many intricate flaws. Loving and protecting her wayward white-one as only a mother could.

Afterward, the boys cried for Lacey. They were the only ones who knew the complete truth.

Lugging those bodies had been hot, humid work. As the sun rose they found a shallow, rocky rapid on the river and watched the clouds of blood washed away in the rapid's spa bath of pressurised bubbles. The morning's cold, mountain water thrashed bloody clothes, hair, faces and bodies clean. Small river guppies feasted on the dried blood, blobs of gristle, and fresh, fleshy chunks that washed downstream. They left the river and the jungle wet and clean to drive home.

They had forgotten just how much oil had been spilled in the house. They hauled all the furniture out. After a few lines, some drinking, and a session, Kenny dragged the hose upstairs and hosed it out, as the others violently scrubbed with mops and brooms. The bleach and disinfectant got a massive work out. Six hours, many, many cones, lines, and drinks later, the house reeked of Pine-O-Clean, but it was spotless. All their killing clothes, rags, mops, the victims' wallets and money, brooms, even the poly-pipe; every little thing went into bags ready to burn. The boys changed into fresh clothes after their showers. Kenny lit a large fire in the

Tribute © Robert Lee Johnston 2016
Email: tributerobertleejohnston@gmail.com

backyard, and they watched while the fire blazed away, till not a thing but ash was left.

In silence. Just how they cleaned the house.

The fire hypnotised them. The boys were dazed, bewildered, confused, confounded, and tired, but mostly relieved.

Hell of a thing, to kill a killer.

Bugs looked at his brothers. 'That was fucking close, man.'

'Too fucking close,' Kenny agreed.

They hugged, patted each other's backs, smiled, and thanked each other. For the next two days no one stirred, except to piss, eat, sniff, smoke, change the music, and return to their respective beds.

After that the trio regained some strength. Kenny drove the boys to the pub. The word at the pub and all over town was about 'some unlucky fucking bloke. His car caught fire, killing him on the dump hill.'

'Shit! Was he local?' Bugs asked.

'Nah, not from these parts, poor bastard!' everyone was saying. 'Shit of a way to go. Sarge is on to it, but can't make hide nor hair of it. Some detectives are on the job now.'

All good, Cozy thought. No one knows shit.

'Let's get pissed, you two.' Cozy tried to deflect any interest. 'Your shout, Bugs.' He rescued him from his present company.

They clashed glasses and drank deeply, after Bugs toasted, 'To Lacey.'

Kenny and Cozy concurred. 'To Lacey.'

Hell Ain't a Bad Place To Be, AC/DC – Song Title
Frank's Wild Years, Tom Waits – Song Title

Tribute © Robert Lee Johnston 2016
Email: tributerobertleejohnston@gmail.com

CHAPTER TWENTY-SIX: KENNY GETS HIS WISH.

His was a tough tree to climb.

The tallest, thinnest, brittle branch that he clung to was impossible for the rest to dangle from for any length of time.

All the drugs the boys consumed loved them. But they always loved Kenny more. His addictive traits ran deeply. He was a binger on food, women, hoarding junk, drugs, drink and motors. It was all or nothing. Fabas indulcet fames, as the saying goes. 'Hunger sweetens the beans.' He became a complete and educated compendium of drugs, coke being the choice pick lately.

A complete disrespect for authority and power ran deeply. Kenny didn't care about airs and graces. What you saw was what you got. Being the raw salt of the earth, he appealed to his pack's sense of humour.

The first time he ever went to court he tried to console the judge with a nervous wink. 'Shit, sorry about all this crap, mate. If I had've scored earlier in the day I wouldn't be here wasting your time.' Kenny shrugged. 'I slept in is all, mate. I was so fucking hungover.'

Tribute © Robert Lee Johnston 2016
Email: tributerobertleejohnston@gmail.com

The judge was pissed off. The whole courtroom went deadly quiet when the judge hollered, 'I'M NOT YOUR, MATE.' Then, 'Blah, blah, blah.'

Kenny looked genuinely surprised. 'Are you hungover too, mate?'

He was sincere, but the judge didn't see it. Kenny was sentenced. He got a small fine and community service. The judge asked him hesitantly if he had anything to say to the court.

'Nah, thanks, bloke. But good on you for asking. I just want to get home and have a bong or three, and chill out.' Standing there in his blue jeans and best clean shirt.

The judge, frustrated, exhausted, asked Kenny to leave. What else could he do? Kenny just swung unknowingly, innocently, on those top branches and vines. If no one was getting robbed, raped, whipped, beaten or hurt, it wasn't a crime in his mind.

But once Kenny was attacked or provoked he would fire up. In his almost Tourette's condition he couldn't hide the truth. If you were being a dickhead he'd tell you.

Something Bugs said reveals Kenny's current mindset. 'What if we bust our arses all our lives for some fucked-up boss. Slave for that fuck until we're sixty. Make him filthy rich and then retire, broken and skint, only to drop dead. Fuck that, man. Fuck that! Were we put here to live, or to work for some schmuck? I choose to live, boys.'

The trio dedicated a lot of hours to that cause. The only place Kenny felt truly at home was around his pack or in the bush growing weed.

He would say every now and then, 'You mob are the only family I got. I'm not one of those blokes who forget family.'

Kenny's dream of football fields of fine weed would be a reality one day. His bush skills and engine 'whispering' would prove invaluable. He would have a hand in setting the new golden standard of fine-tasting herb. His big crop was

Tribute © Robert Lee Johnston 2016
Email: tributerobertleejohnston@gmail.com

coming and every day he collated information to ensure its success. Not long now. All he had dreamed about in prison was that crop. He studied all the maps the small library could lend, looking for small, reliable water sources, a safe distance from stations and land owners. Away from any interstate or local flight paths. He searched for a hard place to get to and with an exit plan if everything went to shit. He met many growers in jail, good ones and bad ones, who had ideas he would take or leave. They helped fill in the gaps. He would learn from their mistakes. Once he got out he dug into his stash of coke and bought himself a newish Cruiser. He poured a fortune into engineering it to be as bush proof as humanly possible. At the same time he accumulated a trailer, tarps, camping gear, a freezer, generators, pumps, tools, and the best seed stock he could get his hands on. Plus a good rotary hoe, plenty of gas, diesel and petrol. Not to mention all the food and entertainment he would need. He would never leave this crop, and live with it night and day. A huge undertaking and a shitload of hard work. Bugs and Cozy would be his only contacts, visiting once every three months to resupply essentials. After three trips of back and forth he had a permanent camp set up. It was fat, and he wanted for nothing once he was comfy. He even had a sink and a shower that drained away far from the camp. The other two loved his spot. It was special; mulga scrub compared to rainforest, but scrub all the same. The country was drier, flatter and more open.

Kenny got to work felling trees, clearing scrub, cathederal ant mounds and roots. He worked bloody hard, shifting rocks and timbers. Once satisfied, he pulled the rip cord on his trusty rotary hoe and made a fine enough tilth to form rows. Hard work breaking rooted, rocky, virgin ground with that bucking, jumping machine. He set up water stations with forty-four-gallon drums filled from the pump. He employed a basic trickle, gravity irrigation system saving lots of back-breaking water cartage. Then he planted seed,

four football fields of the finest herb he could get hold of. It was a hell of a sight, even as seedlings.

Cozy's second visit blew his lid. Bugs had stayed behind in Tribute. All of Kenny's pre-planned systems worked a treat. The fertiliser Cozy brought was going to make things even better, as the girls were getting a little hungry. They bloomed instantly once they emptied some of the one-tonne bag into the irrigation drums. They had never seen so much pot in one place, at one time. The camp was situated right in the heart of that ocean of green. The smell was sweet and powerful. It was like a sugar-cane or maize paddock. You couldn't see through or over it once inside the crop. Some of those plants were truly spectacular. Here and there an exceptional plant was all muscle, huge plants, massive, dense, heavy buds weighing the females down. The odd sack of this sweet beauty got around and its seed was sought after and much admired.

Kenny was the happiest, the freest and the most comfortable that Cozy had ever seen him. The young man, his dreads, and all his earthly possessions, belonged out here.

He had collected books on minerals, gold, trees and soil types; on gunja and how to beat diseases and pests. He had stacks of wildlife references: birds, snakes, spiders, mammals, you name it. There were years of reading. Frozen food, a well-equipped first-aid box, a radio/stereo, alcohol, a full bucket of coke, a tasty sheet of acid, and a good clean water source made for a proud, worry-free Kenny.

He got a bit lonely now and then, but was usually far too busy to notice. He cherished his mates' three-monthly visits. They'd stay a couple of weeks and help with the harder jobs, giving him some company and a break from the girls. They would bring fuel for the generator, movies, alcohol, soap, fresh meat, flour, fruit, some meat pies and some porn for the vaginally isolated one. Kenny was clean, healthy and well nourished. Perhaps the hairiest Cozy had

Tribute © Robert Lee Johnston 2016
Email: tributerobertleejohnston@gmail.com

ever seen him. His dreads were coming together well and suited his dark skin. He had taken the time to plant a great vegetable garden, and it produced an abundance of eggplant, tomatoes, pumpkin, sweet potato, lettuce and capsicum. The two boys went fishing and took Kenny's old rifle to get a nice pig when needed. The little creek never ran dry and contained plenty of red claw, black brim and perch to break up their diet. The pigs and the dingoes were a bit skinnier out here, but the boar tasted great. Kenny never saw any planes or helicopters, so there was no paranoia or any reason to worry: it was a great big dose of freedom. Just what he needed. Just what everyone needs. Cozy stayed an extra week, it was so amazing. He loved it, and they shared heaps of fun and awesome conversation. They never got bored. It was just like being kids in the jungle again, running amok and carefree. Cozy was to come up again in two months with Bugs. The plants were six months old. In two months the dreadlocked one needed to harvest, manicure, dry, cure, weigh and bag it all. If he was snowed under the boys would stay and give him a hand to finish it off. The litter brothers hugged and slapped each other's backs farewell and Cozy left.

Knowing Kenny was happy made Cozy happy. In two months he would have got it out of his system and made a boat load of cash as well. Funny thing was he didn't need the money. He still had his share of the coke. But he had to do it. Kenny had to rebel in that fashion.

Cozy smiled all the way back to Tribute. Kenny was living his dream. Who was he to say it was a good or bad dream? Cozy was happy for his young brother. Bugs asked how Kenny was going.

'Fat and happy. You should see his crop, mate. It's a fucking monster. I knew it was going be big, but it's a boo farm, not a crop.'

Cozy explained the whole set up to him. He had been on the road two days and was tired so he ripped into a

Tribute © Robert Lee Johnston 2016
Email: tributerobertleejohnston@gmail.com

couple of lines to wake up. They talked shit and smoked for a few hours.

***

Cozy was woken early one morning a month or so later by a frantic Bugs. He barged into Cozy's room, flat out in a panic. He was crying and yelling hysterically, obviously devastated about something.

'Hey! What's the matter, mate?' Cozy thought Bugs was hurt and checked him fast over. 'You bleeding, bro? You right?'

'No! Cozy! Kenny! Fuck me! The news! Quick, look mate!'

Cozy got out of his nest and raced with him to the TV. A helicopter was filming a bush scene. Cozy didn't understand. It looked peaceful. Then a rough clearing appeared and the landscape came into focus. A huge crop of dope. Tall, healthy, well-tended females came into view. Cozy recognised the shape of the clearing and the sea of green.

'Oh no.'

They could see coppers with cane knives cutting down Kenny's plants without any respect. The helicopter gave vision of Kenny's fat camp. Cozy was weak and slightly off balance. 'Where's Kenny, Bugs? You seen, Kenny?'

'You have to listen!'

Cozy's ears hadn't heard a word.

'He's been shot, Cozy!'

'Eh?'

'They shot him!'

'Is he okay?'

'No, Cozy. They're saying ... Kenny's dead!'

Cozy stumbled backwards and sat on his arse. The footage revealed three body bags as the camera panned.

'Oh shit.'

Tribute © Robert Lee Johnston 2016
Email: tributerobertleejohnston@gmail.com

A female journalist reported a shootout with a heavily armed grower at the crop sight.

A police officer gave a statement. 'Police employed the services of a local indigenous tracker to find the camp. Once he discovered it he reported to us and escorted six drug squad officers to the site. The suspect was heavily armed and attacked with aggression, firing at and disabling our vehicles. The police tracker was wounded, and two officers killed during the grizzly stand-off. We were forced to open fire on the assailant and, in doing so, fatally wounded him. He died moments later from his wounds. His name is yet to be released.'

The reporter asked how the tracker was doing.

'The tracker is alive, thankfully. He has been evacuated by helicopter and stabilised.'

He was asked how valuable the crop would be.

'The crop has not been weighed and evaluated yet, but it is easily twice as large as any crop discovered previously in Australia. I, on behalf of the police department, would like to, in person, add our sincere condolences to the families and friends of our injured and deceased officers.'

Kenny's mates were inconsolable. In disbelief Cozy front kicked the TV in the guts, punched, elbowed and head-butted walls and the table. He threw a chair at a window and stopped at the sound of broken glass. Stopped dead still, just breathing, lost and foundering.

Bugs screamed, 'FUCK. I'LL KILL THEM. ALL THEM CUNTED FUCKS.'

Snot and tears covered their faces, and they cried heavily onto each other's shoulders. There was a knock at the door, and Cozy, a living mess, answered to a copper's uniform. Sarge. 'I'm so sorry, boys. I didn't know until it happened.' Tears were in his red eyes.

'WAS IT YOU THAT FUCKING SHOT HIM?'

Tribute © Robert Lee Johnston 2016
Email: tributerobertleejohnston@gmail.com

'No, Cozy, no. I had nothing to do with it, didn't know till now. Cozy, I got to ask. They want to know. You two blokes, are you involved with this at all?'

Sarge was tired, sad and upset. He never wanted to see this happen to anyone, let alone Kenny.

Bugs was up at his voice. 'What the FUCK do you want, pig? You got a thick fucking hide showing up here, copper. You swine-fucking maggot.'

Cozy slowly shook his head at Sarge. 'No. Now fuck off.'

He slammed the door as Sarge tried to apologise again. He whispered to them before walking back to the squad car, 'I'm sorry, boys. Kenny ... I'm so fucking sorry.'

Sarge sat and bawled hard before he fired the engine, wiping snot and tears from his face. He looked at his reflection in the mirror. 'What a fucking mess.'

Kenny's brothers were hardened, explosive, brittle, and then broken. Silently they imagined Kenny's last moments. Trying to believe what they had just heard, trying to see it through their friend's eyes.

Cozy told Bugs, 'They took his freedom. He took two of theirs. They just wouldn't leave him alone or give him the space he needed to heal. They gave him nothing but bars and bullets.'

Neither of them saw the damage the bullets had done. His was a closed coffin. He went down fighting. He went on his terms, the happiest Cozy had ever seen him. The best he had been. Kenny would die happy. He hated police and nobodies pushing him around. Kenny pushed back.

He had heard those trucks coming from miles out and thought, I ain't runnin'. Fuck it!

He grabbed all the ammo he could carry, including a few hollow points he had made for his old thirty-thirty. His first shots were to slow them down a bit, straight through the radiators and into the engine blocks of their two trucks. Get them all on foot.

Tribute © Robert Lee Johnston 2016
Email: tributerobertleejohnston@gmail.com

A thirty-thirty punches hard, even into steel. Once they got out of their four-wheel drives Kenny opened up from the safety of distance and cover. He purposely loaded the hollow points, cocked and got a bead. He saw a shoulder and its arm fling off a bloke, cartwheeling into the air awkwardly. He could see the blood misting from where he lay. The copper's screams were loud. He cocked and fired that silky, precise, mechanical lever-action. Cocking, firing. The screams of the dying cop made him laugh. His Tourette's like voice yelled out, 'FUCK YOU ALL! WHY CAN'T YOU POOFTER BASTARDS LEAVE ME THE FUCK ALONE? I'VE HAD A GUT FULL OF YOU.'

Cocking, firing.

'I ain't goin' to jail, fuck yas!'

Cocking, firing.

'I'll kill all you fuckers dead.'

Cocking, firing.

'You maggots. You're fucking dead.' He reloaded his trusty rifle. 'YOU'RE ALL FUCKING DEAD!'

One of the coppers ran to find cover. Kenny took his time, the barrel tracking his enemy. The hollowed-out projectile caved the cop's head in, side on. Covering the steaming cop truck bonnet with claret and bone as it rained bits of brain.

'I fucking told you. I fucking warned youse. Hey, tell Sarge I'm not cleaning that fucking mess up. Ha ha ha!'

He saw a blackfella hiding, crouching, amongst them.

'You dog. Fucking tracker, eh? You're fucking dead too, you nosey bastard.'

Kenny lined him up as he took off and ran. He lowered his aim and paused as he breathed out. 'You won't never track again. You should've minded your own fucking business.'

He fired and blew a gaping hole through the tracker's lower back, instantly paralysing him.

Tribute © Robert Lee Johnston 2016
Email: tributerobertleejohnston@gmail.com

'Not real deadly now are ya, tracker? Bet you didn't see that coming? Eh, which way? Ha ha ha! Track that. You mongrel fucking dog.'

He chuckled coldly and pitifully to himself, shaking his dreads, watching all the bright red oil leak from the tracker's entry and exit wounds.

Kenny spoke matter-of-factly. 'Shit! Well, I'm really fucked now.'

The other pigs saw gun smoke and found the cover Kenny was hidden behind. They opened fire. Kenny ran to a second vantage point and put the copper who was running around with his shoulder missing, like a chook with its head cut off, out of his misery as the thirty-thirty thumped a big hole in his chest.

'Cop that, copper.'

A bullet struck Kenny's ribs, below his chest, punching clean out the other side. His breath was gone. The tiniest hole spat blood. He sat for a second and looked up at the sky. He was winded and in no hurry. He fired a volley of shots into the air in the direction of the shot until he had to reload. That kept them at bay for a bit.

He tried to catch his breath. He had time to relax and wanted a minute to remember. He started thinking about all his orphan kin, all together. When they all were alive, kids growing up. He smiled. Through tears he called out loud to Bugs, Cozy and Evie. 'I love you two, you blokes. I love you, Evie. I'm going to miss you my brothers, my sister. A whole fucking lot. I'm sorry.'

He thought of the others waiting there, buried in Tribute's ground.

'I'm coming, youse. Just … just fucking wait up. I'm coming.'

He sucked in a congested, painful, brave, defiant breath, filling his injured lungs. He stood, turned in the direction of the shot that had hit him and fired back.

'FUCK YOU MARY L—'

Kenny's head was ripped open like a club-struck melon. His shot was too late and less accurate than that of the patient officer who lay in wait.

His fight was over.

In coming days, TV footage would show a mountain of plants being burnt, his half a tin of cocaine, Kenny's killing rifle and the camp itself. The thirty-thirty, cocaine and crop size received the most coverage. The largest, heaviest crop in Australia's recorded history. Ever.

Definitely the bloodiest.

The tall, thin branches and vines Kenny swung from broke and he lost his grip. As he fell he thought, It had been fun up there, peaceful and dangerous. A wicked combination. He smiled happily to himself. I had a ball!

They lost another brother, to anything but natural causes. They had precious few to spare.

Evie saw the news that night, and though names weren't mentioned she knew in her bones it was one of the boys. She rang the farm house. She got no answer because Cozy had destroyed the phone in his rage, so she called Sarge for confirmation.

'I'm sorry, Evie, love. It was, in fact, Kenny.'

She took the news badly. Evie took time off her studies to pay her respects and catch up with her two boys. They howled and huddled together like lost wolf cubs when they laid eyes on each other. Only four people were at his funeral service, other than a few sad cops and the dead coppers' angry families. Bernie paid his respects and helped carry his coffin. The locals were so ashamed of Kenny and what he had done that not one Tributarian came to his service. The mob had to use the undertaker's family to make up the numbers to carry Kenny to the grave. They buried Kenny in Tribute's hillside cemetery, already overpopulated with their friends. The same patch of red dirt where not far away lay Jen, Pops, John Henry, Stirrup, Lacey, and now Kenny. Rev

Tribute © Robert Lee Johnston 2016
Email: tributerobertleejohnston@gmail.com

was buried in there along with Syd and Deidre. They didn't visit those three particular headstones.

You could be forgiven for thinking this sort of thing became easier the more they did it. For Cozy it never got easier.

It was a horrendous, typical Tribute day. Raining hard with gusty wind blowing angry. Bugs brought his trusty, beat-up camping guitar, the same one he took to prison, the first crop, and all their camping trips. He played some Stevie Ray Vaughan, 'The Sky Is Crying.' You could, indeed, see 'tears roll down the street'. The three were lost, phantom limbed and disoriented. They felt guilty, and responsible for their Kenny, and for each of them. A trio wrought by mounting losses and the effort just to suck in oxygen and exist.

It was all too much as Bugs played in the rain, soaked to the bone. They fell apart. Bugs placed the trusty, wet guitar in Kenny's grave, along with some fat buds and flowers. 'Look after this for me, old mate.'

They were just twenty-two years old. Seeing six fallen friends in the ground was particularly hard that day as the remaining three 'g'day'd' them all and tended loyally, lovingly their silent plots.

And just like that, the pack were three.

* *Tears Roll Down The Street, Stevie Ray Vaughan – Song Title (Written by Elmore James)*

Tribute © Robert Lee Johnston 2016
Email: tributerobertleejohnston@gmail.com

CHAPTER TWENTY-SEVEN: SOMETIMES YOU SINK.

"Shine On You, Crazy Diamond".

Pink Floyd — Song Title

Bugs had taken an instant liking to the coke.

He was sucking all the recreation from recreational drugs. He had years and years of supply. Using all day, every day, builds a sturdy resistance, and the more he consumed the more he needed. Bugs took himself out of circulation for a while, to focus on his habit. It filled the emptiness inside him. He needed it so badly he couldn't bear to be far from a stash. Cozy and he had divvied up what was left of Kenny's share between them. Cozy filled ammo tins and buried them. He had sold a little to buy a boxing club and a decent road bike. Other than selling bits and pieces, birthdays, celebrations and anniversaries, Cozy left it well alone. Bugs,

Tribute © Robert Lee Johnston 2016
Email: tributerobertleejohnston@gmail.com

on the other hand, was inhaling so much cocaine that he soon tired of the repetition and traded some for heroin.

Cozy noted cold, subtle shifts in his personality and assumed he was having some discomfort staying away from the coke. He had barely taken any this last month or two in front of him. Cozy was so busy setting up the boxing club and spending more and more time at Mathilda's that a lot slipped his attention. The young couple had decided to move in together when Tilly returned from visiting her parents. Old Bernie dropping dead recently didn't help Cozy's attention. The old timer just didn't wake up one day. Cozy took his passing badly. Bernie had recently told Cozy over a regular, once-a-week beer and tasty, home-cooked meal, 'I'm real proud of you, Cozy. I love you like a father his son. I never got around to having any real family, fighting all the time, and always on the road. If I had my time again, Cozy, I'd want a son like you, mate. I couldn't ever ask for one better. I'm bloody sorry I never pried into what happened at the orphanage, or what you all went through as kids. I just don't know how to talk to people about those things. My old man didn't talk much and, I guess, I got a chip off the old block.'

Cozy loved the old man dearly.

'I would never have told you anyway, Bernie, cos I love you too much. You never stuck your nose in. I could tell when you were worried about me. That was all I needed. Telling you would have been too painful, and Rev may have sent me from you, from Tribute, from my mob. I would be nothing without you. I love you more than any son of yours possibly could. You're bloody good to me, Bernie.'

Cozy carried his old friend and mentor, with Sarge helping the many bearers, to his final resting place on the church's hill. The turn out and the spread at the wake were impressive. Bernie was loved and missed by all who knew his blessed bones. Stories from old fighters and his boxing prodigy were shared at his wake in the main bar of the

Tribute © Robert Lee Johnston 2016
Email: tributerobertleejohnston@gmail.com

Middy. His legend wouldn't be forgotten around Tribute anytime soon.

Cozy would never forget Bernie 'The Wrecking Ball' Burns.

Bugs started falling asleep at the table like the high school kid who'd whited out or drunk too much. He would wake up speaking nonsense and then pass out again. The line on the table in front of him looked like speed.

'Oi, you going to up that, bro?'

Bugs lifted his head and it looked right through Cozy. He mumbled something. It was more of a little heap than a line. Cozy assumed it was speed. He grabbed an unopened pick off the table, put the powder into the spoon Bugs had used, added water, a filter, and then belted it up.

Something wasn't right. Cozy could instantly taste something else. Confused, Cozy wet an index finger to taste the powder left on the table. It numbed his tongue. It's not speed. Something weighty was happening. He sat in the chair and clenched both butt cheeks as he packed a bucket. Cozy smoked, and thought a drink might help take the edge off. He was slowing up and a custard-thick syrup bound his thoughts and body. He felt sick and had to spew. No way could he make the dunny. The kitchen sink it is. Energy and adroit thought left his detached body as he spewed. He felt far beyond himself, lost beyond the world. He woke Bugs.

'What the fuck was that I just jacked up?'

The gibberish Bugs spoke was inaudible.

I'm going to have to ride this shit out, man, on my own. He became paranoid. Had Bugs used pharmaceuticals and mixed up some cocktail? A recipe he learned in jail from the junkies? That was all Cozy remembered later other than puking.

He woke feeling washed out on the couch, to Bugs moaning about how much he had used last night.

'I was sure I saved more than that.'

'I whacked some up.'

Tribute © Robert Lee Johnston 2016
Email: tributerobertleejohnston@gmail.com

Bugs looked up shocked and inhaled sharply.

'Was that smack, Bugs?'

'Yeah. Shit, sorry, man! I should've said. Are you okay?'

'Fuck, man. That was bad.'

'I kinda like it myself.'

'True? Just made me spin out, spew my guts up, and sleep.'

'You get past that.'

'Man, I can do without that shit. That wasn't fun, dude. No fun, Bro-migo. I still feel shithouse. I got to try get some shut eye.'

'I'm into it. It's cool. It numbs everything and gives me time to think.'

Bugs couldn't shake it and savoured his new high. Within months his body gained fat, his mind grew clouded with addled delusions. His shoulders slumped with the effort. Cozy witnessed his best friend's slow demise. Cozy's sense of connection wavered. A black spot was forming on the sun. Cozy hid the powder from him. He'd simply score more. Cozy confronted him, and he'd lie, saying he'd already quit. Bugs became a master at hiding the drug and the resulting high. Bugs's heart didn't trust anymore, not even his pack member. Cozy could barely tell if he was bent or not. He pleaded with him to at least slow down a bit. Other than tying him to a chair, Cozy tried all he could. His slow decline was possibly the most painful tragedy he had ever seen. So Cozy double-bluffed him. He pretended he didn't give a shit. That seemed to make Bugs happier. Any pressure exerted pushed him further away from his mate. Cozy was losing him on many levels. He ingested more and more crap food. All his taste buds wanted was sugary-sweet shit. He consumed nothing of any substance for about a year. He looked bloated and sickly, his weight blew out, his young eyes grew old and deepened in his now bored-with-Cozy face. He aged twenty years in that twelve months. His face fattened and lost its former identity. The more smack he had

Tribute © *Robert Lee Johnston* 2016
Email: tributerobertleejohnston@gmail.com

the more coke his body needed. He'd wake to coke only to sleep off smack. Cozy was finding excuses to not go home, sleeping at the boxing club or Mathilda's. The couple had been spending more and more time dreaming and discussing their futures together. Cozy loved Tilly more than anyone or anything he had ever known.

The black spot on the sun grew. The house was a sty, with old fits carelessly dropped. Packets of empty needle bags, full ashtrays, pot, and take away littered the farm house. The sink and the stink reminded Cozy of Deidre's kitchen. He asked Bugs to stop for a bit and take some time off. Bugs wouldn't, couldn't and didn't. He'd torture himself, and Cozy, for six more excruciating months.

Cozy liked to think the swollen body he found was not Bugs. That it was the hammer's body and that Bugs had died last year when the smack got hold of him. Cozy had warned him that junk is a physical addiction, devoid of any heart or emotion. Particularly when it comes to such a matter as trivial as life. Cockroaches and flies picked and fussed about the blood pooled around his head. The bleeding veins in his brain had cried 'Enough!' Cozy cursed God, Bugs, heroin, coke, everyone he ever knew. The broken man-child hated Bugs for leaving him bloke-less, to fend on his own. Cozy couldn't forgive him. But Cozy couldn't leave him. The kid had loved his almost illiterate mate all his young life. Life looked forever boring without the prospect of Bugs in it. Cozy had loved him so very much, and for so very long.

Cozy recalled old memories that made him smile and then fall to pieces. The remembering whispered inside him like a frozen winter. Bugs amusing them all, impersonating perfectly Sarge, Nixon, their teachers and Winston. Bugs's best were Rev's rants, broadcasting to the heathens. Bugs, with a German accent, always added a Nazi salute, and an index-finger Hitler moustache. He added a high-kicking march when imitating Rev, room permitting.

Tribute © Robert Lee Johnston 2016
Email: tributerobertleejohnston@gmail.com

'Blessed iz ze child who knowz silenze iz eloquenze ...!
Heil Hitler!'

Cozy smiled at a thought, their first trip away from the church grounds together. Five or six years old, to some bloke's farm. The same bloke who taught Bugs the magic power of carrots. He had an old, spacious, cool wooden farmhouse that had deep concrete sinks, with a comfortable verandah. In Cozy's recollections he was a good fella. The two young roosters had worked out how to shoot the rifle when the farmer fired a shot or two into the air one day to scare off chicken hawks. Pull that bolt back, put a bullet up the spout, close it, flick the safety and fire.

'Piece of piss,' they both agreed.

The farmer had to go to town one day, leaving the cockerels alone. They found the rifle and a whole box of shells. It took a couple of seconds to work out the safety switch. Then they were shooting. Bugs wanted to range the weapon to test how far it could shoot, so they scavenged a child-height piece of corrugated iron from the chook shed. Delighted, they shot at it and moved back until the bullets harmlessly bounced off.

Cozy asked Bugs, 'Do you reckon if we took a few steps back from that iron the bullet would bounce off us?'

'I reckon.'

'Righto, I'll yell out when I'm ready. But I shoot you after.'

'Okay. Just don't move once I shoot, otherwise I'll miss.'

Cozy ran off, laughing. 'Make sure you aim high so it doesn't drop to the ground.'

'Don't worry, mate, I'll get you.'

The young blondie got to the iron and took four measured steps back. Cozy grinned in anticipation with one hand covering his eyes, the other his balls. He watched through gaps between his fingers.

'RIGHTO, BUGS.'

Tribute © Robert Lee Johnston 2016
Email: tributerobertleejohnston@gmail.com

'NO WORRIES. HERE GOES. THREE, TWO, ONE.' BANG!

Bugs reckoned that Cozy turned skinny in fright as the rifle clapped hands, trying to reduce his target area by being side on. The bullet hit him just below the hip bone on his meaty upper thigh. It hurt, and he was instantly a tad tropical.

Bugs sprinted to his target. Cozy hopped, moaned, limped, squealed, fell over onto the cold ground drooling, sweating and bleeding. They pissed themselves laughing.

'You should've seen your face!'

'Fucking oww!'

Shit like that.

They had to get the bullet out. It wasn't that deep, but Bugs flat-out refused to let Cozy shoot him. Gingerly they limped away, Cozy's arm over Bugs's shoulder, to the farmhouse to find some tweezers and Dettol. The pain getting that bastard out, with Bugs digging around in there like an epileptic steam shovel, was beastly. All Cozy could do was laugh like a crazed man.

'I gotta get under it, Cozy! Hang on, mate!'

He forced the tweezers around and down on the slug. Finally Bugs got a grip on the slippery mongrel. A bit of blood and material squirted out, so he jammed a cotton ball soaked with Dettol in there. Cozy sucked in air and eggs at that. Bugs finished by wrapping the wound up. He offered Cozy the projectile, and then pocketed the shot when Cozy told him, 'I don't want the bastard.'

'Cozy … you should've taken five steps back, brother.'

Cozy still had the scar, a perfect five-cent-sized circle.

Bugs still had the piece of lead. In a box, with all his ill-gotten booty, under his bed.

✳✳✳

Tribute © Robert Lee Johnston 2016
Email: tributerobertleejohnston@gmail.com

Their kinship and the easy association was struck a mighty blow as Cozy cleaned his dead, lifelong brother. Gently. He told his body, while crying, a Paulette Jiles quotation he had memorised: 'The road to hell is paved with men who didn't know when to quit.'

As he wept, Cozy hoped there was no pain when Death arrived. Bugs's alarmed face testified to panic and suffering. Cozy hoped it was at least fast and merciful. He washed his body on the bed with a bucket, a fresh cloth and warm, soapy water. No man, not even with the cast-iron fortitude of Bugs, could take that quantity of chemical substances daily and live. A cold, hard fact. Cozy rang Sarge after he cleaned the house. He burnt Bugs's blood-soaked clothes and mattress, sacks of smack, and of all his new and used picks lying around. Cozy threw his spoon far away, after bending it and clenching it angrily in his fist. He replaced Bugs's mattress with Kenny's and lay him gently on his back, sleeping peacefully forever in his memory. Cozy kissed Bugs's forehead.

'See you on the other side my … My old, careless one.'

Cozy left after the call. He left his litter brother forever.

Sarge later sadly confided in him that he had found nearly a hundred used fits, stashed carefully in his room, even after Cozy's once-over. Cozy thought he had been quite thorough and removed all the incriminating evidence, but Bugs was always cunning and inventive when it came to hiding stuff from the rest of the world.

Weeks later, Cozy forgave his little brother.

Cozy had just turned twenty-six. His greatest friend was dead.

He had to ring Evie.

The large, wild pack were now … a pair.

Tribute © Robert Lee Johnston 2016
Email: tributerobertleejohnston@gmail.com

CHAPTER TWENTY-EIGHT: HOSPITAL STINK.

"My Back Pages."

Bob Dylan – Song Title

'This is bullshit. Everything's fucked!'

Cozy received the second-hand message and gunned the hardtop flat out to the hospital. A female doctor explained, in a kind of mother-goosey way, to be prepared for the worst. She, along with a male police officer, explained the facts of Mathilda's accident.

The curtains were drawn around the occupied beds in the ICU. A male nurse led Cozy to her bedside tut-tutting and annoying Cozy. He stared for long moments into his eyes with sympathy, making him uncomfortable. Far too much eye contact for Cozy's liking, with his feminine, misplaced sympathy.

I don't need sympathy. I need you to do your fucking job and save my girl.

'Another nurse will be along to help you,' he whispered as he left.

Long, raven-black hair caught Cozy's attention. The curtains were drawn half open, awaiting his presence. She was covered in a thin, white sheet and an assortment of instruments, monitors and the like. He kissed her cheek and then her lips tenderly without disturbing the tube coming out, and whispered her name twice. A female ICU nurse, recording observations on a large chart, came over to Tilly's still, sleeping, machine-aided body and nodded politely to Cozy as she approached. He gave a tear-stained smile as she turned down the volume of various machines that were beeping and whirring. She returned a warm smile.

'Youse two need a bit of quiet, I reckon. If you need anything just press this buzzer, love.'

He nodded and thanked her.

'Can, Mathilda, hear me?'

She told him yes and again smiled softly.

The white hospital sheet hid more than he could clock. Uncontrollable, blistering-hot tears scalded a trail down his cheeks, dripping onto her as he stroked her face. Cozy's breathing became concentrated and deliberate. He needed to see. The kindly nurse whose name tag read 'Alice'— a big girl with an earthy, plump, kind face — then whispered soothingly, 'She's just hanging on, sweetie. There's a lot of trauma going on with our little princess. Are you ready, love?'

'I'm ready.'

Alice gently removed the sheet, exposing his girl.

He exhaled and closed his eyes. His fists were clenched as tightly as his stomach.

'Oh fuck. Oh, baby. No.'

He moaned and whimpered in insulated, insulted agony. The ring he had given her was gone, now in a yellow kidney-shaped dish beside her bed. Her left arm had been amputated just below the elbow. Her chest and torso were

Tribute © Robert Lee Johnston 2016
Email: tributerobertleejohnston@gmail.com

green, yellow and black with bruises. Her ribs and sternum were broken. Thick tubes protruded from her body, bubbling with diluted, bloody, bile-like fluid, drained into shapely glass bottles. Mathilda's lungs were punctured and the resulting air leaking into her body was starting to bloat her. There were deep cuts, lacerations and stitches. It seemed no part of her tiny body was given mercy or quarter. All the while noises of congested discomfort and obvious agony escaped her, like strange, twisted, deluded dream sentences. He could feel under his fingers as he touched Mathilda the stubborn, sharp splinters of glass that remained beneath her soft, pale skin, forming weals like the braille on medication packets. Or an episode of shingles.

A belt of roses from the devil. That was what a doctor had once told him the Vikings called shingles.

Cozy thought of a disturbing phrase by Hesoid: Sleeping a sleep closely related to death, the brother to death.

Her right leg was a stump. Completely gone.

'Argh. Shit no. Be fucked!'

'We couldn't save it, love. The surgeons really tried. They really did their best, lovey.'

A hateful, hot feeling sprang to life. The thought that someone had cut her leg off, and that Cozy couldn't stop them.

Some fucking doctors. Some fucking butchers mutilated my Mathilda. Fucking strangers to us.

Alice sensed his offence. 'Your wife's leg was potentially ...' She placed a hand tenderly on his slumped shoulder and corrected herself. 'Definitely never going to heal, due to massive trauma and loss of blood flow. Her leg was dead, lovey. Infection was inevitable. If that leg had stayed, she wouldn't be here now. And she's not out of the woods yet. I'm so sorry, love.'

Cozy bowed his head, unable to speak. He didn't even register Alice leaving. He stroked his Mathilda, her pretty face, and tried to comfort her. Cozy pleaded and begged.

Tribute © Robert Lee Johnston 2016
Email: tributerobertleejohnston@gmail.com

'Please, wake up. I love you, sugar. I love you, baby,' was all his strangled intellect could muster. Words felt so completely useless. 'I'm sorry, Tilly. I'm so fucking sorry.'

Cozy felt powerless. He wiped the snot from his dripping nose, braced and hardened his mind for her. That's where he stayed for two weeks. Sleeping in a cot-like bed Alice had arranged for Cozy to be close.

***

One night, two weeks later, he woke in a daze to his name being whispered. It was early, three thirty in the morning. He was sure he had imagined or dreamt it. But then he heard Mathilda ask, 'What's happening, Cozy?'

He was up in a flash.

'Baby, you're awake!'

Mathilda was silently crying in pain and confusion.

'Cozy, what's going on, babe?' Her voice was dry and dusty. She screamed a frightened scream. She'd moved her left arm and, after a second's shock, slowly realised.

With a stoic effort Mathilda kicked her sheet off, agitated and confused.

Cozy whispered, 'Honey, baby, you were in a terrible accident.'

She moaned at the flash of a memory. She asked Cozy if this was a bad dream and then fainted fast away upon seeing, vaguely, the stump of her lower limb, where her right leg used to be.

Alice, hearing her screams from the nurses' desk, appeared and tended to Mathilda, patting Cozy's shoulder as she hovered around her.

'We have a little hope, love. By rights Mathilda shouldn't be awake.'

Cozy nodded, too stunned to reply. A terrible sensation enveloped him. It dawned on him that he had no one to tell.

Tribute © Robert Lee Johnston 2016
Email: tributerobertleejohnston@gmail.com

Everyone was gone from view. Cozy hadn't seen Evie for more than a day or three after Bugs's funeral. Each time she had visited Tilly was working away or visiting her parents. Through bad timing and bad luck, the two girls had not yet met face to face. He was all alone. The feeling grew and ate at him. He knew in his heart that Tilly was dying. He'd seen enough people die to recognise its stink. He turned inward, momentarily, deciding not to think like that. He had to tell her parents she was awake.

A new nurse waited politely for Cozy's phone call to end at her work station. She made him aware that Mathilda was awake though heavily sedated, and the doctor had made her as comfortable as he could. A priest was delivering Mathilda her final blessings and the last rites. Cozy waited impatiently outside until the priest left.

Cozy quietly, carefully approached the bed and whispered, 'Hey, baby.'

She turned and smiled. Her faded, pretty smile. The currency of loss and ruin.

'Are you, okay? I'm so sorry, baby. I'm so sorry.'

She moved her head back to make eye contact. 'The doctor says I'm dying, Cozy. I don't have long.'

'No, baby, no. You just woke up! He doesn't know you, know us. He's wrong. They're full of shit.'

She spoke soothingly. 'Cozy, listen to me. It's true. I can feel it. It's heavy and so strong.'

'There's so much I want to say. We got lots to do. You got to fight!'

'We have to say it all now, Cozy,' she continued tiredly. 'I can feel it. I can feel it, baby. Cozy, none of this was your fault, so when I leave, no blaming yourself, okay?'

'What? It's all my fault. I should've been there. Right beside you.'

'Then, we'd both be here. Both be—'

Cozy didn't let her finish. 'I jus wanna be where you is.' He smiled honestly into her eyes at his grammatical error.

Tribute © Robert Lee Johnston 2016
Email: tributerobertleejohnston@gmail.com

'It's not your fault, Cozy. We haven't long so promise me, you.'

Cozy agreed, but by shaking his head. Trying to derail her line of thought, he whispered, 'Does it hurt, baby? Are you in pain?'

'It hurts, babe, cos I'm leaving you. That makes me sad and hurts the most, my sweet Cozy.'

'You're not leaving anywhere, cos … But … You just woke up. Don't think that, honey. You can't … Don't go. Stay. Please stay with me?'

'I'm sorry, Cozy, but I'm weak and too tired.' She locked her exhausted, gentle eyes on her beloved man. 'It's so hard. I love you so much. You know I loved you from the moment I met you? You let me see you, Cozy.'

His body rocked with fits of intense sobs. 'I love you too. Don't go. I'll take care of you no matter what, forever. I love you. I'll do anything.' He broke into fleshy shards right there.

'I know, Cozy, I know.' She relaxed and sighed. 'It makes me happy knowing you love me. I will always love you, you know that? Cozy …? You got to promise me something.'

'Anything.'

'Promise me, when the time's right, promise you will try to meet someone, someone new. When you're ready.'

He recoiled. 'No, don't. You can't ask me that. Please, please, baby, don't ask that of me.'

'If after three years you don't meet anyone, promise me you'll try to meet someone.'

'No.' He sobbed. 'I don't want that!'

'Try. Meet someone you like and talk to them. Promise me?'

'I can't, Mathilda.'

'No one should be alone, Cozy. Also, I don't want you wasting time on revenge. No killing the bloke or hurting him over me. You have to let him go, honey. Forget about him.

Tribute © Robert Lee Johnston 2016
Email: tributerobertleejohnston@gmail.com

Just let him go, and concentrate on you. Write the book you and Bugs promised to write. I'd buy it, and be your number one groupie, Cozy. Revenge, your anger, your hate, will kill you.'

'I can't promise all that, honey.'

'Please leave him alone. Do it for me. Cozy, please, no revenge.'

'No. I can't keep those promises.' Cozy looked far away from her.

'Promise me, Cozy. Twice.' She touched Cozy's face gently and turned it her way. 'Promise me.'

He nodded his heavy head into her only hand. She smiled perfectly at him.

'You, you're a good man. Better than you know. You made me happy every single day. You are perfect to me. For me. I've loved each of our exciting adventures. I knew we would have lots of them as soon as we met that day. That's why I chatted you up. I'll see you again, sweetie, and our adventures will continue.'

A hot lava-lump exploded in his throat. 'Please don't go. You're the perfect one. So perfect. I'm the luckiest bloke around. Cos of you.'

She was fading away.

'Baby, look at me, wait up. You have to promise me something.'

Mathilda focused her weary eyes and smiled sweetly through her tears. 'Anything, baby.'

'Come visit me, Mathilda? In my dreams, when you can or ... I don't know how. I don't know how it all works. But if any time you want to, you drop on in and say g'day. Stay for as long as you want. Haunt me any time you want,' he joked. 'Naked, if you like. Tilly, say you promise?'

She giggled, tired. 'I promise you. I will. I love you.'

'I love you.'

They clung together for the briefest of moments.

The machines' complaining told Cozy Mathilda was dead.

The nurse saw and turned away as Cozy fell to pieces. He kissed her lips and her forehead one last time. A long moment passed. The nurse pulled a sheet completely over her.

'I think she woke to say goodbye to you,' she said, looking sympathetically at Cozy. 'You know? Your Tilly couldn't leave until seeing you off in person and saying goodbye to you.' She was lost in thought. 'That's what love is. Yep. And you two, you got lots of it.'

Cozy broke into a million more smaller shards and had to sit. Just then Mathilda's parents arrived. Upon seeing the young man they did the maths. The three hung their heads and wished the driver hadn't been drinking. Wished that Mathilda had not been on the road while he was on it. Wished she hadn't hit that intersection as he ignored or missed the red light. Mathilda had stood no chance. The driver, due to face trial in a fortnight or so, came out with a cut or two and a broken arm.

Cozy was going to get drunk. Howl at that cruel, hidden moon. It was dark out, so he found a similarly dark bar, with a similarly dark corner, and waited for the crazed drag race of emotions.

He was all alone. The weight of the loss was heavy and cruel. Cozy could feel the emptiness inside him, and no amount of Wild Turkey could fill it. His brain turned primeval, and the urge to destroy formed. Cozy wanted two or three of the biggest, baddest monsters any bastard knew. Just to make it fair. He wanted to torture each of them on their feet. He smiled, the drunken devil, and looked over the line-up of fresh, available quarry.

Rip their flesh and drink their fucking blood. Feel their bones disintegrate under my knuckles.

Tribute © Robert Lee Johnston 2016
Email: tributerobertleejohnston@gmail.com

His hands were clenched into tight fists so intensely they cramped. Cozy inhaled slowly and deeply and glanced at Mathilda's ring in his hand.

Cozy took another gander at the poor fellas he was about to rip apart. All good blokes by the looks. Fair, honest, hard-working men. Innocently having a drink, minding their own affairs. Hurting strangers wouldn't cure him.

'Couple more drinks and I'll fuck off.'

He went to a motel and crashed out, crying.

The next day, Cozy and Mathilda's parents organised and grieved. They were the walking dead. Mathilda's funeral would be held off a week to let interstate family arrive. The driver's court case was less than a week away and the beak had given his council some time to gather their case.

Reading that in the local rag he angrily yelled, 'Get fucked! Lock the bastard up! Fuck youse!'

Cozy stewed. 'Fuck knows, I will knock some fucking pig out if I have to just to get close to him in court and go to prison myself. Just to be near that fuck for the dogs, if I have to. I don't give a fuck.'

Mathilda would be upset and mad at him, embarrassed, and maybe ashamed.

'Fuck it, what can I do? She knows my form. I figure she's just going to have to understand. Everyone's just going to have to fucking get over it.'

He knew all he needed to know, for now: the driver's name. The rest he could find out for himself.

Tom Waits played. It was too easy for Cozy to find the driver's address. He took a few days to learn his routines, his strengths and vulnerabilities. The driver was making the very most of his last week of freedom. He was single, which disappointed Cozy greatly. Drinking and getting laid were highest on his agenda. The hunter sat close enough to him in the pub to overhear him telling strangers, girls and his mates, 'It wasn't my fault.'

He squarely blamed Mathilda and felt victimised.

Tribute © Robert Lee Johnston 2016
Email: tributerobertleejohnston@gmail.com

Fucking victim! Cozy savoured the thought of teaching him the word's true meaning. He pulled a few sympathy fucks here and there, proving any useless dumb fuck could get laid. The window of opportunity was closing.

'Time's up, fuckface.'

Plain as day he figured was best. Just storm in. Cozy knew he was at home alone. He leaned over and picked up a cricket bat from across the back seat of the two-door.

Cozy rested the well cherried old Gray Nic on his lap. His fingers were drumming on the steering wheel hardwood for a moment to focus. 'Fish in the jail house tonight'* played on the hardtop's stereo, making him think of past bloodshed, and keeping ... keeping real. Facing consequences, good or bad. Keeping tough, fighting for life, fighting for Mathilda.

Cozy knocked on the door and the driver opened up. None of this 'who's there?' bullshit. Cozy smiled as the door opened. The driver's eyes widened when he noticed the cricket bat in Cozy's hand.

'G'day,' Cozy told him, and front kicked him in the guts hello. 'You're in big fucking trouble now, fuckface.'

He fell backwards winded, off balance. Cozy dropped the bat.

The winded fella reckoned, 'I'm sorry! Man, I'm sorry!'

Cozy wanted to use hands, and only hands. Get close and personal. He straddled his victim's torso, pinning his arms with both knees, one arm still in plaster from the wreck. Cozy punched, elbowed and clubbed him, with fists and forearms. He head-butted him until his pathetic apologies were rendered silent, until his face was a collapsed, unrecognisable, spat-out red-mango seed.

Cozy was raging. 'It's going to get bloody. Bloodier than your butcher's boots, old mate. You weren't sorry in the pub.'

Cozy kept on ploughing fists into his head.

Tribute © Robert Lee Johnston 2016
Email: tributerobertleejohnston@gmail.com

'I bet you're real sorry now. You piece of shit! I'm putting you down, you mongrel fucking dog.'

There was no response.

'Right now, mother fucker.'

Cozy grabbed his scrawny neck and choked the living out of him. He felt strong and purposeful. His righteous breath skipped in excitement as life faded away under his grip. He whispered menacingly into his dying ear, 'I'm going straight to hell, my friend. When I get there, I will hunt you down and choke you, just like this, twice daily for eternity. I will be your ... Devil.'

Cozy breathed freely, deeply, for the first time since the accident, feeling pure and right as his enemy's body rocked and spasmed. Cozy tightened his grip. He thought of Syd, bleeding out. Pinky and his posse of pussies. The boys drenched in all that blood, that killing night. Then Cozy heard Bugs's voice, relaxed, whispering, 'Fucking wake up, Cozy.'

He turned to see Jen looking on, with her head slightly bowed, a baby in her arms. She was smiling.

Fuck knows, I missed that smile, he thought

Jenny pleaded in a husky whisper, 'It's okay, my brave Cozy.'

They were all in the jungle. All of them. At a favourite swimming hole. A large fire burned comfortably away. Bugs passed Kenny a nicely rolled joint and nodded approvingly to Cozy as he blew the smoke out. Cozy's eyes were focused on strangling this sack of shit. Then he heard John Henry's friendly voice. 'Cozy, wake up, mate.' Stirrup was eager at his feet, wet, with the biggest stick and smile Cozy ever saw. There was proud King Louis, with his single ear. And Bernie, with Pops, cackling happily, stroking Cozy's dingo.

Louis looked on wisely, quietly, behind the kids. Pops whispered from afar, 'We all waitin right ere. You go back now, brudder. She ain't callin fer yer, yet.'

Tribute © Robert Lee Johnston 2016
Email: tributerobertleejohnston@gmail.com

Kenny spoke far too loudly, but it was all of them talking in unison. 'It's all good, man. Let fuckface go, man, and wake the fuck up.'

Cozy let go. He could feel Mathilda near, but couldn't see her. Cozy called out, 'Tilly, I've fucking lost it. I've lost the fucking plot, haven't I?'

He searched for her anew. 'Mathilda? I was with them. Am I dreaming? Have I ...? Am I fucking crazy? I must be crazy ... or lost. Am I lost? I think I'm lost.'

Maybe he didn't belong where he'd just been and maybe now the error had been corrected. He was frightened, his head spinning.

'Is this hell?'

Cozy's hell was when a helpless kid was getting abused in some dirty, fucked-up house.

A smart, pretty girl once told him, Heaven and hell can exist in the same place. At the same time. While that kid's being fucked with in a cold house, the house next door is heaven. They're making love, or welcoming in a newborn. Heaven and hell are here, all the time, with us all. Right now. Fuck wondering what happens next, Cozy, you just got to love them here and now, just in case there is no thereafter.

'Cozy! Wake the fuck up!' It was Mathilda's voice, razor sharp.

'What?' He was confused. 'I'm awake. They're dead. You're dead.'

Cozy found her face in his mind and couldn't take his sore eyes off her. It was as if five seconds had passed since he saw her last. She looked normal. Her face was fresh, her body unbroken. He wanted to stay right here.

It can't be hell. My Tilly's here.

His eyes welled with joy.

Cozy could still hear the boys' voices. Bugs got right in his face. 'Wake the fuck up, BOYO. Right fucking ...' Bugs paused, and then yelled loudly with all their combined voices. 'NOW.'

Tribute © Robert Lee Johnston 2016
Email: tributerobertleejohnston@gmail.com

Cozy woke, confused and fired up. His green eyes wouldn't focus. The whiteness was too bright. Everything's so fucking white.

He felt a hand on his own. Then a flurry of stranger's hands, fingers and activity, a hose or tube. It felt like wet, thick string was being pulled out of his neck and guts, making him wretch.

'Hey, you blokes. Stop it, fucking hell! What's going on, boys?' His throat ached. 'Water.'

Cozy recognised the gentle hand. I know this hand. Blinded, he found the owner's body and touched a thigh. I know this thigh.

He still could only see shapes, vague silhouettes. Thinking out loud this time he said, 'I know this leg.'

Cozy heard Mathilda's voice and yelled in fright, 'Seriously, what the fuck's going on?'

His tightly squeezed eyes gained traction on some vision. But it was a memory, a vision he was seeing. It had to be. First Bugs, Jen, John Henry, Kenny, the old boys and the dogs, and now he could just make out some jellyfish's tentacles, wrapping seductively around a knee.

'IMPOSSIBLE.' Cozy laughed at the sick vision with which he was torturing himself. 'I'm just dreaming.'

Tilly's left hand touched his face, her tiny left hand. Cozy's ring on her finger, her wrists jingling with her bangles and jewellery. Cozy moaned in confused, joyous agony and relief. 'Your arm? Your leg?' His voice felt unused, dulled and dusty dry. Mathilda's face looked gorgeous but tired. Maybe this is my heaven?

He recognised the hospital stench and panicked at the familiar smell. He had many questions. He tripped and stumbled for answers, and squeezed Tilly's hand tightly. For a time he didn't realise how hard it was to breathe. He stared into those sweet, deep eyes, too afraid to blink. 'I thought I lost you.' His heart pumped metallic-tasting adrenaline into his blood. But instead of making Cozy want

to get up and fight, his brain was sent the message that he didn't have to fight anymore. Cozy's exhausted body was telling him, Just lie down for a bit, mate. Let's both recover and rest.

It was the first time he had ever dogged it, ever stayed down. Cozy felt no guilt, no shame, no sky falling in on him. How strange it is.

Cozy struggled to adjust to the immediate surrounds. Colour had finally returned to his world. Mathilda looked as if she'd been crying. She looked so sweet, and slightly beat up; not physically, just tired and run down. She was saying something. Cozy couldn't hear a word through his brain's chatter. All he could summon was, 'What the fuck, babe? What the fuck is going on, honey?'

Strangely, as Cozy asked this he knew, like déjà vu. The answer was on the tip of his tongue but Cozy just couldn't nail it down.

Everything's all fucked up, upside down, and twisted inside out.

All his senses were firing and booting up so fast he needed a minute to work this shit out.

'Mathilda, you look good. You're alive. You're walking? Your leg and arm? You died. Am I dead? Am I dreaming?'

When she spoke her voice was soft and sweet. 'No, Cozy, I'm okay. You're here. I'm here. You're not dreaming. I'm here, baby. Cozy, you've been unconscious for two weeks. It's New Year's in a half hour. We spent Christmas together, here. I was hoping and praying for you to wake up. Merry Christmas, Cozy.'

'Merry Christmas, Mathilda. Sorry for the shit present.'

Mathilda shook her head. 'Cozy, you've been in a terrible car accident.' There was a pause. And then she howled like the high country winds. Cozy was going to touch her, to reach out for her. He felt his arm lift and could feel his fingers search for her, but he couldn't feel her. He looked to see why. There was a stump below his left elbow.

Tribute © Robert Lee Johnston 2016
Email: tributerobertleejohnston@gmail.com

'WHOA. Where's my fucking arm?'

He kicked his sheet off. His right leg was gone. He noticed some jars with fluids, echoing his breathing, the levels moving up and down as he breathed in and out. He held his breath, and the cherry-coloured liquid copied him by staying still.

'Where's my bloody leg? Tilly, where's my bloody arm?'

Tilly broke down and explained that they both had to go. 'The doctors had no choice, babe. The damage was too great. The driver of the car that T-boned you had been drinking all day. He didn't notice a red light. He smashed into the hardtop, right into your door.' Her voice caught on sharp barbs in her throat. 'You were trapped, crushed, in the hardtop for hours before they could free you.'

'It's okay, Mathilda. It's all right. I'll be okay. Will you be all right? How's the coupe?'

Her hand stroked Cozy's face. 'It's written off.'

'Be fucked. Poor old girl. Will you be okay, Tilly?'

'Not without you I won't!'

They both knew Cozy's eyes wouldn't be getting old or his hair grey. He was in the prime years of life. He wasn't going to see his pride years.

'You're going to have to go ahead without me. I'm sore, babe. I'm trashed. I feel heavy and beat up. I have to say goodbye to you now, Tilly. Before I can't. I'm slipping down cold. You're the love of my life, Mathilda, you're my one, my—' Pain, a surge of internal voltage, ran through him. Cozy held his breath. Then he continued, 'My body's hurting, honey. It wants to run away. I'll wait for you when I get there, and get things just right. I'll find a pretty place where you'd like to stay. It's not so far from here, Mathilda.'

'NO! NO! You just woke up! You're confused, Cozy. You'll be okay. I'll take care of you no matter what, baby. Please stay. You have to fight!'

'I can't, sweetie. This fight ... it's beating me. It ain't nothing but heartbreak this bout, Tilly. I can't get up,

Tribute © Robert Lee Johnston 2016
Email: tributerobertleejohnston@gmail.com

Mathilda, and I got a funny feeling I'm stapled down fast. I'm scared, scared I'm never going to taste your kisses again, or smell your pretty hair. I thought I'd live forever, Tilly, with all the wrong I done.'

'Cozy, I have two Christmas surprises.' Mathilda wiped her face. 'We're pregnant, babe! You're a daddy! I'm going to be a mother! Your body has found a way to make life. Sugar, I'm three months pregnant!'

Cozy was overwhelmed. 'I'm so proud of you, baby, and our little one.'

He placed his one hand on her belly. A flutter of images and thoughts charged through his head. I'm a father! Jen, smiling in my dream with a baby. Perhaps it wasn't Syd's child?

He couldn't think straight and was drowning in his mind. He wanted to say so much but the words were hard to retrieve. He smiled and told his Mathilda he loved them both. 'Tell our baby I loved him ... her from the moment I knew he existed. Show him the forest, honey. Let him know I'm in there, and if he looks proper, he'll see me. If you're ever lost, Mathilda, or our baby's lost, I'll find you both. Tell him to look proper. I promise to be around.'

Mathilda cried and promised she would.

'One more surprise, Cozy. Look! Evie's here! She came as soon as she heard. We finally got to meet. We've been chatting the ears off one another for the last week or so. You never, ever went into detail about just how beautiful and crazy lovable Evie is. She's fun and great company. Please, come say hi, Evie. I'll give you two a minute or two alone.'

Evie approached the hospital bed, cradled Cozy's face, kissed his cheek and smiled warmly through her tears. 'G'day, Cozy.'

'Hey, Tenebra.'

'You're a father, Cozy! Your Mathilda's amazing.'

Tribute © Robert Lee Johnston 2016
Email: tributerobertleejohnston@gmail.com

'Thanks. You're finally an Aunt-Evie now. God, how brown are you? You look like bloody Neil Young's "Cinnamon Girl".' Cozy's voice was fading. Have you got a man, Evie?

'I see you're still as white as ever. Cozy, your parents must have been Irish! You're so bloody white. And no, I haven't met a man yet, lots of boys though.'

They chuckled sadly, and he spoke quietly of how much he missed her. He asked her to forgive him all the misery he had caused her.

She held Cozy's face gently in her hands. 'I miss you all the bloody time. And it's real good to see you. And there isn't a single thing to forgive, Cozy, not one.'

'God's a predictable fucking cheat, Evie. How can I get him in a headlock and kick his arse now?'

Evie laughed with him through her tears, imagining Cozy, a one-legged and one-armed arse-kicker. She smiled beautifully. '"It's just a flesh wound". You'll be right, babe.'

Cozy belly laughed. 'Yeah, I'll be right. I promise.'

'You always were a lousy liar, Cozy.'

'We had some times, didn't we, Evie?'

'We … we had them all, Cozy.'

'I'll say g'day to the pack for you.'

She nodded reluctantly and sadly kissed his forehead and both pale cheeks.

'Tell all of them, tell them all …' Evie paused, searching for the words. 'My brother, I miss all of them, so very, very much. You know?' Words tore at her voice. 'I love you all so much. So dearly. Always will. I love you like a brother, Cozy. You're the kind of kid we needed, Cozy. You were the one we clung to when we were all scared to death, so scared we lost our minds and couldn't think. We glued ourselves to you, the cosy one, who wasn't never scared of death. You stole my heart, our hearts, Cozy, but you are a generous thief, and you were born to protect our pack. You're the kind of brother this girl … had always wanted. I wouldn't be

Tribute © Robert Lee Johnston 2016
Email: tributerobertleejohnston@gmail.com

here, or what I am, without you. Truly, babe. I owe you my life, my sanity, my everything. Cozy, I miss you already, hon! Just fight if you can, baby. If you're tired, or you have to stop and can't get up, I understand, sweetheart. I unglue myself from you, with all the love I have. It's okay, Cozy. If you got to go, you go, babe. I won't think any less of you. You put up one hell of a fight. You always did. Please don't stay in pain for me. For anyone, anymore. Shit, I'm going to miss our crucifying Latin together. I'll miss you my brave, bold Cozy.'

Cozy was tiring. 'You owe me nothing, Evie. You did all that and more for me. I reckon me and you, sister, got no debt to each other. Not a single one. I love you. You're my family. My blood. My blood sister. Always will be.'

She squeezed Cozy as tightly as she dared. A moment passed. 'I memorised a phrase you'll like, Cozy.'

'Tell me.'

'Okay. It's about, you know, death.'

Cozy nodded. 'All the good ones are.'

'"The gods conceal from the living how pleasant death is, so that they will continue to live." It's from a poem called Pharsalia, by the Roman poet Lucan. I like that one.'

Cozy took a minute to appreciate the words. 'Me too, Evie. I have one. I fixed it in my memory when the kids and Stirrup died. It reminds me of them somehow. By Edmund Waller, On the Divine Poems. Let me think:

The soul's dark cottage, batter'd and decay'd,
Lets in new light through the chinks time has made;
Stronger by weakness, wiser men become.
As they draw near to their eternal home:
Leaving the old, both worlds at once they view.
That stand upon the threshold of the new.

'It always reminds me of the orphanage.'

Tribute © Robert Lee Johnston 2016
Email: tributerobertleejohnston@gmail.com

'It did me too. Who the hell am I going to tell all my silly sayings now, Cozy?'

'You can still tell me, Evie. I'll be listening out for you.'

Cozy dug deeper and found a drip of energy. 'Evie, please don't let my baby be like me. If it's a boy. Evie, you got to do me one last favour.'

'Of course, Cozy. Anything.'

His words started to slur and stutter. 'If it's a boy, love him for me, really, really hard. Evie, don't let him box, don't let him fight. Keep him from blood. Please, no fighting.'

Evie whispered reassuringly in his ear, 'I promise you, Cozy, I won't let anyone hurt your baby. Your child will be safe and loved. I will help watch over and keep your young one safe. I promise you with all my heart, Cozy.'

He smiled and winked at her. The strain of talking was too much. The racing green around his pupils dissipated.

Tilly, back now, and Evie held Cozy's one hand. Cozy hoped Mathilda would eventually meet a good man, a great man, a proper man. Someone dependable, brave, stable and fertile. A kinder, more thoughtful, better adjusted, longer-lived man than himself. Mathilda was still young enough to have that chance at family and some more kids. Knowing Evie and Mathilda as Cozy did, he was positive they would be inseparable friends.

Cozy's girls would live on.

Where he was bound, he couldn't rightly say. As he lay there adrift, drowning in the short-shadow of his last dusk, he thought how lucky he was to have the two girls he loved, who loved him, holding his hand at the end. And the friends he had made, to quote Jim Morrison and the Doors, 'on this thin route'.* All the life, love, uncertainty and mischief they had shared. Those sweet, rare mysteries explored and discovered. The shared pains and suffering the pack accumulated would handsomely pay for any calamity or ill ledgered against their names. The bloody battles waged for each other, against those who would harm them. This surely

earned each of them a great seat amongst the bravest warriors and Valkyries bound for glory.

Cozy's own fighting days were over. No more fight-game. No more payments in blood. Cozy could retire finally. Without shame or regret. No last minute come-backs. No left arm or right leg put paid to that. All of twenty-six, Cozy would retire and surrender, along with his pride, everything he loved; let it all go. He wondered, Am I abandoning my baby? My girl? Doing what my parents did to me?

Cozy was too tired to think. It was time. Strangely, it felt all right to step down. Better late than never.

Cozy was excited for his child, the love he'd get and the endless possibilities love enabled. Cozy was excited by the thought of seeing his motley, young tribe again.

Cozy had had both friends and enemies die in his arms. By drugs. By disease. By cars. By knives. By fire. By guns. By accident. And by him. Cozy had forgotten half their stories and confused their faces. He had lost a few years, chemically, here and there, so mixed people up all the time. He'd never had the time to grieve any of them. They all fell much too quickly. He wondered if young Jen and John Henry would even recognise him.

Will they have aged? Will they remember? What if they can't stand what I've become? What if they don't recognise the boy inside the man? Am I too old to die young?

Cozy knew deep inside that they would never forget.

One thing had eluded the man-child most of his life. A simple feeling, beset with convoluted requirements or trivial complications. Perhaps taken for granted by many a being who had unwittingly or foolishly stumbled upon it.

The Feeling?

Happiness. For his last, brief moment, Cozy let go of hatred. He let go the rapacious anger that clenched tight his fists, and held fast his life. He embraced that other feeling:

Happiness.

He felt it.

Tribute © Robert Lee Johnston 2016
Email: tributerobertleejohnston@gmail.com

COZY'S END.

Iridescent, winged sapphires lustred within the cloudless sunshine. Two giant, lapis, lazuli Ulysses butterflies glinted and softly danced, fluttering far from their traditional sea-of-green jungle abode. The pair thrust life and colour upon the coastal light while riding a crisp Pacific breeze above a stark metropolis. They beat their colossal wings and gently kissed a closed hospital window.

Tribute © Robert Lee Johnston 2016
Email: tributerobertleejohnston@gmail.com

Ambo = ambulance bearer = paramedic

Arsey = lucky

Barra = barramundi, legendary chromed fish.

Bead = to see or aim

Beak = a judge

Bikes = biker gangs

Blast = a shot = an injection

Bon and Malcolm = rock and roll royalty = look them up

Boo = weed = junga = gunga = cannibis = pot = smoke = smoko = herb

Brace and bits = Got the shits

Bucket bongs = bunger = joint = billy = bong = cone = paraphenalia = I'm sure you're catching on

Buckley's = you got fuck all chance. Eg, ya got fuck'n buckleys of living jumping off that ten storey building

Bullocky = bullock team driver

Bully man = see police

Bungee = mate

Busting his ring = work'n hard

Cack'n ya dacks = pack'n ya dacks = shat or shitting yourself (see also skidmarks)

Captain Cook = to have a look

Cheesy flick = shithouse movie

Chico roll = Aussie pastry

Chuck a whitie = freaking out = passing out

Coeys = co-accused = five-eighth

Come a gutser = to fall

Cricket = a ball game that requires a shitload of alcohol to play and watch properly

Dice'n me? = you avoiding me?

Divied up = divided up

Dog it = yellow = to be a coward, low down maggot

Double dutch = two ropes skipping

Dreamtime = look into it

Duke(s) = Fist(s)

Durry = dart = cigarette

Elbow = pound

Esky's = ice box = cooler

Fair whack = see lagin

Fart arse'n = fuck'n round

Federallies = police = bully man = oink = pigs = fucking cops

Fits = needles = picks

Frangers = condoms

Game of sticks = pool = eight ball

Gammon = to be useless, for something to be shit, even being too proud of yourself. You can also be gammon if you're an arsey bugger.

Gander = to look = squizz = clock

Go commando = commando = bugs' balls free of restraint = freeballing

Go'e = speed = meth anphetamine = whipper

Gray Nic = gray nicholls = a brand of cricket bat

Grunter = good eating fish, grunts like a pig

Gutchy = fucked, rooted

Hard top = coupe = two door = Aussie beast of a fuck'n thing.

Henry Lawson = legendary Australian bush poet

Hill's hoist = Aussie invented, revolving clothes line

Hoyk = chuck = throw

Jackie-jackie = someone who does it all for ya

Jocks = undies

Junk = heroin

Kicker = motorbike's kick starter

Knocked me drink over = skull ya drink

Lagin or lag'n = time inprisoned. A big lag'n usually five years and over. Little lag'n = under that

Tribute © Robert Lee Johnston 2016
Email: tributerobertleejohnston@gmail.com

Landy = landrover

Lawyer cane = the cuts = long rod

Main drag = main street = main h'way

Mallee scrub = a type of jungle

Mickey bull = cleanskin = a wild uncivillised unbranded beast or bull. Can't eat them if their skin is branded. No brand = fresh beef

Migaloo = white bloke

Mouthpiece = lawyer

Mugs away = looser of eight ball has to set em up

Munted = really fucked up, messed up

Nah, yeah = no

Noggin = your head = ya scone

Over the pits = roadworthy

Pannikin = traditional Aussie, unbreakable tin cup

Pick = needle

Queenslander = a house style usually two storey timber

Quincans = Australian Aboriginal bad spirits

Rock-spider = maggot paedoephile = prison's lowest denominator

Screws = screw dog cunts = prison wardens

Seppo = yank = septic tank = seppo = an American

Six cuts = see lawyer cane

Tribute © Robert Lee Johnston 2016
Email: tributerobertleejohnston@gmail.com

Skidmarks = brown stuff you'll find on bugs' jocks if he ever bloody wore any

Skint = broke

Snappy saurus = big lizards = old, giant bloody crocs

Stick magazines = Playboy, Penthouse

Stir = jail

Thunk = what Kenny thunks he thought

Three on the tree = column shift three speed gear box

Towey = shitty = having your rags

V.D. = S.T.D. = venereal disease = the herp

VB song = Aussie beer song on tv

Wag school = cut school = take the day off school

Watch house = police lock up

Werewolf ya = creep up on you

White Ox = rolling tobacco and common tender in prison

Without a stitch = naked

Yeah, nah = yeah

Z900 = Kwacca nine = The Z = Kawasaki Z900 road bike

####

Tribute © Robert Lee Johnston 2016
Email: tributerobertleejohnston@gmail.com

YOURS

My humble sad token
A debt I owe,
Now forever and always unbroken.
I am nothing
Rayless
Never free
Blackish-blue
To live life without
Beautiful
Wonderful, dearly beloved
You.

From Me

ACKNOWLEDGEMENTS

My Wendy. There are no words without you.

To you, brave readers, thank you. Wherever in the world you may be for taking a risk on me and purchasing Tribute, I appreciate the effort you have made to read an independent Australian author.

Very special thanks to Tom Waits and Kathleen Brennan for continually inspiring me.
Shari from Hal Leonard Corporation and Universal Music Publishing Group: Robert, Brigitte and Connie. Thanks for your patience.

The Greatest Cover artist: Robert Scholten.
My Guru, Editor: Phil Newey.

My Absent Friends: Vaughan. Kevin, Clinton, Franko, Gale, Christine, Selina, Guy and Jenny.

My Mates whom I have repeatedly driven crazy with this, that and the other. A big thanks to you lot: Kenny, Simon, Mel, Glen, Seth, Troy, Paddy, Greg, Peter, Cathy, Marit, Farrell and Cindy.

My Important Aussie Test Readers: Shane, Paul, Kenny, Seth, Virginia, Greg, Trish. Cathy, Pete, Tom and Big Rod.

My Important Overseas Test Readers: Marit - Holland, Kourtney - USA, Fee - England, Naija - Denmark.

Tribute © Robert Lee Johnston 2016
Email: tributerobertleejohnston@gmail.com

And not forgetting to thank my sanity for not leaving permanently. The many bottles of Jack Daniels, Wild turkey and Jim Beam. And the countless sacks of prime Boo that assisted in that valiant struggle

My super cool grade eight English teacher. Miss Favier.

The Musicians. Music and Bands: Tom Waits, Pink Floyd, AC/DC, Bon Scott, Malcolm Young, Phil Rudd, Angus Young, Sky hooks, Steppenwolf, The Doors and Jim Morrison, Jimi Hendrix, Janice Joplin, Jeff Beck, Led Zeppelin, Stevie Ray Vaughan, Steve Miller Band, Elmore James, Easy beats, Bob Dylan, Black Sabbath, The Police, Rodriguez, J.J Cale, Queen, Lead Belly, The Who, Willie Deville, Guns'n'Roses, Aerosmith, Motley Crue, Kiss, Humble Pie, Cream, Neil Young, David Bowie, The Rolling Stones, Vanilla Fudge, ZZ Top.

Writers and Wordsmiths: Ambrose Bierce, Henry Lawson, Cicero, Montaigne, Edmund Waller, Lucan, Tiffany Winfree, Thomas Fuller MD, Anton Checkhov, the Reverend Fred Nile, MLC, Thomas Dodd, Suzy Kassem, John Milton, Christopher Marlow, Quintas Curtius Rufas.

The Magazines: Fat Freddy and the Fabulous Furry Freak Brothers, Playboy, Penthouse.

Many thanks.

Robert Lee Johnston

Thank you, dear reader, for choosing my book. If you enjoyed this, please take a moment to connect with me via social media or leave me a comment on my Author's Blog at www.robertleejohnston.com.

Connect with me

Twitter: @R_L_Johnston

Facebook: Author Robert Lee Johnston

Instagram: Robert.Lee.Johnston

Linked In: Robert Lee Johnston

Also by Robert Lee Johnston

A deal has been struck.

The twenty-first century has a visitor. He visits earth for one year each century.

On arrival, he is stripped of his power. The devil is one of us, among us.

Living down under.

Lucifer is on leave. And he's here, in Australia.

Tribute © Robert Lee Johnston 2016
Email: tributerobertleejohnston@gmail.com

www.ingramcontent.com/pod-product-compliance
Lightning Source LLC
Chambersburg PA
CBHW051230260626
47162CB00002B/358